Big Bang or Steady State? Opinions are divided. Supposing there were a third alternative: the retroverse?

"Imagine two parallel universes before the Big Bang," said melanie. "The first, the one we now call the retroverse, had galaxies that went through a cycle of expansion and eventual collapse until all the matter and energy of the retroverse collected in one place.

"This matter and energy form the ultimate black hole, its own gravitational pull compressing what is now just hydrogen plasma until, way beyond critical mass; it has to explode. Not outwards, because its own gravity prevents it from doing so. It takes the only other way out: it implodes, bursting through into this universe.

"This new universe now gained the three physical dimensions of space. Time, the fourth dimension, followed soon after. The new universe was a bit like a tea party, where there are three dimensions taking tea while waiting for time to turn up."

When Jack Fletcher, an ordinary decent criminal, travels through the retroverse, meets his evil stepsisters and discovers he is not who he thought he was, all hell is set to break out, right here on earth.

Also by Patrick J. Stoner

The Jabberwock Continuum

Book 2: The Vorpal Sword Revelation

Praise for The Jabberwock Anomaly

Five stars: witty and well written a superb piece of Sci-fi

This intelligently written Sci-Fi tale brilliantly weaves together a galactic timeline of science, politics and history to deliver a highly additive story, that had me hooked from start to finish. I would recommend this book to any type of Sci-Fi reader; it truly is that versatile. I eagerly look forward to book 2.

Martin Rowe, author of Humanity's Dawn

An easy to read, fast paced science fiction story that has enough twists to make it interesting. The author has come up with a novel idea but gives homage to many well known works of fiction and literature. An intriguing story with a good hook that does make you want to read more. Suitable for teenagers and adults.

Amazon reviewer

The Jabberwock Continuum

Book One

THE JABBERWOCK ANOMALY

Patrick J. Stoner

Published in the UK 2014 by Fascom

Reissued 2024

The right of Patrick J Stoner to be identified as the author of this work has been asserted by him in accordance with the Copyright, Designs and Patents Act 1988

ISBN: 978-0-9957462-9-9

Cover design by Daryl Blasi

CONTENTS

DAY SIXTEEN (cont.)
    FiT: the twenty-first
    FiT: the twenty-second

DAY SIXTEEN (cont.)
    Fit the forty-fourth

DAY SEVENTEEN
    FiT: the sixth
    FiT: the seventh
    FiT: the thirty-fourth

DAY SEVENTEEN (cont.)
    FiT: the thirty-first

DAY SEVENTEEN (cont.)

DAY EIGHTEEN
    FiT: the thirteenth

For Patricia, for everything.

And Purdey and Maisie, for everything else...

Jabberwocky

'Twas brillig, and the slithy toves
Did gyre and gimble in the wabe;
All mimsy were the borogoves,
And the mome raths outgrabe.

'Beware the Jabberwock, my son!
The jaws that bite, the claws that catch!
Beware the Jubjub bird, and shun
The frumious Bandersnatch!'

He took his vorpal sword in hand:
Long time the manxome foe he sought—
So rested he by the Tumtum tree,
And stood awhile in thought.

And as in uffish thought he stood,
The Jabberwock, with eyes of flame,
Came whiffling through the tulgey wood,
And burbled as it came!

One, two! One, two! and through and through
The vorpal blade went snicker-snack!
He left it dead, and with its head
He went galumphing back.

'And hast thou slain the Jabberwock?
Come to my arms, my beamish boy!
O frabjous day! Callooh! Callay!'
He chortled in his joy.

'Twas brillig, and the slithy toves
Did gyre and gimble in the wabe;
All mimsy were the borogoves,
And the mome raths outgrabe.

Author Unknown

"...we occasionally make minor decisions that have enormous consequences to ourselves and others. These decisions are frequently binary and not necessarily open to chance.

"The manipulation of these 'Forks in Time,' or 'FiTs,' resonates with the prevalence of coincidences. There has to be a link."

Professor Benjamin Ashbow, University of Gaia

'I find that, outside of an Agatha Christie novel, the incidence, frequency, and distribution of coincidences, makes their existence unlikely to be coincidental.'

Morgan Cheshire, MI6

"The notion of the characters controlling the writer is as absurd as that of a marionette controlling the puppeteer."

TkRannTk

"Having a pathological hatred of coincidences doesn't preclude their occurrence."

melanie, AIB

FiTs explained

It will not take the astute reader long to realise that there are more than a few oblique references to the books of Lewis Carroll in *The Jabberwock Continuum*.

Although the action of this book takes place over a span of only eighteen Terran days, there are numerous references to what Professor Benajmin Ashbow refers to as Forks in Time, or FiTs. He says:

"These are minor decisions that have enormous consequences to ourselves and others. The manipulation of these FiTs resonates with the prevalence of coincidences. There has to be a link."

Coincidentally, in his fine narrative poem *The Hunting of the Snark*, Lewis Carroll uses FITS instead of chapters, and I have taken the liberty of following his example in labelling these 'minor decisions'.

I have placed them in the text in order of relevance rather than in chronological order, which accounts for the fact that they are not numbered sequentially. However, a glance at the Terran date of these FiTs will, I hope, clarify any confusion in the mind of the reader.

FiT: THE SECOND

Geata Bilé, Earth
Spring 153 BCE

Agnt tre-Kiff was getting old, and walking was becoming more difficult. He pulled rank, persuaded the pilot to land close to the ancient ring, and then go away and leave him in peace. He didn't need long, just enough time to say his farewells to the enigmatic blocks of stone. Like him, they were far from where they had originated.

The afternoon was warm. Pleasant enough, sitting on the spiky green vegetation next to the old stones the locals called the 'Devil's Gate.' But Agnt tre-Kiff had been warned by his meddlesome physician to pay attention to his cooling. He opened the fin on his back to benefit from the prevailing wind.

He stretched out a forepaw to feel the ancient rock, careful that his blunt claws left no mark. His race and tribe had been coming to this isolated backwater to study for over fifty thousand of the planet's years and never left a mark.

Just three thousand local years before, it had been a tribal ancestor, Gudil tre-Kiff, there to watch them start these structures, digging the ditch to create the outer banks. Covert recordings had impressed the young Agnt tre-Kiff enough for him to select exo-history as his chosen field of study.

Early in his career, while compiling his thesis's validations and references, he encountered the anomaly tucked away amongst ancient DNA samples. His seniors had considered his findings and suggested, pointedly, that he ignore his results.

He had done so and resumed his research on the natives. They were funny-looking little things, but fierce. Maybe a bit too fierce after whatever had happened to their ancestors two hundred thousand years earlier.

Although some ferocity might be useful at home, with the current situation; a few of these tiny creatures might prove.... He quashed the thought.

They would do well where they were. Working gold and developing an interest in the world beyond. They had so much promise; tre-Kiff was sorry he wouldn't be able to see how it all turned out. But he had got old, and this was his last visit.

When he was young, he would have known he was being watched sooner, although not much. His eyesight and hearing might be fading, but his sense of smell was still powerful enough to detect one of the natives standing behind a vertical stone. He showed courage.

Agnt tre-Kiff knew he had committed a misdemeanor. He had allowed the being to see him.

He should leave now. Let the native try to persuade his fellows about what he had seen. Best case, they would dismiss him as a fool or drunk. Worst case, a myth of dragons might emerge.

Agnt tre-Kiff hesitated. He wanted to make contact. To talk to this creature. His earlier thought was creeping back. But there would be trouble if he decided on that course of action. Still, one might as well be chastised for a youngling as an egg. He reached for his communicator and opened the translation menu.

His observer was almost certainly from the Atrebates tribe and would speak the Brythonic dialect.

***

Flattened against the stone, Cadeyrn gained control of his pounding heart and the need to suck a lot more air into his lungs. What, by all that he believed in, was it? A lizard of sorts walking on its hind legs like a man.

Cadeyrn knew he faced two options; run, which seemed the better, or kill it and secure his place as the chief of their small group and a better seat at the tribal gatherings. He looked down at Morcant, his son. Would attacking the monster put the boy in danger? Risking his own life was one thing: endangering his son's another. Then the creature spoke.

"Hello," it said, the words carrying across the grass in Cadeyrn's language. "Would you care to come and talk?"

The accent was strange, but the words were clear enough. And somehow, it didn't sound like a threat.

"I only want to talk," the monster added.

"Stay here," Cadeyrn ordered his son and, grasping his spear, he walked out from behind the rock, pushing back his woolen cloak to free up the sword he wore at his belt.

"You speak my language/tongue/dialect, monster/creature," tre-Kiff heard.

"No, my friend, who lives in this box, speaks your language." Tre-Kiff held up a small black device. Cadeyrn considered this for a few moments, weighing up the probabilities. He decided that if monsters existed, so might wizards who lived inside boxes.

Tre-Kiff regarded the man with one eye. Yes, a Gaul: likely fleeing the aftermath of the Punic Wars. He was tall compared to the southern races and Romans. His dark eyes contrasted with pale skin, and he had lightened his hair with a lime wash, then plumped it up like the mane of a horse. His beard was trimmed but leaving mustaches of magnificent proportion.

He wore a simple tunic and trousers made of linen and wool, all in colors defying description other than 'muddy.' A copper torc, not the gold of a wealthy man, sat around his neck.

During this examination, Cadeyrn was studying the lizard. It stood tall. Higher than a horse, with scales shimmering in many colors, as a rainbow or oil spilled on water. Its few clothes seemed designed for show rather than warmth.

The head was impressive. Cadeyrn was familiar with a few reptiles and had heard stories of exotic creatures seen in Rome and Carthage. Giant lizards were considered predators and treated with respect. Except, this one's teeth were not those of a carnivore or an omnivore. They were the teeth of an herbivore. Who could fear anything that ate only grass?

"What are you called?" Cadeyrn asked, the language stilted by the translator.

"I am called Agnt. My tribe is called tre-Kiff. What are you called?"

"Cadeyrn, son of Cadeyrn."

"Tell me, Cadeyrn, son of Cadeyrn, are you from the village over the hill?"

"No. My village is five days' walk that way." He gestured in an easterly direction. "More, when we have livestock and women and children with us."

"Ah yes, I see one of your younglings is keeping special guard from behind the stone. Would he like to join us?"

Cadeyrn turned and called. Morcant emerged, stretching as tall as he could to hide that he had only seen seven summers, gripping his small spear firmly as he walked forward to join his father.

"Hello, young one," tre-Kiff said. "I see you are as brave as your father. That is very good. And what is your name?"

7

"Morcant," the boy replied, holding in check the slight wobble he could feel in his voice.

"And where are you from?" Cadeyrn asked.

"The stars," tre-Kiff said.

"I shouldn't like to live among the stars," Cadeyrn said. "They exist in the dark and are cold."

"Not so; the sun warming you as we speak is a star."

"How can that be? The stars are tiny points of light, and the sun is large and bright."

"When you were walking towards these stones, were they not small? And as you got closer, did they not get bigger? So, it is with the stars.

"Near each star are different worlds like this one, and on these live different people. Some like you, some like me, and some like nothing you have ever seen."

Cadeyrn considered this for a moment. "I understand," he said, "but how do you get to these worlds?"

"I have a chariot, larger than the ships used by the men of the north or even the southern seas. The wizard inside it flies me there."

"Maybe then, I should like to live among the stars."

Tre-Kiff regarded him thoughtfully. He was about to do something not one of his tribe had dared do in all of fifty thousand years.

"Well," he said, holding his voice steady, "perhaps a man as brave as you should get the chance."

DAY ONE

Fiveday 3.5.2834

Tuesday 31st January 2017

For twenty-two minutes after getting the 'Abort Now' signal, mclanic misfilcd data systcmatically.

If, as Terrans liked to say, her cover had been blown, Nel screaming contradictory orders and waving guns would have already surrounded her. They were good at screaming contradictory orders and waving guns.

As she wasn't surrounded by armed Nel, she thought it made sense to wait until her assigned break. The Nel had a steep learning curve in front of them regarding harmonious office management, and leaving early would mean shooting her way out, which was a little extreme.

melanie moved her chair a little and only nudged and annoyed three other clerks. Her previous record was five.

She weighed up the situation. She was more than capable of misfiling and thinking concurrently. Because of the signal, she would leave two days earlier than planned. Which was no hardship. The temperature in the office rarely dipped below forty. Water was a commodity too precious for showers, and at least sixty cloying, home-brewed perfumes were battling for dominance.

It had already become clear that fewer than ten of the two thousand plus Nel in the outpost knew where they were now. It seemed unlikely even they knew where they were going next.

Getting into the base had been easy. melanie had the right documents, though a four-year-old's crayon doodle would have sufficed. In typically perverse Nel fashion, getting out would prove to be a little more complicated.

After twenty-two minutes, the indicator on the wall turned from blue to green, and she could stop what she was doing.

melanie began her break by unleashing a virus into the computer system. Coupled with her weaponized filing methods, the virus should put the project back by several weeks.

She stood up to leave.

Exiting, with others on their break as others pushed in, caused more chaos. As well as creating a new record for upset Nel clerks.

Once clear, while most of the other clerks made for the tiny open space on the top level, melanie headed for the waste and water engineering section, two levels down.

melanie's glove, carrying an exact copy of Technician Vinikar's handprint, opened the composite steel door.

As melanie stepped through, Technician Vinikar said, "Hello, Clerk Malgener, what are you doing down here?" Her accent suggesting origins in one of the northern industrial cities of Nel Prime.

"What do you think, after last night?" melanie said with an attempt at a lecherous smile. "Some more, please."

"Always happy to oblige my favorite Clerk," the technician said as she threw her arms around melanie's neck and kissed her.

"First, though," melanie said, disentangling herself from the other blond, "have you got my pack safe? There's something in there you might like."

"Ooh," Vinikar squealed and pulled the pack from a tool cabinet. "What is it?"

"A surprise," melanie said, taking the pack. "Turn around and close your eyes."

Vinikar turned her back, wiggling her butt seductively as she did so.

Standing behind the technician, melanie draped her left arm over the other woman's left shoulder and across her chest to grip Vinikar's right shoulder, while her right hand gripped Vinikar's chin and snapped her neck.

The body fitted into the tool cabinet with little room to spare, but melanie managed eventually and secured the door. From her pack, she removed a utility belt with a large knife in a sheath and five smaller pockets. After throwing the empty pack into a bin, she wore the belt bandolier style and walked through the section to an inspection cover set into the floor.

She climbed down the ladder inside, closing and locking the hatch above her as she went.

The main sewer was cool, dark, and silent. melanie had expected the drip of water, but there was nothing. It didn't even smell. It was, melanie decided, much more pleasant than the office in which she had recently been working.

melanie's enhanced night vision system showed the tunnel was six meters wide and three high. A tide mark, a meter from the floor, showed the water level during the twice daily flushing.

As soon as she took her first step towards the exit, melanie felt her feet sliding away from her. She had expected the floor of a sewer to be glutinous. The Nel must be flushing large concentrations of silicone through the tunnel and leaving a thin film over the surfaces. Why that was so was something for the chemists to ponder after she got out, which was going to be later than expected on this surface. The exit point was seven kilometers away.

melanie adopted a mix of endurance walking, skiing and skating techniques. It lacked elegance, but she could maintain close to her regular walking speed.

Two kilometers on, she stopped and turned around. Distant infrared light flickered off the scarcely reflective surface of the sewer's walls. Somebody was following her.

Her break had only ended five minutes ago. Being five minutes late didn't result in a search; they just added thirty minutes to the shift.

melanie considered the possibilities. Somebody might have seen her entering the engineering section. They might have found Vinikar's body. The hatch down into the sewer had an alarm.

The soft whirr of electric motors suggested scooters. After a few seconds, the motors stopped for a while, then started again. The pursuers were checking the occasional security recesses on each side. Although, probably, they did not know who or what they were searching for.

A scooter would be faster than walking. Especially on the slippery surface underfoot. Meaning the pursuers would likely catch up with melanie before she reached the exit, and certainly before she blew a hole in it. All things considered, getting caught at the exit barrier would not end well.

Stopping and fighting would have the double advantage of getting rid of the pursuers and gaining both a scooter and a gun. melanie pulled the knife from her belt.

The security recesses were the only available cover, with a front lip level with the tidemark, just over a meter from the floor. They had built the sewer a long time ago, and back then the Nel must have worried about the possibility of losing a few of its own during the flushes.

melanie climbed into the recess on the left. Buried in the Nel DNA were a few human characteristics, and her pursuers would, almost certainly, check the one on the right first.

Settling at the back, she brought her gloved hands up to cover her face, in case a stray beam of infrared light reflected off her skin.

Two minutes later, scooters arrived with soldiers carrying night vision glasses and assault weapons with infrared and sighting lasers. They stopped, and the sergeant sat waiting on his scooter, while the corporal walked gingerly toward the right-hand recess and shone a light into the interior.

melanie dropped silently onto the floor with the knife in her hand, slipped and almost fell. The movement catching the sergeant's eye. He turned, bringing his weapon up as melanie slithered towards him. She grabbed the barrel of the gun in her left hand, shoving it backward into the sergeant's chest, as her right arm struck inwards, driving the knife through his neck.

As the sergeant collapsed, the corporal turned back to check the other recess and saw melanie. Bringing his assault weapon up, he started edging carefully back towards his scooter, incapable of hurrying on the slippery floor.

Equally, melanie could not cross the distance to the corporal fast enough without slipping, so she flipped the knife and threw it. The blade passed through the corporal's uniform and rib cage to bury itself in his heart.

melanie retrieved her knife, slid it back into its sheath, and had just gathered up the corporal's weapon when she heard another scooter whirring towards her.

"Are you there?" the voice came out of the darkness in Nel. An unmistakable tinge of fear working its way to the surface.

Naturally, there had to be a religious officer with them. Making sure the soldiers complied with the word of God.

melanie slid both bodies to one side where they would be less visible, then climbed back up into the recess and crouched down. Cranking up her own night-vision system as she heard the religious officer getting closer.

"I order you to wait," he whined.

melanie unsheathed the knife and then thought better of it. This was a religious officer, and he deserved better. From a pouch on her belt, she pulled out what looked like a pocket watch with an oversized ring for the chain. She slipped the middle finger of her left hand through the ring and pulled out a wire just fifty micrometers thick.

The religious officer paused at the two parked scooters and climbed off his own.

"Where are you?" he called, turning to face the right-hand recess. As he did so, he slipped and fell on his face. It took him three attempts to get into a kneeling position with one hand on his scooter.

melanie silently lowered herself down behind the religious officer and edged forward until she was standing directly behind him.

She crossed her arms and dropped the gossamer necklace, half the thickness of a human hair, around his neck.

"Go with your god," she said quietly and snapped her arms open. His body dropped as his head bounced twice before hitting the wall.

melanie let the thread slide back into the case, cleansing itself as it went, and put the garrote back into the pouch. She picked up the corporal's weapon again, checked it was fully charged, functional and hadn't got any biometric link to the previous owner. It hadn't, and she slung it onto her back. Time was against her; she needed to move.

Climbing onto the scooter, she listened for any other signs of pursuit. She could hear nothing.

The scooter lifted ten centimeters off the ground, and she rode for another fifteen minutes until she saw the faintest gray in the distance and checked her clock. Day was breaking outside and stopping to kill the Nel had caused a lengthy but necessary delay. Although the scooter's speed had scraped back a little time over the slippery floor.

The barrier was mesh, thirty-centimeter-diameter rings of a sixty-millimeter steel polymer mix; more than enough to prevent any of the more dangerous life-forms from getting in but insufficient to stop melanie from getting out. Not with a few strategically placed lengths of explosive tape to help.

Beyond the mesh was an almost vertical slope down to the flat plains. The scooter wasn't designed to tackle slopes, so melanie taped up the few links she would need to blow a hole to get herself through. The scooter could stay behind.

She had just finished fitting the tape when she heard a distant rumble. Fast running water: they were going to flush her out, literally.

She finished what she was doing, and standing closer than she would have liked, pressed the button on the detonator. After a muffled thump, a section of mesh fell out.

14

melanie climbed part-way through the hole in the mesh. Then used the rings to pull herself through and diagonally up and across the barrier. She had barely made the rocks to one side before the mass of water exploded out to arc down onto the plain.

Seconds later, the barrier swung up to let the larger debris out. As melanie scrabbled down and over the rocks, the water flow stopped, and the barrier closed.

Over the years, the impact of the twice-daily waterfall had created a shallow pool where it hit the ground. Most of the water flowed away, but the indentation trapped the flotsam. A flock of two meter tall dodo-like creatures, with a more carnivorous beak, ran up and began breakfasting on the mix of Nel and human bodies and parts. The trapped water turning a muddy red as they shrieked and fought over the tastier cuts.

Down on the flat plain, melanie ran.

The copse of grasses and safety was now seven kilometers away, eight and a half minutes. melanie could maintain close to fifty kilometers per hour when no one was around to ask questions. Or when, like now, she didn't care if they asked questions. Fast enough to keep ahead of the major predators. The smaller variants she could deal with.

The red giant sun's vast face dominated the horizon behind melanie as she ran through the scrubland. Providing she stayed on the baked earth paths; she could keep up her speed all the way to the copse. She settled into a steady pace.

A kilometer from the tunnel, the ground leveled out, with just the occasional outcropping of rocks and plants all the way to the far horizon. Amongst them her target.

Already she could feel the heat of the sun on her back.

A ten-meter-long bright yellow centipede considered her for a between-meals snack. It set off to intercept and then decided she was a little too fast.

A kilometer and a half later, the dodos had finished first breakfast and, like a bunch of avian Hobbits, were looking for seconds. melanie seemed a likely candidate, and they started moving in on her.

melanie glanced at them, assessing their threat. Medium, she decided. Although they were much faster than her, the brain inside the bald head was tiny. The feathers covering the body, a mix of red, orange and yellow, suggested a scavenger warning

15

others off, rather than a hunter. But they had caught up with her and were in hunting mode.

One would close in, worrying at her heels while the others stayed clear. Every few minutes, they swapped, and a new bird would take over the close pursuit. Demonstrating an unexpected level of intelligence.

Without pausing, melanie shot one. Half the flock decided it was enough for a meal and stayed to eat. The other half carried on as before. One was constantly at her heels while the others loped along, reserving their stamina.

She considered shooting a second dodo. They were three kilometers from the copse, and the dodos were getting braver. Even though at worst the animal might trip her over, it would be time-consuming.

The distinctive note of a Nel *Claw-class* flier coming up from behind gave her comfort. Without looking around or slowing, she unslung the weapon from her back. The *Claw-class* fliers were civilian Gaian *Arrow LT-270* fliers with a fancy paint job and couple of guns on them rather than military vehicles.

As civilian light transport, they were more than adequate. Regarded on many planets the same way the Ford F-250, Ford Transit or Toyota Hilux were on Earth.

The crew of the flier would almost certainly want to take her alive. Having her to play with for a while would be part of their prize, so they would overtake her, land, and wait for her to arrive.

She stopped suddenly. Both the dodo and the flier pilot overshot.

melanie raised the gun and fired several rounds at a small vent near the tail of the flier. The vent was an outlet for the cabin climate control, but just above it ran a cable connected to the engine management system. Severing the cable switched the engine off. That didn't matter so much on a civilian transport, where being fired at was not a regular occurrence, but was potentially fatal on a military vehicle.

The second of melanie's shots split the cable open, the flier's engine stopped, and it plowed into the ground four seconds later.

melanie ran on. The pursuing bird, having circled back, took up station a meter behind her as she ran.

As they passed the wrecked flier, one of the uninjured but shaken crew staggered out. melanie shot him just below the

16

knee. The bullet wouldn't kill him, but the dodos now had a much slower and more nutritious target than her.

Two minutes later, melanie ran into the copse and almost into the side of a flier sitting, hidden in the tall grasses. The side door powered up, and melanie faced two troopers behind the muzzles of two large-caliber projectile weapons.

"You recognize what these guns are?" one man said.

"I do, Frederico," melanie said. "So, how are things with you?"

"Excellent, thank you, melanie," he said. "Now, unless you would like me to blow your head off, lean forward, slowly, and look into this light."

"You know, so far, your chances of a second date with me are quite slim, Frederico," melanie said as she carefully leaned forward to look into the retinal scanner. The machine beeped, and a green light flashed.

"It would appear you really are melanie," Frederico said as both men holstered their guns, and melanie climbed into the flier. "Oh, and my wife says to say hello and to stop teasing her husband."

"Tell Yevhena I said, hi," melanie said as the flier door closed behind her.

All three sat down and let the restraints close about them. A slight bump let them know they were lifting off, and almost immediately the flier turned nose up and accelerated at five g for seventy-two seconds.

"I should have mentioned," Frederico said shakily, once the acceleration stopped, "we use the AIs out of *Languid Bloom* class shuttles to pilot these."

"I think I guessed around seventy seconds ago," melanie said as the restraints slid back. "Shouldn't we ban those damned things?"

"Maybe we should," Frederico said. "But probably best we don't discuss that while onboard one. They get a little sensitive."

"I bet," melanie said as she pulled off the blood-streaked blond wig to reveal her crewcut black hair.

"You might need this," Frederico said, handing melanie a cloth. "For your face as well."

melanie looked down and saw blood liberally covered the front of her black uniform. It surprised her that far more predators hadn't come out while she was running around like a self-propelled hunting drag.

Frederico indicated a small door, and melanie went into the flier's tiny lavatory. The mirror suggested she had just come from some pagan festival that involved eating people alive.

She removed the uniform jacket and began wiping her face while she said, "So, why did Lorina pull me out?"

"No idea," Frederico said. "We'll be docking on *Silent Thunder* in a few minutes, and you can talk to her yourself."

"Good," melanie said as she emerged and sat opposite the two men.

She pointed at the second man and said, "You, I don't know, but you look familiar."

"Wynn Koenig, ma'am," the younger man said.

"Any relation?" melanie asked. "Also, do not call me ma'am. Boss is good, or even melanie, but never ma'am."

"Yes, ma... boss," Wynn said. "Rufus Koenig is my uncle."

"We all have our crosses," melanie said with a smile.

"He said something similar when I said I would meet you," Wynn said.

melanie laughed.

"So, what were the Nel up to?" Frederico asked.

"I am not sure," melanie said. "It was an unusual mix. Scientists mainly, and a few low-rank troops. Religious officers, of course. They were running experiments on some Terrans and a lot of their own kind. We believe they will move the entire operation to Earth shortly. I thought one of them might know where on Earth."

Frederico snorted. "Points for optimism."

A slight bump, and the shuttle door opened to reveal a brightly lit hangar deck and a beaming woman in an Aetherian Space Fleet uniform.

"Hello, melanie," she said. "Welcome back aboard *Silent Thunder*. Is there anything on the planet to which an EMP might be detrimental?"

"Hello, Cressy," melanie said. "Only the Nel laboratories,"

"Excellent," Commander Cressida Ricci said and turned slightly, staring into the middle-distance, as she said, "Retroverse, now, anita, if you please."

She looked back at melanie and said, "You will be on Earth in seventy-two hours.

"Meanwhile, Lieutenant Korenjic seems just a little anxious to speak to you, so...." she handed melanie a compad.

18

As Frederico and Wynn climbed out of the shuttle, melanie said, "Hello Lorina, what's the problem?"

"*Boss, at last,*" Lorina said. "*Slight problem.*"

"How slight?"

"*The hunter-squad Bianca Kaninchen sent to Earth is closing in on Caeil Ashbow faster than we thought.*"

"That is not good," melanie said. "So, where is Kaninchen?"

"*On Gaia, as far as we can tell,*" Lorina said.

"Probably not for long," melanie said. "I am on my way now."

FiT: THE FORTY-SIXTH

IST Envoy, orbiting Daedalus 4
16:30 GST Threeday 3.4.2834
(Saturday, 24th December 2016)

"You want me to do what?" melanie said.

"*melanie*," Bianca replied over the comm. "*As we are both aware, you have perfect hearing and perfect recall; therefore, you know exactly what I said.*"

"Okay. I recall hearing you say you wanted me to go to Tarnskill 7 and intervene in a civil uprising. My purpose in asking you to repeat it was to find out if you'd had a sudden mental aberration and might have then recovered. Then I could ask you when we started interfering in the domestic affairs of the Tomalites?"

"*The Tomalites are re-forming some ball of rock, and Gaia is lying third on the infrastructure bids. We want the contract. Corporate thinks your intervention might bump us up two places.*"

"Isn't 'Corporate thinks' an oxymoron?"

"*I shall ignore that,*" Bianca said. "*Get there.*"

"Will do," melanie said. "Just as soon as the order from Rufus Koenig, my actual boss, gets to me."

"*As you mention 'actual bosses,' it reminds me, what happened to Olga Velazquez? Me being her actual boss.*"

"I fired her," melanie said.

"*Why? She was an excellent weapons officer.*"

"She was passing information on our weapons systems to the Bellachi, and if they have it, the Nel have it."

"*Did it not occur to you to check if this was disinformation or not?*"

"Of course. Everything occurs to me. It wasn't. Making Velazquez either incompetent or a traitor. Because it might have been the former, I fired her. If I had thought it was the latter, I would have shot her."

"*You will consult me before making these decisions in the future,*" Bianca said, cutting the connection.

melanie's door slid open, and Lieutenant Lorina Korenjic came in.

"Well?" Lorina asked.

"She wanted to know why I fired Olga Velazquez."

"Didn't she know she was passing information to the Nel?"

"No," melanie said. "Because she wasn't, but she was one of Bianca's spies, and I want to see where she goes from here."

"Technically, as Bianca is head of the intelligence services, and we work for the intelligence services...." She paused, picking up on the look melanie was casting her way.

"Okay, apart from you, we are all Bianca's spies, and it will be difficult seeing where Olga goes; she's disappeared."

"In that, she is no longer on Gaia?"

"In that, she is no longer anywhere," Lorina said. "Which makes a total of two hundred and eighty-seven GCID staff who have gone missing."

"Curiouser and curiouser," melanie said.

"Anything else, or was Olga all you talked about?"

"Not at all. Bianca wanted me to go to Tarnskill 7 and intervene in a civil uprising."

"Yeah," Lorina yelled. "Are you going?"

"Just as soon as I am told to do so by Rufus."

"So, no."

"Correct," melanie said. "How goes the grand plan?"

"Good," Lorina said, waving a compad. "Team A, Robert Sunter's little band of misfits, is complete. But an odd development.

"I received an internal memo from Colonel Kaninchen requesting I include Greta and Georgia in the team."

"Any explanation for this request?" melanie said.

"Some crap about Sunter's mother being an old friend, and she realized he had some 'weaknesses' due to 'inexperience' and two officers as experienced as the Dee-Dum might prove invaluable."

"I'm going to assume she didn't use the term 'Dee-Dum' to describe her daughters?"

"No, of course not," Lorina said.

"Any other requests from on high you haven't told me about?"

"Should I mention this is the first time we have been face-to-face for several weeks, that—as per your instructions—written reports on either team are to be kept to a minimum and encrypted, and that it only happened two days ago?"

21

"My suggestion is that you shouldn't mention it, no."

"Good, and yes, there has been another request from on high, *requesting* we also add Zara Chang to Sunter's team."

melanie stared at Lorina impassively for several counts and then said. "If that is your idea of a joke...."

"When it comes to this mission, my sense of humor is worse than yours, if that is possible," Lorina said. "So, no, it isn't my idea of a joke."

"Does Bianca know where she is?"

Sort of," Lorina said. "She knows the real one is dead. She prefers not to know the whereabouts of the one she thinks is her, and she is only vaguely aware of the existence of the one we think is her."

"Fun, isn't it?" melanie said.

Lorina considered for a moment. "Yeah. Mostly, it is," she said.

"What are you doing with these requests?"

"I will stop using the word 'request' for a while," Lorina said. "At least until the urge to wiggle my fingers around, like speech marks, goes away. But, I will simply comply. Like a good little lieutenant."

"That will raise suspicions," melanie said.

"Well, not exactly comply," Lorina said, ignoring melanie's comment. "I have told the Colonel that, although I am not overly pleased, it will be done, and all three will be in Sunter's team."

"I must say, using Sunter was inspired," melanie said. "It was inevitable he would tell his mother and his mother would tell Bianca. This means Bianca now has solid evidence you are planning something; she has a ready source of information and needn't investigate further."

"Why, thank you kindly, ma'am," Lorina said and executed a very awkward curtsey.

"You do remember my two options were to promote you or execute you and that I could reverse my decision?"

"Not a day goes by I do not thank you and the fates for my deliverance," Lorina said with a grin.

"Glad to hear it," melanie said. "Where does Sunter think he is going?"

"Earth," Lorina said. "I told him Earth, even though he didn't ask. He will tell his mommy, so Bianca will know I told him we were going to Earth. Bianca will also know I wouldn't tell him our true destination. Suggesting we are not going to Earth. But she will also know you are involved, and there has been a high probability for some time that you will go to Earth. One cancels out the other."

"Excellent," melanie said. "What have you told the Dee-Dum?"

"Not much," Lorina said. "I told them they would join the Sunter team at their mother's request, and travel orders would follow. This means they will just do as they are told, so it's a result for us.

"In fact, I'm putting them in our team. Mommy wants them close to you, and that's what mommy will get."

"What was Bianca's reason for including Zara Chang?"

"Apparently, her parents are also family friends of the Colonel, and they think it will be good for their little girl."

"They have only met twice, to my certain knowledge, so they are not family friends," melanie said. "Not that Bianca has family friends; if she did, as Zara's parents know Zara is dead, they'd not be amongst them."

"Yes, but here we go; I'm not sure the Colonel knows we know Zara is dead. Or she knows we know but doesn't know if we know she knows. At three in the morning, I worked out at least four more levels of that, but it made my head hurt, so I'm not doing it again."

"Have you told our Zara?"

"Yes, I did. She thought it was hilarious."

"She would," melanie said. "So where is she?"

"Jericho."

"What the hell is she doing out there?"

"We have friends in low places. In this case, a whole gaggle of friends who will remain *friends* all the time I pay them overly large quantities of UCs to provide the services we want."

"Okay, and so, to Team B," melanie said. "Unless you were about to mention some other little surprise?"

"No. And Team B is good."

"How are Lemasolai and Gulab going to react to seeing Zara Chang?" melanie asked.

"They don't know she's dead, of course," Lorina said. "Her death was well hushed up by you and the Colonel, which helps. Especially as, officially, neither of you knows. Other than that, Chiyo Lemasolai will notice in five seconds, considering her past with Chang. My options were to drop her from the list or, eventually, confide in her. I opted for the latter. She is very good at what she does, and if I drop Lemasolai, I need to drop Gulab. She and Chiyo are a real double act."

"I agree," melanie said. "Have you arranged to spring Olafsen as well?"

"As far as I'm aware, he isn't in detention."

"With his record, he will be by the time you leave."

"Very true," Lorina said with a nod. "The others are all in place. Iwasaka and Johannsen know what's happening initially, as they are coming with me to Romstrum. The others in the team currently do not know they are in a team. What they, plus around eighty extras, all think they know, is that I have selected them to go on an exercise that may or may not involve going to an asteroid for several weeks."

"How's Tamara Finkel?"

"As normal as Finkel gets. We've only just got her back after she was with you on the Aetherian freighter, and she is slightly weirder. What were you doing there, anyway?"

"Building a trans-planar pha-pho transmitter," melanie said.

Lorina shrugged. "Yeah, whatever. Miguel, Gary and I all think Chiyo will suggest something is 'going on' and get ignored because that's what she always says, but Finkel will figure out that there really is something not right."

"It's what I would think, too," melanie said. "So, equipment?"

"All here," Lorina waved the compad again. "Weapons, food, munitions, materials for the shuttle conversion, and all the extras discussed."

"Talking of shuttles?"

"A small hitch. Section-J has your T3, for some reason, and they won't let it go. I have no idea why they had it in the first place unless you used it to tell Bianca yours is bigger than hers."

"It's having a little work done right now," melanie said without expression. "But when it's complete, it'll be on its way to Romstrum."

"Yeah?" Lorina said, grinning. "How did you manage that?"

"I told the creep who runs Section-J that if he released or delivered it to anyone other than me, or my designated agent, I would kill him, his entire department, and all their families. Up to and including second cousins."

"I suppose he believed you."

"Of course, he believed me. I meant it," melanie said. "Is all the transport in place?"

"All the Aetherian transport is, yes. I will leave the Gaian transport until much closer to the date, and I will make multiple bookings to muddy the waters a little."

"Okay, final dates?" melanie said. "I am arranging for the shuttle to be delivered on one-six-five. You should be there on the same day. Be careful; I suspect your old friends Briony Sigurðardóttir and Gabriel Lee will be the delivery pilots."

"Not good," Lorina said. "They will question why it is me rather than Robert Sunter arriving. In theory, he is going from Gaia to Earth. Romstrum is on the route, and they will have assumed he will go there to meet you."

"Could you not say you wanted to carry out your own inspection before handing it over?"

"I could. If I wanted an implausible excuse that looked like a series of large holes held together with improbably thin ice," Lorina said. "Or, I could say Sunter is delayed, and rather than leave a T3 shuttle unattended, I went there to look after it."

"That might be better," melanie said, not sounding convinced. "I will arrive the following day with Caeil Ashbow. The rest of the team must get there within the next two days."

"As arranged," Lorina said. "They will arrive on the second day, but it will give you time to re-register."

"Okay," melanie said. "Keep our team in the dark until just before you pull them out. I don't want any rumors starting."

"Exactly what I was going to do," Lorina said, bristling slightly.

"I know you are good at your job," melanie said. "It doesn't stop me from having concerns. So, just in case...." she handed Lorina two square plastic cards. "Mission authorizations. One from Colonel Sligo and the other from Caesar. My name isn't on them, which will help."

"Wow," Lorina said, slipping the cards into her pocket. "How will they stand up under scrutiny?"

"With no problems, they are both genuine."

Lorina raised an eyebrow.

"Caesar and I have an arrangement, and Sligo would rather I didn't talk to his wife about his mistress, or vice versa, or to Internal Affairs about some of the contracts he signs."

Lorina laughed. "Okay, and you sound very certain about when you will get to Romstrum and that you will have Caeil Ashbow with you."

"I am. Very certain."

25

"Why are you finding him? I mean, I know who he is and what happened and all, but with everything else, why now?"

"Bianca is putting together a squad to wipe out a few people on Earth she dislikes. Caeil's name will be at the top."

"Why? He was a baby when his parents were killed."

"But not just any baby, he was Sarah and Benjamin's baby," melanie said. "He was safe all the time Scallon was looking for him because Scallon enjoys living on Earth. A professional team will be different."

"Is that where you are going next?" Lorina asked.

"No," melanie said. "There is a Nel research facility that is being moved to Earth. One of them might just know where their base is on Earth. So, I am going there first."

"Okay, boss," Lorina said. "It's always the same. Just as things get busy, you take a vacation."

26

DAY FOUR

Twoday 4.5.2834

Friday 3rd February 2017

"What time of night is this to be calling on a frail old spinster lady?" Agnes Good said, making a show of looking up at melanie.

"Why? Do you know any?" melanie said.

"No, probably not," Agnes said. "Come in and try to walk around the ceiling lights. I take it from the length of those legs you have been teasing the Nel again?"

"Only temporarily," melanie said. "I was trying to get a better idea of where the Nel might hide down here when Lorina called me out."

Agnes ushered melanie into a comfortable living room. The large, over-stuffed, and predominantly dark red furniture gave the impression it existed only to be where it was. Pictures of rows of children all spruced up for the annual class photograph encrusted the matt white walls.

In front of the fire, an elderly Springer Spaniel woke, regarded melanie with suspicion for a moment, thumped her tail on the floor twice, and went back to sleep.

Over the fireplace was an oil painting of two women standing before a large country house. Their dresses suggested the scene was from the second half of the nineteenth century.

"Trying to find the Nel base, were you?" Agnes said, gesturing towards a chair. melanie sat down.

"Yes," melanie said. "A total waste of time. I don't think any of the Nel knew, or cared, where they will be when they get to Earth."

"Probably," Agnes said. "Anyway, Lorina told me the situation, and you are only a couple of days earlier than intended, so it was all ready."

She handed melanie a buff folder.

"You have heard of compads and computers?" melanie said, looking at the folder with horror.

"I have," Agnes said. "Paper files kept Caeil safe for years."

"You have a point," melanie said and opened the folder.

"You need to find the orphanage first," Agnes said. "In the pack is a magazine article from which you could work it out, even if you didn't already know."

28

"Anjelica is going to work on Clive Walker-Russell, lure him into the right area so he can spot Caeil as David Massey. And there is new software you can use to spot Caeil being Pierre Gomez."

"Is Caeil anybody else?"

Agnes sighed. "He was William Dean originally, as you well know, but then, after leaving the school, he was Danny Glover, Danny Pollard, Jack le Bois, David Massey and Pierre Gomez. His new real name is John Card Fletcher, but he calls himself Jack."

"Ah," melanie said. "I have been waiting for a Jack Fletcher to turn up."

Agnes looked at melanie the same way she had looked at generations of school children when they said something silly.

"Of course you were, dear," she said.

"Does he have an occupation?"

"Do you read my reports?"

"Rarely," melanie said.

"No shit," Agnes said. "He has been a bouncer in a strip-club, muscle for a loan shark, a van driver, and now he robs banks."

"Okay," melanie said. "It makes you wonder what we let loose on the world when we saved him, doesn't it?"

"It does," Agnes said. "Although he was such a nice little boy as William Dean. So, what are you going to do with him?"

"Get him off Earth and onto a freighter to Aetheria. He can stay there until Kaninchen is dead, and then I will bring him back."

"You can't use him in this operation of yours?"

"I can't see how," melanie said. "Caeil's a Terran now. He has no skills we need, and I'm not sure I want a career criminal as part of my team."

"Absolutely not," Agnes said, and they both laughed.

DAY ELEVEN

Threeday 5.5.2834
Friday 10th February 2017

"What the fuck is he doing?" Jacob Scallon said, almost to himself.

The monitor's image, hacked from the bank's security system, showed a gray-carpeted, gray-walled corridor lit by the inevitable fluorescents. A cleaner's trolley, the wheel on the front right corner wobbling, came into view, pushed by a tall, somewhat plump man, his limp synchronized to the erratic progress of his trolley.

"He's robbing them," melanie said from the corner of the room.

Scallon swung his chair to look at her, sitting in the gloom. "What?"

"He's stealing their money."

"When did you get back? When did you come to that conclusion, and when were you going to tell me?"

"Two minutes ago, fifteen minutes ago, and I just did."

"Where were you anyway?" Scallon said.

"Breaking into his flat," melanie said. "It's not far away."

"Find anything worthwhile?"

"Nothing," melanie said.

As they watched the screen, a door opened, and a man, suit jacket off and tie askew, appeared and waved at the cleaner.

"Who's he?" Scallon said.

"Steve Smith, the bank's security boss," melanie said.

Scallon swung round in his chair and said, "Yeah, why is he calling him into his office?"

"Who knows?" melanie said. "Maybe he figured it out too?"

"You reckon?"

melanie sighed. "No, I don't reckon. Smith looks like a man in need of a cleaner because Smith is a bit of a slob and because Smith has an appointment in ten minutes with the police."

"Oh, okay," Scallon said.

melanie shook her head, knowing someone would tell him she had done so at the first convenient moment.

Steve Smith prided himself on being calm in an emergency. Not so this evening, he thought, surveying the litter of papers, used cups, sandwich wrappers, and other detritus on his circular meeting table and in the already overflowing bin. Under normal circumstances Julia, his secretary, would have dealt with this in her quiet and efficient way. But these were not normal circumstances, and tonight Steve had sent her home early along with the rest of the team.

"Go home, get some rest, and let's start again fresh in the morning," he had told them. He expected howls of protest at the idea of working over the weekend and wasn't disappointed.

Tony Wilson had started it all, staggering through Steve's door carrying a laptop and enough sheets of print-out to wallpaper a small flat while saying, "Hi Steve, we've got a problem."

Three hours and a missed lunch break later, Wilson went back to wherever he and the others of his kind hid, and Steve called the police. The young detective constable he spoke to had taken his name and number, but as soon as Steve told him the problem, the DC said, "*May I stop you there, sir. Sergeant Willis will phone you back in five minutes.*"

"Sure," Steve said, a little surprised. It almost sounded like they were waiting for his call.

Steve's phone rang four minutes later, and a voice said, "*Mister Smith?*"

"Yes."

"*Detective Sergeant Willis, Wood Street police station.*"

"Okay, thanks for calling me back," Steve said.

"*Not a problem, sir,*" Willis said. "*My DC has given me the basics; can I ask you how many people are aware of what has happened?*"

"Sure, probably three guys in the IT department." Steve was glad he hadn't said 'three geeks.'

"They spotted the anomaly while running some pattern recognition software they have devised. Also, three of my team and my secretary."

33

"Can you keep it at that? Detective Inspector Alex Monroe and I would like to meet with you, say, eight o'clock this evening? And just you, if that's okay?"

"Not a problem," Steve said.

He had been a detective chief inspector with the Metropolitan Police prior to early retirement and knew inspectors didn't carry out interviews. They might do it in the movies and on TV, but the constables and sergeants did all the legwork in the real world.

He waited for five minutes and called Wood Street again.

"DS Willis, please," he said to the desk sergeant, who answered. The extension rang, and Steve heard, *"DS Willis."* It sounded like the man he'd just spoken to, and Steve was going to hang up.

"Sorry, wrong number," he blurted.

"No problem; see you at eight," Willis said.

As a detective, Steve's success had been due in no small way to his cynical attitude toward everything he heard. Now Steve had good reason to believe Willis was who he said he was.

A meeting at eight o'clock on a Friday evening after all the staff had left for home, or the pub, concerned him. Not that he couldn't guess what was going on. Behind these anomalies lay something serious. Something that might even originate inside the bank. But right now, Steve's primary concern was his apparent inability to deal with a bit of rubbish.

As he wondered where he might lay his hands on a couple of plastic rubbish bags, he heard the familiar squeak of the cleaner's trolley. He could visualize the man, tall, a bit podgy with a slight limp, and a cleaning cart with a wonky wheel. He had an odd name, Pierre, something, but not something French.

Steve opened his office door as the man drew near. The cleaner had earpieces and an ancient Walkman around his neck and seemed oblivious until Steve waved his arms about.

The trolley wobbled to a stop.

"Pierre," Steve said with a smile, "I have rubbish that needs taking away. Can you help?"

Dark brown eyes stared at him for a second, seemingly not comprehending, then the cleaner reached up to pull out the earpieces. He wore rubber gloves, yellow on the right hand and blue on the left. Steve repeated his question, and the man said, "Yes, sir, no problem, no problem." He spoke with an odd but recognizable French accent—almost as if tainted by an undertone of Scouse—and followed Steve into the office.

The cleaner pulled the required bags from his cart, began collecting the rubbish, and crushing it down to make room for more. He loaded the debris onto his cart and returned, waving a duster and an aerosol. "Sir, you want?"

"Yes, please, thank you," Steve said, stacking the papers he thought he might need for this evening.

Pierre got to work erasing the last coffee cup rings from the table, dusting off, and straightening the chairs.

At one point, Steve turned. Pierre had disappeared, then surfaced from beneath the table. He held a sandwich carton aloft in his yellow glove, like a diver with a recovered silver artifact from a sunken Spanish galleon.

The phone rang, and as Steve answered, he glanced at the clock: just after eight o'clock. Time up. Thanking the man, Steve ushered his cleaning savior out of the office. Pierre Gomez set off again on his rounds, his progress observed only by a single security camera set high on the corridor's wall.

GCID office, Belgrave Road, London
19:55 GMT
(20:55 GST)

"So, how is he robbing them?" Scallon demanded. "Exactly."

"I don't know, but he is," melanie said, crossing her improbably long legs. "There is no other explanation."

Scallon regarded her silently, knowing she was probably right. She was always right.

"Fuck and double fuck," Scallon said. "I need to stop working out what he is doing or how he is doing it because, like, who gives a fuck, and get him secured."

"Not yet," melanie said. "Soon."

"How soon?" Scallon said. "Bianca fucking Kaninchen is not in her office, and that stupid fuck Katelyn Fofana won't tell me where she is. We don't know, but she could be on her way here and showing up any time now. What the fuck am I going to tell her?"

"Actually, Bianca fucking Kaninchen is already here, and what the fuck *are* you going to tell me?" said a familiar voice from the door in the corner, causing Scallon to swing round in his chair.

"Here's an idea; you tell me everything. From the beginning."

"Hello, Bianca," Scallon said, standing up and glowering at the underling who had let her into the room unannounced. "How're things with you back in the real world?"

"Well, thank you, Jacob. Now, how about somebody gets me a cup of decent coffee and a decent Cognac? I'm probably going to need it."

Scallon nodded to the underling, who hurried away to get coffee and brandy in the sure and certain knowledge he had not heard the last of this.

Bianca turned and looked at melanie.

"Hello," she said, "I am Bianca Kaninchen. Head of the Gaian Central Intelligence Directorate. You bear a striking resemblance to somebody I thought we employed, but who my office has extreme difficulty finding."

"Hello," melanie said, still seated in the gloom. "My name is melanie. I am employed by Rufus Koenig, head of the Aetherian Intelligence Bureau. And you remind me of somebody to whom they have seconded me, at no cost, to assist in the Nel situation. Providing Koenig may call me back whenever he has important work to be done."

"Hmm," Bianca said. "And yet, here you are."

"And yet, here I am," melanie said. "I was passing and thought I would drop in, see if I could lend a hand. It has been fifty-nine years and no results."

"Has anything changed since your arrival?" Bianca said.

"Judge for yourself," melanie said and rose to her feet.

Bianca looked at her and asked, "Are your legs getting longer?"

melanie smiled and held up one foot for examination, revealing a long thin heel on her booted foot. "No. Just a fashion victim."

"Don't the locals notice?"

"I don't wear these boots outside," melanie said. "Or rarely."

"She's two meters ten in those damned boots," Scallon said. "She gets approached by a scout from a fucking modeling agency every time we go out, even in flat shoes."

"Hmm," Bianca said. "Well, if you have no positive news for me, at least you have a fallback career lined up."

"Yes, I do," melanie said. "As the future head of AIB,"

Bianca stiffened but knew this was one of many areas where she would not best melanie.

36

The underling returned carrying a tray with coffee and brandy. Scallon directed them towards a small informal seating area with three brown sofas and a coffee table. He seated them, melanie to one side, Bianca to the other, and himself in the middle. Bianca abhorred being 'trapped.'

They were in an open-plan office like thousands of others across London. Fluorescents scattered amongst the white polystyrene ceiling panels illuminated pale biscuit-colored walls and checker-board gray carpet tiles. A row of office partitions, modified to protect the room from a broad spectrum of surveillance equipment, stood before the windows.

Several agents scattered around the room, were staring intently at monitors, desperately hoping they wouldn't be spotted and sent on errands, so they could continue listening to Jacob Scallon taken down a peg or two, maybe more.

Three desks pushed together in the center of the room carried yet more monitors and several cases, open and disgorging cables and wires in a multi-hued cascade. The monitors were visible from the brown sofas.

"Did you raid a museum for all that?" Bianca asked, pointing at the displays.

"It's current Terran," Scallon said. "Just in case we get visitors."

"We cannot be forever burying civil servants in the basement," melanie said.

"I would," Bianca said.

Scallon sat hushed for the few minutes it took Bianca to nestle. Bianca took a couple of sips from her cup and offered as close to a benign smile as she was capable of before jabbing a finger at melanie.

"Well, have you found him or not?" she said.

"It looks like it," melanie said.

"Then why haven't you picked him up?" Bianca said.

"I was waiting for you to arrive and Caeil to get home," melanie said. "He lives near here."

Lancaster and Lancashire Bank
20:05 GMT
(21:05 GST)

Steve cast a quick eye around the office. It was all in the 'light oak' plastic, rather than the 'ash' plastic or the 'natural pine' plastic, which made up the company's parameters for individualism. Although he had brought in his own Recaro chair, eliciting much tutting from office services.

Steve swung open the tiny locker door and exchanged a grimace with his reflection in the mirror. He didn't look almost fifty-one, and most of the time, he didn't feel it. The hair was thinning a bit, well, more than a bit, although it would take someone tall to notice the bald spot developing at the back. Other than that, he passed muster.

He checked his tie was straight and buttoned the jacket of his dark blue 'bankers' suit, then shot his cuffs correctly. He had been with the Lancaster for less than a year and was still finding his feet. All so different from his days as a copper.

Back then, his disheveled look was almost the norm, and only the occasional fast-track jockey looked as if he took his suit off at night to sleep. Steve was now surrounded by bankers with dark suits, dazzling white shirts and loud ties.

He'd bought a couple of expensive suits when he'd joined the bank, but no amount of tailoring could disguise the fact that he looked like a gorilla on its hind legs. Or a rugby player.

It had been twenty years since Steve Smith last picked up what he regarded as a 'proper-shaped ball,' but as well as the physique, he still kept the mental attitude of a rugby player. To him, the word 'try' was synonymous with winning, and while he was happy to weave around those standing between where he was and where he needed to be, if all else failed, he would still put his head down and go through the middle.

He didn't feel so much out of his depth as out of his comfort zone. A bit like the bank that employed him.

Two brothers, Fowler and Grosvenor Neith, had established the Lancaster and Lancashire in seventeen fifty-two as a commercial bank, with offices at one end of the newly constructed Saint George's Quay in Lancaster. The location suited the local business community's needs when the port gained prominence, particularly in the slave trade.

Not resting on their laurels, soon after founding the Lancaster Bank, the brothers went to New York and founded the grandly titled but modestly accommodated Artemis Banking Group.

After the abolition of slavery throughout most of the British Empire in 1833, the 'Lanc', as it had become known, continued to handle local businesses' requirements through to eighteen fifty-four when the original building was closed, and the bank moved to London.

The bank chose its new home, built in the neo-Palladian style, because it conveyed a certain gravitas and inspired confidence, and because it sat within the square mile of the City. The stylized Red Rose trademark was the only remaining link with Lancaster or Lancashire.

The bank only serviced businesses, and over the years it added branches in the United Kingdom's industrial areas, following the trends from heavy engineering to high-tech as the world changed.

Walking towards the lifts, Steve wondered idly about the DI on his way up. Steve had rarely had any dealings with the City of London police, even when working for the neighboring Metropolitan force, so he hadn't any contacts to check out who this guy was. The name suggested a Scot, but that was jumping to conclusions. Chances were, he was born and bred in Tooting.

The lift doors opened, and a man who could only have been a policeman emerged, followed by a youngish woman in a business suit. Wide-set blue eyes gazed at him steadily from beneath a blond fringe.

Of course, Steve realized, the name Alex Monroe didn't mean he was necessarily either a Scot or a man.

"Hello," he said, "I'm Steve Smith."

The two visitors produced warrant cards like conjurers, and the woman said,

"Hi, I'm Alex Monroe, and this is DS Ben Willis."

Ben Willis saw the look, the slight dilation of the pupils as Steve Smith looked at DI Monroe. No chance, Willis thought. He glanced around at his boss, waiting for her to take the lead, and saw how she looked at Smith. Well, well, Willis thought, this might get some of the starch out of her knickers.

Steve shook hands and escorted them back to his office, where he offered coffee and the few biscuits he'd found secreted in Julia's desk. They chatted for a while; Willis, at least, was ex-Met., and they shared a few contacts. Once the ritual of establishing who knew who was complete, they turned their attention to the business at hand.

"It was some of the bright young things in IT that discovered a pattern in failure to repay loans," Steve explained. "I'm not an accountant, so I don't have all the details, and normally I would have a couple of them in here to explain it, but it seems these repayment failures centered on just three branches. When we spoke to the branches concerned, they had no recollection of authorizing these loans. Records, yes, but no one remembered the people or the actual authorization."

"Everything checked out, codes were all in place, everything as it should be?" Alex asked.

"Yes. But do I understand this isn't something new to you?"

"No, it's not new. They have robbed two other banks in the same way in the last five years," she said.

"I've heard nothing about this," Steve said.

"You wouldn't," Alex replied. "It happened before you joined the Lanc, and the banks in question didn't want publicity, so it was all hushed up."

"So much for the banks sharing this sort of intelligence. How much did they get with the other two?"

The two police officers exchanged significant glances at Steve's comment about shared intel, which was no surprise.

"About nine million from one and eleven million from the other, so they are probably going for around the same here," Alex said.

"I don't think so," Steve said, "they have only had us over for about one and a half million."

"So far," Ben Willis said. "This could go on for weeks, if not months. This gang sets up fifty or sixty loans over six or seven months. Each loan is for a little below two hundred and fifty thousand. Initially, the loan repayments are all on time. They pay them from the loan itself, a bit like a Ponzi scam. Then the repayments stop.

"For some loans, the last repayments will have come in within a few days of the cut-off point, so it will be another month before the next one is due. Genuine borrowers don't make payments all the time. The banks send letters and reminders out, and so on, through the normal process. It could take months to determine what is a genuine loan with a small repayment problem and what is not."

"Jesus H Christ," Steve said. "But how are they doing it?"

"That's what we asked our tame geeks," Ben answered. "Once translated, what they say is, if the computer says 'yes', then the loan goes through, and if someone can manipulate the bank's computers, they will say 'yes'. At which stage, there is no cause for alarm; what is happening is nothing out of the ordinary."

40

"Yes, I understand," Steve said, "but if someone can easily muck about with the system, why not just take the money in one hit?"

"That's the clever bit," Alex said. "Loans for ten million aren't just dealt with by computers; there's human interaction. Shift ten million out of the bank, and questions get asked immediately, and trails followed. Non-repayment on a small loan gives the thief a lot of time to cover his tracks. Fifty loans for a quarter of a million to buy machinery or expand a business are bread-and-butter stuff. We suspect they pulled the plug on the repayments about two weeks ago, and our thieves are sitting in a bar in the Caribbean, as we speak."

Steve let out a long sigh. "I suppose all the money they borrowed has long since become something anonymous and portable?"

"You just summed it up," Alex said with a wry smile. Steve thought it to be a lovely, wry smile.

"Have you anything to go on now, anything from the previous two robberies?" Steve asked.

"Sorry, but right now, we have nothing," Alex said. "Our first choice was one of the terrorist organizations. We had a word with Special Branch, who had a word with Five and Six about any large windfalls. Nothing."

"I was looking at the villains proper," Ben said. "Twenty million so far, probably another ten from here; I was sure someone would know something. Not a sniff. By which I mean they don't know, not that they're too frightened to talk, they just don't know."

"Suggesting," Steve mused, "this gang isn't part of the scene. They don't have records or criminal contacts. Unless it isn't a gang but an individual."

"We think it is an individual," Alex said. "Who knows about banking rather than robbing banks."

"Yeah," Steve said. "My first thought when I heard about these anomalies was that they originated inside the bank. My money would have been on a branch manager somewhere, paying for a lifestyle he can't afford. But with two other banks, I assumed it had to be a gang.

"If it isn't, then for that level of expertise, it will be someone here and at a senior level."

"Now you know why we wanted this meeting kept secret," Alex said and cast a long glance at the coffee machine.

41

FiT: THE EIGHTH

Manhattan Island
09:22 Local Sunday 12ᵗʰ May 1754
(14:22 GST Fiveday 6.3.2390)

Grosvenor Neith stood where, one day, 6ᵗʰ Avenue and West 57ᵗʰ Street would cross. The flier behind him humming.

"*Test number one*," Fowler Neith said over the comm.

The flier hummed louder; almost immediately, Joshua Nimrod yelled in triumph and emerged with a bar of gold.

"Returning your gold," Grosvenor said.

After a pause, Grosvenor heard Fowler say, "*Received*."

They waited a few moments before the next test, and this time Joshua appeared from the flier, waving a rabbit.

At a little after ten-thirty, Fowler himself arrived, and the brothers shook hands.

"Uncanny," Fowler said. "I know it isn't the same place, but it is identical to Caeloeterra."

"I look forward to seeing the other side," Grosvenor said.

"You will, brother, and soon," Fowler said. "Once we have both banks built."

"Tomorrow, we will mark out the area," Grosvenor said. "And on Tuesday, the first contingent of Irish arrives."

"Yes, ours started four days ago," Fowler said. "They won't work Sunday, so we thought it would be a good test day."

"How are you finding them?"

"Argumentative, easy to rile and drunk most of the time. But they can dig. That's why the British used them to dig their canals."

"What happens after the gates are installed?"

"The section they are digging first is over there," he pointed south. "Just big enough for them, their families, and all their belongings. I suppose you will do the same?"

"Of course, we can't have any loose ends," Grosvenor said. "I doubt anyone will find the remains for several hundred years. And I doubt I will care when they do."

DAY ELEVEN (Cont.)

Threeday 5.5.2834

Friday 10th February 2017

GCID office, Belgrave Road, London
20:10 GMT
(21:10 GST)

"When will he get home?" Bianca said.

Before melanie could answer, an aide said, "Commander, please excuse the interruption; there is an urgent comm for you."

As melanie rose, Bianca said, "Couldn't you patch it through?"

"It's probably Koenig," melanie said. "It won't take long."

Two doors down from the office, the comm room contained a desk, chair, and a military-spec comm unit.

"melanie," she said.

"*melanie. Rufus Koenig,*" said a voice from the speaker. "*What are you doing on Earth?*"

Then followed a conversation full of accusations and counter-accusations that would have told anyone listening, which there certainly would be, very little. Other than that melanie and her boss were fighting.

In reality, melanie was having another conversation, hidden in the digital carrier provided by her argument with Rufus Koenig. An argument generated by a computer aboard the Aetherian freighter *Silent Thunder*.

"*I just got a 'call-me' bleep from you,*" Lorina Korenjic said. "*So, I'm calling you.*"

"Bianca just turned up," melanie replied through her neurolink.

"*How did she know where you were?*"

"I don't think I am the main reason she's here," melanie said, "We found the lost boy."

"*Wow. That would have been difficult.*"

"You know sarcasm is wasted on me, don't you?" melanie said. "I should have known she would be here immediately after we found him."

"*I suppose Scallon ratted you out as soon as he realized you had found him?*"

"He did," melanie said. "But I now have a problem. I was going to grab Caeil tonight and load him onto *Silent Thunder*. I would have got off on Romstrum to meet you with the equipment while Caeil was on his way to Aetheria.

44

"Now, Bianca will want to take Caeil back to Gaia, non-stop, on *Encounter*. I must go with her, or Caeil won't live to see his birthplace."

"*I see what you mean,*" Lorina said. "*Although I'm looking at the fleet disposition, and it says* Encounter *isn't near you. It shows* Envoy *in Mars orbit, which is odd because* Envoy *dropped our team at the asteroid not too long ago.*"

"It will be *Encounter* 'ganged to show up as *Envoy*."

"*Yes, melanie, I know. I was being disingenuous. While locating your equipment, which I sincerely trust includes all the bedding we need*?"

"It does, but why get it from Earth?"

"*Most Gaian bedding is manufactured on Earth, but why pay extra to have it shipped all over the galaxy?*"

"Reasonable."

"*Ah, there it all is, just checking the manifest for bedding, and it is in our New York warehouse, and it is now... almost there... almost there... almost there... now, scheduled for delivery to* Envoy, *by any other name, and then on to Romstrum.*"

"But Bianca will still not want to stop at Romstrum," melanie said.

"*In theory, she gets no choice.* Encounter *is still a freighter. If there is cargo aboard, the AIs have no option but to stop and deliver. I will send you the number of the shuttle taking it down. I suggest you are on it, with the boy-wonder if necessary.*"

"*Okay, and I just had an idea, so* Encounter *has to stop at Romstrum.*"

"What idea?" melanie said.

"*Nothing to worry your pretty little head about because it involves mis-routing freighters and causing distress to pilots.*

"*Also, because I am so very good at my job, I have arranged a disposable drop-shuttle. Meaning, seconds after you leave the airlock,* Encounter *will accelerate at four billion g and slide back into the retroverse. They won't even know you have gone.*

"*And do not tell me it cannot accelerate at four billion g. I know, I was being whimsical.*"

"I would never dare correct you," melanie said. "But why a drop-shuttle?"

"*You will have Caeil with you. Bianca will not want him leaving; any standard shuttle will get checked. Nobody will*

45

bother checking a drop-shuttle. They aren't safe for anything but cargo and lunatics like you."

"Well thought," melanie said. "Except how am I supposed to get Caeil down in a drop-shuttle? They aren't... Yes, I, see?"

"*Thought you would, boss.*"

How is everything else?"

"*Everything else is good. Everybody is where they should be and heading where they should be going. Although there will be a lot of bitching when some get to travel straight back.*"

"Good work," melanie said. "I shall end my conversation with Rufus and get back to the fun."

"*Okay, boss, talk soon,*" Lorina said.

***

As melanie followed the aide to the comm room, Bianca turned to Scallon.

"How long has she been here?" she snapped.

"A week," Scallon said.

"A week? And it never occurred to you to tell me?"

"I told you."

"Eventually."

"I thought you knew," Scallon said. "She had orders from you."

"You mean, you thought she might not be legitimate, but that she had a better chance of finding Caeil in a few days than you did in the five years you have been here and then you would take the credit."

"No, ma'am."

"Do not 'ma'am' me," Bianca snapped. "This little sinecure is over."

Bianca looked deep in thought and then said, "I have a hunter-squad down here. Think yourself lucky I don't switch targets to you."

"Yes, ma... Colonel."

They sat in silence for several seconds, and then Bianca said, "Was it Rufus?"

Scallon looked up to see melanie was back, walking soundlessly as usual. He would be glad when she was gone.

"It was," melanie said. "There seems to be a considerable interest in why I am here."

46

"It must be pleasant to have so much interest shown in one's location," Bianca said. "So, when do we pick Caeil up?"

"Three, maybe four hours," melanie said. "It depends if he finishes his shift, and I suspect he won't do so tonight."

"Why?" Scallon said. "What did you do?"

melanie came close to a rueful shrug. "I inserted a memo into the bank's IT division this morning to review some procedures. Just to check that all was well."

"If you only realized he was stealing from them half an hour ago, how come you alerted their IT people to this earlier today?" Scallon asked. He could see melanie scoring a few points here and wouldn't let it be a total walkover.

"I had my suspicions a while back," melanie explained. "But I only received confirmation that something was happening just before I told you. I needed to work through a lot of telephone calls, and bankers do like to chat."

"Hmm," Scallon said pointedly.

"I take it Caeil works in this bank," Bianca said, waving her hand at the screen. "Can we see his office instead of this person?"

The monitor showed the man with a limp pushing a trolley with a wobbly wheel along a gray corridor.

"He is Caeil," melanie said. "He's the one robbing the Lancaster and Lancashire Bank."

melanie was looking straight at Bianca as she spoke and picked up the almost imperceptible swivel of Bianca's eyes towards Scallon and the equally imperceptible shake of Scallon's head. What a pity that neurolink traffic was undetectable; the ether would be alight, she imagined.

"So, right where I came in," Bianca said, her demeanor very casual. "How do you think he's doing it?"

"We have no idea," melanie said.

"No," Bianca said with the exaggerated composure of one who already has the answer; but wants to stretch out the moment. "But I do. He's invisible. Nobody notices him any more than we notice cleaning and repair 'bots back home. The only difference is we de-bug all our 'bots about six times a day."

"Who the hell would bug us?" Scallon said and got a withering look from Bianca that softened slightly when she realized he was attempting irony.

"In any large organization," Bianca waved her hand at the screen, "nobody thinks people like him can do anything they shouldn't. He is not very bright, or he wouldn't be a cleaner, they think, which only goes for those who know he exists. Most of the people in those offices assume magic cleans their desks. They leave; there are coffee cups and scraps of paper everywhere, and the next day they have a nice clean space with all their documents in a nice tidy pile.

"People get careless in familiar surroundings. It happens in our own offices. People leave screens on, notes on compads, passwords written on desks and keys lying around. It's okay; they are safe, surrounded by friends. It doesn't matter. All he had to do was slowly build up the information he needed. Extremely crude computers run everything here, and making those computers do what you want is simple. Even for someone without melanie's talents, or those of that strange female with the blue hair she employs, all they need is a few passwords, and from there, it is just a few short steps to being in total control."

Scallon stirred from where he had perched on the edge of a desk. "So, when does this robbery take place?"

"That I don't know," Bianca said.

"Okay. What next?" Scallon asked.

Bianca Kaninchen grinned. "How far from here does he live?"

"A ten-minute walk," melanie said.

"With your legs, perhaps," Scallon said. "Fifteen is more accurate, but we can drive there. Because of the one-way system and traffic, it takes a little longer, but it's more comfortable."

"It is eight-thirty, local," Bianca said. "Do you have somewhere I could nap for an hour or so?"

FiT: THE NINTH

Neith Bank, Manhattan, Caeloeterra
11:05 Local Thursday 8ᵗʰ December 1774
(15:05 GST Twoday 5.2.2425)

Fowler Neith said, "They are late." He had been leaning nonchalantly against the marble fireplace dominating the room for some time and beginning to find the pose tiring.

"Give them a little latitude," Grosvenor Neith said. "We are some distance out."

"Not quite eight kilometers."

"Miles, brother, miles, if you please."

"Not quite five miles, then."

The door opened, and a secretary came in and said, "Messrs. Haym Salomon and Robert Morris, to see you, gentlemen."

He stood aside, and the two men walked in, the brothers moving forward to shake hands and offer drinks, either hot or alcoholic.

Brandy dispensed, the four settled in the more comfortable chairs around the fireplace.

"You are a goodly journey from the city," Haym said. "Do you not have problems with the local tribesmen?"

"To the contrary," Grosvenor said. "We have excellent relationships with the Lenape. And any travelers to our enterprise will find themselves safer than on the streets of New York." He paused. "Although, perhaps not, if they happen to be wearing a red coat."

All four laughed.

"But do you not consider it possible the city may never reach you? Or is that your plan?" Robert Morris asked.

"It will reach us," Grosvenor said. "Thirty-seven years from now, in the year eighteen-eleven, the city fathers will commission a plan for this great city of ours, and this bank will stand on the corner of 6ᵗʰ Avenue and 57ᵗʰ Street."

Morris and Salomon exchanged glances.

"You speak with enormous certainty," Morris said.

"I do," Grosvenor said. "My brother and I have made a deal of money in a short amount of time. Something frowned upon in England, I might add. Money in England is only acceptable if the person who made it had the grace to die at least five generations earlier.

"We made our money because we discovered a book, many years ago, containing a list of prophecies written in the sixteenth century by Philippa Flowers, one of the witches of Belvoir."

Morris and Salomon sat, waiting for more.

"Are you not familiar with the case?" Grosvenor asked.

"We are not," Morris said.

"There were three witches, mother and two daughters, accused of killing the Earl of Rutland and two of his sons. Consuming communion bread caused the death of the mother, Joan Flowers, Margaret was hanged, and Philippa fled.

"She gained sanctuary from an ancestor of ours and lived out her days on his farm. In her gratitude, Philippa wrote a journal containing one hundred and forty-three prophecies. Our family has followed these prophecies to this day, and they have never been incorrect."

"Do these prophecies mention our current situation in any form?" Salomon asked, casually.

"They do indeed," Grosvenor said. "The language is a little contorted, as one might expect from the era, but the message is clear. Should the colonists elect to secede from Britain and the rule of King George, the consequent war will be short, brutal and establish British dominion for all time.

"And the facts speak for themselves. The British, unusually, are not at war with anyone, although the East India Company will probably soon be fighting the Maratha Empire in India, which will hardly count.

"King George, Lord North and Parliament will look at ways to keep their many colonies under control; and have the army do so. The Americas are proving difficult, and France and Spain are always looking for ways to increase their holdings here.

Hence the passing of the Intolerable Acts and closing the port of Boston. Coupled to which the Quartering Acts are not only a further restraint on liberties but an indicator that the British bring many more soldiers to this country."

"You say any revolution is damned?" Morris said. "Should there be any who wish to revolt, of course."

"No, not at all," Grosvenor said. "The prophecies suggest a properly funded revolution might be successful. And they suggest it will be hunters who provide what is required."

"The natives?" Morris said. "In what form?"

Grosvenor laughed, "No, not the natives. Our family name, Neith, originated in Scotland. But it is also the name of the ancient Egyptian goddess of war and hunting."

"Ah, I see," Morris said.

"Look at the facts.

"The British army is large, well-equipped and well-trained. But they are at their best fighting other national armies such as those of France and Spain. They would not be so successful against an army of the common people. Especially if those people had access to the funding for modern weapons and proper instruction."

"And, in a hypothetical situation," Morris said, "where a group was looking for financial assistance in such a manner... you would, perhaps, be aware as to whom they could persuade to broker such a deal?"

"Why, of course," Grosvenor said. "We are in contact with the governments of France, Spain and the Netherlands. Through them, we could readily broker loans. And we ourselves could even provide monies to assist in such an endeavor."

"In what form?" Morris asked.

"From us," Grosvenor replied, "French Livres, Spanish Reales, silver or gold bullion, British pounds if preferred."

"And loans from you would need to be paid with what interest and over what period? Hypothetically."

"I believe we would be willing to forgo interest," Grosvenor said. "Equally, there need be no haste in repaying the principal. Once a revolution is won, you will need to reform the financial well-being of the new nation.

"Although we might be looking for some small assistance with a project to the west of here."

"I understand," Morris said. "How far west?"

"Currently in flux between French and Spanish rule, that far west."

"I see no problem there," Morris said.

DAY ELEVEN (Cont.)

Threeday 5.5.2834
Friday 10th February 2017

Lancaster and Lancashire Bank
20:15 GMT
(21:15 GST)

Pierre Gomez pushed his trolley into an empty third-floor office and adjusted the volume control on the Walkman hung around his neck. In his earpieces, he heard Steve Smith saying, *"...suggesting this particular gang isn't part of the scene. They don't have records or criminal contacts.*

"Supposing it is a gang and not an individual."

A woman's voice: *"We think it is an individual who knows about banking rather than robbing banks."*

Smith: *"My first thought when I heard about these anomalies was that they originated inside the bank. My money would have been on a branch manager somewhere, paying for a lifestyle he can't afford. But with two other banks, I assumed it had to be a gang.*

"If it isn't, then for that level of expertise, it will be someone here and at a senior level."

The woman: *"Now you know why we wanted this meeting kept secret."*

There's a bit of a turn-up, Gomez thought. He'd had an inkling something was up when he'd arrived at work and heard Steve Smith would be working late. It didn't take a genius to work out that when the security boss holds after-hours meetings and doesn't invite his secretary; it has to be time to stick a bug under the table and find out what's happening.

Gomez expected to hear a fresh scandal concerning one of the directors about to break, and Steve should be vigilant. Ya de ya de yah.

He had not expected to hear of the geeks running some intelligent analysis system. Now, of all times. It wasn't fair. Now was still the best time of the year for him to work. Once Guy Fawkes' Night, on November the fifth, was over, everyone's thoughts turned to Christmas, the office party, and anything other than work. Over Christmas, it was like, well, Christmas; he could whack loans into the system at four a day, with nobody around to notice. Then came January, which everybody seemed to reckon had forty-one days; it lasted so long. Those who didn't have a cold had the flu, and they all suffered from a lack of sunshine and general malaise. The last few loans went in, and everything just rattled along. He made his dispositions with the takings, bouncing the money around the world in and out of a series of banks in countries where bank managers regarded criminals as their best customers, not their worst nightmares.

Okay, they'd peeled away the top layer of his little scam. So what? The money was all gone, but they didn't know where or how much. They also thought it had to be an inside job, and better yet, at a senior level. It should take them a while before they worked down to the cleaners. Even so, it was now time to move on. He was only staying on to ensure nothing untoward happened, and now it had his work here was done. He would finish his shift, as usual; no need to wave a big flag over his departure, it would be the last anyone would ever see of Pierre Gomez.

Lancaster and Lancashire Bank
20:55 GMT
(21:55 GST)

Steve Smith looked up from the pad on which he had spent most of the last twenty minutes busily scribbling notes.

"To get up and running on this," he said, "I am going to need some additional clout, which means I need to talk to a couple of people up on the top floor. They have all been here for five years, at least, so I think we are fairly safe, providing no ancillary staff is involved."

"I can't see any of them bothering for only ten million," Willis said. "They'll get that in bonuses."

Steve laughed. "Good point. Most of them couldn't have thought this up in a fit, anyway."

"What's going to be your first line?" Alex asked.

"Well," Steve replied, scratching his temple, "HR is going to squeal like stuck pig over this, but whether it's a gang or someone working alone, someone on the inside is feeding them information. My first line will be people who have moved over from the other two banks that were robbed. It should take only a matter of hours, mainly because anyone who comes into or moves within the banking industry gets their references checked properly. Next, there is the possibility our primary culprit is still working for the first bank and has recruited help in the other two, although I suspect that is far less likely. Too dangerous."

"And then?" Alex prompted.

"And then I will need to look at the entire staff. I'll start here, but the thieves could be in a branch. I will need to brief other members of my team, but most of them are ex-coppers and would have no better chance of dreaming up something like this than that lot up on the top floor."

"Assuming they are all ex-coppers," Willis said.

"They are all hand-picked," Steve said.

"So I believe," Alex said. "I heard you called back through the main switchboard to check on Ben."

Steve smiled. "Wouldn't be the first time there has been a robbery by villains pretending to be coppers."

He's got a sweet smile, Alex heard herself think. He's a little old, maybe fifty, but that's only eight years older than me.

"Good point," Ben said. "Maybe not your security people, but there will be people running around in offices like these who may not get the security vetting they should.

"The guys who fix your computers, the telephone engineers and maintenance people. Are they employed directly or supplied by outside contractors?"

"Bit of both, really," Steve answered. "The computer people are all in-house and properly vetted because they often have access to sensitive information."

"Maybe we should look at them as well," Alex said.

"I will," Steve said, seeing that his relationship with HR would hit an all-time low shortly.

"How about the maintenance people?" Ben persisted.

"We have office services in-house," Steve told him. "They sometimes bring in outsiders to do a specific job. But I think they would need to be in regularly and not during office hours for something like this."

Ben and Steve looked at each other and said, "The cleaners," in unison.

"Where do they come from?" Alex asked.

"They are all from an agency, and most don't speak much English," Steve said.

"Or one of them is just pretending he can't speak much English," Alex said.

Pierre Gomez stared out of the bus window with the words, *"Or one of them is just pretending he can't speak much English,"* running through his mind on a continuous loop. Fuck it, he thought. Another hour or two was all I needed. I could have finished my shift, and then I'd have had the entire weekend. But no, that bloody DS had kicked the whole thing off by saying, *"The guys who fix your computers...."* The pillock. Then Steve bloody Smith had to bring the cleaners into the frame. All because Pierre had helped him out and reminded him the lower orders still existed. No gratitude, some of these people.

On the other hand, Pierre thought, if I hadn't turned up and dusted his bloody table, I couldn't have stuck the bug underneath it. But then, if I hadn't turned up and dusted his bloody table, maybe he wouldn't have thought of cleaners. He decided he had fallen into one of those circular arguments that could run and run. So best get off.

If they were wondering about cleaners, they would start by looking at those who had left recently as the likeliest of suspects. Then, they might look at those still there. So, he should be in the clear. A dangerous word 'should'. As in, 'Your brakes should be fine'. Not the sort of word he wanted to entrust with his future liberty.

If they had interviewed the cleaning staff there and then, he would have been in a very vulnerable position. Getting out of the building could have become complicated. As it was, leaving when he did meant it would take a while before anyone noticed. Either way had its disadvantages; he just hoped he had chosen the right path.

The ache in his upper leg—a penalty of spending too many hours walking around with one shoe higher than the other—had gradually worsened in the cramped bus seat, and he shifted position slightly. It was an essential part of the Pierre Gomez disguise; they would never forget the limp. Still, he thought, get home tonight, and that pain in the ass will end. He smiled faintly at his own small joke.

He turned his mind to what he needed to do over the next forty-eight hours. Writing it down was the sort of mistake that brought down empires, so everything had to be memorized.

Not quite everything. Getting from Gomez's flat to the hard drives was something he did at the end of every working day. The difference was that this was the last time, and he would need to double-check everything was clean.

From then on, it became more complicated.

The bus pulled up in front of Victoria railway station, and he limped through the station's main concourse and exited onto Buckingham Palace Road. Further down, he turned left, over Eccleston Bridge towards Belgrave Road, and girded himself for the last fifteen-minute limp to the door of the small basement bed-sit Pierre called home.

As he passed the passport office, three people walked out of one of the Georgian buildings further down the street and climbed into a white van through its side loading door.

They were an odd group, even without the added oddity of entering a van rather than, say, a taxi or car. Of the three, the girl attracted his attention the most. She was tall. God, she was tall. Pierre was six feet two in his bare feet, but she had to be a head taller. He estimated close to seven feet, but—he glanced down—those heels had to make up for six inches.

She wore trousers and a jacket made from black leather with the oil-on-water iridescence of scales. Gomez wondered if it might be snakeskin but dismissed the idea.

She turned slightly as she entered the van, and her gaze swept past Gomez without pausing. As it did so, he saw a long, elegant neck and a face with a near-perfect bone structure allowing her to carry off the military-grade crew cut. Her large, intelligent almond-shaped eyes were a piercing cobalt blue, contrasting with skin hinting of a Mediterranean heritage.

The older woman might have been tall, but she seemed like a little old lady next to the girl. As for the man, the suit and his impenetrable shades suggested that he had watched *Men in Black* once too often. He just didn't have Will Smith's ears.

Belgrave Road, London
22:15 GMT
(23:15 GST)

58

The van door closed, and the vehicle moved out into the evening traffic.

"You two have suddenly gone very quiet," Bianca said.

"Did you see the man walking past?" melanie asked.

"The one with the limp? Of course, I saw...." Bianca stopped. "That was him?"

"It was," Scallon said.

"So why didn't we grab him there and then?"

"Right outside our offices?" melanie asked. "Which are almost next door to the passport office, a building with discreet but extensive surveillance running twenty-four-seven? I can't think."

"There is no need for sarcasm," Bianca said. "I have had a long day, and I'm not as young as I used to be."

"At least we know he is on his way home," Scallon threw in to help douse the flames a little.

Belgrave Road, London
22:30 GMT
(23:30 GST)

Pierre was about to cross Lupus Street into St Andrew's Square when the sound of a van's side door sliding open slightly dented his concentration.

"Excuse me," her voice said, husky, with a slight accent.

Testosterone can be a real bitch, Pierre thought, knowing he should ignore her, but he paused as he knew he would.

"Can you tell me please where is St Andrew's Square?"

Pierre turned to look. The tall girl in the skin-tight snakeskin he had seen a few minutes earlier at the other end of Belgrave Road. It would have been sufficient warning, had his brain been in receipt of its full quota of blood.

"Oui, she is 'ere, across the street," Pierre said, hoping that keeping in character might quell the senses screaming warnings at him.

"This way?" she asked, pointing to the right.

"Non," he said, getting closer, "it is over...."

He felt something cold on his neck and thought, "You fucking idiot," before consciousness fled the scene.

"Where and when are you being collected?" melanie asked Bianca.

"Scar House in the early hours of Fiveday," Bianca said. "Why?"

"Couldn't you have arranged something a little closer a little sooner?" melanie said.

"No, or I would," Bianca said. "Several large consignments are going out from London and Birmingham, and we don't want to make ourselves too obvious. Besides, I had meetings before then."

"It suits me," melanie said. "I want to get hold of some of Caeil's computer equipment, and we have time in hand. If we can go to St Andrew's Square, I must get into one of his apartments."

"How many apartments has he got?" Scallon said.

"Four to my knowledge," melanie said. "He moves from one to another and shifts identity as he goes. He is either cautious or clinically paranoid."

"What would he have to be paranoid about?" Bianca said.

"What indeed?" melanie replied.

IST Valiant Sky, Jericho System
23:55 GST

Rufus Koenig had been waiting, alone, in the room inboard of the airlock. As Zara walked through from her shuttle, he fell into step beside her.

"Welcome to *Valiant Sky*," he said.

"Thank you, Rufus," Zara said. "It's good to be back."

"My pleasure," Rufus said, although he was sure the young woman with the unusually blond hair striding beside him had never been on the ship before.

He escorted her through *Valiant Sky's* labyrinthine interior to her cabin. They met nobody during the journey, and even the surveillance cameras seemed preoccupied with the ceiling.

As they walked, Rufus talked. He told her the rest of the team would join *Sky* in the next twelve hours. Zara would come aboard, officially, approximately seventy hours later. Until then, she should always remain in her quarters.

Zara nodded. She understood this. She should; having helped put together the basic plan.

Where she had been and where she was supposed to be coming from were two different places. Where the others were coming from was in between the two. So, she needed to stay out of sight for a while. Then she could join them when they reached where she was supposed to be.

The cabin in which she would stay had an enormous bed, a bathroom big enough to party in, and even a kitchenette. Zara wasn't certain why she had it, except for coffee, but if she felt the urge to prepare a meal, there were a few frozen dinners in the freezer.

She had several screens and access to all the Aetherian and Gaian channels. All were showing repeats of the same Terran crap.

Maybe it wouldn't be too bad.

DAY TWELVE

Fourday 5.5.2834

Saturday 11th February 2017

"That's it," Steve said, tossing the last of the files onto the table. "None of the cleaners have left in the last four months. So, if it is a cleaner, he or she is still working here."

"It was a bit of a long shot," Ben Willis said from what was fast becoming his usual position, making yet more coffee.

"Whatever the outcome of all this," Steve said, looking at the scattered papers in front of him, "we'll launch a massive sort out with our cleaning contractors on Monday morning. It looks like we could have anyone wandering around here at night. The security checks they carry out are bloody useless. Like their bloody manager."

"I shouldn't expect a Christmas card from him either," Ben said.

"No, he wasn't happy at having to go and dig out this lot," Steve agreed.

"The problem is we have no way of knowing if any of these names are real. They could have worked at other banks or other cleaning companies," Alex added.

The phone on Steve's desk rang, and he walked over and took the call. After a short, one-sided conversation, he turned to the other two and said, "We may have a break. That was the cleaning company manager again, and it looks like one of their people didn't clock out. As far as they can tell, the guy isn't still here, so it's probable he left before the end of the shift at eleven o'clock, although the manager does not know when, or if, he actually left."

"Do you have a name?" Ben asked.

"Yes, Pierre Gomez. Oddly enough, he was in here a few minutes before you two arrived. He gave me a hand, clearing up the mess my lot made this afternoon. So, we know he left, if he left, between eight and eleven."

Alex was scrabbling through the pile of files on the table and said, "Give me a hand to find this guy's file, Ben. And we may need an interpreter."

"Hang on a sec., boss," Ben said and asked Steve, "Where was this mess?"

"On the conference table. Gomez gave it a wipe-over and helped straighten the chairs and everything. Why?"

Ben dropped to his knees and crawled under the table.

"I think he must've lost something," Steve said to Alex with a smile.

"His marbles? His chances of making inspector?" Alex laughed.

"Okay, boss," Ben replied, emerging from under the desk, "But I don't think we need an interpreter. I think Mr. Gomez understands English very well." He held a tiny device attached to a piece of Blue Tack between his finger and thumb.

"I suspect I know the answer to this," Steve said, "but what is it?"

"This," Ben said, "is a bug, and it means our friend was listening in while we discussed the possibility of it being a cleaner. So, what would you do in his shoes?"

"Probably not go home if he has any sense," Alex said, opening a file, "but we have to start somewhere. I have an address in Pimlico. I'll ask the Met if they would be kind enough to break the front door down for us. We need to talk to Mr. Gomez."

St Andrew's Square, London
01:10 GMT
(02:10 GST)

The police carrier turned into the top of the Georgian-style square and cruised down the road without headlights, blue flashing lights, or two-tone horns to announce itself.

As they approached number one hundred and eleven, a very tall woman walked out of number one hundred and thirteen and climbed into a white van just before it pulled away.

"That's handy," the sergeant said. "Save us double-parking."

The sergeant and six other officers in protective gear climbed out and walked up to the front door of number one hundred and eleven. As they approached the front steps, a petite, fierce-looking lady wrapped in a voluminous toweling dressing gown pulled the door open.

"Can I help you, gentlemen?" she asked.

"And you are?" the sergeant asked.

"Mrs. Parrot and I live here, mind you." She pointed to an open door in the corridor behind her.

"Best go back in then, my love," the sergeant said as the contingent of policemen advanced on the doorway to the basement.

IST *Valiant Sky*, en route to Romstrum
11:45 GST

The freighter materialized from the retroverse at a little under one percent lux. The onboard AIs dipped into the control systems of the shuttle ahead, bringing the smaller vehicle up to just three meters per second slower than the larger one.

Beneath *Valiant Sky*, the retrieval dock lowered, and the AIs slowed the shuttle to a relative stop inside the dock before the freighter slid back into the retroverse.

On the shuttle, after a final-sounding *thunk*, Sergeant Chiyo Lemasolai opened her eyes and said, "Is it over?"

Examining a strand of bright blue hair for defects, Sergeant Tamara Finkel said, "There have been very few incidents with a freighter picking up a shuttle. It's safer than virtually any contact sport."

"So what?" Chiyo responded. "I don't like it."

The shuttle lurched as it settled onto the freighter's hangar deck.

"What was that?" Chiyo said. "I thought we were down?"

"We are now," Tamara said with a smile.

"So, what happens now?" Chiyo asked. "Zack, you must know."

Sergeant Zaccaria Vartanian looked up from his compad and said, "That's odd; just after take-off, we got a message from Lorina. I was sure I saw you sitting beside me, gripping my arm."

"I wasn't listening," Chiyo said. "Tell me what's happening."

Zack sighed and said, "We get wherever we are going on Threeday of next week, and when we get there, Lorina will tell us what happens next."

"'Threeday'," Chiyo yelled. "Almost a fucking week away."

"Wow, numeracy to add to your skills," Tamara said. "Speaking of which, do you need to swear so much?"

"I know, and next week I get to learn readin' an' writin' just like the smart kids," Chiyo said. "Meantime, yes, I do like to fucking swear."

There were several clicks, and the shuttle's door cracked open. Rufus Koenig stood beaming at them from outside.

"Welcome to *Valiant Sky*," he greeted the nine members of the GCID contingent in the small passenger compartment. "We have accommodation prepared, and I alerted the kitchens that you might be hungry."

"Excellent," Chiyo said.

"She's feeling better," Zack said.

"You might be interested to know we will pick up your colleague Zara Chang in three days," Rufus added.

"Be still my beating heart," Chiyo said.

"Sarcasm, Sergeant Lemasolai?" Rufus asked.

"Sarcasm, Master Koenig," Chiyo confirmed.

Asteroid orbiting 73. 4β.6αα69α.36α43 β.4975α2
12:50 GST

Lieutenant Robert Sunter was both deliriously happy and upset.

Sunter was a good soldier. Father Jocelyn had been a soldier and retired early as an honorary general in the army. Father Claude had served for four years as a young man. His mothers, Mariel and Desiree, had served in their youth, and he had followed the family tradition. An air-tight, precision-machined round peg in a precision-bored round hole.

To date, this had not been the easiest of missions. Robert had been told they were on their way to Romstrum, a notoriously hot planet, after a journey that should have taken no more than seventy hours. Instead, after over two hundred hours, they had arrived on an asteroid only a few degrees above the ambient temperature of space, itself only a few degrees above absolute zero.

On the plus side, the accommodation was enormous, and very well equipped. Artificial gravity to match home, but it could be disabled in some rooms, lowering to five percent of standard. There was plenty of space. Lots of excellent food and drink. A gym and exercise facilities. The entire cache of virtually every movie and tv program produced on Earth, Aetheria, or Gaia.

But back on the negative side, it also contained another group of Gaians. It took him a full ten minutes to realize just who they were.

melanie's private army was one of those myths to have persisted for many years. The theory was that among the GCID, melanie had hidden a group of her choosing. Nobody knew who they were. Except everybody knew Lorina Korenjic was one of them, and she wasn't there.

But the theory, in its various retellings, had names that constantly cropped up. Tamara Finkel, the technical high priestess, was one. Dan Olafsen, a demolitions expert with a death wish, another. The legendary, if misnamed, fire triem of Sophia Gulab and Chiyo Lemasolai featured regularly.

All square pegs trying to fit into round holes and failing.

Robert knew there had been a plan. He also knew Lorina Korenjic had put together the project, and it was, therefore, fail-proof. Robert desperately needed to know that what was happening was not a failure, but part of the plan.

The message from Lorina Korenjic for the Sunter team was to remain and the others to leave in the shuttle, still sitting outside, had come as no surprise. He shrugged. A few weeks in a warm, well-equipped refuge, far from Bianca Kaninchen and her inquiries into his well-being, was not something to dread.

But none of this made Robert Sunter either deliriously happy or upset. What made Robert Sunter both deliriously happy and upset was already advancing on the office he had commandeered. Sashura Boutillier was the sexiest and most beautiful woman Robert had ever met and he loved her passionately, but apart from when duty called, she never seemed to notice he existed.

***

Sergeant Sashura Boutillier crept closer to Robert's lair with her heart in her mouth. She did not know what she was going to say. From the first time she had seen him, she had loved him. But the Lieutenant reduced her to a stuttering wreck, unable to say anything meaningful.

She tapped on the door and waited for Robert to call, "Come," from the other side.

As she stepped inside, she felt herself tense. She still did not know what she was going to say.

Just then, Corporal Michiko Dimopoulos pushed past her and said, "Hi Lieutenant, can I have a word now Sergeant Boutillier is here?"

"Umm, yes," Robert Sunter said. "What is it?"

"We are going to be on this rock for quite a while," Corporal Dimopoulos said. "We have everything we want, which will make a bit of a vacation.

"But it won't if you two do not figure out that you are besotted with each other. As the rest of us did weeks ago. Please do something about it. Because the two of you moping around might trigger mutiny."

DAY THIRTEEN

Fiveday 5.5.2834

Sunday 12th February 2017

Pierre was just awake, letting his mind wander around the inconsequential dross it favored in the slow process of waking up.

The memories of his encounter in the street sidled in to remind him he was an idiot and needed to find out where the hell he was. But with discretion.

The wind's moaning, and the synchronized rocking of where he lay suggested a vehicle of some sort. Probably the same damned van.

No engine rumble, tire noise, or the sort of swaying he'd expect in a moving vehicle suggested they were stationary. Despite being wrapped in a blanket, he was cold. Suggesting they had been stationary for some time.

It wasn't a lot. He needed visual information.

Showing as much restraint as he could, he cracked one eye open the tiniest amount. Peering around, he could just about make out that he was in a van, illuminated by a couple of small low-wattage lamps on the roof.

Ahead of him, he could just see the backs of the two women. The tall one with the crewcut and the other one—whom he had not noticed earlier—had shoulder-length blond hair. Leaving the third one, the black guy. He could be anywhere; there were seats behind where he lay, he was sure.

He doubted these people were the authorities. Not even the security services, unlikely to be involved anyway, pulled stunts like this. These people had to be criminals, so he could lose the last haul of money. Or maybe they were terrorists, and he might die as well.

A contrived throat clearing came from the row behind and told him where the wannabe Will Smith was sitting.

"Ah, Caeil," the blond woman smiled as she turned to face him. "You are awake and, I am sure, desperate for tea or coffee."

"Caeil?" How the fuck had they come up with that name? He had never used it, and nor had anyone else. The only place he had ever seen the name was on the files he had removed when he left the orphanage.

Several thoughts, all starting with the word 'but', flashed up in a clump.

The most dominant was that these *were* security services, just not British. Somebody had stolen his parents' bodies from the morgue after the accident. Suggesting dear old mum and dad were into some serious shit and maybe some equivalent of Ernst Stavro Blofeld and SPECTRE existed and were seeking revenge.

"Coffee?" the younger woman asked.

He nodded. Although a dedicated tea drinker, he knew tea and vacuum flasks were a terrible mix.

He reached for the mug and realized his wrists were in plastic handcuffs. Added to which, his work overalls, various bits of padding, his re-engineered boot to provide his distinctive limp, and the wig he wore as Pierre were all gone. Instead, he wore his own jeans, a T-shirt and a pair of trainers. The last time he had seen any of these items, they had been in the first flat in one hundred and thirteen St. Andrew's Square. Which was not good. Although not as bad as them finding the second flat.

"Do you take cream?" crew cut asked.

Using the word 'cream' suggested an American. The English said 'milk'.

"No thanks," he said.

She poured the coffee and asked, "Sugar?"

"Lots, please," he said, and she spooned it in until he eventually said, "Stop."

She stirred his coffee, and he took a sip.

"Good coffee," he said.

"Thank you," the blonde woman said. "It is my personal blend."

"Then you have an exquisite taste in coffee," he said. "Which merely leaves the question, who the fuck are you and why am I in this van?"

"Funny, I was sure your first question was going to be 'Where am I?' in some form," the younger woman said.

"You do this a lot, then?" he said.

"It happens. You know how it goes," she said.

"Not really, no, I don't," he said. "I don't do a lot of kidnapping these days."

"You should," she said. "Although, truth be told, it doesn't make as much money as you do robbing banks."

"To answer your question," the older woman interrupted, deciding the nonsense had gone on long enough, "this young lady's name is melanie, the not-so-young man behind you answers to either Jacob or Scallon and I.... well, I answer to nobody. However, my name is Bianca Kaninchen."

"What do you want?" Pierre said.

"Hah, I knew that would be your second question," melanie said.

"An hour or two of your time," Bianca said.

"Hmm, and then?"

"Whatever you like," Bianca said.

"My name isn't Caeil," Pierre said. "Does that alter things?"

"Not really," melanie said. "Tell me which one you would like us to use. Caeil Ashbow? William Dean? Danny Glover? Jack le Bois? Jack Fletcher? David Massey? Pierre Gomez? Your atrocious French accent has slipped a little, by the way."

He sat and stared at melanie helplessly, as if the big kids had just invaded the sandpit and stolen all his best toys.

"How the fuck do you know those names?" he said. Nobody knew all those names; nobody. Each one was on a closed track, separate from all the others. It was impossible.

"Jack Fletcher seems to be the nearest thing you have to a general-purpose name," melanie said. "Shall we go with that?"

He shrugged. "It will do." He had a million questions and no idea which to ask first. While he figured it all out, Jack Fletcher would do as his name. He couldn't think of it as his real name because he knew it wasn't. The only real one might have been Caeil Ashbow, and even then, he wasn't too sure.

Jack wasn't too sure about running away at the moment, either. He didn't know where they were, but it was February, it was England, and the wind was howling. Dressed in jeans and a T-shirt with his wrists bound, his chances of survival were minimal.

Although it was always possible, he was in a warehouse in London, and a couple of guys were outside rocking the van and making howling noises. But it was unlikely.

"Look, Caeil," Bianca said, "we wish you no harm. We have DNA proof you are the son of Benjamin Ashbow and Sarah Gunter. They were friends and colleagues, and I have spent considerable time and resources on finding you. I'm just sorry it has taken so long."

Interesting, he thought. Those were the names on the documents he'd liberated, so these people might know something.

"Really?" he said. "So, who were they? Or, while we are at it, who are you?"

"That is quite a story," Bianca said. "We will be somewhere a lot more comfortable shortly, and I can answer all those questions. Is there anything else I can tell you?"

"You said we would be 'somewhere a lot more comfortable shortly', but we aren't moving," Jack said. "How does that work?"

"It's coming to us," Bianca said politely.

"So, where are we?"

"The Yorkshire Dales."

"Okay," Jack said. "So do we just sit and wait?"

"Yes," Bianca said. "I understand your impatience, but you would not believe me now if I told you the truth."

"Try me," Jack said. "I'm very trusting and gullible."

Bianca laughed, "I doubt it, but just for fun, suppose I said you were born on a habitat called Gaia, currently in orbit around an orange dwarf star eighteen thousand, eight hundred light-years from here. Would you believe me?"

"Yes, of course I would. I always thought I was an alien," Jack said. He fell silent; it was apparent they weren't going to tell him anything sensible. Unless...?

Bianca said, "I didn't say you were an alien; I said you were born on...."

Before she could say any more, melanie said, "Two minutes, everyone," and slid the side door open.

"Time to get out," Scallon said in Jack's ear.

They climbed out of the van. Freezing stilettos stabbed Jack's face and soaked into his clothes until Jacob Scallon pulled a poncho down over his head. It covered him to just below the knees.

A minute later, as they stood in the near pitch blackness, a blast of warm air surged past, and Jack felt, rather than saw or heard, something arriving. It might have been vibration just outside the aural or visual spectrum. He didn't know, but one second, they were standing facing a blackness hiding an empty chunk of Yorkshire, and the next, they weren't. They were standing facing a blackness that was there, in front of them, and radiating heat. Ticking, the way hot metal ticks as it cools, all accompanied by a faint smell of ozone. He couldn't determine the size or whether it was mechanical or organic. It was just there. He swallowed, and his ears popped.

"What the fuck is that?" Jack demanded.

"Our ride," Bianca said.

Only just audible over the wind, Jack heard a new series of noises in the narrow range between clanks and clicks, followed by a faint whirring as a widening band of red light revealed a doorway two meters from the ground.

A short and steep ramp folded out to stop just in front of where they stood. Two figures hurried down it; the first stopped in front of Bianca and said, "Good evening, Colonel Kaninchen."

"And good evening to you, Sergeant Himaro," Bianca replied. "This is Mr. Fletcher, and he is having trouble walking. So, if you would be so kind...."

"No problem, Colonel," the sergeant replied as he and his companion took Jack's arms and helped him hobble up the ramp into a small red-lit room. Bianca and melanie joined them, and they waited while the door slid closed. The red lighting changed to white, causing Jack to screw up his eyes a little.

A second doorway slid open, leaving Jack with the strange feeling it should have gone 'whoosh'.

Himaro bundled Jack into a brightly lit corridor. In a few paces, they were in a cabin, and Himaro removed Jack's poncho and dropped him, firmly, but not roughly, into one of the dozen airliner-style seats. Cushioned safety bars slid out to hold him in place.

Bianca and melanie sat down facing him, and similar restraints slid out of their seats. Maybe they picked up a job-lot at an auction of second-hand amusement park equipment, Jack thought. Although, overall, he had to confess; it appeared well done.

"Not long now," Bianca said.

Jack ignored her. He was still trying to figure out what was going on, and he was failing. Why were they continuing this charade? What was it they could want that all this hokum could help them get?

Unless? The sly thought creeping in. He'd always said he was different; how much more different could you get? And it seemed kind of exciting.

But then, if his parents had been alien and their bodies snatched to stop the authorities from noticing they had green blood, pointy ears, or two hearts, how come he didn't have any of those things? Nor did these people come to think of it. Well, not the pointy ears, at least.

A low-frequency vibration built in intensity and finally leveled. After a few minutes, following a couple of stomach-churning moments, as if they were being driven too fast over a hump-backed bridge, everything settled down to a distant hum.

A red bar around the room at ceiling height switched to green, and the safety restraints slid back into the seats.

"Here's the deal," Bianca said immediately. "I want you to do exactly what I tell you for the next twenty-nine minutes. Then, you will get to choose between two options. One of those options is for us to safely deliver you and your hard drives...."

"You have my hard drives?" Jack yelled.

The hard drives had been in the second flat in one hundred and thirteen St. Andrew's Square. Not good.

melanie held up a leather bag and shook it.

"Are they intact?"

"They are," melanie said. "I liked your destruct system, wired to the office light, but I got around it."

"Clever," Jack said.

"As I was saying," Bianca continued. "We will safely deliver you and your hard drives to any location in the world you want, and we will put an extra ten million dollars in one of your bank accounts in the British Virgin Islands. Plus, you'll never hear from us again."

"What's the other option?" Jack asked.

"You stay with us."

"My head tells me to opt for 'any location' and the money. Rio would be lovely."

"The twenty-nine minutes aren't up yet, so it doesn't matter. Once they are up, if your head still wants Rio, then that's where we'll take you."

"I don't seem to have much choice right now," Jack held up his wrists to show the handcuffs, "so I agree to do as you say."

The handcuffs and ankle restraints clicked open.

"Do we still have an agreement?" Bianca asked. "I promise you we mean no harm, and you will soon understand what's happening."

Jack shrugged. "Why not? I still don't have many options."

"Fewer than you think," Bianca said as the door slid open, and a man wearing an orange one-piece suit walked in and put what looked like a similar garment onto the seat.

"This is Simon Singh, who will keep you out of trouble. Take your shoes off and put that on," Bianca said, pointing to the orange suit.

If it came to an escape across Yorkshire in mid-winter, Jack thought, this suit might be better than what he was wearing. He had to admit, to himself, at least, Bianca's offer had his interest. He had been expecting something more like 'do as we say, or we shoot you in the head' to secure his compliance rather than attempted bribery.

Jack pulled on the baggy suit—close-up, it looked like a pair of mechanic's overalls—over his clothes. The front appeared to fasten with Velcro, but as he pulled the two halves together, they began fusing themselves together to form what had to be a water-proof seal. He completed the outfit with matching boots and gloves that sealed themselves to the suit in the same manner.

"Very fetching," Bianca said.

"Orange isn't my color. I feel like a complete prat," Jack replied.

"Another three minutes," Simon said. "We can go to the lock."

Bianca smiled and said, "Come on, let's get this done." She left the room with melanie, Jack, and Simon trailing after her, back to where Jack had come through earlier. He and Simon walked in.

"Okay, and we are going where exactly?" Jack asked.

"Just outside," Simon replied.

"Oh right," Jack said. Then the thought struck him. We're on a submarine. They hadn't been in Yorkshire but at the seaside or a Scottish sea loch.

The outer door closed, and a series of green lights appeared.

Although nothing made sense, Jack saw the traces of a pattern emerge. Although not why Captain Nemo and his crew had kidnapped him. Again, give it time.

Unless? Maybe they were Russians? It might explain the accents. Supposing dear old mum and dad had been spies for the KGB? Perhaps they had had some sort of spy kit built-in, and the Russians needed the bodies back? So why wait thirty-five years to find him now the cold war was all over? Come to think of it, why did they need to find him at all? He was not likely to have any spy kit or know any secrets. He hadn't even been old enough to walk when everything had kicked off.

"First, you'll need this," Simon said, and Jack brought his attention back to the present. He looked down at what resembled the sort of small backpack walkers might carry. Simon helped Jack into the device, held in place by a couple of clips and more self-sealing material. Jack noted Simon was already wearing a backpack. Or maybe an aqualung?

"Finally," Simon said and produced a pair of helmets looking very much like the full facial Shoei NXR he had for when he managed a ride on his Honda Fireblade.

The big difference was that the helmet Simon held had a flexible aventail attached to the bottom to cover the neck and sit over the shoulders.

Simon attached a pair of coiled cables from the backpack to his own helmet and slipped it on. The aventail wriggled itself into a tight seal.

"Your turn," he said as he plugged the two leads from Jack's backpack into the second helmet before putting the contraption over Jack's head.

"You should have three green lights and one red just above your eye line," Simon's voice came through the speakers in Jack's helmet.

"Got 'em," Jack said.

"When I close the visor, the red light will become green. If any of the lights change color or go out, tell me."

"Don't worry, I will," Jack said, with feeling. He'd tried scuba diving once, years ago, and hated it.

Simon reached over and touched something on the side of Jack's helmet, and the clear visor snapped down and seated itself.

A lamp on the room's wall changed from steady green to flashing amber, which steadied before becoming a flashing red. Jack's suit felt a little strange, almost as if it were being inflated from the inside. He glanced down at his arm and saw it was much less wrinkled than it had been. Which was odd; the room they were in should be filling with water, not having the air removed.

Simon clipped a line between Jack's suit and his own and turned to a panel on the wall. He flicked it open and pressed buttons on what could have been a keypad for an ATM.

The outer door slid open. Jack was expecting the sea's murky darkness, fish, seaweed, passing sharks, and maybe even a giant squid. What he saw was a mass of tiny points of light.

Then he realized. They were stars. Not the feeble white pinpricks of light he'd seen on a clear winter's night out in the English countryside or even the denser display he'd once seen in Australia. Here was a sense-pulverizing show of red, blue, white, yellow, orange, and green. Whoever created the universe had got in Jackson Pollock as an interior designer.

Christ All-fucking-mighty. It was true. They were in space, not under the North Sea, heading for Mother Russia. They were in a spaceship. He was a bloody alien, after all.

It occurred to Jack that he had stopped breathing a little earlier. He took in a lungful of air.

Jack had never been religious. He thought 'believers' were, at best, weak-minded and at worst psychotic. But standing on the edge of the airlock right then, he could understand why man had looked at the heavens and experienced the need for there to be a higher power. The vastness before him, let alone what lay beyond, was too much for the human mind to comprehend. It had to end somewhere, so what came next? Or beyond that?

Jack felt a little light-headed and grasped the edge of the airlock door.

"Fucking hell," he said.

"We were expecting something a little more profound, to be honest," Simon's voice sounded in Jack's ear.

Jack laughed. "Yes, sorry."

"Come on," Simon said and stepped through the door, clipping on a second safety line as he went, and floated away until the cord stopped him. Jack hesitated. He hadn't got a head for heights, and this was very high. He took a moment and followed. As Jack stepped through, he felt his stomach and its limited contents, unfettered from the usual downward drag of gravity, rising. For a moment, he was unsure how far north they might be going.

Expecting something of the sort, Simon said, "Turn and face back into the airlock. Fix your sight on something solid until it passes."

Jack obeyed. Nausea and the panic having risen almost as quickly as his stomach's contents subsided. He stayed where he was for a minute and turned his head to look outwards.

"Fantastic, isn't it?" Simon said over the radio. "Come on, let's go around the other side. There's something there you will want to see."

Alongside the outer doorway were several handholds, a narrow ladder recessed into the hull. Using just his hands, Simon climbed, with Jack close behind.

On the top of the ship, they moved into the reflected light from the Earth, turning beneath them. They watched as Sydney and Brisbane saw a new dawn.

"We have only ten more minutes of oxygen," Simon said. "Is there anything you'd like to see before we go in?"

"No, can we just stay here for now?" Jack replied.

"No problem, man," Simon said, and the two floated on the end of the safety wires in silence, watching the Earth recede until the oxygen alarms sent them back to the airlock.

Shuttle *Baleful Moon*, Kuiper Belt, Terran system
01:10 GST

"That's it," Vadim Cole said, staring at the floating wreckage on his screen.

"Considering its location, Master Cole, I am loath to even take it under tow," Micha Ogoe said.

"You will have no argument from me, Captain," Vadim said. "I want to send in camera drones and see what's inside. Then we will destroy it and the drones. Then I suggest we get as close to the star as we can and let it burn off anything hitching a ride."

"That's damned close with this," Micha said. "The Gaians might be a bunch of arrogant pricks, but these T3 shuttles are tough."

"So, you like our new toy?"

"A shuttle this size with retroverse capability. What's not to like?" Micha said, with schoolboy enthusiasm. "Can we have another fifty, please?"

Vadim laughed. "Sorry, but there are only two of these."

"Where's the other one?" Micha said.

"Hmm," Vadim said. "Does the name melanie mean anything to you?"

"If you mean the Gaian...?"

"I do," Micha said. "Best you not let her hear you calling her Gaian. She and our boss, the incomparable Master Rufus Koenig, conspired to combine a Gaian T3 shuttle and Aetherian rabbit-punch. The cost was considerable and unlikely to be repeated, ever."

"Pity," Micha said. "The drones are going in."

Vadim Cole returned to the screen and watched the tiny drones' progress into the carcass of the derelict ship. The hole in the side, although partially blocked by a chunk of ammonia ice, provided a way in.

The flight deck held two figures. Humanoid, perfectly preserved, and well over two meters tall, they wore military uniforms. In the compartment behind the flight deck sat two much shorter humanoids. Bellachi.

The camera drones forced their way past a mix of aluplas and ammonia ice chunks into the passenger compartment.

Two more of the tall, uniformed figures sat in the forward-facing seats. The camera spun and, in the rear-facing seats, sat three more humanoids. These were shorter and wore clothes bearing no resemblance to military uniforms. Cole still recognized what they were.

"Shit," Vadim Cole said.

Micha Ogoe had known Master Cole for twenty years and never heard him swear once.

"Get DNA sample readings sent back, then destroy the thing and get us out of here," Vadim said. "Make sure we get a roasting. Take us past the star, and I want to feel flames on the outer skin and hear the alarms screaming. Understand me?"

"Yes, sir," Micha said.

"Then into retroverse from solar orbit. Let's see if an instantaneous seven-thousand-degree shift in temperature is enough."

Shuttle *SVC 2-486*, en-route to Mars orbit
02:15 GST

As the inner door of the airlock slid open, Jack stepped through and almost collided with Bianca.

"Well?" she asked.

"Oh yes," he replied, trying to wipe the grin off his face and failing. "Absolutely, bloody amazing."

"Good, I'm glad you enjoyed it. You wouldn't get me out there at gunpoint."

"Now I understand why you didn't tell me anything. There's no way I would have believed this."

"If you recall, I did tell you. But I don't think you were quite ready to believe me."

"Er, no, good point, I wasn't. But right now, you can tell me Darth Vader is real, and I'd believe you."

"Who?"

"Yeah, him too." Jack was burbling.

Bianca looked confused, and melanie had a word in her ear. Eventually, Bianca said, "Ah!" and beamed at Jack.

"Now," she said, "back to our agreement. Anywhere in particular in Rio? Ipanema's a bit run-down these days, but there are some elegant properties...."

"Stuff Rio, I'm on a spaceship; who needs Rio?"

Bianca laughed. "I'm pleased to hear you think so. Now let's get you out of that ridiculous orange suit. We have got a lot to talk about."

Jack turned, shook the startled sergeant's hand, and said, "Thanks, Simon, that was the most awesome experience of my life."

"My pleasure," Simon said.

Jack turned and followed Bianca the few steps back to the room with the aircraft seating. melanie showed him how to make the suit unseal itself.

The suit discarded and his feet back in trainers, he sat down opposite Bianca.

"Before we start, would you like a drink or something to eat?"

"I'm not hungry, but a drink would be good. Do you have any Scotch?"

"Of course," Bianca said.

melanie volunteered to get them. There was a clinking of glass on glass, and she returned with two large crystal tumblers with generous amounts of whisky.

Jack took a sip from his and said, "Excellent Scotch."

"It's a forty-year-old Tomatin. It is rather good, isn't it?" Bianca agreed.

"Are you not joining us?" Jack said to melanie.

"I won't, thank you," she replied. "I have a liver complaint."

Bianca snorted, and melanie glowered briefly, which struck Jack as odd. Did these people find liver complaints funny?

"You know," Jack said after a pause, "I have a million questions and no idea where to start."

"So, why don't I start, and you jump in and ask questions as and when?"

"Sounds good to me."

"Then I'd better start again with the introductions. My name is Bianca Kaninchen, and I am a colonel in the Gaian Central Intelligence Directorate. This young lady is melanie, and she is one of my operatives...."

melanie snorted this time.

"To be precise," Bianca said, "melanie works for the Aetherian Intelligence Bureau and has been on loan to my department for some years.

"The gentleman we left behind is Jacob Scallon, my bureau chief for Europe."

"Okay," Jack said, "now you mentioned Gaia when we were in your van. You said that I was born there. I thought you were just talking crap to keep me quiet. How does it all work? I mean, am I an alien or something?"

"No, you're not an 'alien' how you mean it. Gaians originated on Earth. For example, one of my grandfathers was born in Germany in eighteen sixty-one, and one of my grandmothers was born in France eleven years later."

"So, no Klingon blood then?" Jack asked.

Bianca looked perplexed.

"A fictitious species from a Terran science-fiction television serial," melanie said.

"No. No Klingon blood," Bianca said, treating Jack with a smile that suggested she was chewing a lemon. "Have I reassured you a little?"

"It's a start. Is there more?"

"Yes," Bianca said, "there's a great deal more.

Jack yawned. "I'm sorry," he said, "but I feel like I have had a long day. Is there any chance I could get some sleep? I'm suddenly having difficulty keeping my eyes open."

Bianca pulled an old pocket watch from her jacket and said, "It is getting late, and I have had a busy day myself. Let me get melanie to find you a bed, and perhaps we can talk first thing in the morning?"

"Sounds good to me," Jack said.

"If you come with me," melanie said, "I'll find you a berth. It won't be much, but we will transfer to the *Encounter* tomorrow."

"Anywhere will do," Jack said as melanie led him down the narrow corridor into a small cabin. It had four bunk beds and a door to a lavatory, shower, and washbasin. melanie gave him a quick run-down on how it all operated and left him to sleep.

Jack kicked off his trainers, stretched out on a bunk, and he was asleep before he had pulled a blanket over himself.

***

melanie returned to the room Bianca had taken over to find her sitting at one of the screens with a refreshed tumbler of Scotch.

"I take it his Scotch wasn't pure malt?" Bianca said.

"Not quite," melanie said. "But Jack needs sleep, and I thought you had had a long day and were tired."

"Don't talk nonsense, melanie; I haven't slept for more than four hours a night in twenty years.

"So, what were you doing on Earth that led to this find?"

melanie shrugged. "Rufus wanted me to look into the Aetherian office in London. Nothing major, but I was passing. So, while there, I made a courtesy visit to the Gaian office."

"Without informing me?"

"Bianca, I am seconded to you for some of my time. My role is to pass on information I have gleaned on the Nel that might benefit Gaia. Providing it is not detrimental to the best interests of Aetheria. My boss is Rufus Koenig; he pays my salary. You don't. Therefore, I am not one of your tame puppy dogs like Scallon. Please do not treat me as one, or I will see that Rufus terminates this arrangement."

Bianca glowered at melanie for several seconds and then said, "What do you think of Caeil? Now we have found him."

"Interesting," melanie replied, sitting on the couch. "He's taking all this remarkably well. It is only a few hours of subjective time since I grabbed him off the street. By rights, he should be screaming blue bloody murder."

"I think you've been spending too much time on Earth," Bianca said drily. "Was that some Terran expression?"

"I would agree," melanie said. "Given the option, I would never go there at all, but none of us gets exactly what we want. Indeed, it was a British expression, I believe."

"Humph," Bianca muttered. "Anything else?"

"Excellent control of fear, rather than fearless. Bright and extremely devious."

"You think so?"

"I do," melanie said. "So, what will you do with him now you've found him?"

85

"I have no idea," Bianca said. "I should have given it some thought. He might like the idea of joining GCID. He might just want to go back to Earth."

"I am not sure he is GCID material," melanie said.

"Why not?" Bianca said. "I would have thought he is precisely what we need. Or do you want him for the AIB?"

"No. Same problem. We need team players, too."

Bianca made a snorting sound. "From even the greatest of horrors, irony is seldom absent."

"Lovecraft," melanie said. "I said we needed them; I did not say I was a team player. Anyway, as Wilde said, or stole, 'Irony is wasted on the stupid'."

"Hmm," Bianca said. "Oh yes, and before I forget. Following what you said earlier about not working for me, why did you arrange for Robert Sunter to come to Earth? Not that he has arrived. Only he works for GCID and me."

"I did not arrange for him to come to Earth," melanie said. "I arranged for him to go to Romstrum."

"Didn't you arrange for that T3 of yours to be delivered there as well?" Bianca said. "Why could you not have returned to Gaia and collected it yourself?"

"I was too busy sorting out the mess Scallon was making of a simple task," melanie said. "You know, he could have found Caeil years ago if he had used even his limited mind. I believe your pet dog likes Earth and was in no hurry to find poor lost Caeil."

"You won't deflect me that easily," Bianca said. "I have had to provide a freighter and two pilots to get your damned shuttle to Romstrum. I have lost a platoon and one of my best officers to go to Romstrum separately, although I do not know what they will do or how long they will be gone. Yet, as you point out, you are not a member of GCID or answerable to me."

"I am a commander in GCID, as a courtesy," melanie said. "Also, as I just said, I have been wasting time on Earth sorting out a mess your incompetent staff could not. That has delayed my schedule for Koenig's work, which I could only retrieve by having the shuttle delivered.

"Coupled with all that, if it had not been for some minor functionary in Section-J doing someone else's bidding—the name Katelyn Fofana springs readily to mind—everything would have been far more straightforward.

86

"And if you consider Robert Sunter and his troupe of clown marionettes amongst your best, then I despair for GCID."

"I concede your point about young Robert," Bianca said. "He is not overly bright, but his mother is a friend. I trust he will come to no harm in whatever you are doing for Koenig?"

"He will be safe enough," melanie said. "The biggest danger is self-inflicted injury through not obeying orders. Although my shooting him is always a possibility."

"I would have thought you would have used Korenjic," Bianca said. "You two seem to have an exclusive working relationship. Even though, yet again, she works for me."

"Korenjic has been getting a little too full of her own self-importance," melanie said.

"Korenjic has always been too full of her own self-importance," Bianca said. "Changing the recognized natural order and putting those who do not belong there into positions of authority has consequences."

"I am guilty as charged," melanie said. "Although part of your deal with Rufus is that you don't pay me, but I have the pick of staff."

"Yes, I need to re-read that agreement," Bianca said.

IST *Echoing Forest*, en route to Romstrum
02:55 GST

"Tamara," Lorina said. "How are things with you?"

"*Wondering if you were still alive.*" Tamara's voice said over the comm.

"Why wouldn't I be?"

"*You communicate with us daily for months, this mission starts, and your comm stops working. Ergo, you are dead.*"

"Far from it," Lorina said. "Hypothetical question for you. Could you send a message to *Enterprise* from Bianca Kaninchen that neither the *Enterprise* itself nor the crew could tell was fake?"

"*Yes. Plus, all the signal confirmations. What do you want it to say?*"

"They need to leave immediately for DV8, or anywhere else you can think of."

"*Of course*," Tamara said. "*I take it you want me to send this message when the* Enterprise *has a certain shuttle on the ground? So, where will it be when I send the message?*"

"This is purely hypothetical," Lorina said. "I am not entirely sure we will do this at all."

"So, *Romstrum 3*, then."

"Why do you think that?"

"*I don't think that. I know that*," Tamara said. "*It is where* Valiant Sky *is going, so that is where we are going. It is where Echoing Forest is going and, therefore, where you are going. It is where* Encounter, *doppelganging as* Envoy, *is passing by, so that is where the Commander is going if* Encounter *were to stop long enough. So, where else would that shuttle be going?*"

"Possibly," Lorina said. "So, in this hypothetical situation..."

"*Yes.*"

"Yes, what?"

"*Yes, I can send a signal from* Enterprise *to* Encounter *to say that they have had to leave a shuttle on Romstrum and as they,* Encounter, *have cargo for Romstrum, will they collect their shuttle? The shuttle with Briony Sigurðardóttir and Gabriel Lee on board?*"

"You are far too smart for your own good," Lorina said. "Please keep what you think you know to yourself."

IST *Echoing Forest*, en route to Romstrum
03:22 GST

"*Is all well?*" melanie asked over the comm.

Lorina Korenjic glanced across at Miguel Iwasaka, sleeping peacefully beside her in the most enormous bed she had ever seen, and said, "Not bad."

"*I was hoping for a little more detail*," melanie said crisply.

"We went retroverse almost two hours ago. It's almost three-thirty in the morning; Miguel is sleeping, probably exhausted after...."

"*Not that much detail*," melanie said.

Lorina giggled. "Okay. *Valiant Sky* picked up Zara from Jericho just before midnight on Threeday, as scheduled, and Koenig tucked her away in one of their diplomatic isolation cabins. The team and their equipment arrived on *Sky* at eleven forty-five yesterday morning and are complaining already. The other team is on an asteroid awaiting orders I might be too busy to issue, ever.

"I have arranged it so *Encounter* will stop at Romstrum to collect Sigurðardóttir and Lee after *Enterprise* had to leave before they were recovered, on the orders of Bianca Kaninchen."

"*Ingenious,*" melanie said. "*How are you doing?*"

"We are on *Forest,* and I have to say that when this is all over, I am signing up with the AIB because the accommodation you people get on your boats is far better than we get on GCID freighters."

"*We could buy your loyalty that cheaply?*"

"My loyalty you have," Lorina said. "But I would sell my soul for this bed."

"*I read something similar in a lavatory block on the second floor of GCID.*"

"'Course you did. Except you don't use the bathrooms in GCID, and you certainly have never been down to the second floor."

"*True on both counts,*" melanie said. "So, *how is the trip going?*"

"Well, as well as comfortable, these things are fast, and we will get to Romstrum around twenty-thirty on Oneday, just after they deliver the shuttle."

"*Good.*"

"How goes it that end?"

"*Okay,*" melanie said. "*The game continues, and I think we have reached a state where we are both aware of what the other one is doing, and we are both hoping that the other will make a slip, and we can get our own way.*"

"Your usual game of chess with invisible pieces, then?"

"*Exactly.*"

Shuttle *SVC 2-486,* en route to *IST Encounter* in Mars Orbit 03:30 GST

After her conversation with Lorina, melanie returned to her cabin and settled to read the backlog of reports that kept accumulating.

The figure that materialized did not surprise her.

"Oh my," she said. "A hat-maker disguised as Oscar Wilde has just appeared in my room."

"As you well know, I am Lewis Carroll, not Oscar Wilde," the figure said.

"I would know that if you didn't erase my memory of you after every meeting," melanie said.

"I do no such thing," Carroll said.

"You must do," melanie replied. "Because I can recall nothing you have said that is of any use from our many meetings."

"Nonsense, I told you where to find Caeil's father and where to find the parents of your little wolf pack."

"I will allow you that, but a little help with me contacting the other me would have been useful."

"Really, melanie?" Carroll said. "Do you genuinely believe that it is possible to phase photons without them being close?"

"Tamara did it," melanie said.

"No, she did not," Carroll said. "You were both communicating through a bridge I set up."

"Ah," melanie said. "So, are you going to help me find the Nel base on Earth?"

"I will," Carroll said. "But you know the rules. I will naturally exercise some restraint while working on my own demise."

The figure disappeared, and melanie resumed reading reports until her compad buzzed.

IST Valiant Sky, en route to Romstrum
03:25 GST

Rufus Koenig pored over the message from Vadim Cole, recognizing it would remain the same no matter how often he reread it. He visualized the icon that connected him to melanie and pressed it mentally.

"*Master Koenig, do you never sleep?*" she replied almost instantly. He was about to ask her the same thing and decided it was pointless.

"I was sleeping," he said. "But I thought I'd wake up and tell you that the residue on your Nel uniform was silicone, and the scientists think there is a weapons laboratory in that base."

"*I would believe many things of you, Rufus,*" melanie said. "*But I do not believe that you woke up to tell me that. So, give.*"

"As it's you," Rufus said with a chuckle. "Two hours ago, I got a call from Vadim Cole. He's on *Baleful Moon*, our new retroverse capable shuttle."

"*They are quite rare, I hear*," melanie said. "*But I don't suppose you called me at this hour to tell me about a vehicle, either.*"

Koenig said, "I did not. When Cole called me, they were on their way towards Sol to give themselves a radiation soak."

"*They'd been in the Kuiper Belt, I assume.*"

"If that's what the Terrans call it, yes. They found the missing Nel ship."

"*The one that didn't exist, so couldn't be missing?*"

"Yes, that one."

"*Anything interesting?*"

"Unfortunately, yes. There were passengers. They were Venatori."

"*Now, that is interesting*," melanie said. "*Oddly, I see nothing unfortunate in that at all.*"

"More to the point, we believe they were Hochadel."

"*Why do you believe they were Hochadel?*" melanie said.

"DNA," Rufus said.

"*The Hochadel are only a caste of the Venatori; surely they wouldn't have a different DNA?*"

"That was our thought, but *au contraire*," Rufus said. "When we took the DNA samples of those in the shuttle, we expected to find three strains: Bellachi, Nel and the Terran-Aetherian-Gaian group, which normally covers the Venatori. We found four. The fourth strain was totally new."

"*Are you sure the bodies were actually Venatori and not some other species, Tomalite perhaps?*"

"Now, why didn't we think of that?" Rufus snapped. "We simply went by the name tags on their suits. They clearly read Prince Louis Venatori and Duke Constantin Venatori, and we decided that was all the proof we needed."

"*My apologies Master Koenig,*" melanie said.

"No apology necessary, melanie," Rufus said. "We ran the DNA through every system to which we had access. And no, they weren't Tomalites or any other humanoid race on record.

"We also ran through our records and Gaia's, and while we have DNA records from before the banishment of the Venatori and even the Niederer Adel caste, we could never test a member of the Hochadel caste.

"We are both elated and terrified by this result. While proving a connection between the Nel, the Venatori and whatever is living on that Nemesis ship, we have discovered something we dislike."

"I agree," melanie said. *"This is going to change things."*

"It will," Rufus said. "Does that include your current plan?"

"I think not," melanie said. *"It may improve its viability. We now have a direct link between the Nel and Venatori; therefore, I can get to the Venatori, and Caeloeterra, through the Nel."*

Shuttle *SVC 2-486,* en route to *IST Encounter* in Mars Orbit 03:28 GST

"First thing," Bianca snapped into the comm. "Is that damned shuttle on its way to Romstrum?"

"Yes, Colonel," Katelyn Fofana, Bianca's confidential secretary, replied. *"It left thirteen hours ago, on* Enterprise. *Briony Sigurðardóttir and Gabriel Lee will take it down to Romstrum 3 and hand-over to Lieutenant Sunter."*

"Good. Any difficulties from Section-J?"

"Some," Katelyn said.

"melanie blamed you for any delays."

"She would, and in this case, I would like to take the credit, but it was down to them. They had just got their hands on a T3 shuttle that is retroverse capable, and there is no such thing as a retroverse capable T3. Plus, the generator, rabbit punch, MAM, and SQUID are Aetherian. So, when I told them they had to give up their new toy before they took it apart and ripped a hole in Gaia, there were tears."

"I am not surprised. The moment a T3, with that sort of mass, arrived, they would get all excited. What I don't know is why melanie brought it to Gaia, or why such a thing exists."

"That occurred to me also," Katelyn said. *"I would have thought she would have kept it a secret."*

"Unless she wanted to send me a message?"

"Possibly," Katelyn agreed. *"So why let her have it back?"*

"My people installed the items I requested while it was with section-J?"

"They did."

"That should answer your question. I am replying to her message with a brief note that reads 'BOOM'.

"Now, where is Sunter?"

"He and his people left some time ago, in an Aetherian freighter. They could be on Romstrum by now, but I doubt it. It is more likely they are sitting on that freighter waiting for the shuttle to arrive. There is no way they could survive the days on Romstrum without it.

"Added to which, the welcoming committee would have told me the moment they made contact, so they could get the rest of their payment."

"Speaking of the welcoming committee," Bianca said. "I trust you stressed their role is to rough them up a little. I don't want anyone killed, especially as I have requested that Greta and Georgia join that team. Along with Zara Chang...."

"But Zara Chang is...."

"Dead. Yes, I know. But I have someone else taking her place."

"Understood, Colonel." Katelyn said. *"I have made it clear to them that any serious injury or deaths could mean a visit from GCID troopers and a universe of pain."*

"Good," Bianca said. "My daughters and Zara can look after themselves in a fight, but Robert Sunter can not, and his mother is a close friend of mine. I just want him discouraged from staying on board that shuttle.

"Once it is just melanie, Korenjic too if that works, and my three girls, melanie can be disabled and that shuttle destroyed.

"The only problem we have now is that we do not know when, how or where melanie is going to rejoin her shuttle."

"I may have some ideas?" Katelyn said.

"Go ahead," Bianca said.

"First, I believe that melanie finding Caeil so quickly was possible because she knew where he was all along. She would have left him there, were it not for you setting the hunter squad on his trail. And had you not arrived when you did, melanie would have taken Caeil aboard Silent Thunder, *which was in the vicinity, and he would be on his way to Aetheria by now."*

"So far, so good," Bianca said.

"Thank you," Katelyn said. *"However, you did arrive when you did, so melanie had to go along with you taking Caeil back to Gaia on* Encounter.

"Coincidentally, shortly after your arrival, Korenjic transferred a consignment of household goods from Silent Thunder *to* Encounter, *despite* Silent Thunder *being scheduled to*

drop cargo on Romstrum and Encounter *having no scheduled stops.*

"The means of delivery was to be a disposable drop-shuttle. It was, I suspect, intended to be melanie's escape route.

"I was going to exceed my authority and persuade Encounter's *AI to ignore the drop on Romstrum, as it is only household goods and, therefore, non-urgent. However, I decided against.*

"As Caeil's self-appointed protector, she can't take him with her in a drop-shuttle and can't leave him alone with you. That means she intends to travel all the way to Gaia with you.

"Once she gets to Gaia, she will undoubtedly have some idea of how to get Caeil away to Aetheria or wherever she plans to hide him. But we have that time too."

"Excellent," Bianca said. "I think you may the answer there."

"Thank you, Colonel," Katelyn said. *"It was merely a tactical consideration that I trust fits with your strategic planning."*

"Yes, it does," Bianca said, recognizing that Katelyn had diplomatically reduced the importance of what she had done by deferring to her boss, and thereby extended her life. People who could out-think Kaninchen tended to die young.

"Okay. Let me know if anything happens that shouldn't," Bianca added.

"Yes, Colonel, of course."

"And have you recalled the hunter squad?"

"Yes, I recalled them," Katelyn said. *"They were making excellent progress. They were following leads from Manchester to London and suggest that they would have completed within three weeks. Terran weeks, that is."*

"That was quick," Bianca said.

"Yes, it was," Katelyn said. *"They suggested that the mission was well within the capabilities of a local field officer, and one with the commander's abilities should have completed the assignment in days."*

"Were they suggesting that Scallon is incompetent?"

"Not at all," Katelyn said. *"They suggest nothing. They say clearly that, in their opinion, Jacob Scallon is incompetent."*

"They got that right," Bianca said.

Shuttle *SVC 2-486*, en route to *IST Encounter* in Mars Orbit 03:30 GST

Very few things, good or bad, ever caused any disruption to melanie's disposition. Confirmation of a link between the Nel and Venatori caused a seismic shift. It proved that, despite the official Gaian stance to the contrary, the Venatori had survived their banishment. Collusion between certain factions on Gaia, the Nel and now the Venatori were indisputable.

This was what she had always suspected. That out there, somewhere in the galaxy, the Venatori were plotting their revenge. Now she was certain, she could determine why they were collaborating and how to demolish the Venatori.

It also justified the elaborate plan, based on the then unproven assumption of collusion, that she and Lorina had conceived and then Lorina had developed.

That still left the problem of what to do with Caeil, or Jack, as he now was.

The plan had always been to leave him where he was. Scallon would never find him, and, with a bit of luck, he could have lived out his life on Earth unaware of his heritage.

After all these years, Bianca had become impatient about finding Caeil and killing him. melanie had always thought that the killing of Caeil Ashbow was a project Bianca was saving for her retirement.

Whatever had caused Bianca's change of heart, melanie had promised Caeil's parents she would look after him if anything ever happened to them. She had done just that.

And now she was going to get him away from the danger that was Bianca Kaninchen. The question was, where to?

Aetheria was the obvious choice, but it was an open society, and Gaian assassins would easily find him there.

Once they were aboard *Encounter*, melanie would locate the drop-shuttle that Lorina had organized to get them down to Romstrum and make sure Jack could survive in it. But first, she needed to persuade Jack to come with her.

Swagman Inn, South Figueroa Street, Los Angeles
19:31 PDT Saturday
(03:31 GST)

"Vilishu, would you like to make a name for yourself?" the voice on the phone asked. She would have hung up if the caller hadn't been speaking Nel.

"Who is this?" she said in English. It might be a test. More likely, a prank from some of the other officers in the building across the road.

"That you don't need to know," the voice said. Male, but not entirely. Androgynous. Nel.

"The Gaians have posted that Envoy *is in Mars orbit on a routine collection and deployment."*

'So?" Vilishu said.

"That is not Envoy. *That is* Encounter *with a transponder running illegal data. Both Bianca Kaninchen and her tick-tock bitch will be aboard shortly."*

"What are you saying?"

"I'm saying a smart girl like you ought to get up there and check it out. But you'll need to move fast; it's leaving in nine hours."

.

Shuttle *SVC 2-486,* en route to *IST Encounter* in Mars Orbit 09:00 GST

Jack woke to find melanie standing beside the bunk.

"Breakfast time," she said and was back out of the door before Jack had time to react.

Grumbling and still half asleep, Jack motivated himself into the shower and stayed under until he felt human again.

When he emerged from the cabin half an hour later, showered, and dressed in the new clothes melanie had left for him, she was standing outside.

"Bianca's waiting," she said and set off down the corridor.

"Tell me something," Jack said, trying to keep up. "How did you find the security system for the hard drives?"

She looked at him as if he was an idiot. "The hard drives were in devices intended to wreck them, so I simply followed the wiring."

"The wiring was in the wall."

"Yes, I know."

Jack decided he wouldn't get much information out of melanie—he was better off with Bianca.

She was in the shuttle's mess room, eating a croissant and drinking coffee.

"Get yourself something to eat and some coffee," she said, waving regally at the various plates and jugs scattered around the table as Jack flopped into the chair opposite. "We'll be docking with *Envoy* in about ninety minutes."

"Which is what?"

"It's the vehicle that will take us to Gaia."

"Why aren't we going in this one?"

"This is a planetary shuttle," melanie said. "*Encounter* is an IST or Inter-Stellar Transport."

"Which is it?"

"'Which is it?', what?" Bianca asked.

"You said it was called *Envoy*, and melanie said *Encounter*."

"Did she?" Bianca said. "Unlike you to make a mistake, melanie."

"Isn't it?" melanie said. "The vehicle we are going to be meeting is actually *Encounter*, but it is sometimes politic to use the name of a sister vehicle. In this case, *Envoy*. It is a practice usually known as doppelganging."

"Makes sense," Jack said. "Will we be going outside again?"

"No. We won't," Bianca said forcefully. "We dock with it like civilized people. However, as you seem to enjoy space and the like, I've got you a seat on the shuttle flight deck for docking."

"Thank you; I will enjoy that."

"No doubt. It's the sort of thing your father would have enjoyed."

Bianca stopped eating and looked at Jack. "You must have a lot more questions; where would you like to begin?"

"I haven't a clue. I just keep going around and around in circles. So, I suppose I want to start at the beginning: with my parents."

"What do you know about them?" she asked.

"Nothing much. They died in a car crash when I was about nine months old. I grew up in an orphanage, and when I left, I received a copy of the file on them, but there wasn't a lot in it. They were academics of some sort, I think."

"I think it was more a case of, when you ran away, you stole your file, rather than it being given to you when you left," melanie said.

Jack shrugged. "Po-tay-to, po-tah-to."

"Yes, your parents were academics," Bianca said, ignoring melanie's comment. "Your father, Benjamin Ashbow, was a professor of English literature at the University of Gaia. His specialization was in your nineteenth century. Your mother, Sarah, was a lecturer in Terran history at UG, specializing in the industrial revolution; she was in line for her professorship.

"Do you know anything else about them?"

"Yes, after the accident, their bodies disappeared from the hospital morgue," Jack said.

"Was that in the file, too?"

"Sort of. There was a note to that effect. Along with a few intriguing references for me to follow up later, when I learned how to use a computer properly. Not that it helped much."

"In that case, I'd better tell you what happened that night," Bianca said. "Your parents had traveled to the north of England for a few days. On the A1 Road, just north of London, they were involved in a collision with another car and killed.

"As is standard procedure, I sent out a team to recover their bodies, and you, of course. They found your parents, but you had disappeared. There had been some confusion at the scene. A passing doctor said you were in the other car. Naturally, you went to the same hospital as those passengers.

"When I recovered your parents' bodies, the authorities went into a panic, decided you were at risk, and took you into hiding. I imagine there was a great deal of idle speculation about foreign spymasters and drug barons."

"So why did you remove my parents' bodies?" Jack asked.

"Enhancements. The post-mortem would have revealed non-terrestrial gadgetry. You may have noticed your handcuffs opened all on their own. That was me, using what we call a neurolink—it's like a little remote-control device in your head—to open the lock. Quite a useful thing, but likely to cause a bit of a problem in nineteen eighty-two England."

"I can imagine," Jack said. "Then what?"

"Then nothing," Bianca said. "We tried to track you down and kept running into problems. Computerized systems were still something of a rarity back then, and there is nothing more secure than a hand-written ledger tucked away in a closet somewhere."

"That's for sure," Jack said and stared into space for a moment. "Hang on a minute. You just said that you sent out a team to recover my parents and me. It was thirty-five years ago. How old were you at the time? Ten?"

"No, I was... let me see... sixty, I think, when we lost you."
She looked at melanie, as if for confirmation, who nodded.

"Yeah," Jack said, "but that would make you ninety-five now."

"I know how old I am only too well, but we have a different length of year from yours. As far as I'm concerned, I have been looking for you for sixty years. That's sixty Gaian years. Thirty-five of yours or thereabouts. I'm trying to convert everything to your years, but I'm afraid I'm not very good with numbers."

"So, you're trying to tell me you are ninety-five now?"

"I am very sure that if your mother were still alive, she would tell you it is vulgar to discuss a lady's age, but yes, I am. What makes it worse is that I'm one hundred and sixty in Gaian years."

"I thought that after the spacewalk, the surprises might be over. Are there any more?" Jack stared at her for a long while then added, "If it's any consolation, you don't look ninety-five."

"That's very kind of you, providing you don't mean I look older than ninety-five. As far as surprises are concerned, yes, I'm afraid there are a few, but nothing to worry about."

Shuttle *SVC 2-486*, en route to *IST Encounter* in Mars Orbit 09:15 GST

"There are few things I worry about more than people telling me there is nothing to worry about," Jack said.

"In this case, they really are not," Bianca said.

"Okay, so what is this Gaia, a planet?" Jack said.

"No, it's a habitat, which is an artificial planet. Most habitats are in permanent orbit around another planet."

"Some orbit stars or even moons," melanie said.

"Why?" Jack asked.

"Manufacturing plants, prisons, leisure facilities," Bianca said. "Additional living space. Gravity-free environments."

"Some are the top end of an orbital elevator system," melanie said.

"Oh yeah, I know what you mean," Jack said. "Arthur Clarke invented that."

"It was in use a few million years before Mister Clarke was born," melanie said. "But if you are familiar with his work, you may recall the vehicles in *Rendezvous with Rama*; they were a form of habitat."

"Gotcha," Jack said. "It's in orbit around some orange dwarf thing."

"At present, yes," Bianca said, "although it will move on shortly."

"Cool," Jack said. "So, how many of you live on this thing?"

"A little over ten million Gaians and a few thousand other species; what I suppose you would call aliens. They are largely diplomats, trade mission staff, sales and business representatives, visiting academics, students, tourists, and a few who just like living with us because they choose to."

"'Ten million'," Jack repeated. "Fucking hell, how big is it?"

Bianca looked at melanie, who said, "It's a cylinder, three hundred kilometers long and a hundred in diameter, say a little over ninety thousand square kilometers. It's one of the larger habitats, but they come bigger."

"It's a giant spaceship," Jack said.

"If you like," Bianca said. "But we don't use the term 'spaceship'. We say 'space-vehicles'."

"Okay," Jack said. "Any reason?"

"Let us say there was some unpleasantness regarding a certain Admiral, and we dropped all naval terminology."

"May I ask what sort of 'unpleasantness'?"

"No, you may not. We don't speak of him," Bianca said.

They sat in silence while Jack attempted to process all the new information. It wasn't proving easy.

Eventually, Jack said, "How come all these humans live in this habitat? What I mean is: how did they get there?"

"Just over two thousand of your years ago," melanie said, "a Saurian archeologist called Agnt tre-Kiff was visiting Earth—a place you call Stonehenge fascinated him—and met a Celtic trader named Cadeyrn.

"Saurians are a lizard-like species; they are harmless herbivores, but they would have been regarded as dragons back then. Much to the amazement of scholars since then, Cadeyrn didn't kill Agnt tre-Kiff and wear his skin as armor.

"Instead, Agnt tre-Kiff recruited Cadeyrn to create a mercenary army of Terrans to fight for the Saurians."

"Okay," Jack said. "So, Earth is *not* mostly harmless after all?"

100

"Far from it," melanie said. Jack was unsure if she had picked up on the reference or not.

"As I recall, nobody has ever suggested it is," Bianca said.

"I believe Jack was quoting Douglas Adams, the Terran author of *The Hitchhiker's Guide to the Galaxy*, a work of fiction very popular on Earth."

"Never heard of it," Bianca said.

"No, probably not quite your thing, Bianca."

"So, they became the Gaians?" Jack asked.

"After a fashion," melanie said. "First, the recruits lived on a continent on the Saurian home world where the climate suited Terrans better than Saurians. Then, seventeen hundred years ago, half of these humans bought a habitat, named it Gaia, and set off. Those that stayed behind called their continent Aetheria to stay with the whole 'mother-of-the-gods' theme."

"How do you mean, 'bought a habitat'?" Jack said.

"Much the same as in you may have bought your flat in London. They don't give them away," melanie said.

"Okay," Jack said. "So how come you all seem to speak English? Is there some sort of translator working here?"

"We don't seem to speak English," melanie said. "We speak English. Better than some English people, I might add. Translation machines always sound like somebody who hates reading to others, reading to others.

"In the early days, Cadeyrn recruited in Europe and to the Roman Empire's furthest extent. So, Latin was the most common tongue. Later, they looked further afield; the Indian sub-continent, China, Japan, north and south America, Africa, Russia. Any race that liked a fight got to join.

"Time passed, Cadeyrn and his son Morcant grew old and died, and new generations continued the recruitment. Earth was always going through one major catastrophe or another, allowing us to come along and recruit people who would otherwise have died. During the Black Death, in the middle of your fourteenth century, one hundred million people died. Nobody noticed that Gaia recruited over one hundred thousand, and Aetheria over half a million. The other Terrans assumed they had died."

"How did you recruit them?"

"Easy enough," Bianca said. "In Europe, we recruited the priests first, and then they did all the hard work."

"Yes, clever," Jack said.

"Then, in your fifteenth and sixteenth centuries, we hit the exploration and colonization period. We did very well from that. Colonists are adventurous, and once they get where they are going, many find it difficult to settle. Like soldiers returning from war, they want a bit of excitement in their lives. We offered them just that."

"So, they all got to learn Latin?"

"To begin with, of course. It needn't be difficult. There are techniques using sleep-hypnosis that are extremely effective."

"Why did you switch to English?"

"Elizabeth the First," melanie said. "Her father Henry the Eighth had removed Britain from the influence of Rome and the Pope. That not only changed religion in England, it also changed everything else. It permitted what was close to free-thinking without fear of the Inquisitors removing bodily parts.

"Some scholars, your mother included, believe that without Henry and the English Reformation, the industrial revolution might have been delayed by decades or even centuries.

"Under Elizabeth, the British seemed to galvanize themselves as a race, and before long, they had an empire that stretched around the globe. Giving rise to the expression that 'the sun never sets on the British empire'."

"That's because God wouldn't trust an Englishman in the dark," Jack interjected.

"I concur," melanie said. "But that freedom had allowed the British to create products they could trade globally, and trade requires a common language. If it hadn't been for Henry and later Elizabeth, that would have been French or Spanish."

"I am still not sure why you needed to speak English," Jack said.

"What do you suggest we spoke?" melanie said. "Klingon?"

Jack laughed. "No, but why English? Why do you need a language of Terran origin at all?"

"We just told you," melanie said. "Trade."

"You trade with us?" Jack said.

"Of course we do," Bianca said. "There are seven billion of you on Earth, and that means you have the economies of scale to produce many items far cheaper than we."

"Such as?" Jack asked. "What could people who lived on a three-hundred-kilometer-long spaceship need to buy from Earth?"

"melanie, can you help on this one?" Bianca said.

"I can try," melanie said. "Primarily, anything you can produce in great quantity at low cost. Many minor components like fixings, nuts and bolts, some machinery, simple power tools.

"A classic example. Every species in the galaxy with technology produces power tools. Terran power tools are the only ones designed to fit the human hand. Domestic pharmaceuticals, furniture, ceramics, clothing, small weapons...."

"Weapons?" Jack said.

"I thought you might pick up on that," melanie said. "Beam weapons of the sort used in your science-fiction movies need a lot of power to be effective and are expensive to make. So, we stay with projectile weapons. Heckler and Koch, Glock, and SIG Sauer are popular amongst our military personnel, and we couldn't make anything as good for the same cost.

"We re-barrel some tactical shotguns we buy to handle our own ammunition. Larger military weapons we get from Aetheria."

"Let's not fixate on the hardware," Bianca said. "The population of Earth is seven hundred times that of Gaia. This allows the breadth and the depth of inspiration and talent to produce art, literature, poetry, music, fashion, cinema, and even television to be, through synergy, thousands of times greater. We have our own musicians, writers and artists, but they can only work so fast.

"With all our technology, we still couldn't match Hollywood, Pinewood or Bollywood for the creativity and diversity of Terran cinema. We can access practically every film made on Earth from the beginning of cinema until about six hours ago, and do you know what is at number seven in the list of most-requested films?"

Jack shook his head.

"*Star Wars*. Although I confess, I've never seen it. That was why I was a little confused over who this 'Darth Vader' might be."

"We are closing in on *Encounter*," melanie said, "time for Jack to go."

"Yes, you probably won't want to miss this, but we will talk later. We can meet for lunch."

"Okay," Jack said, "I'll look forward to that."

FiT: THE FOURTH

Terran Senate, Saurian Prime
19:00   13.56.17834 (Saurian Standard Date)
(Sunday 13th March 236 AD Julian calendar)

Senator Aethelwig Fearson stopped to admire the fish in the pond. They were a new species, a vivid green cutlass blade shape with an extended caudal fin tipped in orange. According to the sign, they were carnivorous and liable to remove any fingers placed within reach. Fearson thought they should put a similar sign over the door to the Senate.

He resumed his walk. The evening was pleasant, still warm from the day's heat, the sun glinting through the green-blue sky, painting the horizon with hues of peach and yellow.

The gardens between the Senate and accommodation were a delightful sight at this time of day, and the number of senators present outside of the building always outnumbered those inside.

Beneath a knot of oaks taken from Earth before Cadeyrn had been born, the cluster of seats was the unofficial headquarters of the 'habitat' group, and Senators Hamza Portius, Drest Umbrius, and Fáelán Herminius had gathered already.

"Hurry, Aethelwig, your wine is getting warm," Hamza called.

Fearson continued at the same pace. He would be delighted when togas were no longer fashionable, and he could go back to trousers. He could walk at the speed that suited him when he didn't have to worry about tripping over his skirts.

"Any news?" he asked as he sat down and accepted the goblet of wine.

"Yes," Drest Umbrius said. "The Saurians say we can have our hundred billion UC at zero percent interest and pay back the principal whenever it's convenient. Or not bother if we don't feel like it."

Fearson's head spun around to look at his friend. "What?" he almost yelled.

"He's teasing you," Fáelán Herminius said. "Don't you think we'd have yelled it out loud if we'd heard anything?"

"Yes," Fearson said. "Silly of me, really."

They had known from the beginning that borrowing one hundred billion Universal Credits would never be a quick process. The decision involved governments, not just banks, and few governments wanted the Terrans to get too mobile.

Indeed, most governments were against the Terrans existing away from their home planet. Some even proposed that the rest of the galaxy would benefit if they wiped out the Terrans. The only problem was that the only race capable of such a genocide was the Terrans.

Allowing them the freedom of their own habitat, without Saurian control, just seemed like a shortcut to galactic suicide.

The Terrans, self-programmed to disagree, thought otherwise.

Not that there was anything fundamentally wrong with the planet on which they lived. The Saurians had given the humans a vast continent that they could call their own. But it was still on someone else's world, and there were still terms to be met.

Although fighting for the Saurians was hardly problematic. Few races were interested in taking on the Terrans. Once negotiations broke down, all the Saurians needed was to mention their Terran mercenaries and negotiations restarted instantly.

But that was not the point. Humans were still at the beck and call of a race who were, in some ways, their masters. Acquiring their own habitat would allow them to dictate their own destiny.

Contrary to expectations, the Saurians were not against the plan and had even helped in the first approaches to the central banking associations.

However, there had been some resistance from other humans. There were only just over two million of them, and they expected that half that number would go. And that meant half the soldiers who provided the primary source of income for the Terran community.

The counter argument was that, in the equivalent of three hundred and eighty-nine years since Agnt tre-Kiff and Cadeyrn had met, the population had risen to its current level from just eight of Cadeyrn's immediate family. Primarily by recruitment from Earth, where there were plenty who would willingly escape the usually short and brutal life they faced, for that offered by people with flying chariots. Therefore, numbers would soon build up, and those who went off traveling were never more than a few weeks away, should the need arise.

Gradually, both sides worked out ways that the two factions could remain allies and friends. Mainly because the advantages of being allies far outweighed the disadvantages of being enemies. It was merely a matter of synergy.

Under the four oaks, the group drank wine, nibbled on cheeses and olives, ate fruit, and took calls from colleagues, wives, husbands, and friends. They weren't waiting for anything, because nothing was going to happen tonight. Or tomorrow. Or next week. But it felt right that they spend this time together, just in case.

"Julius Sidonius is on his way over," Drest Umbrus said. "Is there a vote this evening I've forgotten about?"

"I don't remember," Fearson said, and the others laughed.

"Good evening, Madam Senator, gentlemen," Sidonius said.

"Good evening," Fearson replied.

"I come from Brun tre-Kell. He bade me tell you that as of one hour ago, the Saurian government has approved the loan."

The four senators sat staring at the usher in silence, none daring to speak in case it broke the spell.

"Thank you, Sidonius," Fearson said, eventually. "Thank you very much."

"That was truly my pleasure, Senator," Sidonius said and turned back to the Senate building.

"It's real," Fáelán Herminius said, holding up a compad. "This is from Brun tre-Kell's office."

Hamza Portius lifted a large container of wine from the cooler and said, "We must drink to this. We are getting a habitat."

"Yes, we are," Fearson said, his voice little more than a whisper. "We are getting a habitat."

FiT: THE FIFTH

First Minister's Office, Zone C3, Gaia
19:00 GST (Gaian Standard Time) Oneday 1.1.0001
(Saturday 17th August 340 AD)

"First Minister, the last shuttle has left for the surface, and we will leave orbit in seven minutes," Gaia's principal AI said through the neurolink.

"Thank you, Captain," Elash Amrit replied, out loud, as he looked up from his desk screens. He had difficulty understanding sub-vocalizing and was reluctant to upgrade to the newer units, where he just had to think of a response. Too dangerous for a politician, he decided.

Amrit realized the momentous occasion deserved commemoration. They'd had functionaries up all day, attempting to eat and drink their way through Gaia's stores, but they were all gone. Back to the planet they would always call Saurian Prime, and to the new nation of Aetheria.

It was inevitable. When they bought Gaia, it had no name, and they had been wrangling over it for years. There was the 'Cadeyrn' faction, as was to be expected. Then those who had pointed out that once they had recruited Cadeyrn, he simply sat on his increasingly fat backside and played at feudal chieftain for thirty years. It was his son, Morcant, who had created the Terran nation of which they were all part. Equally, many wanted the name of Aethelwig Fearson, the man who had started the entire project, to be honored. But they had all ceded to the idea that the name should reflect their roots and 'Gaia' had won.

Almost immediately, those who were staying behind decided they needed a name for the continent they called home, and if those who were leaving were going the classical route, then so were they.

The name Aetheria had been postulated, discussed, and selected in a fraction of the time it had taken the Gaians. A fact the Aetherians loved to drop into conversation whenever possible.

By and large, it had been an amicable split. The Gaians weren't rebels. They just wanted something a little more from life than fighting the Saurians' battles for them. Not that they did much of that anymore. After the equivalent of four hundred

Terran years of having hordes of humans descend on them for any minor infringement of Saurian territorial or access rights, most of the enemy races had decided to go and pick on someone else.

Amrit was leaving behind some of his own family. A daughter from his first 'chaco', as the young now called a cohabitation contract, but then he was also leaving his first partner. Nothing is ever entirely bad.

Gaia had no control room, flight deck or bridge of any sort. There was no need for such a thing. The AIs controlled the ship. It usually didn't matter, but right now, Amrit thought, it would have been nice to have somewhere to gather. Now that all the decisions had been made and the die cast.

Instead, Amrit flicked on the main screens in his office and called in his immediate staff. They came in carrying two sacs of wine and assorted tumblers and brought chairs into a semi-circle to watch.

Amrit tried to get the rear-view camera images on the screens and failed until one of the junior assistants came to his rescue.

Saurian Prime sat centrally in the screen, a large green ball with white end caps feeding the broad rivers that divided the nine continents.

They watched, chatted, and reminisced until the planet was a tiny dot, and the AI said, *"About to enter the retroverse,"* and all the screens went black.

DAY THIRTEEN (Cont.)

Fiveday 5.5.2834
Sunday 12th February 2017

"Goddammit, I'm bored," Zara Chang snarled at herself in the mirror.

She grinned. Calling up improbable deities from other species was not cool. It reminded her of Terrans, who went to Italy and then started saying 'Ciao' to all their friends.

She relaxed the smile and stared hard at the face in front of her. They'd done an excellent job. Zara Chang was a pretty girl, as the face staring back testified. A nose that men would call cute. The mouth was too big, but men liked that. The psychology behind that said a lot about male egos.

Her blond hair was... well, awful. She'd toned it down a bit, gone for the dirty blond look, and ended up looking like a dirty blond. She grinned again and knew that needed work. Zara didn't grin; she simpered. Yes, she was good at that. But not grinning. Or snarling.

The body was okay. No, perfect. Not too big on the boobs, but enough. The only thing that wasn't right was the eyes. They were big and blue and had long lashes she could flutter in times of distress. In fact, they were terrific; but under the surface, it all went wrong.

Maybe boredom manifested itself that way. Maybe hours of watching crap Terran films and TV programs and trying to exercise without space showed up in the eyes.

She had thought it wouldn't be too bad.

Zara remembered the thought and cursed both it and herself.

That had been Threeday evening, and now only Fiveday morning, and she had got it wrong. It would almost be worth mixing with the others, except somebody, call them Tamara bloody Finkle, would figure out that if she were coming from where she was supposed to be coming from, then she wouldn't be rendezvousing here and now. Tamara would then decide to share this intelligence with everyone.

She had to talk to somebody; she pulled out her compad. A single button and a familiar voice said, "*Ah, sister mine, how's things?*"

"Dreadful," Zara said. "I hate you with a deep and abiding hatred that only your slow and tortured demise at my hand will reconcile," she continued with little emotion. "It being you that got me into this."

"*Not going well, then?*" her sister replied.

"No, it isn't, and it's your fault," Zara said. "And my arm itches."

"*How is it my fault?*"

"Must have been. It can't be mine," Zara said. "You allowed me to be part of this."

"*How long now?*"

"Two days, give or take a few hours."

"*Then you'll get some company.*"

"I don't need company, especially not that company. I'm not sure Chiyo Lemasolai is my BFF. More, my WEF."

"*I'll bite; what's a 'WEF'?*"

"Worst Enemy Forever," Zara said.

"*Obvious, now you mention it.*"

"It's also likely that the others don't like me."

"*The other women don't, no. But the men tend to. Which is usually why the women don't.*"

"I suppose so, not that I care about them, but I am going stir crazy. I need to run, feel the wind in my hair...."

"*Kill a passing gazelle and eat its still-beating heart, raw?*"

"Possibly."

"*Talking of the wind in your hair....*"

"Do not go there," Zara said. "You should see what they've done to me. I look like a porn star."

"*That should improve your popularity.*"

Shuttle *SVC 2-486,* en route to *IST Encounter* in Mars Orbit 10:30 GST

melanie led Jack around a curving corridor. He had never given much thought to what the flight deck of a space vehicle might be like in real life. Now on his way to visit one, his mind was bouncing between the old NASA shuttle *Enterprise's* flight deck and the bridge of its namesake in *Star Trek.* Based on what he'd seen so far, the NASA shuttle seemed to be the most likely destination for the smart money. So gray metal with lots of controls, switches, display screens, flashing lights, and gauges.

A door slid open, and melanie ushered him through. He had been mistaken both ways. The room was dark, with just enough light to see the two seats that could have come from any mid-range sports car. In front of the seats and curving round them through one hundred and eighty degrees, a meter-high video screen showed a few stars. There seemed to be none of the controls, switches, display screens, and gauges he had expected—just a pair of tiny joysticks to the sides of each seat.

"Sit there," the woman in the right-hand position said, gesturing towards the other seat. As Jack sat, restraints dropped over his shoulders and held him firmly in place.

"We reduce the inertial field slightly through the flight deck, so we can get some feel for what's happening."

"I see," Jack said with all the confidence of the blind.

"Oh, and I'm Patrizia Sanchez, by the way."

"I'm Jack," Jack said.

"Oh, they told me you were called Caeil."

"I was, but I changed it."

"You changed your name from Caeil to Jack?" she asked. From her tone, he could tell the switch hadn't met with her approval—time to change the subject.

"You normally have a crew of two, yeah?" Jack asked.

"Yes. That's normally Jenny's chair; only she wanted to get ready. Her new boyfriend is on *Enc*..., err, *Envoy*. They are at the real cuddly, smoochy stage, and she's not much use right now, so you might as well enjoy the view."

"I know it's *Encounter*, really," he said.

"Good, I knew I would get it wrong."

Jack glanced over at the woman flying the vehicle. She had long dark hair, slim and gorgeous, and she had a certain poise that Jack liked.

"No boyfriend for you on *Encounter* then?" he asked casually.

She cast him a sidelong look and smiled slightly. "No," she said, "I don't think my wife and three children on Gaia would like it."

Jack shrugged and said, "No, I don't suppose they would."

The three-dimensional image on the curved screen altered and swam with the shuttle's trajectories, the *Encounter*, and a multitude of small objects that Jack assumed were things they would not want to hit.

"Where are we?" Jack asked.

"Guess," Patrizia said, and the screen filled with a heavily pockmarked reddish-gray section of terrain.

"What is that?"

112

The view pulled back slightly until Jack made out the circular shape and decided it could be an impact crater.

"The moon?"

"No. Wrong color. What comes after the Earth, moving outwards?"

Jack muttered to himself and said, "Mars, fourth planet out from the Sun."

"Correct. So, what was that you were saying, some sort of mnemonic?"

"Yes, it goes "My Very Easy Method Just Sets Up the Nine Planets." Mercury, Venus, Earth, Mars, Jupiter, Saturn, Uranus, Neptune, and Pluto."

"Very good, if inaccurate. Pluto isn't a planet. Despite what the astronomers on Earth think."

"I think it's called a dwarf planet now," Jack said.

"Still wrong," Patrizia said. "We refer to it as a planetoid, but there are hundreds of objects in your solar system that could justifiably be called planetoids, making the mnemonic unwieldy.

"Whatever it is, it's somewhere I like to keep away from."

"What Pluto? Really?" Jack said. "Why?"

"Its second moon, you call it Hydra, isn't a moon."

"So, what is it?"

"It's a Nemesis ship."

"A what?"

"You heard, and that is all I am saying on the subject," she said in a tone suggesting that the topic was closed, and then shuddered.

"Okay," Jack said and fell silent.

After a couple of minutes, Patrizia said, "That mnemonic you recited. Are you interested in astronomy?"

"No, but many years ago, I knew a girl who I thought was into it in a big way, so I learned that to impress her. That's when I found out she was into astrology. So, it was a total waste of time."

Patrizia laughed. "It came in useful today."

"I suppose so, except that it doesn't tell me how far from Earth we have come."

"Out to Mars, it varies, but if it's any use, on the trajectory we used it was...." she looked at a display on the curved screen, "just over one hundred and twenty million kilometers."

"Christ, in what, a little over eight hours?"

"Yes, it takes a while."

113

"I thought that was bloody fast."

"Not out here it isn't. We maxed just over two percent of light. That's about as fast as civilian shuttles go. A military shuttle would get to four percent lux, but an IST like *Encounter* can reach seven hundred and fifty kilolux on a long haul."

"What's a 'kilolux'?"

"A thousand times the speed of light."

"A thousand times? This ship, sorry, this vehicle we are going to can go at seven hundred and fifty thousand times the speed of light?"

"That's top speed. Average is around five-fifty, cruising around six-fifty to six seventy-five."

"I thought it wasn't possible to exceed the speed of light. Didn't Einstein discover that?"

"Where you live, he may have done. Out here, that discovery pre-dates him by a few thousand millennia. Although he was right, you can't. Not here, but it's possible in the retroverse. Some experimental vehicles are hitting a megalight. But they are just all engine."

"Wow. A million times the speed of light. So, what's a 'retroverse,' then?"

"Something about which you need to ask somebody a lot smarter than me. Anyway, it's time for me to start earning my pay and get this thing lined up for docking with *Env.... Encounter.*"

Jack settled back in his seat and watched the screen, now showing empty space. Small boxes popped up with snippets of data that disappeared almost as fast as they appeared.

Following a bleep, two extra boxes appeared on the screen and Jack got his first proper look at *Encounter*.

Weaned on a steady diet of Hollywood starships, he was expecting a gleaming white monster sprouting gun turrets and strange devices, the purpose of which he wouldn't even be able to hazard a guess. Instead, he saw a stubby cylinder with a sludge-gray hemispherical cap at what he supposed was the front end. Directly behind the cap was a yellow ring and then a much longer sleeve in a grubby gray green.

"Is that it?" he asked.

"That's it," Patrizia said. "A little different from the Star Destroyer, *Devastator*?"

"How do you know the name of an Imperial warship?" Jack laughed.

"We have three boys, and they are obsessed with *Star Wars*. My luggage consists entirely of books, models, and games. Plus a few extras like cosmetics and clothes, of course."

"Well, there aren't many mothers back on Earth who know any ships from *Star Wars*."

"I bet they know the *Millennium Falcon*, though."

"That one they might," Jack said.

"Except few mothers on Earth have a job on a real starship," Patrizia said.

"No, they don't," Jack said. "Odd that."

The view of *Encounter* had shifted slightly. "What's the yellowish band for?" Jack said. "Just behind that gray lump at what, I suppose, is the front."

"The gray lump is ice," she said. "It's an ablation shield. It's there to absorb the impact of small chunks of matter that might be in the way. The yellow rotating section behind the shield is the habitation, and the gray-green part is the cargo hold.

Jack could just make out that the yellow band was turning around the central part of the hull. The cargo section seemed stationary. But behind that, and difficult to see, was another section that had to be matt-black.

"Any idea how big it is?" he asked Patrizia. "It is difficult to get a sense of scale."

"I think it's about one hundred and fifty meters in diameter and five hundred meters long, something like that," she said. "Grosses something like half a million tonnes. That's excluding the power unit, of course."

"Which is the power unit?" Jack said.

"Not everybody can see it," Patrizia said, "but is there a fuzzy section behind the cargo holds?"

"Yes, there is."

"That is the power unit. It isn't here; it's in the retroverse."

"Okay," Jack said. "I suddenly have a lot more questions to ask."

The shuttle slowed and rolled until it moved with *Encounter's* vast bulk directly overhead. They edged closer until it felt as if the top of the shuttle was almost scraping the underside of the other vehicle. Ahead, a rectangle of bright green lights lowered itself out of *Encounter's* hull. Jack had an almost overpowering urge to hum *The Blue Danube,* but restrained himself.

"That's our docking bay," Patrizia said.

"Is it big enough?" Jack asked, trying to keep his voice steady.

"It was when I left," Patrizia replied with a grin.

He felt a slight pull as the shuttle slowed to match *Encounter's* speed, barely feet above their heads. Tiny judders moved the vehicle around as Patrizia made the final adjustments.

"I normally let the RAIs take it in, but I like to do one landing in ten manually, to keep my hand in."

"Of course," Jack said. "So, what's that? Some sort of grain?"

Patrizia laughed. "Not 'rye.' It's spelled R-A-I, and it means Restricted Artificial Intelligence, a sort of supercomputer really, not a full-function artificial intelligence."

"I see," Jack lied again.

The shuttle passed through the rectangular gateway into a bright, cavernous docking bay and dropped onto the deck, followed by four distinct thumps.

"That's the landing clamps," Patrizia said. "The dock is now balancing artificial gravity with the shuttle and filling with air."

They had docked with *Encounter.*

IST Encounter, **Mars orbit**
11:15 GST

With the shuttle locked down, the docking bay rose back into the body of what Jack took delight in thinking of as the mother ship. The docking crew, wearing black, white, green, blue, yellow, red, and orange spacesuits closed in. The colors identified the wearer's function, and it became apparent that the majority, in red suits, seemed to have little function beyond staring at computer tablets. Even with tablets rather than clipboards, maybe things weren't so different in space, Jack thought.

A tube slid out of the wall facing the shuttle and latched onto the nose, directly below the flight deck.

"That's the passenger walkway," Patrizia said, "they'll be coming for you any minute, I should think."

"Probably," Jack said. "Well, thanks for that."

116

"No problem," Patrizia said. "Wait 'til I tell my boys I met a genuine Earthman."

As she spoke, the door to the flight deck slid open, and melanie called Jack through to disembark.

He followed her down a deck and out through a tunnel, not that different from the things they used at airports, back on Earth.

They caught up with Bianca in a windowless room, about eight meters square. Sliding doors stood at the opposite end, and seats lined the side walls. Bianca sat in one.

Jack looked at melanie for a moment.

"It's the transfer car," she said, without waiting for the question. "To match the speed of the habitation ring."

"I thought so," Jack said. "Most of my reading is science-fiction.

"I assume you use artificial gravity here and on the shuttle?"

"We do," melanie said. "The ring itself uses a mix of centripetal and a-g."

The doors of the car closed behind them, and Jack felt the car move sideways. The acceleration was gradual. Far less than a train or even a London bus.

"So, how does a-g work then?" Jack said.

"Do you have a doctorate in quantum physics?" melanie said.

"Not yet," Jack said.

"Ask me again when you do," melanie said.

"I will," Jack replied. "Meanwhile, isn't there a dumbed-down version for the savages?"

"Do you mean the version where ultra-short photons power a surface of diamagnetic plates?" melanie said. melanie said.

"That's the one," Jack said.

A minute passed in silence. The car had stopped accelerating, but from the very tiny vibrations, they were still moving.

"Is it broken?" Jack asked.

"No," melanie said. "Three shuttles arrived around the same time, and the two ahead of us are also unloading. So, several cars are trying to let passengers out at the more popular gates simultaneously."

"Mmm," Jack said.

"'Mmm'?" Bianca said, sitting beside where they stood.

"Yeah, 'Mmm'," Jack replied. "It just all seems a bit overly complicated. That's all."

"You have some insight into vehicle design, based on 'most of my reading is science-fiction' that we may have missed in the last two millennia?" Bianca said, sounding a little annoyed, which brightened melanie's day.

"Not really," Jack said, pretending not to notice he had annoyed Bianca. "But melanie said 'the ring itself uses a mix of centripetal and a-g,' I believe."

"Yes."

"Why not just use the artificial stuff all over? It would save on all these ring things and make it all so much easier."

Even Jack noticed that the other people in the car were waiting for Bianca's response.

"It is a safety feature," Bianca said. "Should the a-g fail, the centripetal force means that the passengers wouldn't suddenly find themselves in a zero-gravity situation."

"Okay," Jack said. "So, how often does artificial gravity fail?"

"It hasn't," melanie said. "Not in the last two thousand one hundred and seventy years, anyway."

Jack noticed the venomous look Bianca gave melanie.

"Okay," Jack said. "So why not use full a-g in the ring during docking and stop the thing rotating. The shuttles could dock directly. You would save a lot of time."

"He has a point," melanie said.

Bianca said nothing.

"You said Gaia is a cylinder, so does it rotate?" Jack persisted.

"No, it doesn't," Bianca said, trying to control her temper.

"Gaia wasn't designed to spin," melanie said.

"Okay," Jack said. "I only wondered."

"Don't you have an expression about how curiosity killed the cat?" Bianca asked.

"Yes, we do," Jack said and turned to face Bianca. "We also have one about how satisfaction brought it back. You know, I wouldn't need to ask so many questions if you had left me where I was."

melanie glanced over at Bianca and smiled.

They stood in silence a little longer, then Jack said, "Patrizia mentioned 'the retroverse.' What's that?"

"Very complex," melanie said. "I will give you the dumbed-down-for-savages version when we are sitting down and comfortable."

"Okay," Jack said.

With only the slightest sensation of movement, the car moved gently sideways.

"That felt odd," Jack said.

"I've just added inertial dampening to the 'dumbed-down' list," melanie said to Bianca as much as Jack.

The doors slid open into the main lobby of *Encounter*'s habitation ring.

Jack followed melanie through into an open area and experienced a sudden mix of *déjà vu* and intense disappointment.

"I have a couple of things to do," Bianca said, catching up with melanie and Jack. "So melanie will keep you entertained for an hour or so." Then she disappeared into one of the connecting corridors.

"You look a little disappointed," melanie said.

"Yeah, sorry," Jack said. "I suppose I was expecting something a bit more *Star Wars* than this. I thought there would be aliens and things. This looks vaguely familiar, I suppose."

"You think it looks like every airport you have ever seen," melanie said.

"Yes, I do," Jack said. "Look at it. Bars, restaurants, and shops. All it needs is a Tie Rack."

melanie laughed. "You are right. But what I find most worrying is that we have been using this style for several centuries. How did your airport designers get to use it?"

"Yes, that is worrying," Jack said. "Maybe I should save my feelings of *déjà vu* for JFK or Heathrow then?"

"That's about it," melanie said with a smile.

"By the way, I am sorry I riled Bianca," Jack said. "There is something I don't like about her, and it got the better of me."

"You need never apologize for annoying Bianca," melanie said. "Now, shall I show you to your quarters? Then, perhaps, I can answer some more of your other questions. I know there is a lot for you to catch up on."

They set off across the concourse, and Jack said, "Who are all these people, and where are they going?"

"Most are families, going home from various offices on Earth," melanie said. "There are anything up to three thousand of our people down there at any one time. Mainly buying the things Earth manufactures that we don't. There is a regular rotation where two or three hundred of them will go home after we drop their replacements."

"What are you doing?" Jack said. "Invading?"

"No. *We're* not," melanie said.

"That sounded ominous."

119

"Not really," melanie said. "English is not my first language, and I still get the inflections wrong."

"Oh?" Jack said, wondering what her first language was, considering what Bianca had said earlier.

"That's another complex story that we can save for another day."

"Okay," Jack said. "But I am putting together my own list."

"No doubt," melanie said.

They climbed a flight of stairs to the upper deck and walked to Jack's quarters. Jack found the journey quite disturbing. The circumferential corridors on the habitation ring always appeared to be running uphill ahead of him. But when he turned around, they were running uphill in the other direction as well.

Strange though that aspect of *Encounter* was, the dark gray flooring and light gray walls were reassuringly familiar. The brightly painted doors in the corridor provided some relief from the drabness.

melanie finally opened a blue door and ushered Jack into a small sitting room with two sofas and an extensive entertainment system. Through a short corridor, flanked by a well-equipped bathroom on one side and a kitchenette on the other, was a bedroom.

"I'm making coffee," melanie said as Jack walked back past the kitchenette towards the lounge.

"Thanks, the coffee you guys' use is excellent. Although I'm going to be walking up walls if I keep drinking it at this rate."

"Sit down; I'll bring it through."

Jack slumped in a chair and looked around. Dotted around the bare white walls were a series of prints of what Jack took to be flowers, though they were like no flowers he had ever seen. The furniture had a comfortable feel to it, although it looked like the sort of items he could have bought in any upmarket department store on Earth.

"This is for you," melanie said and placed a small pouch on the table. Jack opened it and found his hard drives, his watch, wallet, and phone.

"Thank you," Jack said. "How did you get all of this?"

melanie placed the coffee tray on a low table and sat on the couch opposite Jack.

"My pleasure," melanie said. "I have my ways."

M   elanie clearly knew much more about Jack than she had told Bianca. Suggesting there had to be a reason.

"No porthole," Jack said. "Can I get an upgrade?"

"No," melanie said. "There aren't any windows or portholes in an interstellar vehicle. Any human looking out of a window in the retroverse would go insane. So not a good idea."

"I might circle back to why a human would go insane," Jack said. "Meanwhile, what's the retroverse?"

"Hmmm," melanie said. "That's difficult. We have already established you don't have a doctorate or even a degree in physics, yet you want me to explain a concept that some physicists might be hard-pressed to understand."

"I read a lot of science-fiction," Jack said with a grin.

"Yes, so you told Bianca," melanie said. "And, of course, having read a lot of science-fiction always trumps a degree from MIT."

"Okay," Jack said. "You are obviously far too important to be stuck with nursemaiding me, so why don't you fuck off and count paper clips or whatever other vital task you have been assigned?"

melanie sat opposite Jack, the two glowering at each other. melanie had found Jack's limit for dealing with arrogance and off-handedness.

"My apologies," melanie said. "I realize that you have a lot to learn."

"No apology needed," Jack said. "I just don't know where to start with all this stuff."

"I understand," melanie said. "Let's go back to the beginning. I presume you know it is not possible to travel faster than the speed of light?"

"Yes," Jack said.

"You aren't going to mention, 'E = mc^2' or 'Einstein'?"

"No," Jack said. "Should I?"

"Preferably not," melanie said. "And are you familiar with the origins of our universe?"

"If you mean the big bang, yes, I am," Jack said. "If you have discovered something else, then no."

"The big bang holds good with us too," melanie said. "What do you know about that?"

"Err," Jack said, digging up something from a documentary he'd watched on TV a long time ago. "I think there was some sort of singularity that became energy and matter and stuff, somehow?"

"Do you know what a singularity is?" melanie said.

"Not really," Jack said, aware that he was getting out of his depth. "Something tiny but infinite?"

"No, but it will do," melanie said. "It was the energy of the universe compressed into something incomprehensibly tiny."

"More or less what I said," Jack mumbled.

"Where do you imagine this singularity was at the time of the big bang?"

"Where?" Jack said. "You mean like... I have no idea what that means, err, wherever the center of our universe is now, I suppose."

"Soon after the big bang, yes, that might be the case, but I meant just before the event?"

Jack wished he hadn't started on this line of questioning at all, but he wasn't going to back down now. Especially after suggesting that melanie's primary role was counting paper clips.

"Umm, where the center of our universe was going to be?" he said tentatively then added, "Or is?"

"Not quite," melanie said, "it was in an inverted form of our universe."

"Like a parallel universe?" Jack said.

melanie paused, deliberating her response, then said, "Yes and no. Yes, it co-exists with our own universe spatially, forming a parallel universe. No, in that the usual concept of a parallel universe—what we would call an alternate plane—is a universe that exists in parallel with ours and that may be similar, or even identical, to ours.

"I am talking about the antithesis of our universe, the negative image, the retroverse. Unlike alternate planes, the retroverse exists."

"Okay," Jack said.

"You understand what I am saying?" melanie said.

"Not really," Jack said. "Or what this has to do with faster than light travel or why I can't have a window."

"I'm getting there," melanie said. "Imagine two parallel universes before the big bang. The first, the one we now call the retroverse, had galaxies that went through a cycle of expansion and eventual collapse until all the matter and energy of the retroverse collected in one place."

"Like water pools in the lowest place."

"Close enough," melanie said. "This matter and energy form the ultimate black hole, its own gravitational pull compressing what is now just hydrogen plasma -- everything else has long

122

gone -- until way beyond critical mass; it has to explode. But can't. Not outwards, at least, because its own gravity prevents it from doing so. Therefore, it takes the only other way out, and it implodes, bursting through into this universe."

"The big bang," Jack said.

"Indeed," melanie said. "Although the big whoosh is more accurate. All the hydrogen atoms, plus a minuscule amount of helium and an even smaller amount of lithium, entered our universe and expanded once more. Over the next hundred million years, these basic elements formed the primordial stars.

"These were short-lived stars and died in supernovae, where they created the heavy elements. Although some became the supermassive black holes forming the pivotal points of the galaxies. The rest formed matter that became the stars, planets, dark matter, reefs, black holes, anti-matter, black stars, cloud folds, and nebulae in all the galaxies and all the spaces in between."

"So, the big bang was really more of a whoosh and just the starting point, not the main event it's dressed up to be?" Jack said.

"To a point, yes," melanie said. "Matter formed, although it was more like a hydrogen fog, and this universe now gained the three physical dimensions of space. Time, the fourth dimension, followed soon after." She smiled. "The new universe was a bit like a tea party, where there are three dimensions taking tea while waiting for time to turn up."

IST Encounter, **Mars orbit**
11:35 GST

melanie had clearly said, "The new universe was a bit like a tea party, where there are three dimensions taking tea while waiting for time to turn up."

Regardless of the circumstances, it would have been a curious expression. A *non sequitur* of epic proportion.

Except, Jack knew of a tea party where three characters, a hatter, a dormouse, and a March hare, attended a tea party with the clock perpetually reading six o'clock, as they waited for time to arrive. All in an obscure children's novel entitled *Alice's Adventures in Wonderland*.

123

Jack knew little of his parents. They had died while he was a baby, but his father had left him three novels and two hand-written notebooks. The novels were *Alice's Adventures in Wonderland* and *Through the Looking-Glass, and What Alice Found There*, the sequel to *Wonderland*, and a separate work altogether called *The Hunting of the Snark*. One notebook identified Charles Lutwidge Dodgson, a nineteenth-century mathematician, writing as Lewis Carroll, as the author of all three novels.

Curiously, in the first half of the notebook, Jack's father had written of Dodgson as a well-known figure, in the second half he accepted what Jack had discovered for himself. Nobody, including the supposed publishers, had ever heard of the books, Dodgson or Carroll. Even Dodgson's supposed work as a mathematician was accredited to others.

Jack had long decided that the books were most likely printed privately, possibly as a gift for a favorite niece. He was also reasonably sure that nobody else had ever heard of them.

During the short time that Jack had known melanie, he had gathered the impression she did not make idle mistakes. That a purpose lay behind her use of an analogy from an obscure book.

Jack could only suspect that melanie was testing him to see if he was aware of the books. Although why she would do so remained unclear.

melanie watched Jack's reaction to her labored reference with interest. He knew what she meant. He had the books and had read them. That was promising.

"So, if time doesn't exist," Jack said, bringing the conversation back in line, "then there is no speed of light limit. Is that why the universe is bigger than it should be?"

"In what way?" melanie said.

"It's fourteen billion years old and ninety-three billion light-years in diameter," Jack said. "If the maximum speed of everything is that of light, the universe should only be about twenty-eight billion light-years in diameter."

"An interesting hypothesis," melanie smiled, looking at Jack as if he were an unusually intelligent lab rat. "Except objects traveling away from each other cannot exceed the speed of light, relative to each other, either, so it would be fourteen billion light-years in diameter.

"While you are close enough on age, the actual diameter is at least two hundred billion light-years and growing."

"Okay," Jack said, "How come the universe is that big?"

"The expansion of a universe is the exception to the rule for the speed of light, in one sense. The universe is still expanding, it is still accelerating, and it is not traveling faster than light. But space is creating more space as it goes, giving the illusion of faster than light travel."

Jack looked blank.

"Imagine a dead straight superhighway from New York to Los Angeles. You set off from New York at one hundred kilometers per hour, the legal speed limit, and drive for ten hours. As you perceive things, you will have covered one thousand kilometers.

"At which point the police in Huntington County, Indiana, pull you over for speeding. What you are unaware of is that behind you, the superhighway has been stretched. New York is now three thousand kilometers away, and, as you have only been driving ten hours, you have been averaging three hundred kilometers per hour. You have, to the police, exceeded the speed limit."

"Okay," Jack said, looking a little less than persuaded by melanie's argument. "And space expands by stretching?"

melanie considered her options and chose, "Close enough."

"Jesus," Jack said. "Will it stretch, or expand, or whatever it does, forever, or will it collapse one day?" Jack said, dredging up his only question on the topic.

"Both," melanie said. "Using the standard five-dimensional spherical model of the universe, but reduced to three dimensions, if the big bang happened at the north pole and expands outwards, it will reach the south pole in another hundred billion years or so. There it will collapse back into energy until it reaches a critical point and burst back into the retroverse, and the entire cycle starts over."

"Ah," Jack said. "Does that mean that, meanwhile, the retroverse has no energy, no matter, and no time?"

"Correct," melanie said.

"No time and therefore, there is no such thing as the speed of light to act as a barrier," Jack said.

"Yes," melanie said.

"Okay,"Jack said. "Patrizia said something about *Encounter* being capable of traveling at seven hundred and fifty thousand times the speed of light. Is that right?"

"Yes. Although *Encounter* is a military freighter. A civilian cargo vehicle can normally only manage five hundred kilolux. That's...."

"Yes, I know about them; a kilolux is a thousand times the speed of light. That's awful quick."

"Not as quick as we'd like," melanie said. "This galaxy is currently one hundred sixty-three thousand Terran light-years in diameter. At five hundred kilolux, which is long-range cruising speed, it would take *Encounter* over two thousand eight hundred hours, one hundred nineteen days, to get from one edge of the galaxy to the other. The tea clipper *Cutty Sark* once sailed from England to Australia in seventy-three days, and that didn't have engines."

"Okay," Jack said. "This retroverse is the fast track to the other side of the galaxy, but it's another universe; how do you get into it? I mean, wouldn't you need to live there to take advantage of it?" Jack asked.

"No. You live in London and use the tube by going in at one point, traveling across town, and coming out at another underground station. You don't need to live underground."

"I see what you mean. All you need to do is enter the retroverse, travel across the galaxy, and come out back into this universe."

"Exactly."

"How do you do that? Pop into another universe, as it were?"

"Easy enough; the retroverse is another universe occupying the same space as this one but in a parallel plane. To get from this plane to the retroverse, we create a rabbit-hole."

"'Rabbit-hole' is a ridiculous name," Jack said. Another oblique reference to that book.

"Really? You think?" melanie said, "They call them 'wormholes' on Earth. Now, that is silly."

"Fair point," Jack said and sat thinking for a few seconds. "Then how do you go about creating a rabbit-hole?"

"With a rabbit-punch," melanie said. "Which is primarily an electromagnet."

"Okay, that all sounds vaguely understandable," Jack said. "Why can't I have a window?"

"There is nothing in the retroverse. The human mind cannot accept the notion of either infinity or nothing and goes into melt-down."

"I know how it feels," Jack said.

126

Jack was feeling tired. Science, real science, wasn't his favorite topic. He preferred the fictional variety where such things as faster than light travel were explained away with a few words, a piece of folded paper, and a pin.

What he was experiencing now was a bit like talking to a Ferrari enthusiast and getting overwhelmed in talk of double-overhead camshafts and how to balance six twin-choke Weber DCOE carbs with a Swiss army knife and a drinking straw. Time to get back to fundamentals, like what it did to the gallon.

"Next question, how do you power this lot? This vehicle, I mean. Nuclear reactors?"

"Not really," melanie said.

"That sounds peculiarly ominous," Jack said, wondering if he shouldn't have stayed away from everything technical. "In that case, what do you use?"

"A synthetic black hole. It spins and generates electricity in the terawatt and upwards scale."

"What's a terawatt?"

"A trillion watts, a one followed by twelve zeroes, and Gaia's black hole generates zettawatts, which is a sextillion or twenty-one zeroes."

"Christ, what do they need that sort of power for?"

"The containment fields, primary drive, rabbit-punch, artificial gravity, life support, maneuvering engines, powering factories, and homes. They all use lots of power, and wind farms have proved to be a bit of a failure."

Jack laughed. "No shit. What do containment fields contain?"

"The synthetic black hole," melanie said. "Those fields take up twenty-five percent of the output, and if they fail, there is a sort of cosmic swallow, and the entire vehicle disappears."

"Happen often?"

"No."

"What about the primary drive? Because I sort of imagine four enormous rocket things at the back end with blue lights."

"Sadly, our vehicles don't have any outward signs of activity when under power."

"Shame, so how do they work?" Jack asked.

"The actual propulsion is through a matter/anti-matter or MAM drive where anti-matter repels matter, but matter attracts anti-matter. The anti-matter presses away from the matter, but the matter tries to catch up, causing the anti-matter to push away again."

127

"Like a slinky going downstairs?" Jack said.

"You have this innate ability," melanie said, "after I have reduced an explanation to the lowest level of simplicity, of finding a sub-basement."

"Thank you," Jack said.

"Which is where the next problem comes in," melanie said. "To get up to speed needs high levels of acceleration. For example, getting to five hundred kilolux in an hour requires an acceleration in the order of forty billion G."

"Wow," Jack said. "No pressure then?"

"Witty," melanie said, not sounding particularly amused.

"While MAM drives will, theoretically, provide those levels of acceleration, in doing so, they would flatten themselves and any vehicle to a molecule thick film in the first milliseconds.

"Therefore, the second part of the drive is called 'SQUID'. Not the acronym writers' finest hour; it stands for a sub-quantum inertia-less drive.

"'SQUID generates a field about the vehicle at an atomic level that can move every atom within the field at an equal rate of acceleration. The MAM power unit moves the field generated by SQUID. The field moves everything inside it, including the ship, the MAM and the SQUID field generator itself, and we get to accelerate up to speed without turning our passengers to jam."

"Talk about lifting yourself by your bootstraps," Jack said.

"It is precisely that," melanie said.

"Good, that explains it all as well as I can cope with," Jack said.

"Glad to help," melanie said. "Now, we should see about meeting Bianca for lunch."

IST *Valiant Sky*, en route to Romstrum
12:30 GST

"I don't care what you say, that is not Quidditch," Abdul Wei said as he thumped down at the table. "It's not even quidditch. A novel form of ze-ball maybe, but Quidditch it is not.

"For the record, calling this a broom," he held up a two-meter length of alloy tubing with a saddle, stirrups, and handgrips, "does not alter the fact."

"What do you mean by, 'it's not Quidditch, it's not even quidditch'?" Setu Anastassiou said.

"One has a capital 'Q.'"

"Yeah? Okay, so what?"

"With a capital 'Q' it's what Harry Potter played. With a small 'q', it's the game they play on Earth," Abdul said. "Or wait, is it the other way around?"

"Seriously, they play whichever one it is on Earth?" Elise Jarmo said. "Without a zero-gravity environment? How?"

"They sit astride brooms and run around the field," Abdul said, wishing he hadn't.

Elise boomed with laughter and turned to the rest of the Gaian team as they walked into the dining room. "Did you hear that? And I thought our lot was lame."

"It's just a bit of fun, and it's no lamer than football," Abdul said, knowing he was on fragile ice.

"What?" Dan Olafsen said. "Are you calling 'the beautiful game' lame?"

"No," Abdul said. "I'm just saying that quidditch is no lamer than football, and football is not lame."

"American football is," Sophia Gulab said.

"Wash your mouth out with soap, woman," Zack Vartanian yelled. "You are talking about a real man's game, not that girly substitute they call soccer."

"Real men play rugby," Elise said, throwing a highly inflammable topic onto the first sparks of argument and standing back.

"Rugby?" Abdul, Dan, and Zack screamed in unison.

"Gentlemen," Setu interjected. "I believe the ladies are winding us up."

"Oh, Setu," Elise wailed, "why must you give us away when we were having so much fun?"

"Because I want my lunch, and that argument never ends well."

"Which sounds like my cue," Martin Anatol said, appearing from a side door.

Like most Aetherian and Gaian intelligence services vehicles, *Valiant Sky* was a military carrier with accommodation for various political, military, diplomatic, business, and intelligence staff who needed a travel facility between outposts that combined security and discretion.

On occasions, different traveling groups preferred or even required that discretion to extend to total isolation. To make this possible, they could reconfigure the accommodation to provide areas that kept different groups away from, and even unaware of, each other.

Each area, depending on size, contained cabins, a lounge, a dining room, and a gym. This time, with only three different groups aboard, the largest of the three also gained use of the zero-gravity gym. Best of all, a Martin Anatol and his team, known throughout Gaia and Aetheria as the best food providers in the galaxy, ran the kitchens.

"Martin, what delights have we to look forward to today," Setu, the team's self-confessed gourmet, gushed.

"Today is a surprise," Martin beamed. "A light white wine, Terran in origin, will serve as an apéritif."

As he spoke, two server-bots sprang out of traps in the walls and delivered glasses of pale wine.

"I could get used to this," Sophia Gulab said.

"Especially after the trip out," Zack said.

"Yeah, about that," Chiyo said, sipping her wine. "Doesn't all of this strike you as odd? We've heard nothing from either Lorina or the Commander, apart from that recorded message in the shuttle. Added to which, we are on an Aetherian vehicle?"

"Here we go," Elise said. "Come on, Chiyo, no conspiracy theories today."

Chiyo laughed, "Okay, not today."

"You know, she has a point," Tamara said.

"She does?" Elise said, wishing she had just let it go.

Tamara had a stratospheric IQ, a dress sense that defied description, a shopping fetish, and Marge Simpson's blue hair, but if she thought that something smelled fishy, a trawler was bound to be nearby.

"This time, yes," Tamara said with a nod of her head to confirm her point.

"How?" Setu said.

"Okay," Tamara said, "think what's happened so far."

"Go on," Elise said, and the others stopped talking in smaller groups and gathered around Tamara.

"There are a few minor details that aren't right," Tamara said. "Let's start with the command structure.

"We area Gaian unit and yet have melanie, an Aetherian, as our commander. Our second in command is Lieutenant Lorina Korenjic, former wild-child and the only GCID officer to be commissioned without attending the officer training academy. A lieutenant who has more power...."

"That's not fair," Elise said.

"I was not being rude about Lieutenant Korenjic," Tamara said. "I was merely pointing out that she did not go to OTA, and that is probably why she is such an outstanding officer. But she has more power than some colonels. Most colonels, in fact, except Kaninchen."

"And your point is?" Zack said.

"Singularly and collectively, those two are undoubtedly the two finest officers in GCID, although neither, technically, is a GCID officer."

"That point I cannot deny," Zack said.

"Thank you," Tamara said. "Now, it occurs to me that two such spectacular officers, if assembling a team, would want the very best and they put together what we often call 'melanie's secret army'."

"It's a myth," Elise said.

"That's a stupid story for cadets," Zack said.

"It doesn't exist," Abdul said.

"Oh, it exists," Tamara said. "But it's so secret, those in it don't know they are in it."

"Crap," Chiyo said. "Who are they then?"

"Us," Tamara said.

Chiyo kicked off the laughter, but it spread through the others, apart from Tamara and Abdul.

"You know, she might have something," he said.

"Oh, come on," Elise said.

"Think about it," Abdul said. "We are a team of eleven sergeants. Nine here and two with the lieutenant. All specialists."

"Plus, the fragrant Zara Chang will be here shortly," Chiyo said.

"Okay," Abdul said. "Twelve sergeants, all of whom have a reputation for unconventional methods. All of us could have gone to the OTA, but none of us did so because we all broke the rules and/or the conventions. We didn't fit.

"But I bet not one of you could name someone in your specialization, whatever their rank, who is better."

"He's right," Elise said. "We are all at the top in our field. There are a couple of other names, I could add, but we are the *crème de la crème* of GCID."

"If you are right," Chiyo said. "We aren't that secret anymore."

"Yes, we are," Tamara said. "I doubt anyone, other than the commander and the lieutenant, knows where we are. And most will think we are on that asteroid."

"How do you work that out?" Chiyo asked.

"Look what has happened to us over the last few days," Tamara said. "First, we are told we are going on an exercise. To an asteroid—a very remote asteroid, way beyond many other suitable asteroids—where we will be for several weeks. No comms allowed and no information on what we will do there, and, just for good measure, our commander is off to Earth, our lieutenant and her favorite sergeants are off somewhere else, and we will be on our own.

"Big fanfare, then we are loaded onto *Envoy*—which, right now, is officially in orbit around the planet Mars in the Terran system, although I suspect that is *Encounter* in disguise—and lugged right across the galaxy.

"Now, here's the thing," Tamara said and placed a small bowl, a wine glass, a flower vase, a salt cellar, and a coaster, each about forty centimeters apart, along the length of the table.

"The small bowl is Jericho," Tamara continued, "and eighteen hundred and forty light-years away is the wine glass, representing the asteroid we were on. Fourteen thousand seven hundred and twenty light-years from that is a flower vase that is Earth. More precisely, Mars orbit, which is near as we can get with a freighter. Another eight thousand two hundred light-years along, we have a salt cellar for Romstrum, and another ten thousand six hundred light-years beyond that is Gaia represented by this coaster.

"As you can see, this isn't to scale, and they aren't really in a straight line, but let's not get too wrapped up in detail."

The others all nodded and exchanged cautious glances. With Tamara, they would have expected a three-dimensional holographic display with precision scaling. Tamara just didn't say things like 'let's not get too wrapped up in detail' unless something far more critical had taken her attention.

"We were on Gaia, right?" Tamara started over.

"Right," Chiyo said.

"After leaving the coaster Gaia, we passed salt-cellar Romstrum, although at some distance, flower vase Earth, close enough to pick up a shuttle, and finally to this wine glass asteroid where we were shoved into another shuttle and sent

132

down to the surface. As soon as we had disembarked, the shuttle took off, and, once it was back aboard *Envoy*, they left."

Tamara looked around the table. Everybody was nodding their heads in agreement.

"Anybody who matters on Gaia now thinks that we are on an asteroid, because that is where the Gaian freighter left us. And being Gaians, that is where the authorities think we will stay. After all, we have no way of going anywhere else.

"One hour after we got down, a shuttle arrived from the Aetherian freighter *Lucid Tsunami*, carrying Lieutenant Robert Sunter and his team, supposedly on their way to meet the commander on Romstrum. A journey that should have taken them sixty-six hours. Instead, they were on *Tsunami* for two hundred and nine hours, but being Sunter, he had not questioned this.

"Anybody who matters on Gaia now thinks that Robert Sunter is on Romstrum, because that is where the Aetherians have told them he is. And who is ever going to think Robert Sunter important enough that the Aetherian government would lie about his location? Not that anybody, apart from his mother, will care where he is."

"Meanwhile, *Lucid Tsunami* left orbit immediately after dropping the shuttle, containing Robert and his pals, as opposed to the standard practice of waiting to retrieve its shuttle after a drop.

"Within minutes of arrival, Sunter received a recorded message from Lieutenant Korenjic telling him he was no longer going to Romstrum but taking over from us on the asteroid. A few minutes after that, we got recorded orders from Lieutenant Korenjic that we were to board the Aetherian shuttle in which Sunter had arrived.

"That is an odd series of events."

"What's odd about that?" Setu said. "Sunter thinking, he is going to one place when going to another is normal. We regularly get recorded messages from Lorina. The commander is Aetherian and often uses Aetherian freighters. So, what?"

"Agreed on all points," Tamara said. "I suspect we all received recorded messages from Lieutenant Korenjic to prevent us from asking her why the change of plan, which we would have done if she had been calling us live. But we should also consider that as the messages were pre-recorded, this was pre-planned."

"Why take us out to the asteroid to bring us all back?" Setu said.

"A smokescreen, maybe?" Elise said.

"That was my theory," Tamara said.

"You know all the kit was for them," Dan Olafsen said.

"Shut up, Bang," Chiyo said.

"No, wait," Elise said. "Bang, what do you mean, 'all the kit was for them'?"

"On the asteroid base, I went into the stores," Dan said, "and although we had our personal kit with us, there were crates in there marked with the names of their team and none for us."

"Why didn't you mention it at the time?" Elise asked.

"I tried, but Chiyo kept telling me to shut up," he said.

"That's fairly conclusive," Setu said, "but I still don't see why any of this was necessary."

"It's simple," Elise said. "If the powers that be think the commander has Lieutenant Sunter with her, they may be a little less concerned than if, for example, we were with her.

"So, having seen Robert Sunter set off in the right direction to be with the commander and us safely packed off in the opposite direction—figuratively, if not literally—they can forget about it."

"That all makes a twisted sort of sense," Setu said. "So what about the shuttle?"

"Ah, yes, the shuttle," Tamara said. "The shuttle that brought Lieutenant Sunter's team down was not from *Lucid Tsunami*, but from *Valiant Sky*."

"How do you know?" Setu asked.

"The words *Shuttle 7. IST Valiant Sky* over the rear hatch was a bit of a clue," Tamara said.

"Okay, now that is interesting," Elise said. "Both Aetherian vehicles, but why would the civilian *Lucid Tsunami* be carrying a shuttle from the military *Valiant Sky*?"

"At this stage, the more interesting question might be, how long was the civilian *Lucid Tsunami* carrying a shuttle from the military *Valiant Sky*?" Tamara said.

"I suppose you know the answer," Setu said.

"I don't know the answer, definitely," Tamara said. "But as far as I can tell, the last time *Valiant Sky* and *Lucid Tsunami* were within shuttle swapping distance of each other was six weeks ago.

"I know the shuttle could have been left somewhere by *Valiant Sky* three days ago and picked up by *Lucid Tsunami* two days ago. But the two hadn't occupied any common space for several years, before both being in orbit around some planet on the edge of Arthronine space six weeks ago."

"Another freighter could have transported it from one to the other," Setu said, "if it was that important."

"Unlikely," Sophia Gulab said. "*Valiant Sky* is a full-on military vehicle. *Lucid Tsunami* is a civilian, after a fashion. All the habitation crew is civilian, but the operational team is Aetherian military.

"With military crews, all operations are confidential. With civilian crews, all gossip is a trade commodity. A shuttle transferred from one IST to another, by a third, might as well have its movement orders broadcast on a news channel."

"So, six weeks it is then," Setu said. "So, if the transfer happened then, the plan must have been put together a long time ago."

"It looks like it," Tamara said.

"But why that shuttle?" Setu said.

"Because we needed it to get aboard the *Valiant Sky*," Tamara said.

"But civilian and military shuttles are identical," Setu said. "We could have used a shuttle from *Lucid Tsunami*."

"Or they could have stopped and sent a shuttle down for us," Elise said.

"No, they couldn't," Tamara said. "It had to be that shuttle."

"Why?" Setu said.

"Here is an extract from *Valiant Sky's* log," she said, projecting a blue screen into the air from her comm so they could all see it.

"Here is where *Valiant Sky* dropped out of retroverse," she said, indicating a point on a red line on the screen. "They were down to ten percent lux, thirty thousand kilometers per second. The vehicle maintains that speed, to within five hundred kilometers per second, until it re-enters the retroverse. With us on board."

"That's not possible," Cornelius Vartanian said. "We traveled in a shuttle. There is no shuttle capable of either that speed or the acceleration needed to get to that speed."

"I agree," Tamara said. "It's not possible."

There was a pause. Everybody was waiting for Tamara to say something.

"What sort of shuttle was it?" Tamara asked Cornelius as the screen disappeared.

"An Aetherian F7 or F8. The F8 is just an F7 with a few extra bits."

"Size?" Tamara said.

"From memory," Cornelius said, "eighteen meters long, five wide, single deck. Four stub wings, each with a Gonzalez engine unit with swivel nozzles for both lift and horizontal travel. Nothing new or innovative in its technology.

"Interior is basic. The front eight meters have the flight deck and passenger space for about twenty-four without kit. The rear half is all cargo space."

"Correct," Tamara said. "From Sunter landing to us leaving in that shuttle was two hours and four minutes. As soon as we were off the ground, we accelerated to a speed of thirty thousand kilometers per second in forty minutes.

"An acceleration of twelve thousand five hundred meters per second squared.

"When we stopped accelerating, *Valiant Sky* was exactly five thousand meters behind us and traveling, maybe, thirty meters per second faster, but slowing to match our speed in a little under two minutes later."

"But..." Cornelius said and was 'shushed' by Elise.

"As you probably know, normal docking procedures take place at between five and thirty kilometers per second," Tamara continued. "We were traveling at thirty thousand kilometers per second."

"But relative speeds between the two vehicles is virtually zero," Elise said. "What difference does it make?"

"Angular variation," Tamara said. "If the two vehicles are not precisely parallel, at thirty k, they will go out of alignment by a long way in no time at all."

"As I just said, that's not possible," Cornelius Vartanian said.

"Yet, here we are," Elise said.

"But there is no shuttle that could do that," Cornelius said.

"Yeah, there is," Tamara said, looking at Cornelius. "In fact, the Aetherians have four SQUID plus MAM equipped shuttles. They don't have rabbit-punches, so they aren't retroverse capable. But they are all capable of getting to thirty thousand kilometers per second at twelve thousand five hundred meters per second squared and without squishing the passengers. All four are aboard *Valiant Sky*.

136

"Well, they are now. One was aboard *Lucid Tsunami*."

"That does sort of explain why we were given a *Valiant Sky* shuttle," Setu said.

"Where do they put SQUID and MAM in a shuttle?" Cornelius asked.

"Where would you put it?" Tamara asked.

"There isn't room for... Oh! The cargo hold."

"Right again," Tamara said. "That's why Sunter's team had all their kit pre-delivered. There was no room in the cargo space. We just dumped ours over the spare seats, as usual."

"So," Elise said, trying to move on from shuttles, "we have a smokescreen, so that the powers that be, which is a long-winded way of saying, 'Bianca Kaninchen', doesn't know that we are going to somewhere, presumably to meet the commander, but almost certainly Lorina. Or that Sunter is still on that asteroid. But we still do not know why."

"Or why the tight schedule?" Zack said.

"Is it tight?" Chiyo asked.

"More than you can imagine," Tamara said. "*Valiant Sky* had come from the Jericho system, which is just over eighteen hundred light-years from that asteroid...."

"How do you know where it had been?" Elise asked.

"I have my sources," Tamara said.

"You hacked into the Aetherian system," Elise said.

"I have my sources," Tamara repeated.

"What's Jericho?" Sophia asked.

"You have led a sheltered life," Setu said. "Jericho is one of those places where, if you want something illegal, you will find someone who will supply it. And I'm not talking a few hi'n'lo tabs. I mean banned weapons, berserker 'bots, neural gases, bio-weapons and every illicit item of electronic kit the collective intelligence of this galaxy has put together for evil intent."

"Oh, okay," Sophia nodded.

"So, Doc, how do you know so much about Jericho and hi'n'lo tabs?" Chiyo asked Setu, smiling in what she sincerely hoped was a winsome way.

"I spent six months there before entering med-school," Setu said. "How do you think anyone gets through med-school without tabs?"

"Hmm," Elise said and turned towards Tamara. "And you have been hacking into Aetherian security services systems and discovered... What?"

"I have it on good authority," Tamara stressed, "that *Valiant Sky* left small bowl Jericho, just eleven hours and fifty minutes, before collecting us from the wine glass asteroid. They came out of the retroverse for precisely one hundred sixty-two seconds, grabbed us, and re-entered the retroverse before accelerating back to their previous speed of eight hundred and fifty-five kilolux.

"I believe that this is all part of a convoluted plan...."

"This is Lorina Korenjic's work," Elise said.

"You've worked with her before?" Setu asked.

"Yes," Elise said. "She is a planner. I mean, when Lorina puts together a plan, it is a work of art built with engineering tolerances. This plan has her mark on it."

"Isn't there a contradiction here?" Setu said. "It was considered necessary to drop a freighter out of retro at ten percent lux, to pick up a shuttle that isn't supposed to exist. That suggests a tight schedule. But, for it to work, they moved the shuttle from one vehicle to another six weeks ago.

"If they knew six weeks ago, surely there was time to arrange a more leisurely pickup?"

"Unless the idea was to make several things happen all in the same narrow time frame," Abdul Wei said.

"That makes sense," Elise said.

"We still don't know what it is all about," Cornelius said.

"Nor will we until the commander or Lorina decide to tell us," Elise said. "So, where are we going next?"

"We have two more scheduled stops," Tamara said. "The first is in the Terran system, and that's on Twoday next, about eight-thirty in the morning. We are going to drop off one passenger and pick up another three."

"The passenger we are dropping off, I do not know," Tamara said. "Okay, I have an idea; in fact, I know, but it's not relevant to us. What is relevant to us is that we are picking up both the Dee-Dum and Zara Chang, supposedly."

"Fucking kill me now," Chiyo said. "I thought getting Chang back bad enough, but the Dee-Dum? What can we have done to deserve such cruel punishment? Maybe we can get them to turn around and take us back to that asteroid for a twenty-year stretch?"

"They aren't that bad," Dan said.

"Fuck, you aren't still carrying a torch for Greta, are you?" Chiyo crowed.

"No," Dan said, blushing slightly.

"Who are they?" Setu asked.

"Fucking hell, Setu," Chiyo said. "Where have you been?"

"Busy," Setu said. "On Jericho."

"Okay, fair enough," Chiyo said. "Greta and Georgia Kaninchen are Colonel Kaninchen's daughters."

"Oh them," Setu said. "So, what was it you called them?"

"'The Dee-Dum,'" Chiyo said. "It's short for Tweedledee and Tweedledum; their stepfather gave the nicknames to them. Nobody knows where the names came from, so I suppose he just made them up."

Setu shrugged. "Okay," he said. "I am just trying to process who married Kaninchen to become their stepfather. I will have nightmares now."

"No, he married their birth mother, Sarah Gunter. She left Kaninchen for him."

"Brave," Setu said. "And dangerously stupid, I would have thought. Who was he?"

"Benjamin Ashbow."

Setu shrugged again.

"Even in your busy life, you must have heard of Benjamin Ashbow?" Chiyo said. "Professor Benjamin Ashbow, from Gaia U?"

"I don't remember him," Setu said.

"You wouldn't; he and Sarah died before we were born," Elise said. "On Earth, I think. In an accident."

"You do surprise me," Setu said. "Although, them living to a ripe old age would have surprised me more."

"There was this enormous scandal at the time," Elise said. "My father told me there was this rumor that Kaninchen was involved, but nothing official."

"I'll take your word for it," Setu said.

"But you have heard of Greta and Georgia."

"Oh yes," Setu said. "I've heard of them. Isn't their sister...."

"Ahhh," Chiyo yelled. "Do not mention that name in polite company, or you'll get seven years of bad luck."

"I heard that if you say her name three times, she will appear and kill you," Elise said.

Zack Vartanian snorted with laughter and suppressed it when Elise glowered at him.

Chiyo said, "This passenger on board now, that's not her, is it?"

139

"No, I don't think so," Tamara said.

"I will not sleep if it is," Elise said.

"Shame. That's the only time you stop talking," Cornelius said.

The others laughed, and Elise pretended to be offended, but not for long.

"I know what I was going to ask," Chiyo said. "When you mentioned picking up Zara and the Dee-Dum, you used the word 'supposedly'."

"Mmm," Tamara said. "I'm not sure... Something isn't right. The Dee-Dum are on their way to Earth from somewhere and will get there in time to meet us. But Zara Chang isn't on Earth and doesn't seem to be anywhere else."

"Good," Chiyo said.

"The *Valiant Sky* has just come from Jericho, and it occurred to me it was there to collect her," Tamara said. "That she is already on board and will appear next Twoday as if she has just come aboard when she has been here all the time.

"But the only problem is that I cannot see Zara Chang as the sort of person who would go to Jericho."

"I agree," Elise said. "She isn't the type. But then I couldn't see Setu going there either."

"True," Tamara said.

"Why would she do that?" Setu asked.

"I don't know," Tamara said. "Except most people who have just 'come from Jericho' keep it to themselves because if you went to Jericho, you went there for something illegal."

Everyone turned and looked at Setu, who shrugged.

"Zara would probably prefer us to think she hadn't been to Jericho, and the easiest way to accomplish that would be to pretend she had boarded when we get to Earth."

"There is a certain logic there," Elise said. "We get to this vase, or as it's better known, Earth, next Twoday, and then I suppose the next stop has to be Romstrum, of all places."

"How do you know?" Tamara said.

"Because you identified the salt cellar as Romstrum, so I kinda figured it fitted into the plan somewhere."

"You are right; there is some sign that might be our destination," Tamara said, "but what happens when we get there, I do not know."

At that moment, the food arrived and putting the proper plates in front of the right people took several minutes.

"So, here we are," Chiyo said. "Although where we are going is an unknown quantity."

"I think it is Romstrum," Tamara said. "Two reasons for that. The first is that Lorina told us we would get where we were going on Threeday next week.

"Because of our route, that is when we will pass Romstrum."

"Okay, and the second reason?" Elise asked.

"When we were talking about the shuttle that got us to *Valiant Sky*," Tamara said, "I didn't mention that rumor has it there are two T3s out there with full retroverse capability."

"Is this a Tamara rumor?" Elise asked. "Meaning, you know, but can't talk about it because you hacked someone?"

"Maybe," Tamara said.

"What's a T3?" Bang asked.

"Medium-size shuttle," Tamara said.

"You know those shuttles prospectors favor?" Cornelius said. "Thirty meters in diameter, two decks, about six meters tall, looks like a... I don't know. What do they look like?"

"A fat frisbee," Setu said.

"I know the ones you mean," Bang said. "But what's a frisbee?"

"I'll tell you later," Setu said.

"These are for real?" Cornelius said. "The T3s, I mean."

"I believe so," Tamara said. "They are deeper than a normal T3, about eight meters tall, with the SQUID and MAM in the extended lower part and a LiRo rackium-fueled cold-fusion generator in the center core."

"What's 'rackium'?" Bang asked.

"I suppose if it doesn't explode, you wouldn't know," Tamara said. "It is the densest material in the galaxy...."

"After Bang's head," Chiyo said and got a laugh from everybody, including Bang.

"Okay," Cornelius said. "So, where are these T3s?"

"One of them has disappeared totally, possibly destroyed in an accident. Or the Aetherians have it tucked away somewhere. The other one, hence reason two, is on its way to Romstrum."

IST *Echoing Forest*, en route to Romstrum
12:55 GST

Lorina watched the discussion among the team members on her compad and grinned. It was a good thing that Tamara Finkel was on their side.

"What's funny?" Miguel Iwasaka said from one of the other desks in the cramped office.

"Tamara has figured out the first bit of the first stage," Lorina said.

"Good," Gary Johannsen said. "When we get to Romstrum, she can explain it all to me."

"It is quite simple, really," Lorina said.

"No, it isn't," Miguel said. "You and melanie understand it because you have been working on it for the last twenty-four years and think that everybody else understands it as well."

"We just want to find Caeloeterra," Lorina said. "What's so complicated?"

"There's no such place?" Gary said. "It's fictional, like all those places they write about on Earth. Like Middle Earth and Lilliput."

"What about Disneyland?" Miguel asked.

"Yep, 'fraid so," Lorina said.

IST Encounter, **Mars orbit**
12:55 GST

Bianca stood waiting in the area by the docking gate. She led melanie and Jack straight into what purported to be an Italian restaurant called *Gli Pazzo Cappellaio*. Jack misread the ornate sign over the door as Pizza, not Pazzo, which didn't inspire confidence, but it pleasantly surprised him once through the door because it was nothing special.

The bar was near the door, the ideal location for a quick drink or an apéritif. Beyond it, the room opened up to hold a dozen wooden tables and an assortment of bentwood chairs. The walls were decorated with posters of New York, adding to the authenticity. In Jack's experience, few restaurants in Italy, other than spring-loaded tourist traps, had posters showing Rome on their walls. For the aspirational restaurateur somewhere like New York, London, or Sydney—wherever some cousin or brother had gone to make his pile—this added the right note. But for Jack, the clincher was the smell. Like they had marinated the furniture in garlic, olive oil, and Italian cheeses and charcuterie.

142

They treated Bianca like visiting royalty and escorted them to a table near the back that, Jack knew, had to be where she always sat.

"This isn't what I expected," Jack said.

"Good," melanie said.

Consulting the menu, Jack discovered that, with a few exceptions, the food was just everyday Italian fare. While melanie and Bianca both ordered the lasagna, Jack went for tagliatelle Bolognese.

The food turned out to be excellent, and they did little but make small talk, eat, and drink the *Nobile di Montepulciano* that Bianca had selected. Then dessert was under consideration.

Jack had just decided coffee was probably a safer option when Bianca said, "We have a problem."

"Yes," melanie said as a confirmation, not a question.

"What is it?" Jack said.

"A Nel vehicle has just docked," Bianca told him. "You stay here and ignore us. melanie and I will be at the bar."

Bianca and melanie moved to two stools at the bar, and waiters descended to clear the table of everything except the debris from Jack's lunch, making it look as if he had eaten alone. Just to complete the picture, a small cafetiere and the other coffee essentials arrived.

Meanwhile, the other diners were being moved to new locations, screening Jack from being seen clearly by anyone coming into the restaurant. They all seemed to accept this as part of the regular daily routine.

The door of the restaurant swung open, and the most beautiful woman Jack had ever seen walked in. He acknowledged it hadn't been very many days before that he had thought melanie was the most beautiful woman he had ever seen. He shrugged mentally, yes; it was fickle, but what the heart wants...

She was even taller than melanie, and her midnight blue uniform couldn't disguise a similarly slender figure. The severe cut of her dark-blond hair failed to detract from the classically perfect face it framed. Enormous blue eyes surveyed the room disdainfully.

Oh yes, a super-bitch of the old school, Jack thought. In his time, he had dated a few slightly shorter versions of this woman. Calculators on perfectly formed legs whose only interest in him had been his spending power. Not that he cared. It was a mutually beneficial arrangement; both parties got what they wanted and moved on. Nobody got hurt.

The two men with her were even taller and wore the same blue uniform. Many women—and not a few men—would, he conceded, find them quite attractive, too.

He was close enough to the bar to hear the woman say, "Colonel Kaninchen, I thought I might find you here." She had a slight accent Jack couldn't quite place. That and the forty-a-day huskiness were a beautiful mix, he decided, remembering that melanie's voice had got him where he was now.

"Captain Vilishu, how nice to see you," Bianca responded in a voice purring with vitriol. "Tell me, did you mean here as in the bar, or onboard *Envoy* or in Mars orbit?"

"Possibly all three, Colonel. Although rumor would suggest the first of those was probably the most likely. We are both aware that this is *Encounter*, doppleganged to *Envoy*. An illegal practice throughout the galaxy."

"'Doppleganged' eh?" Bianca said. "Have you heard of that, melanie?"

"Vaguely," melanie said. "I believe it refers to the, as Vilishu says, illegal practice of altering a vehicle's electronic signature to mimic another vehicle.

"For example, if the Nel assault ship *Blood Claw* wished to hide its presence, it could disguise itself as the Nel freighter *Dominator*, currently parked on the far side of the Terran moon. Supposedly."

Vilishu's face darkened in a blush. "Can you not bring your tick-tock companion to heel?" she snapped.

Jack assumed this reference to melanie must be some sort of slur—a 'tick-tock' had to be a type of dog, perhaps—in the language of these people, whoever they were. 'Nel' was the word Bianca had used. Something else for the list, Jack thought.

"Only with great difficulty," Bianca said. "As to your earlier remark, 'rumor' is a very particular word in the English language, Captain," Bianca said. "It means 'gossip,' and the underlying implication is that it is voluntary. It doesn't apply to anything wrung out of some wretch in one of your torture suites."

"Thank you, Colonel," Vilishu said with a smile that extended no further than the lips. "I would say I will make a note, but I would hope that it will not be necessary to use such crude sounds before much longer, and I only need to speak Nel."

"Oh, good. You are all returning to Nel."

144

"No, Colonel, we are not."

"Pity," Bianca said. "Well, now we have covered the pleasantries, let's get down to business. What do you want?"

"Certainly, Colonel," Vilishu cooed. "May I ask what you were doing here?"

"Certainly, you may ask."

There was a pause that seemed to stretch forever.

"Well?"

"Well, what?" Bianca replied.

The silence in the room was almost audible.

"What are you doing here?"

"I permitted you to ask. I said nothing about responding. But I will say whatever it is, it is entirely my business and none of yours."

"On the contrary, Colonel, I think it is my business."

"Then we will have to agree to disagree."

"You Gaians think because your ancestors once lived on that lump of rock you call Terra, that you have rights in determining its future. You do not."

"Do you believe that you have rights?"

"At least as much as the Saurians."

"Yes, that argument might gain favor amongst the 'anything for a quiet life' species you like to intimidate with all your religio-militaristic crap. It does not impress Gaians and never will."

Vilishu laughed. "Am I to take that as some sort of threat? Haven't you noticed, neither the Gaians nor your friends, the Aetherians, frighten anyone anymore? Nobody cares what you say or think or do. You are, what is the expression? All washed up?"

"Well, you won't be the first punk species to underestimate us, and you probably won't be the last. So, if you have nothing else, I'd like you to get your backside off my vehicle before I forget myself and have you escorted out of an airlock to which your shuttle isn't connected."

"I'll leave when you have answered my question; what are you doing here?"

"No, you're leaving now, and there are three gentlemen outside the door with weapons that will make a real mess of your pretty little uniform if you decide otherwise."

The pause stretched on. Two alley cats staring each other down.

145

"I shall return to my ship. From there, I shall put the same question to you while keeping my finger on the weapons' trigger. I imagine you will not want to enter the retroverse this close to Earth. Anyway, these old freighters have too many tells for you to escape that way."

"You would fire on an un-armed freighter?" Bianca asked.

"Only in cases of the severest provocation or by accident. I do not know which it will be in your case. Not that it matters. Nobody is going to say a word, not even your Gaian High Command."

Vilishu turned to go.

"Just one minor point before you leave," Bianca said.

Vilishu turned back with a tiny smile, anticipating victory.

"I asked if you would fire on an un-armed freighter?" Bianca said. "You said you would. Not that it surprises me, but here's the thing.

"You are right, this is *Encounter*, and that means she isn't your standard un-armed freighter; she has no tells and could run. Fast.

"But she is a GCID freighter, so won't be running from you and your stupid little toy ship. One reason for that is that right now, there is a rail gun, loaded with very dirty fission ammunition, on a remote-controlled ordnance platform sitting about ten kilometers directly behind your ship's ass."

"You're bluffing."

"Possibly. Are you willing to gamble that the last thing to go through your mind, other than a lump of spent plutonium, will be, 'so, she wasn't bluffing'?"

Vilishu spun around and, followed by her little retinue, walked out past three combat-suited men carrying stubby guns.

Bianca waited a full ten seconds at the bar before she and melanie turned back towards Jack's table. A waiter materialized and placed the largest brandy snifter Jack had ever seen in front of Bianca.

"What's going on?" Jack asked.

"Now that, Jack, is a very long story indeed," Bianca replied, after taking a large sip from her glass. "I need to talk to several people. Perhaps melanie will explain the situation regarding the Nel." With that, she stood up and walked out of the restaurant.

***IST Encounter*, Mars orbit**
14:35 GST

"Katelyn," Bianca snarled into her compad once back in her office. "I want blood."

"Anybody's in particular?" Katelyn Fofana asked.

"Vilishu's will do, to begin with," Bianca said. "That bitch dared to board *Encounter*. I want her dealt with."

"I will get on it, Colonel."

***IST Echoing Forest*, en route to Romstrum**
14:35 GST

"Is it true you were boarded by that Nel woman with the bad attitude?" Lorina said a little too loudly.

"All Nel women have a bad attitude," melanie replied. There was no picture on the compad, so Lorina thought she was probably busy shepherding her new charge.

"In fact, all the Nel have a bad attitude," melanie continued. *"But in this case, I assume you mean Vilishu?"*

"I do. So, how did she find out *Encounter* was 'ganging *Envoy*?" Lorina said.

"Someone must have told her," melanie replied.

"Yeah, but who knew and amongst them who...." Lorina paused as realization sunk in. "You. You told her."

melanie laughed.

"Why?"

"Because Jack needed to know whom we would need to deal with first, and the only way to meet Nel that I can think of is to annoy them. They don't much go in for social calls."

"Good thinking," Lorina said.

"Where are you now?"

"In the retroverse, so I'll just look out the window and have a look. Or I could say that we get to Romstrum in just over two days. Which seems like forever right now."

"We will be almost exactly twelve hours behind you."

"And our shuttle?"

"Still on its way."

"Good, we'd look pretty stupid sitting on Romstrum without a shuttle."

147

"Not really," melanie said. *"Tamara Finkel may not know where the other one is, but I do.*

"Now, I must go; I am about to explain to Jack what the Nel are all about."

"The whole truth?"

"Of course not. Bianca will have bugged his room and will want to hear me telling Jack the sanitized version. I shall leave it to others to reveal the whole story."

IST Encounter, Mars orbit
15:30 GST

melanie arrived at Jack's suite to find him sitting on the sofa with a large cafetiere and two cups on the small table.

"I think I might need this," he said.

"You might," melanie said as she sat down. "But I need to keep this to the basics; I have things to do.

"First, though," she said, placing a plastic disc on the table, "you will need this."

"What is it?" Jack said.

"A combination ID and a sort of charge card. You might need a few things; if you take this with you, you can get whatever you need."

"I need a Ferrari," Jack said.

"If you can find one on *Encounter*, buy it. It's your money."

"How come?"

"Something like life insurance your parents carried."

"Hmm," Jack said. "Thanks."

"Now," melanie said. "Bianca promised you an explanation of what Captain Vilishu and the Nel are up to."

"Yes, you didn't exactly strike me as best buddies," Jack said. "I take it calling you a 'tick-tock' was some sort of insult?"

melanie laughed, "No, we're not exactly best buddies. So, yes, that was an insult.

"There is a Gaian restaurant chain; I believe there is one on *Encounter*, called *Procrastination*. The décor is all old clocks, and the servers are obsequious robots with exposed cogs, wheels, and springs. They are called 'tick-tocks'."

"Meaning Vilishu thinks you are obsequious to Bianca?"

melanie smiled. "Yes."

148

"Either she has never seen you two close up, or she hasn't quite grasped the meaning of the word. Do you two even like each other?"

"Not at all," melanie said. "Should we?"

"Good point," Jack said.

"But that is of no importance," melanie said. "What is important is that the Nel are at war with an insectoid species, called the Arthronine.

"War between species in the galaxy is rare because it is unnecessary and expensive. Earth is small and finite, and your wars are usually over territory and/or ideology—political or religious.

"The galaxy is, technically, finite, but not small, at one hundred and sixty-three thousand light-years across and two thousand light-years thick at the hub. At last count, it contained just over four hundred eighty-seven billion stars with twelve hundred forty-three billion planets."

"That's a lot more stars than I thought," Jack said.

"Based on what you can see from Earth, or the Hubble telescope, it would be," melanie said.

"Okay," Jack said.

"In the galaxy, there are, currently, only one thousand one hundred seventy-six species with the ability to travel through the retroverse and therefore between stars. Until a relatively short time ago, all those species were evenly spread throughout the galaxy.

"Meaning each one had, on average, some nine billion cubic light-years of space and over four hundred million stars and a billion planets in its own backyard. As even the most expansionist species have discovered, there is a natural limit to how far they could expand their empire before it broke down, and that is well inside that volume."

"In what way 'broke down'?" Jack asked.

"The usual mix you would expect on Earth," melanie said. "Social entropy, lack of communications, the law of diminishing returns, over-stretched supply lines, local situations and local politics, taxation without representation.

"The size of any species' sustainable sphere of influence varies, of course," melanie continued, "but on average, it is between one and two thousand light-years in diameter, and the same depth as the galaxy is thick locally. That contains space for something in the order of fifty million stars and anything up to

149

five thousand planets capable of sustaining their kind of life, to call their own. Plus, they can mine the resources they need from more than seventy million other less inhabitable planets.

"What all this means in real terms," melanie said, "is that there is plenty of room, and war over territory is a largely redundant notion."

"That doesn't stop the odd border dispute, and occasionally one species will decide another species has taken too much space or has assets within its sphere of influence that could be shared more equitably. Which is how we got involved in the first place, removing a species that were blatantly mining planets in Saurian space. They were mining an element that was more difficult to extract in their sphere than in the Saurians'. The Terran mercenaries resolved that with hardly a shot fired."

"What about ideology?" Jack said.

"Rarely an issue between sovereign nations if they aren't trying to share the same finite land space. Within a species or nation, the disaffected group can overcome any differences by moving to another planet to practice their beliefs. Although that can have its own problems.

"The common form of war in the galaxy is a rebellion within a sphere of influence. Rebellions are frequent and usually nasty with unfortunate consequences for both sides."

"What causes them?" Jack asked.

"What causes any war?" melanie said. "Two sides who both think they are right, and the other lot wrong. I have long thought that the preferred end of a boiled egg to open was a far more compelling reason for war than the series of events that led to the first Terran world war."

"You are probably right," Jack said. He paused.

"So, despite all this, the Nel are involved in a war with these insects," Jack said. "When did all this happen? I mean, are we talking about hundreds of years ago, last week, or what?"

"By your calendar," melanie began, "the Arthronine first used the retroverse in nineteen seventy-two and the Nel five years later.

"Which was part of the problem," melanie said. "Not only did the Arthronine and the Nel discover the retroverse almost simultaneously, but their home planets are also fewer than four thousand light-years apart.

"Although if common sense had prevailed, that need not have been a problem. The expected expansion of their spheres of influence to the sustainable maximum would have left a two thousand light-year gap between each territory's outer edges.

"Unfortunately, there were those who saw additional profit in reinforcing the paranoia of the two."

"You mean other species were causing problems between the Nel and the Arthronine, simply to make money from a war?"

"You think that never happens on Earth?" melanie said with a smile. "But there needn't be an actual war, just as long as both sides buy enough weapons to match the weapons the other side are buying."

"That I can see," Jack said. "But I assume it didn't stop there in this case?"

"No, it didn't," melanie said. "The Arthronine and the Nel began expanding towards each other, but in no other direction."

"Somewhat inevitably," melanie said, "they reached the mid-way point, the real war between them began, and they both expanded sideways. As a result, they ended up with two bell-shaped volumes of space pressed mouth-to-mouth."

"A sort of three-dimensional front line," Jack said.

"Yes," melanie said. "The actual interface area is now a disc approximately a thousand light-years in diameter, two hundred light-years deep and contains some three million stars."

"Where they are fighting their war."

"Yes. But don't get any wrong ideas," melanie said. "This isn't *Star Wars*. We do not fight wars with spaceships and laser weapons. The vast distances and speeds of travel in space mean no battles between imperial cruisers and rebel alliance ships.

"This war is being fought planet by planet," melanie said. "The soldiers arrive on a planet and set up a base to provide a jumping-off place for the next system. Much as the Americans island-hopped towards Japan in your latest world war."

"Which brings me to ask," Jack said, "what are the Nel doing on Earth?"

"The Arthronine have a large and well-disciplined army of fighters," melanie said. "The Nel do not. They have a social structure controlled by a priesthood using what I can best describe as advanced brainwashing. This provides them with an army that is so disciplined, nobody ever does anything without direct orders from a superior. To make matters worse, in their wisdom, the priesthood has created an intense fear of death that renders their army useless. They are all cowards."

"Why?" Jack said.

"Fear is an essential tool in maintaining total control. They created the army before the war, when bravery was not a requisite," melanie said. "Their job was to make sure that any members of the civilian population who escaped the psycontrol system were dealt with. It takes no bravery to sit in an armored vehicle and gun down unarmed civilians. Just blind obedience."

"That's for sure," Jack said.

"Fighting planet-by-planet against a foe like the Arthronine is not for the faint-hearted," melanie said. "Seven years ago, they found that just five thousand light-years away from their home planet, and in the opposite direction from the Arthronine, is the ancestral home to one of the most feared species of warriors in the galaxy."

"That was handy," Jack said.

"I'm talking about Earth," melanie said.

"Ah, not so handy," Jack said. "I didn't realize that. Are we feared?"

"Oh yes," melanie said. "The Nel are paranoid that Gaia will join with the Arthronine against them, or even help them recruit Terrans to fight on their side. Especially as they have directed all their war effort towards the Arthronine planets, and Earth is behind them. As a result, they have a presence on Earth and make things as difficult as possible for us when they can."

IST Encounter, en route to Romstrum 3
16:15 GST

melanie had left at sixteen hundred, citing an urgent call and leaving Jack wondering what she had meant by, 'make things as difficult as possible for us when they can'.

He had the distinct impression that melanie had not told him the whole truth. However, she had returned his hard drives and given him his watch, phone and wallet—his: those belonging to Jack Fletcher, not Caeil, or Pierre or David. Clarifying that she knew who he was before he had confessed.

How she had found the links between all those aliases over the years baffled him. He was sure that melanie had been the prime mover in that, rather than Bianca.

Bianca, he did not trust. He didn't know why not; he just didn't. Not that he totally trusted melanie. But of the two, he thought melanie was marginally more trustworthy.

152

Not that it mattered. He knew they had embroiled him in some elaborate machinations, undeniably power politics, where he was only a pawn.

While he considered this problem further, he was going to indulge in a little retail therapy. It always worked for Amber Gullifoyle, the closest thing he had ever had to a best friend. But maybe that was because she only ever used his money.

After pocketing the black disc melanie had given him, he strolled down to the main concourse and its stores.

A general store had all the toiletries he might need, but no staff. Not that it mattered. A machine by the door took all his purchases and promised delivery to his suite within the hour.

The electronics store across the way took his phone and transferred all the data to a smart new compad. They would deliver his old phone to his suite, along with a charging lead, within the hour.

Further along, a clothing store had jeans, shirts, a jacket, some trainers, underwear, and socks.

He stopped at a deserted bar for a drink and then went back to his suite. His purchases were on the sofa, waiting for him.

IST Encounter, en route to Romstrum 3
17:55 GST

Jack was getting used to what his new compad could do when a gentle musical tone and a woman's voice announced that *Encounter* had just entered the retroverse.

He was a little disappointed. He had been expecting flickering lights, a surge of acceleration, a klaxon, running feet in the corridors.

The clock on the compad screen told him it was six o'clock and too early for dinner, so he read on, and what seemed like minutes later, he realized another hour had passed.

He showered and changed and, feeling a little hungry, walked back to one of the cafés near the docking gate.

Procrastination, the restaurant that melanie had mentioned, was open, and he walked in. A robot, looking like a collection of random clock parts with wheels, took him to a table.

"Sir, may I humbly suggest a drink before you place your esteemed order, sir?" the machine said. It had a round clock face.

The hour and minute hands moved to ten minutes past ten in a smile. The menu lit up on the table.

"Double, single malt Scotch, no ice, please," Jack said.

"Sir, is that a two, as per your instruction of a double, or one as per your instruction of a single, sir?" The hands had dropped to twenty minutes to four in dismay.

"You have single malt, Scotch?" Jack said.

"Yes sir, we do, sir," the robot said.

"Good. I want two shots of that in one glass," Jack said.

"I understand, sir," the machine said and whirred away.

Jack glanced at the menu with mounting trepidation. He was sure that the name of every dish would be a pun. But apart from a possible excess of dishes featuring thyme as an herb, there were none.

A note on the menu told how the robot waiters were called 'servitors'. A term derived from Oxford undergraduates who paid for their tutelage by carrying out menial work in the college. There was no mention of 'tick-tocks'.

The servitor came back with the Scotch, and Jack ordered a steak, salad and a half-bottle of dark red wine from an Aetherian vineyard.

While Jack waited for his meal, he looked around. The walls, furniture, and even the floor featured clocks. Anything circular was a cog, a coiled spring or a clock face and anything straight one of the hands or a pendulum.

He was sure the decorators had had a plan. But it looked as if they had turned up with a couple of dump trucks full of random clock parts and kept working until they had used them all.

The food arrived, and Jack was halfway through one of the best steaks he had ever eaten when he saw it. In one corner of the room was a drawing of a white rabbit. It stood on its hind legs, wearing a checkered jacket and plain waistcoat. It held a furled umbrella under one arm, and a pocket watch in its hand.

According to the hand-written notebooks Jack had, one John Tenniel had drawn that rabbit in the early eighteen sixties for inclusion in Lewis Carroll's *Alice's Adventures in Wonderland*. Unlike Carroll, Tenniel had existed. He just hadn't drawn that rabbit.

Jack stopped eating and stared at the print. This was no coincidence.

While explaining the retroverse, melanie had said, 'The new universe was a bit like a tea party, where there are three dimensions taking tea while waiting for time to turn up'. Jack was sure it had to be a reference to the hatter's tea party, but had no idea how she knew about the books.

The three books and two hand-written notebooks had come to Jack, supposedly from his father. One notebook covered the books themselves, the other the author, Lewis Carroll. Curiously, although neither notebook contained anything to suggest the books were unusual or rare, the latter halves of both suggested that they were suddenly unknown. As if the world had woken up one day and the original books and their author had been erased.

Jack's own research at the British Library and at the books' publishers, Macmillan, had drawn a blank. Neither had heard of the author or the books.

Christ Church, Oxford, where the author, using his real name of Charles Dodgson, had supposedly held a Mathematical Lectureship from eighteen fifty-five until eighteen eighty-one, respectfully denied any knowledge of the author or his works.

The facts were evident. Charles Lutwidge Dodgson had never existed. Lewis Carroll had never existed. *Alice's Adventures in Wonderland* had never existed. *Through the Looking-Glass, and What Alice Found There* had never existed. *The Hunting of the Snark* had never existed. Yet, in the house Jack considered home, three bound volumes and two notebooks proved otherwise.

It occurred to Jack that melanie might have seen the books. She looked about his age, but as Bianca's apparent and actual ages were so far apart, that might also be the case with melanie.

He hadn't known about the books until he was fifteen and had taken them, along with the rest of his files, when he left the orphanage. If melanie were fifteen years his senior, she would have been thirty years old by then, although it seemed unlikely that melanie could have known where he was then.

Another question was the significance of the books. If any. But then, if the books had some importance, why had melanie not simply asked him about them?

After dinner, his mind still racketing through everything he had been hearing and seeing since his first meeting with melanie and Bianca, he decided he needed something stronger to drink. As his foray into space looked likely to be short, what he needed was somewhere a bit like the Cantina in *Star Wars*, with a band and a purple saxophonist and green belly-dancers. Somewhere down in the dark underbelly of the ship... the vehicle, he

155

corrected himself. Somewhere the beautiful people didn't go and where gangsters and whores and villains hung out.

Being a GCID vehicle, *Encounter* didn't have a dark underbelly. Instead, he found the *Encounter Inn*, trying, with little success, to emulate an eighteenth-century British man-of-war's interior. It was under-populated, with not a gangster or a whore to be seen.

As for villains, he was the closest they had in that evening, and he wasn't that bad. White-collar thieves don't have quite the panache of, say, an armed robber.

That's how he'd started, back in the bad old days, after he'd met Julia and fallen in love and she had disappeared. He often wondered about her. More often than he would have liked. She was almost certainly not called Julia Pattle anymore. He hoped that whatever the reason for her disappearance and wherever she had gone, she'd been happy.

He thought he'd seen her, years later, one chilly Saturday morning in Chiswick, of all places. She'd been walking towards him, a young girl beside her, chatting away and laughing at something silly. The sort of thing at which mothers and daughters laugh.

Halfway through his third Scotch, Jack decided he would go back to his cabin as soon as he had finished his drink. He had a lot of thinking to do and, although the whisky wouldn't answer questions, it might make him forget to ask himself a few, and that might not be a good thing.

He was about to leave when a woman sat three stools down at the bar. Jack noticed her hair first. It was black, thick and wavy and fell almost to her waist.

She ordered a white wine and took two sips before she looked around the bar.

Jack was the only single male in the place, and she smiled. Jack smiled back and began wondering if she was going to make the next move.

It wasn't vanity. The professionals always made the next move. Time was money, and they couldn't wait around for men to summon up the courage.

"Hi," she said. "I'm Aurora."

Yeah? I bet you aren't, Jack thought, but said, "Hello, Aurora, I'm Jack."

Aurora moved up next to Jack, confirming what he had suspected. She was a professional. Maybe she was just what he needed right now.

"Perhaps you can help," Jack said. "I'm new here, like really new, in that I didn't know this existed a few hours ago, and they gave me this disc. No idea what it's worth, or how it works, or whether everybody takes it or what."

Aurora looked at the disc. "You must be Terran," she said.

"That obvious, huh?"

"Just a bit," Aurora said. "But this isn't like a Terran credit card; this is cash. Everybody takes cash."

She touched the edge of the disc, and it glowed red, then went back to black.

"You touch the edge," she said. Jack did so. The disc came alive to show a little numeric pad in green.

"The disc is yours, and nobody else can use it. Tap in a number and place your disc next to someone else's disc and you pay them whatever sum you have shown. In Gaian dollars."

"Simple as that?" Jack said.

"It is, and in stores or places like this, you needn't even do that. They will take a retinal scan and charge you without you taking the disc out of your pocket.

"But then, as you are wearing Aetherian made jeans and a Gaian shirt bought on *Encounter*, you probably knew that."

"Yeah, I did," Jack said with a smile. "But you can't talk about the weather here, can you?"

"Very true," Aurora smiled back. "So you know, your drinks were costing you about three dollars each."

"They are great," Jack said. He had meant, "That is great," but he had caught sight of Aurora's cleavage and been distracted.

"Why, thank you, kind sir," Aurora said with a warm smile.

"I am sorry," Jack said. "Where I come from, we don't say things like that to a lady."

"Well, you can say it to me," Aurora said. "I like it. So, do you want to get out of here?"

"I would," Jack said. "But they probably didn't give me a lot of money on this card, and if you were thinking of going somewhere expensive..."

"Barry, lend me your reader," Aurora said to the barman, who placed a small tablet in front of her.

Aurora said, "Touch your card and place it on this thing."

Jack did. Aurora looked at the screen and said, "That's enough. Let's go."

***

Jack followed her into another section of the habitation ring and to a small apartment.

As soon as they were inside, Aurora held up her finger to her lips to stop Jack from saying anything. She pulled a pad from her purse and flicked it on, waited two seconds until it beeped, and said, "Sorry, Jack, not your lucky night."

Jack thought he had walked into a situation and that a pimp or boyfriend was about to appear. He looked around for a makeshift weapon. A chair would have been ideal.

"My name is Amrita Ghatak. I work for melanie," Aurora said.

"So, you are not a..."

"Yes, I am," she said. "Why? Oh! Well, after we've talked, yeah..." she shrugged.

"Okay," Jack said. Now they were in a brighter light; he looked at Amrita and thought she reminded him of someone. He couldn't remember who, but the impression was strong.

"What do you want to talk about?" he said.

"You met with melanie today?"

"Yeah."

"She told you how wars, what wars there are, work out here?"

"Yeah."

"That was the truth," Amrita said. "Then melanie told you the Nel were on Earth because they were scared the Gaians and Aetherians would recruit Terrans and sneak up behind them?"

"Yeah."

"The room was being bugged by Colonel Kaninchen and what melanie told you was what Kaninchen wanted you to hear," Amrita said. "If she hasn't done so already, melanie will tell Kaninchen that she lied to you because she did not want to upset you with the truth."

"Okay," Jack said. "I wish I had some idea what the fuck is going on around here, but can we start with you telling me what is the truth about the Nel being on Earth?"

"Sure," Amrita said. "The Nel are on Earth to raise an army."

"Okay," Jack said, "but didn't they tell me that the Saurians recruited some bronze age Brits on Earth? Isn't it the same thing?"

158

"Not exactly, no," Amrita replied. "We recruited volunteers. The Nel want slaves."

Jack stared at her and, after a long pause, said, "Slaves? Are you fucking kidding me?"

"I don't think the recruitment of four billion slaves as cannon fodder is a suitable topic for 'kidding', do you?"

Jack felt the blood draining from his face and a metallic taste in his mouth. He concentrated on not vomiting.

"Billion? You did say four billion?" he said. "That cannot be."

"I'm afraid it can," Amrita said.

"But that's over half the fucking population."

"Yes," she said, pouring him a glass of water. "Drink this, and then take nice steady breaths, or you'll hyperventilate."

Jack gulped at the water and managed to inhale enough to set him coughing and choking.

When he had recovered, he said. "How? How could they enslave billions of us? We'd fight them."

"It isn't that simple," Amrita said. "As melanie told you, Nel society is hierarchical and maintained with neural implants and a cocktail of drugs in their water and food that keeps them in order."

"She said, 'brainwashed'."

"Close enough," Amrita said. "The Nel plan to use these techniques to subdue the Earth's population, then put them on the front line against the Arthronine.

"Fortunately, and I use the word in a relative sense, the cocktail they use on their people doesn't work on Terrans. Yet. But they have been working on it for years, and they will get there."

"So, what is anybody doing about this?"

"By anybody, I assume you mean the Gaians and Aetherians?"

"Yes," Jack said. "They are descendants of Earth."

"Nothing," Amrita said. "Gaia and Aetheria have tiny defense forces, mostly ceremonial these days. Gaia is a giant spaceship, and, faced with any threat, it just leaves the area. Once in the retroverse, it is undetectable. Aetheria is under the Saurian defense net and would be difficult to breach. Neither needs anything beyond its own part-time, volunteer defense services on the ground.

"Even if we had massive armies, if either of us should take any action, we could well incur the collective wrath of much of the rest of the galaxy, where the consensus is that if the Nel and Arthronine want to kill each other, so be it. Terrans are no different. You see reports of war on TV. If your own nation is not involved, do you care?

"To the rest of the galaxy, the destruction of the Earth's population is merely collateral damage and better seven billion dead Terrans than other species getting involved in a broader war."

"Seven billion," Jack interrupted. "You said four billion. How come it just went up?"

"The four billion is what they'd use as soldiers," Amrita said. "The other three billion would grow food, work in factories, breed more soldiers, and when they get beyond economic utility, used as a food source."

"Fucking Christ, you mean the Nel would eat them?" Jack yelled in horror.

"No, of course not," Amrita said. "They would be reduced to a suitable protein form and used in intensive agricultural processes to create vegetable-based meat substitutes. Mainly for the Terran soldiers."

Jack tried to take that in and gave up. "Okay," he said. "So, why does Bianca not want me to know why the Nel are really on Earth?"

"Because Bianca is Venatori..."

"Who the fuck are they?" Jack said.

"The Venatori are a dynasty, banished from Gaia centuries ago, but still with many supporters on Gaia. They are involved with the Nel. How we do not exactly know, but the Venatori will not be in the subservient position, of that we are sure. And they are the real enemy."

"Meaning she doesn't want anyone interfering in the takeover," Jack said.

"Exactly," Amrita said.

"How about Aetheria? They may have a tiny army, but is there nothing they can do?"

"They are doing something," Amrita said. "While the Venatori have split Gaia, the Aetherians have remained undivided. They live in the best of all possible worlds. But not the Panglossian acceptance of Leibnizian philosophy and fake optimism for acceptance of what God has provided, but in a truly

160

optimistic philosophy of being in the best possible world because they have made it so."

Jack stared at Amrita for several seconds and said, "I haven't the faintest idea what you just said."

"I said that...."

"No," Jack said. "Let's move on. So Aetheria is helping. How?"

"melanie."

"melanie?"

"Yes. Tall, beautiful, terrible hair."

"I know who melanie is," Jack said. "So, what can she do?"

"She has a small team," Amrita said. "A group of specialists in various disciplines who can use their abilities to dissuade the Nel from remaining on Earth. That team is largely assembled and on its way to a planet called Romstrum 3, which we will pass shortly. From there, they will go back to Earth."

"It would need more than a small team, surely?"

"Not at all," Amrita said. "An army would be too... much. Armies make a lot of noise; they like marching, running around in tanks, and blowing things up. What we need here is a small team that will use a scalpel, not a chainsaw, to eradicate the cancer. Ideally, this needs to be done without spooking the locals."

"I see what you are saying," Jack said. "So melanie is jumping ship?"

"She is."

"Pity. I quite like her. She's scary, but in a good way. Bianca, I didn't warm to."

"You could go with her," Amrita said. "You could join the team."

"I don't think so," Jack said. "I'm not much of a team player."

"Very few members of this team are," Amrita said. "That's why melanie picked them and has trained them over the years."

"But she's only known me for a few days," Jack said.

"Perhaps," Amrita said. "But she is a quick study."

Jack sat silently, thinking this through. The Earth might be his adopted planet, and his early days on it may not have been enjoyable, but he had not suffered in the way some people did and were still doing. He hadn't ever been starving, tortured, or enslaved. In later years, his fortunes had changed, and he had become a relatively wealthy man. It was still home, so he wasn't

161

just going to sail off into the galaxy and let this happen without putting up a bit of a fight.

"I just hope I'm doing the right thing," Jack said, the sea-mist of self-doubt creeping in. "But I'll go if there is anything useful I can do."

"I would think so," Amrita said. "You planned and executed some very imaginative bank robberies. I'm sure you could plan some very imaginative ways to persuade the Nel to go back home."

"Er, hang on a second," Jack said. "Planning a bank robbery is one thing, but it bears bugger all resemblance to what's needed here."

"You would be surprised."

"You sure?"

"Absolutely," Amrita said. "You'll be the man who saved the planet."

Jack laughed. "I don't think so. You need to be able to fly or get bitten by a radioactive spider first. Absolute minimum, you have to be an American."

"Well, you'll be the Englishman who saved the planet," Amrita said. "At least it's different."

"When do I have to decide on any of this?" Jack asked.

"Tomorrow..." she glanced at the clock on the wall. "Later today."

"Okay," Jack said. "But one last point, how big are these giant insects the Nel are fighting?"

"The Arthronine?" Amrita said.

"Yeah, them."

"Huge," Amrita said. "The size of a horse."

FiT: THE FORTY-FIFTH

Asteroid orbiting, 72.β4.732βα8.93β08α.βα7389
16:30 GST Sixday 1.4.2833
(Friday 13th May 2016)

"Jalimek, get in here. Now," Captain-Colonel Polikar said into the communicator on his elaborately carved desk.

Almost immediately, the door opened, and Jalimek shuffled in, his gray jumpsuit crumpled and grubby.

"Yes, sir. How may I be of assistance?" The Bellachi kept his eyes lowered, trying not to appear nervous. Polikar looked at the creature with disgust. Bellachi were scum in their natural form, but this thing had Nel blood, judging by the lightness of the hair. He shuddered at the vision of a Nel and a Bellachi mating.

"In there," he pointed towards a second door from his office, "Get it cleaned up."

"Yes, sir, at once," Jalimek said, scurrying to the door indicated. He knew what to expect by now: the female trooper's body strapped to the frame didn't shock or even surprise him. "Will you want the skin preserved, sir?" Jalimek asked from the doorway.

Polikar considered. "Yes. I almost got the whole thing off in one piece before the bitch died," he said eventually.

"Well done, sir. I will put Malgenaff on to it right away."

Jalimek called in a clean-up unit and spent the time until it arrived carefully gathering the pale skin and putting it with the blond scalp.

The sudden blat-blat-blat of the alarm made the Bellachi flinch, and he rushed through to where Polikar sat watching the progress of the latest incursion on his wall monitor array.

"Nothing for you to stop work for," Polikar said. "Just a minor breach in section seven."

"No sir," Jalimek said, but hovered near the door, unable to tear his eyes away.

On the main screen, a detachment of Nel troops was firing into one of the tunnels. The lights were gone, making it impossible to see what they were shooting at. Not that there could be any doubt.

163

Out of the darkness of the tunnel scuttled the first Arthronine, its lower pincers snipping off the left arm and right leg of a Nel soldier, the upper arms probing for eyes and softer parts.

As the creature's eight legs straddled the body of its victim, the triangular head and multi-faceted eyes swung to find the next target. A burst of heavy projectile fire ripped it apart, and it crashed down onto the Nel.

The dead Arthronine half blocked the three-meter-high tunnel; a second Arthronine, its upper body bent forward, ran over its companion and into the Nel gun position. The video feed died.

Jalimek cast a glance over at Polikar. The Nel was getting off on this, watching his own kind being butchered.

Polikar switched the monitor to other sections of the complex. There were new breaches in sections #Six and #Eight, which were linked by a short tunnel to #Seventeen, where they were.

The Arthronine were overwhelming the Nel by force of numbers, and the Nel officers were finding it more challenging to force the troops forward.

Minutes later, sections #Nine and #Ten were overcome, the swarm of insectoids filling the tunnels, ripping the Nel, and smashing equipment and supplies.

"Jalimek, fetch my luggage," Polikar said.

"Yes, sir," the Bellachi said, dropping the skin on the floor and picking up the handle of the trunk Polikar kept packed for such emergencies.

Polikar strode towards the door, and Jalimek, forty centimeters shorter at one meter eighty, ran along behind, pulling the trunk. They turned right, moving swiftly along anonymous plasticized corridors illuminated by harsh white lighting panels. Other Nel, with the same idea, were going the same way, the officers ordering any lower ranks to do their duty and fight as they ran.

"Sir, if I might suggest," Jalimek said.

"What?" Polikar swung round, his face darkening with anger that a Bellachi dare suggest anything.

"There is a service tunnel through to section #One from here," Jalimek said quietly, eyes downward, fearing retribution.

"Where?" Polikar snapped.

Jalimek pointed to a small service hatch.

Polikar stared at Jalimek and considered the situation. Section #One was the designated lifeboat and the way out.

164

To take the advice of a Bellachi was a massive loss of face, but the alternative might be a massive loss of life.

"Yes, dolt, I know there is," Polikar said. "I was merely waiting for you to open the door. Or do you expect me to do everything around here?"

"I beg your forgiveness, sir," Jalimek said and pulled open the low doorway for Polikar to duck in.

Jalimek followed, and the two half-ran, Polikar half-crouched, the twenty-five meters to the *Vengeance-class* shuttle that formed section #One.

It was filling fast; Polikar barged his way through and onto the ramp. As Jalimek fell behind, he found himself grabbed by a Nel lieutenant.

"Where are you going, Bellachi scum?" the lieutenant asked.

"My master is...." Jalimek waved towards Polikar.

"Trying to sneak away, thinking to take the place of a Nel officer, you cowardly shit," the lieutenant spat.

"Let him go," Polikar barked from the ramp. He would have left Jalimek. The lieutenant was just as capable of dragging a trunk as the Bellachi, but the servant had his uses.

Still gripping Jalimek's throat, the lieutenant looked up and recognized Captain-Colonel Polikar. His grip slackened. "Sir, my apologies," he said, his voice a little unsteady, "I thought this Bellachi was taking the place of a Nel."

Polikar drew a pistol and fired, the projectile obliterating the young officer's face. "He is. Yours," Polikar said.

As the lieutenant's body dropped, Jalimek scampered up the ramp.

"Thank you, sir," Jalimek said as he reached Polikar.

"I didn't save you; I saved my trunk," Polikar said and walked on.

They could hear firing from the tunnels leading into the shuttle dock. The ramp closed, and the vessel lifted off from the planet.

Polikar found a suitable, if utilitarian, cabin and was comfortably installed when Jalimek brought him a bottle of Tolak.

"Good news, Jalimek," the Nel said.

"Yes, sir?" Jalimek replied, wondering if it would be good news for him as well.

"I have just come off the comm from High Command. I have a new assignment."

"Where, sir?"

"I don't recognize the coordinates. But far away from the Arthronine. A pity, as I like to be close to the fighting. But duty calls."

"Yes, sir, I'm sure," Jalimek said, trying to keep any tone that might be misconstrued from his voice.

"It is a pre-retroverse planet in a single star system. Third out of eight, I believe. A temperate climate and a population of seven billion humanoids."

"Sorry, sir, is that good?" Jalimek asked.

"Oh yes, Jalimek, that is very good."

DAY FOURTEEN

Sixday 5.5.2834

Monday 13th February 2017

IST Encounter, en route to Gaia
08:00 GST

Jack had got back to his suite at a little after two in the morning, and after a restless night he had woken at seven and lay staring at the ceiling.

At eight o'clock, he called Amrita and arranged to meet that evening.

Jack had decided that, for whatever reason, he did not trust Bianca, he sort of trusted melanie and largely trusted Amrita. She reminded him of someone he trusted in his past; he just wasn't sure who.

From her, he might find out what he needed to know about the Gaians, the Nel, the Venatori, and what those books had to do with it all. In the meantime, he needed to read whatever he could find on the subject of the Venatori.

IST Encounter, en route to Gaia
11:05 GST

"Colonel," melanie said as she walked into Bianca's office. "I need a few moments of your time."

Bianca looked up and regarded melanie with a suspicious eye. "When did you start calling me by my title?" She asked.

"Since I needed something," melanie said.

"That figures," Bianca said. "What do you want?"

"I need *Encounter* to drop out of retroverse at Romstrum so that I can disembark."

"To join your team there?"

"My team, no, but I need my shuttle. Rufus is sending me somewhere else."

"What about your team?" Bianca said. "What happens to them?"

"I have arranged other transport," melanie said.

"I do hope so," Bianca said. "The surface temperature in daylight on Romstrum is not survivable by humans."

"As I am aware," melanie said.

"I mention it because Robert Sunter's mother is an old friend of the family. Also, although it had slipped my mind, I asked Korenjic to include Greta and Georgia into Robert's team."

melanie shrugged, well aware that nothing ever slipped Bianca's mind. "Oh, that came from you? I thought Korenjic had chosen them herself. Any reason? Not that it matters."

"No good ones," Bianca said, "but I thought my daughters, although pilots, might guide Robert a little, this being his first command."

"It makes sense," melanie said. "They don't out-rank him but have far more experience. It sounds like an excellent idea."

"I also asked her to include Zara Chang."

"There's a name I haven't heard for a while," melanie said. "What is she doing these days? Still gathering degrees on Garner-Valathien 4?"

"No, she left there around three years ago; she's been traveling. Studied on Earth for a while."

"Then that's good," melanie said. "Is her mother a family friend, too?"

"Not to my knowledge," Bianca said. "But Zara has always struck me as one of those young people who would fritter away their lives in academic studies but could be so useful in other areas. This mission shouldn't be too risky, and they need an opportunity to stretch themselves a little."

"As I said, no problem, especially as Korenjic and Sunter are okay with it."

"You know," Bianca said, "I'm surprised you didn't want Korenjic to lead the Earth team."

"So is she," melanie said. "But, apart from her rebellious streak getting worse, she's become an administrator. She organized the kit and transport impeccably but argued about every detail. That is why I got her to take another team on an exercise."

"I'm not sure I understand," Bianca said.

"Most of the new generation in GCID have little or no real experience dealing with an enemy force. That's something that Sunter and Zara Chang lack, and I think that you are doing precisely the right thing in putting them forward for the Earth team. Let them experience a bit of genuine fear; we can pull them out in a heartbeat if it all gets too much for them.

"But, apart from the other thing, Korenjic has been office bound for years; she hasn't even been on a training exercise for far too long. So, she can get in some training, and then, maybe,

169

next time a mission like this turns up, I might let her have a shot."

"Very sensible," Bianca said. "Are you not joining either team?"

"No," melanie said. "They don't need me interfering, and as I said, Rufus has other plans for me."

"I assume you have already booked a shuttle to take you down," Bianca said.

"I don't need one. There is a consignment of household goods that are going down in a disposable drop-shuttle. I can ride down in that. It will save you having to go into orbit or wait for your shuttle to return."

"Then I see no problem at all," Bianca said.

IST Encounter, en route to Gaia
13:10 GST

Bianca opened her office door, and the steward pushed the trolley to the dining table. He spread a fresh white tablecloth before setting out silverware and glasses.

"So, what do we have today, Angelo?"

"Gazpacho followed by fabada astruiana, Colonel," Angelo replied. "I thought a bottle of the Dominio de Pingus...?"

"Excellent choice," Bianca said.

"Thank you, Colonel. Will that be all?"

"Not quite, Angelo," Bianca said. "I understand melanie will leave us tomorrow evening. She is riding a disposable drop-shuttle down to Romstrum.

"I would consider it a personal favor if, just before she goes, you would kill Caeil Ashbow—he calls himself Jack Fletcher now—and that whore, Amrita Ghatak. If you can make it look as if Ghatak murdered Ashbow and was killed, evading arrest, that would be perfect. It needn't be too obvious; nobody is going to care."

"It will be done," Angelo said. "Or I can probably capture him, and you can kill him yourself?"

"That would be kind," Bianca said. "But I have reached the point where I simply want him dead."

"I understand, Colonel," Angelo said and turned to leave.

As soon as the door had closed, Bianca sat down to her meal and called Katelyn Fofana.

"Katelyn," Bianca said. "I have arranged for Angelo Demirci to kill the Ashbow brat tomorrow, just before melanie leaves for Romstrum. Arrange for Demirci to meet an untimely end soon after, would you?"

"*Consider it done*," Katelyn said.

IST Encounter, en route to Gaia
20:05 GST

Stopping briefly for a sandwich at lunchtime, Jack had worked steadily through Gaian and Aetherian histories to find out what he could about the Venatori. The results were not a lot to show for the time it had taken.

The Aetherians were a lot more outgoing than the Gaians, but it wasn't their history, and there were differences between the two accounts. Gaian reporting suggested that either the Venatori regime had never happened or that it hadn't been that bad. As, no doubt, versions of Mao Zedong's reign might differ between those who had lived under his regime and outsiders.

***

The door alert took several seconds for him to identify and then deal with. When he managed both, he found Amrita standing outside. She was wearing a summer dress, all bold flowers and décolletage.

"Had a good day?" she said as she draped herself over a sofa.

"Possibly the best day of my life, ever," Jack said.

"So, no, you haven't."

"So, no, I haven't."

"Learned lots about the Venatori?"

"If I take out all the contradictory bits, no, not a lot. Except that I thought history got written by the victors."

"Would it make it better if you took me to dinner? Somewhere other than that Italian place, Colonel Kaninchen likes."

"My pleasure," he said.

"Yes, that reminds me," Amrita said. "Your pleasure." She grabbed Jack's T-shirt and dragged him toward the bedroom.

DAY FIFTEEN

Oneday 6.5.2834

Tuesday 14th February 2017

Alex Monroe wasn't surprised to see Steve Smith's name come up on her mobile phone screen as it vibrated and skittered across the desk. They had spoken a lot since their meeting at the bank the previous Friday.

"Hi Steve," she said, "what can I do for you?"

"*Alex, good morning,*" Steve said. "*I have a hypothetical question for you.*"

"Go ahead."

"*If, hypothetically, you had sent me four CCTV clips, which of course you didn't, as that would be against many commandments, what would I be looking at, hypothetically?*"

"Purely hypothetically," Alex said. "The first clip is Gomez walking towards the Passport Office in Belgrave Road. The second is after he passed the Passport Office, but the critical bit is the white van. We can see three people getting into it. One of them, we think a female, is damn near seven feet tall, although she is wearing killer heels. But it makes her easy to spot."

"*Got it,*" Steve said.

"Clip three is from the bottom of Belgrave Road, on the corner of Lupus Street. Gomez walks behind a white van and never emerges."

"*Got it,*" Steve said. "*Is it the same van?*"

"It is, apparently, the same make and model," Alex said. "But as it's a white Ford Transit and there are like a million of them in London, who knows?"

"*That's for sure,*" Steve said. "*Question one is, did he get in the van or go into a house behind the van?*"

"Agreed. Is there a question two?"

"*Yes. If Gomez got into the van, did he climb in or was he dragged in?*"

"That was what we thought," Alex said. "But we are reasonably confident that he has some connection with the van because clip four shows our very tall lady leaving the house next door to the one in which Gomez lives, carrying a bag of something."

"*I'm surprised they weren't spotted by the guys in the Met's carrier?*"

174

"They weren't just spotted by them. That clip is from the carrier's dash cam and the carrier parked in the space they were vacating."

"No number plate, I suppose?"

"Yes, we got a plate, and yesterday morning, Devon and Cornwall police went to interview the owner in Truro. Mister Penrose, it seems, between our capturing the van on CCTV on Friday night and Monday lunchtime, had not only converted the van into a camper, but he had also taken his wife and kids on four holidays in it."

"Cloned then."

"Looks like it."

"Have your people had a look at Gomez' flat?"

"They have, and the short version is that it was a waste of dusting powder.

"They reckon he never so much as had a cup of coffee in there—no food, no prints, no fibers, no clothes that have been worn. There was a hair they found in a comb, but they haven't managed a match...."

"That sounds odd. No prints, yet a hair in a comb."

"That's what we thought, especially it appears all he did was go into the block to collect his mail and nothing else."

"What about eyewitness reports? Surely someone had to see him coming in and out?"

"They did," Alex confirmed. "He went off every evening at four o'clock and came home anytime between eleven p.m. and one a.m. We have a Mrs. Parrot, believe it or not, to thank for that, not that she spends much time looking out the window, of course."

"No, they never do. But what about shopping trips, weekends, that sort of thing?"

"Not according to Mrs. Parrot. Not that she checked, mind you."

"Alex, is there any chance I can have a look at the flat?"

"Officially, none, especially as we have had the Met. clumping around in their size twelves. Off the record, how about I pick you up in ten minutes, and we'll have a look-see?"

"Great, and I'll try not to 'clump' too hard." He hung up, leaving Alex to cringe; she'd forgotten Steve was ex-Met.

175

"I know just the place for lunch," Amrita said when Jack opened the door. "My treat."

"That's not normally the way it works," Jack said.

"Oh, you sweet old-fashioned boy," Amrita cooed. "Thing is, I am an independent woman who don't need no man to buy her lunch. Anyway, it's on expenses, so melanie is paying."

"Then I shall be delighted," Jack said.

They went up round to the far side of the habitation ring and down a level to find a small restaurant offering a fusion of Chinese, Japanese, Thai, Korean and most of south-east Asia's cuisine.

"Have you been here before?" Jack asked once they were seated.

"No," Amrita said. "I just picked one of the few places on *Encounter* where Kaninchen's surveillance systems are currently down."

"Good," Jack said. "Can we talk?"

"We can."

"I'm in."

"That wasn't difficult, now was it?" she said. "What persuaded you?"

"The Venatori," Jack said.

"Interesting," Amrita said. "Did they visit in the night?"

"No," Jack said. "I'm a great believer in old-fashioned, one-person-one-vote democracy. In history, there has never been a war between two democracies because voters don't like 'em. Voters tend to die in wars.

"Terran history is stuffed full of too many examples of small groups who have decided that they know better than the people and can grab power without the inconvenience of elections.

"Hitler, Stalin, Mussolini, Mao. Right and left and in it for the power, nothing else. Maybe some of them actually believed that they were doing it for the common good, but I doubt it.

"Have you ever read *Animal Farm*?"

"No," Amrita said.

"You should," Jack said. "A guy called Eric Blair wrote it, under the pen-name George Orwell, to expose the dangers of communism. I should add that Blair was not some extreme right-winger; he was a dedicated socialist. But the same dangers are there from extremism in either direction."

"By somebody called George Orwell, was it?" Amrita said.

"Yes, why?" Jack said.

"Is there a character called 'Napoleon'?"

"Yes, why?"

"I just solved the other bit of that photo on melanie's wall," Amrita said.

"I have never seen melanie's wall," Jack said.

"You will," Amrita said. "So, what has this to do with the Venatori?"

"Everything I have read suggests the Venatori were just such a group. I want to help stop them. I am not much of a team player. But I will try to adapt. I will do what I can to help melanie defeat the Nel and then defeat the Venatori."

Jack's compad made a peculiar noise, and Amrita said, "Are you going to get that?"

Jack pressed buttons laboriously until he could read the message.

Welcome aboard. melanie

"I thought you said the surveillance systems were down?" Jack said to Amrita.

Amrita laughed. "No," she said. "I told you that Kaninchen's surveillance systems were down. Currently."

"Okay, you have me there," Jack said. "So, what next?"

"We are going to play ze-ball this evening."

"I'm not much good at anything that includes the word 'ball'."

"It's a zero-gravity game."

"I'm not much good at anything that includes the words 'ball' or 'zero-gravity'. Or 'game' now I think of it."

"It doesn't matter. That is where we are going. It is unlikely that we will get there. While it is most likely that we will fall in with bad company on the way there and end up on a one-shot shuttle. An experience that may make you think that ze-ball is great fun."

St Andrew's Square, London
11:30 GMT
(12:30 GST)

177

Alex found a place to park outside number one hundred and eleven, and Steve climbed unsteadily out of the passenger seat. Alex wasn't a bad driver, just a little fast.

Alex produced keys and let them into the block and down into the bed-sit flat, that was the supposed home of Pierre Gomez. They narrowly missed Mrs. Parrot, who needed a fresh input of information to retain her status as the primary source of gossip in the street.

"I see what they mean," Steve said as they stood in the middle of the tiny room. "Nobody ever lived here, that's for sure."

"Not without contemplating suicide, anyway," Alex said.

The single grimy window, looking out into a dingy yard, let in little of the weak February sun. Whatever light that fought its way through the grubby net curtains was immediately sucked in by the pale, institutional green walls.

A brown and white poster for the *Mirondela dels Arts* in Pézenas was the only decoration.

"This isn't a room; it's a set," Steve said.

Alex laughed. "You better believe it," she said. "All the crockery, kitchen utensils, everything, has been through a dishwasher. What, amongst many other things, this room does not have, is a dishwasher."

Steve looked over at her. She was wearing a dark blue tailored suit, with a shortish skirt and white blouse, a business-like and feminine mix.

"So, if he didn't live *here*, where did he go?" she said.

"We are sure he came down here, are we?" Steve said. "I know this was his address, but once inside the front door, he could have gone elsewhere. Up the stairs rather than down."

"Not a chance," Alex said. "We checked all the other flats. The other residents are all too old or too short or too fat to be Gomez or were present at a residents' watch committee meeting one afternoon when Mrs. Parrot saw Gomez leave."

"What about down here in the basement?" Steve asked.

"Nothing. Originally, this was where the kitchens, sculleries, and pantries were. Some of these houses along this road have two or three flats in the basement, but not this one. There is just this flat, a room full of the residents' spare furniture and other junk, and a couple of other empty storerooms. None even have a door, and forensics says nobody has been in any of them for months."

"How about a cupboard?"

178

"No cupboards either. We even checked the stored furniture, and nobody has moved it. Most of it is only still standing because the woodworm are all holding hands."

Steve laughed. "How about other ways out apart from the inside stairs?"

"There is a tiny backyard, with solid walls all around. No windows or doors, other than the one from this basement."

"There is the old tradesman's door out into a sort of basement level yard in front. It took twenty minutes with cans of WD-40 to get it open. Anyway, Mrs. Parrot has a perfect view of the stairs, from the second step up to street level, from her living room window."

"Hmm," Steve said. "Did she or anyone else ever see anyone, apart from Gomez, coming down here or going up?"

"Again, they say not."

"He didn't live here," Steve said. He opened the wardrobe. It was empty. Not that he expected anything different.

"Did you take his clothes?" Steve said.

"Yes," Alex said. "All bagged up and in the evidence locker. Although the lab thinks the sizes were all fake."

"Yeah? Why? Why would they think that?"

"When he first started as a cleaner, the company loaned him some overalls and a pair of work boots. They had his sizes on record, even though they only supplied one set."

"And all the stuff here?"

"All for a shorter, fatter man. Even the boots were two sizes too big."

"Christ, he bloody well thought this through," Steve said. "Every time we think we have something on this little bugger, it turns out it's not real. He has created a false identity and then scattered red-herrings along the way. I suppose these notes on the size of overalls he borrowed are genuine?"

"I think so," Alex said. "It wasn't like a precise fitting. Overalls, size XXL long, that sort of thing. They told him to help himself to things that fitted and then dropped a scribbled note in his file on the size he took so they knew what to get back when he got his own."

Steve fell silent, lost in his own little world. He was working his way through a problem, and she was just going to let him run and see if he came up with the same solution she had.

"So, he knew we would come in here one day and find his clothes, and that would tell us how tall and what sort of build he had."

"Uh-huh," Alex said.

"He created this false identity to lead us away from him, mainly by providing us with things we might remember. His height has to be genuine; you can't fake that, well, not by much, but he probably wasn't as chubby as he appeared, and he probably wasn't French, or Spanish, and probably not as swarthy, and... oh, Jesus H Christ, he didn't have a limp, did he?"

"It's possible," Alex said. "Forensics reckon the shoes they found in the cupboard were worn down with a power tool of some sort, not by wear and tear."

"He's a clever bastard," Steve laughed as he sat on one of the chairs.

"Isn't he, though?"

"It is now Tuesday," Steve said, "and we have no name, no fingerprints, no DNA samples. Even every description we have is suspect."

Steve sat, gazing at the wall for several minutes, and then said, "How about this? We know Gomez left here every afternoon for work and returned in the early hours of every morning.

"We know, with some certainty, that while he was supposed to be here, in this flat, between the early hours and four in the afternoon, that he was not actually in this flat.

"We are also quite confident that Gomez left not only this flat, but this building, soon after he got here every day and then came back before he had to go to work.

"We are equally confident he would know very well that Mrs. Parrot would know every single person who came into this building and who left it, and when. She would also have known that he was the only person who would have a reason for coming down to this basement and would have recorded anybody else. This means that even if he changed his clothes and appearance and lost the limp, Mrs. Parrot would have noted his arrival and departure times. In fact, she would have probably called the police to find out why this man, who was not a resident, was coming and going."

"I will assume that you are about to reveal the solution, my dear Holmes?" Alex said.

"No, I'm not, because I'll be damned if I know," Steve said, then grinned. "But you know that if you eliminate all the impossible bits, whatever is left, no matter how implausible, has to be the answer."

"It's 'improbable' not 'implausible'," Alex said.

"Try not to be a smart-arse DI Monroe," Steve said with a grin. "It is very unbecoming in one so young."

"Why, thank you for that, gallant sir," Alex said. "So, what can we eliminate?"

"Hmm," Steve said. "Well, so far, we have eliminated the possibility of him living in this flat. We have eliminated the possibility of him going to another flat in this building. We have eliminated the possibility of him going out through the front door upstairs. And we have eliminated the possibility of him going out the door down here. What does that leave? However implausible or improbable?"

"No idea," Alex said.

"No, me neither," Steve said. "Unless there is another hidden door."

"It's a Georgian terrace, not a medieval castle with a secret passage," Alex said.

"No, I suppose not," Steve said in a resigned tone. He stared at the room for a while and smacked his hand down on the small and rickety table.

"Shit," he said. "You remember those CCTV clips you didn't send me? One of them showed that van in this street."

"Yeah," Alex said.

"We think, although very much like everything else to do with this case, we don't know, that there was possibly contact of some sort between that van and Gomez?"

"Speculative, and nothing even the dimmest QC, wouldn't get thrown out in a heartbeat, but yes."

"So, the white van was first seen outside the passport office. The very tall girl was getting in as Gomez walked past. It was next seen further down the street and Gomez certainly started to walk past, but we never saw him emerge. We think he ended up inside, willingly or otherwise."

"Agreed," Alex said.

"Then, when the lads arrived to break down the door, the same very tall girl came out of the house next door and got into the same white van. Gomez may not have been inside that van, but I suspect he was, although whether alive or dead, I don't know."

"So far, so good," Alex said.

"Suppose for a moment that the tall girl worked for a rival mob who thought that instead of stealing the money from the bank, they just take it from Gomez."

"Feasible," Alex said.

"Gomez will not have stolen thirty million quid and hidden it under the mattress. He will have it tucked away in some dubious tax haven somewhere and getting at it will require all sorts of computer magic.

"To get at it, tall girl snatches Gomez off the street and they cut off his fingers with a pair of secateurs until he tells them where to find the computers they need. Which, if he has any sense, will be after the first pinkie.

"Tall girl and friends come straight to this street and tall girl goes in to pick up a laptop or maybe a memory stick. Who knows?"

"Sounds good to me," Alex said.

"The thing is," Steve said. "She didn't come out of this building. She came out of the one next door. Because I suspect that is where Gomez actually lives. Or lived."

"And how did he get from here to there?" Alex said.

"You said it first. There's a secret passage."

"You mean, you think there really is a secret passage?" Alex said.

"I don't know," Steve said. "But it is what's left."

"Okay, so, let's find it."

"It has to be in that wall," Steve said and pointed at the wall opposite the door. "It's the one that is shared with the building she came out of."

"That makes a certain amount of sense," Alex said, looking around carefully. "So where's the door?"

"Pretending to be a piece of furniture. Not a stand-alone piece of furniture like a wardrobe because Gomez knows we'd be looking behind it to see what fell down the back, but a built-in piece, like a kitchen or bathroom cupboard."

"Not the kitchen," Alex said, pointing at a line of nineteen fifties style cupboard units and a cooker from a couple of decades earlier. "It backs onto the wrong wall."

"Then let us have a look at the bathroom," Steve said.

They went through into the cramped bathroom, and Steve pointed at the waist-high, once white cupboard at the head of the bath, showing the results of being in a humid atmosphere. Not, Steve suspected, that Gomez had ever used the bath here.

"That has to be it," he said.

Steve took hold of the cupboard and tugged, but it didn't move. It was never going to be that easy.

"What's odd," he said, "is that this looks like a piece of cheap, flat-pack furniture, and one tug normally pulls the back wall right out. It's only glorified cardboard."

Dropping to his knees, he opened the door and looked inside. It was empty.

"You don't have a torch, do you?" he asked. He had long since stopped being amazed by what women carried in their handbags, along with a small pharmacy and several varieties of tissues.

Alex handed him her phone. "No, not a torch, but..."

Alex turned the phone over and tapped the torch icon, bringing up a beam of white light.

"Ah, thank you," Steve said and shone the light into the cupboard's empty interior.

On the slime gray back of the cupboard were four green-tinged wooden battens, each an inch and a half wide, three-quarters of an inch thick, and three inches long. In the center of each was a large screw head.

Steve was not the sort of man who could do things about the house. But he was sure that four fixings and screws that size, to hold one small cabinet in place, was over-kill.

He stared at the battens for a while and then said, "If Gomez usually went out this way, he couldn't have screwed this thing back on the wall. Those aren't fixings; those are some sort of catch or locking system."

"Could be," Alex said. "Assuming this isn't just another red herring."

Steve jiggled one batten. It turned a little stiffly, but it felt like it was supposed to turn, rather than just being loose.

"Hmm," Steve said.

"Any joy?" Alex asked.

"Sort of," Steve said.

"Have you tried saying 'Open Sesame'?" Alex asked. There was a palpable silence.

"There are four blocks in here, and they all turn, and I just need to see how far they turn."

After several minutes of turning battens and pulling the cabinet, Steve said, "It has to be it, but I've tried turning them ninety degrees, a hundred and eighty degrees and the full three-sixty, and still it won't shift."

"Suppose it's just some of them you need to turn, and if you turn them all, it locks it again?" Alex said. "Like a combination lock."

"Why would that work?" Steve said.

"I don't know," Alex said. "Why would that work? Let's ask the man who has had his head in a cabinet for the last hour, shall we?"

Steve grunted, stuck his head back inside the cabinet, turned all four battens around to what he sincerely hoped was their original positions.

Steve turned the top left and gave a tenuous tug to the cabinet, but it remained solid. He twisted the batten back to where it had been and tried the same thing on each of the other three. Nothing happened.

He started again with the top left and then with one of the other three in turn. Nothing happened.

Next, he turned the top right. He didn't bother trying the top left as well; he'd already done that. Instead, he turned the bottom left and felt the cupboard shift.

"Gotcha," he yelled in triumph, leaping to his feet and pulling the cupboard out on deeply recessed rubber-tired wheels to reveal a large hole in the wall behind.

"My God, you were right," Alex said.

"But you were right about turning two battens thing," Steve said, beaming at Alex. "I was about to give up and get a crowbar."

"We'll call it a joint victory, then," Alex said.

"Sounds reasonable," Steve said. "Now, let's see where this takes us, shall we?"

He pushed his head and shoulders into the hole, then he disappeared altogether.

A few seconds later, Steve's voice came through the tunnel. "You have to see this."

Alex shrugged, dropped on all fours, and crawled through the tunnel.

The tunnel, which had painted walls and ceiling and a carpeted floor, measured just under two feet in length.

She emerged into a well-lit bathroom.

"Interesting, eh?" Steve asked.

"Very," Alex replied, standing up and redundantly dusting herself down. "Whose flat is this?"

"No idea," Steve said, "but it doesn't look like it got much use either."

"In that case, I'd better make a phone call and find out," she said.

While Alex was talking, they looked around the flat. It appeared almost as sterile and empty as the one they had just left, except there were a pair of jeans, some underwear, socks, a T-shirt and a pair of trainers in the wardrobe.

"Do you think we now have some idea of Gomez's size or are these another red herring, do you think?" Steve asked.

Alex shrugged and went back to her phone call.

"According to the letting agent," Alex said, a few minutes later, as she put the phone back into her bag, "this flat has been empty for some time. At the express wishes of the owners who are keeping it for their son."

"Any idea who the owners are?" Steve asked.

"Not yet," Alex said, "but if it's anything like the building next door, we'll be running around for weeks chasing up dead ends and finding out it's a company in some banana republic where we have no prospect of getting any accurate information."

"Well, it's fairly obvious that this is not where Gomez hangs his hat at night, either. I reckon he just uses this place to change his clothes before disappearing out of the front door, or upstairs into another flat as someone else. This is the equivalent of running down a river when the dogs are in hot pursuit."

"Which means what, exactly?" Alex said.

"In the old days, blood hounds used to pursue convicts escaping from the chain-gangs, and they would try to shake off the dogs by running along a stream, so their pursuers lost the scent.

"Then they could emerge from the stream somewhere else, and the dogs would have a problem picking up the scent."

"I came to City police from Dorset; we do things a little differently from you lot in London, down there. We abolished chain gangs a while back now."

"Ha-ha," Steve said. "But our trail will now go cold."

185

Alex considered this for a moment.

"That's true," she said. "But it occurs to me that Gomez would be in the same situation here, as he was back in the first flat. He can change his clothes here and become someone new. But he can't just walk in and out of the flats whenever he feels the need. He needs to have a reason to be in this block, like living here. Or to be seen to be living here."

"You have a point," Steve said. "We will need to check out who lives in the other flats."

Alex looked lost in thought for several seconds and then said, "Not all of them, no. The safest place to go would be another flat in this basement," she said, pulling open the front door and pointing at the door opposite. "There, for example."

"Lead me through that one," Steve said.

"Certainly," Alex said. "Gomez arrives in the first flat dressed as Pierre Gomez. He touches nothing, so there will be nothing for forensics to find. He comes through the wall into this flat, still wearing Pierre Gomez's clothing. Here, he changes into the clothes of someone else. He didn't make it home last time, so his fresh clothes are still in the wardrobe.

"From here, he goes home. One way would be up the stairs and out into the street," Alex said. "But that has several risks attached. People will notice him coming and going. Somebody will realize that there are two flats down here, and he doesn't live in either."

"You know," Steve said. "That is a very rural attitude. Most people in London couldn't give a damn."

"Possibly not as much, but they notice in their home environments. You know what neighbors are like, even in London.

"So, he needs to 'live' in this building at least part-time. He must be able to pass the other residents coming in the front door and not arouse suspicion. He has to belong."

"Yes, that fits," Steve said.

"Now, if he lived in one of the flats upstairs, then someone is going to spot him coming up from down here and ask questions," Alex said. "At worst case, it will be something they tuck away for future reference. You know how it goes, 'Yes, I often wondered why Mr. Bloggs, who lives on the third floor, was always coming up from the basement.' Although, 'always' means they were spotted twice.

"But if he has both flats, then there is no reason for any of the other tenants to come down here, ever. He can slip across the hallway unseen. That means nobody will ask him what he's doing. He can come in through the front door and come down here without raising questions."

"That all fits," Steve said. "We need to look in that other flat."

"I had better organize a warrant or someone who can pick locks," Alex said.

"Funny that," Steve said.

IST Encounter, en route to Gaia
16:00 GST

melanie opened the shuttle's small hatch and climbed in. Should any of the many professional snoopers on *Encounter* be curious, they would assume she was checking the cargo.

The sole purpose of a disposable drop shuttle was to get cargo from an orbiting freighter to the ground. The operative word was 'cargo'. Nobody ever used a DD-S to transport humans because humans died when traveling in one.

But not always. Especially when Lorina Korenjic had made all the arrangements.

Victoria Station, London
15:28 GMT
(16:28 GST)

Alex sat on the terrace of the Wetherspoons pub, looking out over the station concourse. It was before the main evening rush, and the last of the ladies who had lunched were scurrying for their trains back to Kent and Surrey and Sussex, so getting one of the bright aluminum tables and a couple of chairs hadn't been too difficult. Steve was walking towards her, carrying a tray with a pint of lager and a coffee.

I bet there's no Mrs. Steve at home, she decided regarding the slightly ill-fitting suit and the badly ironed shirt. Not that she felt a wife's job was getting suits dry-cleaned or shirts ironed, but having a woman around usually made a man a little more conscious of what he wore. Mind you, she allowed, he wasn't the right shape for a suit; a rugby jersey and a school tie around his forehead would have been more in keeping. But, she thought, surprising herself as she did so, he is rather nice.

Steve, carrying the tray towards the table, had also been thinking about Alex. His overriding thought was that she was out of his league. She had to be ten years younger and a career copper if ever he had met one. She was always so immaculate, even after climbing through a tunnel; while he had emerged covered in dust, she had come out almost unscathed. She was gorgeous and must have loads of admirers, so he stood no chance.

Steve said, "I hope this is better than Mrs. Parrot's awful tea."

"Wasn't it just," Alex agreed. "But, for someone who never really looks out of the window, 'mind you', she is a mine of information. She has to be worth a dozen CCTV cameras."

"CCTV makes better tea," Steve observed.

"True. But what did you make of all that?"

"I'm not sure where to begin," Steve said. "I mean, Mrs. Parrot didn't have much more to contribute than before. She saw the white van leave but thought it had been outside from around eleven forty-five."

"That would have been from just after they parked it at the junction of Belgrave Road and Lupus Street," Alex said. "So, it was there for the best part of an hour as it was seen leaving at ten past one when the Met turned up.

"I wonder when Mrs. Parrot sleeps?"

"She probably doesn't, just hangs upside down from the ceiling, thinking of new ways to spoil a cup of tea."

"Don't be unkind," Alex laughed. "You'll be old one day."

"I already am," Steve said.

"Hardly," Alex replied. "In your prime, I'd have said."

"Er, yes, um, so what did you think of the second flat in number one hundred and thirteen?"

"The one I haven't been in because I do not have a search-warrant, and I do not know anybody who picks locks?"

"That one," Steve said with a grin.

"According to Willis, who will deny everything, the supposed tenant is David Massey, a financial consultant, but there was little sign of occupancy. He probably just uses it as an office. Which means he can come and go, whenever he likes, easily. But, so far, no record of a David Massey working as a financial consultant. That's from any professional bodies, HMRC, PNC, DVLA, or any other organization with letters instead of words.

"Also, somebody had removed parts of the computers," she said. "It also looks like those devices wired to the light switch were designed to zap hard drives. Wipe them clean. Not standard equipment with financial consultants, I would have thought."

"So, our suspect, known as 'tall thin girl', was in there for an hour. Time enough to collect hard drives from the zappers, plus anything else incriminating."

"She seems like a traceable lead," Steve said. "There can't be too many women that tall in this country."

"No, and that friend of Mrs. Parrot, Miss Pleasance Daresbury, seemed to be quite positive in her description," Alex said and flipped open her notebook.

"Miss Daresbury had a visit by a tall, thin, possibly IC2 female and an even taller IC3 male about ten days ago, she thinks, looking for her neighbor Caeil Ashbow. Ashbow is never there, and it's five years since she last saw him and so forth and so on."

"Unusual name, "Caeil Ashbow,"" Steve said. "Sounds Celtic."

"Yes. I've passed it on to Ben Willis to run through the alphabet soup, but he hasn't come back to me yet," Alex said.

"Why am I not surprised?" Steve said.

"Okay," Alex said. "After that, the girl came back on her own and asked about visitors to Ashbow's flat. Miss Daresbury told her that, apart from a friend who sometimes stayed, the only visitor was our friend David Massey, who picked up the post. She, Miss Daresbury, that is, told the girl how to contact Massey and assumes she may have done so."

"At which point, presumably, she forgot all about it because it wasn't that important," Steve said.

"Yes, that seems reasonable."

"Until Mrs. Parrot happens to glance out of her window at ten past one in the morning and sees a tall thin girl leaving the building in which Massey has a flat."

"That sounds about right," Alex said. She looked pensive for a moment and then said, "You know, the other thing that I found interesting was that Miss Daresbury didn't really remember what Caeil Ashbow looked like, except that he was a bit over six feet. The same height as Massey and Gomez."

"What are you saying?" Steve asked.

189

"I'm just wondering aloud," Alex said.

Steve looked at his watch. "Well, there's not much else we can do now, so maybe we ought to call it a day. It's Valentine's, so I imagine there is some young man all geared up to take you out somewhere romantic this evening, and you'll want to get ready."

Alex laughed. "No such luck. How about you? Got your wife a nice present yet, or do you want to skive off early so you can get into the shops?"

"Not me. Divorced five years ago," Steve said. "Coppers' hours aren't always the best way to matrimonial harmony."

"I'm sorry," Alex said.

"Don't be. We keep in touch at Christmas and birthdays, and she's remarried and seems happy."

They sipped their drinks in silence for a couple of minutes.

"Of course, if you've got no plans...." Steve said, at the same time as Alex said, "Perhaps we could...."

They both broke off, laughing.

"That would be lovely," Alex said. "I'll give you my address; perhaps you could pick me up about eight?"

IST Encounter, en route to Gaia
19:30 GST

"Perv," Amrita said with a smile as Jack lay in bed and watched her dressing. "Get out of bed, into the shower and dressed. Bianca wants to see you. I sent her a message that you would see her on the way to ze-ball."

Jack groaned, walked into the shower, and stayed in just long enough to get clean before walking back to the bedroom.

He dressed, as usual, in jeans, a T-shirt and trainers. Amrita was wearing a summery dress with a full skirt and a fascinating neckline.

"This is for you," Amrita said, showing him a black spacesuit.

"What's it for?" he said.

"Ze-ball."

"Are we really going to that?" he said.

"We aren't, but this will also be useful where we are going,"

"Cool," Jack said. "Do I need to put it on now?"

"Not unless you want to look like a total dick, no. Put it back in the bag."

190

Jack left Amrita in a café and walked around to Bianca's office.

"Can't stop," he said. "I'm going to learn to play ze-ball in zero-gravity."

Bianca looked at the bag he held, with the black garment poking out. "So, I see," she said. "With Ms. Ghatak?"

"Yes, with Ms. Ghatak."

"Then I shall not detain you," Bianca said. "Tomorrow, perhaps around oh-nine hundred, we could meet. We should look at your plans for the future."

"Good idea," Jack said. "I will need a job. Probably not much call for bank robbers where you come from."

"No, not a lot," Bianca agreed.

GCID Operational Base, Romstrum 3
20:30 GST

"He'll be okay in a minute," Gary said.

Miguel, still dry retching, was not sure if he would ever be okay again.

"They ought to ban those damned things," Gary added.

"I agree," Lorina said.

In her experience, life consisted of good things and bad things, and traveling on an Aetherian, *Languid Bloom* class shuttle was deeply embedded in the shitty end of the bad stuff. Almost as bad as traveling in a disposable drop-shuttle, as she had just arranged for her boss.

Although she had met no one who had been stupid enough to do it. So, maybe not.

Unlike disposable drop shuttles, LB class shuttles had seats, engines, and complete environmental control. For some obscure reason, the Aetherians had blessed them with deranged AIs as pilots and the shuttles were renowned for converting every landing into a barely controlled crash. The one that dropped her, Miguel and Gary, was, if anything, one of the worst of its type. That it had left bare seconds after the three had disembarked was a wise decision on its part.

"Any movement?" Gary asked, partly to cover the sounds of Miguel's newest heaving fit.

191

"No," Lorina said and looked at her compad. "The shuttle from *Enterprise* to pick up the pilots should land soon. I shall just message Tamara."

"This place is turning into the galaxy's largest shuttle park," Gary said. "Are there any more on their way?"

"I hope so," Lorina said.

"I'm okay now, I think," Miguel said with heavy sarcasm, joining them, the moonlight making him look even paler than he was.

"Good, let's greet our delivery drivers, shall we?" Lorina said, and the three picked up their packs and walked towards the building in which they could just see the vehicle they were here to collect.

Officially, it was a shuttle, but considerably larger than the others arriving and departing the small area outside the building.

"Sergeant Korenjic," a figure said, stepping out of the deep shadows beneath the shuttle's bulk.

"Captain Sigurðardóttir," Lorina said, ignoring the rank slur.

"We were expecting Lieutenant Sunter," Gabriel Lee said, emerging from behind Briony Sigurðardóttir.

"Robert is on his way," Lorina said. "Typical of you junior officers, he is late, and I will reprimand him when he gets here. Now, I am sure you have other errands to run, and deliveries to make, so let's get this thing handed over, shall we?"

"Listen, you..." Lee said, but Sigurðardóttir raised her hand to stop him.

"Let him speak," Lorina said. "Things are usually slack in the GCID, but threats to senior officers are one area where they are not. So, if you want to test who is the senior officer here, be my guest."

"You did not go to officer training school," Lee said.

"No, I didn't, but then I knew what I was doing. A week in that place, and I would have lost the ability to think for myself. It seems we have enough sheep, and they don't need more delivery drivers."

"Come on, let's get out of here," Sigurðardóttir said and flicked a small packet in Lorina's direction. Lorina caught it with one hand.

"I haven't checked the vehicle over," Lorina said.

"Who cares," Lee said, and the two walked towards the far end of the compound where the lights of a descending shuttle from *Enterprise* were visible.

The shuttle had barely touched the ground when Sigurðardóttir returned, screaming incomprehensibly.

"Oops," Miguel said.

Lorina waited until the pilot was close and said, "Whatever is the matter, Briony, dear?"

"*Enterprise* has left orbit," she said. "You must have had something to do with it."

"I don't think so," Lorina said. "How could a mere sergeant make a freighter leave? That would take a senior officer. With lots of power."

"You bitch," Briony yelled. "I will have you kicked out of GCID for this and don't think that tick-tock is going to save you."

"Never mind," Lorina said. "Can we give you a lift anywhere?"

"Fuck you," Briony screamed. "*Encounter* is on its way with the colonel on board. Then we'll see who laughs last." She turned and ran back to the shuttle.

Lorina stood and watched it take off.

"I see relations between you and Bryony haven't improved much," Miguel said.

"No," Lorina agreed. "Nor has that scar of hers."

She opened the packet she had caught and removed several plastic strips. "But at least they left us the keys. So, shall we make it secure?"

"Yes, boss," Gary said.

Gary took a strip and climbed the front ramp. A few seconds later, the airlock door opened, and he walked in.

"At least they left it locked," he shouted down.

"Even so," Lorina said. "It's Sigurðardóttir and Lee we are dealing with. Be careful."

She and Miguel followed Gary into the airlock, where he closed the outer door and opened the inner.

"Gary, you're with me; we'll do the upper deck," Lorina said. "Miguel, you do the holds."

"Okay, boss," Miguel said and set off around the inner corridor while Lorina and Gary climbed the stairs to the upper deck.

"A quick initial inspection first, and then we'll check for real," Lorina said.

"Opposite directions or follow-the-leader?" Gary asked.

"No, follow-the-sergeant," Lorina said with a grin.

"Typical. Officers sending in the poor common soldiers while holed-up away from all the action."

"Such is the way of the world," Lorina agreed and followed Gary as he investigated each of the cabins in the outer ring.

On the fifth cabin, Gary said, "That's odd," as he walked in. There was a crash, and Lorina rushed in to find out what Gary had tripped over.

IST Encounter, en route to Gaia
22:20 GST

"melanie," Bianca said over the comm. *"They have just informed me that Lorina has arrived on Romstrum to take charge of that shuttle."*

"Yes, I am aware of where Lorina is," melanie replied.

"Fortunately, we had to come out of retroverse to allow you to disembark, so we can pick up the pilots easily. Do you know anything about Enterprise?"

"I know a few things about *Enterprise*," melanie said. "Were you after a specific detail?"

"Yes. Where is it going?"

"I don't know where it is, let alone where it is going," melanie said. "Have you lost it?"

"No, I have not lost it," Bianca snapped. *"Where is Sunter, then?"*

"He's lost too," melanie said, "but on his way. There was a delay caused by his incompetence, and I did not want a shuttle sitting on the ground unattended. Certainly not on Romstrum."

"Why was I not informed of this?" Bianca snapped.

"It is a minor operational glitch; I have dealt with it. If it would help, I will dispatch all operational questions and my intended response before answering in the future. Shall I send them to you or Katelyn Fofana?"

"There is no need for sarcasm," Bianca said.

"When it comes to questioning my operational decisions, sarcasm doesn't come into it. I have sent the actions file to Katelyn, and I will await your permission for any further actions."

melanie closed the comm. After blocking further incoming messages from Bianca, melanie called Lorina. There was no answer. Which was curious.

Dinner, in a mock Provençal restaurant, had been excellent. The Gaians certainly knew how to eat well, Jack thought. The conversation had wandered around ze-ball and been flirtatious. It was unclear if surveillance was in force, and they had to appear like a couple with little more on their minds than a game and then sex.

"My friend has just messaged me to ask if we were going to the game," Amrita said. "So, maybe we should go?"

"I suppose," Jack said, showing little enthusiasm.

He paid, and they made their way round to one of the transfer cars into the non-rotating cargo section of *Encounter*. On the other side, point-one g artificial gravity was in operation from the elevator up to the ze-ball arena.

"Walk, slowly," Amrita said. "Put each foot down before you pick up the next one."

"I thought that was the definition of walking," Jack said.

"For most humanoids, yes, but you walk fast and tend to break into a trot every few paces. The a-g will drag you down after a few meters, but it isn't a cool look."

The ze-ball spectator area was almost empty. "It's a play night, not a proper match," Amrita said.

"It really isn't my sort of thing," Jack said, watching twenty players flying around in a two-hundred-meter diameter sphere and firing what looked like fluorescent tennis balls at each other.

"Why not?" Amrita said.

"I don't like heights," Jack said. "I went outside when we were on the shuttle leaving Earth, and that was okay, but I don't want to make a habit of it."

"Oh dear," Amrita said. "So, we had better get our ze-ball suits on. Not much of this section has a breathable atmosphere."

"Especially the bit where we are going, I suppose," Jack said.

"Absolutely right," Amrita said and bundled Jack into a small cabin. She immediately started stripping.

"Ah," Jack said. 'so, ze-ball is ..."

"No, it's not," Amrita said fiercely. "I am... I was wearing a dress. Dresses do not fit inside spacesuits. I have removed mine, and I am replacing it with pants and a T-shirt. While I am doing so, get into that suit."

"Why did you wear a dress?" Jack asked.

Amrita paused and stared at him. "I enjoy wearing a dress," she snapped.

At that moment, Jack realized Amrita reminded him of his old school matron. He had very mixed feelings about that as he pulled the spacesuit on over his clothes.

"Suits you," Amrita said with a smile.

"Don't be sarcastic," Jack said, putting his watch and compad into a sealable pocket.

Jack followed Amrita down several narrow passages, where passengers would never tread, trying to walk slowly in the low gravity until they reached a circular hatch in the wall. Amrita opened the door, and Jack followed her through into a tiny chamber with a second circular hatch opposite.

"We will need breathers from here," Amrita said and pulled the hood of Jack's suit over his head. Once it fitted snugly, she clamped on a clear face mask and switched on the lights on each temple. As soon as she had completed Jack's suit, she bundled up her hair and forced it into her own hood before fitting her face mask.

"*These are not like the full suit with the hard helmet,*" she said through the earpieces in the hood. "*They are for fooling around, playing ze-ball. But they will do for our needs.*"

"Okay," Jack said.

"*There is enough air to last one hour,*" Amrita said.

The room depressurized quickly; Amrita opened the second door and led Jack through into a circular room with a hole taking up all but a small lip of the floor. Opposite the door, a ladder ran from the darkness above down into the darkness below.

"*Get onto the ladder,*" Amrita said as she clipped a safety line to Jack's suit.

Jack reached out towards the ladder.

It was too far away for him to reach, and he was now leaning out at a dangerous angle over a hole in the floor that had no bottom. Amrita shoved him so that he half fell and half leaned out over the chasm until his outstretched hands grabbed the rungs of the ladder.

"You nearly pushed me down that fucking hole," Jack snapped as he swung his feet forward to land on a rung. His arm

196

and leg movements felt slightly suppressed as if he were wading in water or dreaming.

"*Hardly,*" Amrita said. She was floating above the chasm and pulled herself closer, using the safety line. She reached around Jack, grabbed the ladder, and pushed herself downwards, disappearing into the darkness.

"*Let go of the ladder, Jack,*" Amrita said.

He gripped a little tighter.

"*Jack, let go of the ladder,*" Amrita said, but louder.

He took his feet off the rung and let go with his hands, gritting his teeth and waiting for the sudden downward plunge. He stayed where he was until a jerk on the safety line started his descent.

After what seemed like ten minutes, but was closer to sixty seconds, Jack decided to help. He grasped the ladder and pushed himself down.

"*Ow,*" Amrita said. "*You just kicked me in the head.*"

"Sorry," Jack said. "I was helping."

"*Well, don't,*" Amrita replied.

Two minutes later, Amrita said, "*Now you can grab the ladder.*"

Jack reached out and grasped a rung of the ladder, stopping his descent. Looking down, Jack's head torch illuminated the soles of Amrita's shoes beneath him.

"What are you doing?" he asked.

"*Turn this way up,*" Amrita said.

Jack turned himself over until he was what he thought of as head down.

Amrita's feet moved away from him and disappeared out of sight.

"*Come on, Jack,*" she said.

Jack pushed what was now upwards on the ladder and rose out of the ground, next to Amrita. She pulled him sideways and down onto a walkway that linked to his boots.

"Where are we?" he asked.

"*The spine,*" Amrita said. She pointed in one direction and said, "*To the habitation ring.*" She pointed the other way and said, "*To the engines.*"

They stood on a flat walkway, a meter wide, with red lights down one side and blue down the other. Two meters over and up a little, on each side, was another walkway at an angle to theirs. That pattern repeated over their heads and down the other side.

Jack counted twelve sets of lights, including their own, and, he supposed, twelve walkways.

"*Let's go,*" Amrita said. "*Be careful, there are side spars like the one we came out with every fifty meters. You can't fall down them, but they will trip you up.*"

They set off, Jack placing one foot down before lifting the other one up.

They passed two more side spars in the floor and were close to a third when Jack saw a few blue lights go out on the next walkway across. As if a head had popped up out of the ground and then ducked back down.

"See that?" Jack said.

"*No,*" Amrita said. "*What?*"

As she spoke, a sky-diving ninja came out of the spar from where the head had appeared and flew straight at them.

Jack had stopped, and the safety line attaching him to Amrita had brought her to a stop. Jack didn't think he had time for explanations; he sat down heavily and yanked hard on the safety line. Amrita fell onto her butt, then her back as the ninja passed over her and crash-landed on the next walkway over.

"That," Jack said.

Amrita was already getting to her feet, unclipping the safety line, and throwing herself towards their attacker.

Jack looked around. It was possible there were two of them. And the second one was already inbound.

Jack could handle himself in a fight, especially if the other guy was standing on the ground. Fighting flying guys was new, so he needed his assailant's feet on the floor.

Jack crouched down, waited for a split-second until the incomer had compensated, and aimed for the lower target, then stood and moved backward. He had it in mind to punch this one in the head, but in the semi-darkness and against a moving target, that wasn't so easy. He missed, but his fist scraped across the tubing for a face mask, and Jack gripped and pulled.

Amrita stepped up onto the walkway with a large, stained knife in her right hand.

"*Where's the other one?*" she said.

"Over there," Jack said, pointing with the mask in his hand. "I was trying to drag him down, but I only pulled his mask off."

"*Then, I needn't find him,*" Amrita said. "*He'll be dead by now.*"

"Okay," Jack said. A little numbed because he had just killed someone.

"S*o, let's go*," Amrita said, and the pair continued steadily along the spine of the vehicle to the rear of the cargo section.

Jack was just beginning to think they were walking back to Earth when melanie rose from a side spar in front of them, the zombie rising from the grave in a hundred killer-B movies.

"*We had a problem*," Amrita said. "*Two of them. Jack saved my ass by pulling me down on my ass and then dealt with the other one.*"

"*How?*"

"*He ripped his mask off.*"

"*Nasty way to die*," melanie said. "S*till, good work. Bianca must be getting impatient.*"

"*You think?*" Amrita said with a giggle. "*Now I must bid you farewell.*"

"*No, you are coming with us*," melanie said. "*Bianca wants you dead, too. We can get you off Romstrum on* Valiant Sky *after the rest of the team arrives.*"

"*Okay, boss*," Amrita said. "*Can we get these masks off?*"

"*You can, shortly*," melanie said. "*Follow me.*"

melanie turned and dropped, headfirst, back into the side spur from which she had emerged. Amrita and Jack followed.

Jack was still trying to work out if they were descending or ascending when melanie took them into an airlock. The increasing sound of air rushing in and a sudden increase in weight came as a relief to Jack.

Amrita and melanie took off their masks, and Jack followed suit.

"Let's go," melanie said and led the way from the airlock along a broad corridor with, to Jack's relief, full gravity, lighting, and atmosphere.

"Couldn't we have come in this way?" he said.

"No," Amrita said in a tone suggesting that line of conversation was now closed.

"So, who were those two guys?" Jack said.

"A couple of Bianca's thugs," melanie said.

"Why are they trying to kill you two?" Jack asked.

"They weren't," melanie said. "They were trying to kill Amrita and you."

"What for?" Jack said. "I realize Bianca has issues with you, but what have we done?"

"Amrita, it was nothing personal," melanie said. "They were going to frame her for killing you."

"Okay, so what have I done?"

"You didn't." melanie said. "Your mother did. She left Bianca for your father. That is why Bianca had them murdered. You, she wants dead because you remind the world that Sarah left her. And nobody leaves Bianca."

Jack's legs went a little weak, and he sagged. Amrita grabbed him and started pulling him along.

"Bit too much info in one burst there, boss," she said.

"Probably," melanie said as she stopped at a large door and punched in a code. The door slid open, and melanie walked through with Amrita and Jack close behind. The door slid shut.

In the middle of a uniformly gray room sat the bright yellow doughnut shape of the disposable drop-shuttle, directly over an orange and black striped hatch.

"This is our ride," melanie said. "It was designed to carry cargo. *Only* to carry cargo and not passengers. So, it has no real engines, heating, cooling, or even oxygen."

melanie turned a handle on the side, a hatch opened, and all three climbed inside. Crammed into cages around the outer walls were crates, boxes, and bags. A pile of bedding, mattresses, duvets, blankets, quilts, and pillows dominated the center of the floor.

"They don't have real engines," melanie said, "but they have four chemical rockets with enough power to kick the vehicle out of orbit and start the deceleration and descent to where the parachute can deploy.

"That deceleration will reach ten Terran standard gravities for a while. It will be bad but survivable. As these vehicles don't have seats, I have lashed down this bedding onto the cargo deck. We will lie, strapped down, on that.

"It will be uncomfortable. It will probably render us unconscious, but it will be much better than the hard surface of the deck and we will get down."

"Okay," Jack said. "May I ask why they don't have seats?"

"Because nobody but a deranged lunatic would travel from orbit to the surface in a disposable drop-shuttle," Amrita said.

"Precisely," melanie said.

"But we are?" Jack persisted.

"Yes, we are," melanie said.

200

"Why couldn't we have used one of those shuttles that brought us up from Earth?"

"Bianca wants you dead," melanie said. "She would quite like me dead as well, but because I work for an Aetherian called Rufus Koenig, who has a history of getting bad tempered towards those who kill his people, Bianca would need to be very discreet when killing me.

"You she could cut you open and eviscerate you in the middle of a public area on *Encounter*, and nobody would say a word."

"And this has what to do with shuttles?" Jack asked.

"If you were on it, she would blow it up as soon as it was clear of *Encounter,* and my death would be part of a tragic accident. That means I have to get you off *Encounter* by some means that are impossible."

"Okay," Jack said. "And nobody but a deranged lunatic would travel from orbit to the surface in a disposable drop-shuttle."

"Now you've got it," melanie said.

"Makes sense. So how about the heating, cooling, and oxygen?"

"All handled by the suits," melanie said. "Ze-ball suits are normal spacesuits, but black. As ze-ballers are the only people who want black spacesuits, it gets forgotten that they are real spacesuits."

"What's wrong with a black spacesuit?"

"Seriously?" Amrita said.

"In space, you need to be seen," melanie said. "Against the sky. It stops things from running into you and makes it easier to find you if you get untethered. Not a lot, but some."

"A black spacesuit is dangerous," Amrita said. "Probably more dangerous than traveling in a disposable drop-shuttle. Except it isn't."

"Okay," Jack said. "That was a dumb question."

"Got any others?"

"Sort of," Jack said. "I'm not big on coincidences, so how come you have a load of bedding to deliver just when you need a load of big, soft, squishy stuff to protect fragile human bodies from a mix of high-g and inflexible decks?"

"It isn't a coincidence," melanie said. "When we get down to Romstrum, you will meet Lorina Korenjic, my number two, and a logistical genius, who arranged for this bedding to be here."

"Brilliant," Jack said. "So what happens when we meet up with your logistical genius?"

"We wait," melanie said. "My shuttle is there, and the rest of the team will join us shortly."

"Then what?" Jack said.

"We have a slight detour and back to Earth."

"I just came from there," Jack said.

"Yes, but that is where the action is right now," melanie said.

Jack was setting up a new battery of questions when melanie said, "We will come out of the retroverse soon, I suggest we get settled in.

"When we come out, we will be very close to the planet. There is nothing for the EMP to damage on the surface of Romstrum, as the indigenous species live underground. But as soon as we come out, we will drop."

"Okay," Jack said.

"When we get down to the surface, we might be in the middle of a situation," melanie said. "Amrita and I can talk through our neurolinks. If I introduce Amrita as Sergeant Carroll and you as Lieutenant Sunter, say nothing and go along with it."

"Sure," Jack said. It seemed simple enough.

What concerned him more was the choice of name melanie had assigned to Amrita. 'Carroll'.

Again, coincidence - or testing the water?

FiT: THE TWENTY-FIFTH

Valiant Sky in retroverse
20:50 GST Twoday 3.4.2776
(Sunday 5th September 1982)

Albrecht Torre looked up as the door opened and melanie walked into his office.

"You called me," melanie said.

"I did," Albrecht said. "Bad news. Bianca Kaninchen is on her way to Earth aboard *Encounter*. And, for reasons best known to themselves, Sarah and Benjamin have gone along, taking Caeil."

"That is not good," melanie said. "Kaninchen must have told them that all is forgiven. Benjamin is an academic. I can forgive him for being stupid, but Sarah knows Kaninchen never, ever forgives or forgets."

"Our opinion also," Albrecht said. "Sky is now heading for Earth at as close to eight hundred megalux as we can achieve."

"Thank you," melanie said. "And our ETA?"

"We will drop you in Earth orbit around nineteen-hundred GST. Benjamin wanted to visit a place in the northern part of England. We can have you on the ground around twenty-one hundred."

"Thank you, Albrecht," melanie said.

The door opened and a younger man walked in.

"This is not really the time," Albrecht said, "but melanie, may I present Rufus Koenig. I am training him to take over as my successor in a few years.

"Rufus, may I present melanie, probably the most efficient agent in the GCID. And the one person in the galaxy I am heartily grateful works for us in the AIB."

Koenig stepped forward and took melanie's hand. "I am truly pleased to meet you, ma'am," he said. "Master Torre has told me of your many adventures together."

"Lesson one, young man," melanie said, "never believe a word a spymaster tells you. They lie professionally."

"As I am becoming aware," Koenig said.

FiT: THE TWENTY-SIXTH

A1, Great North Road, Hertfordshire, England
22:15 BST Wednesday 8th September 1982
(22:15 GST Fiveday 3.4.2776)

"Right then, we're all done. We'll leave you to it."

Police Constable Robert Jones turned to look at the fireman walking towards him.

"Yes, thanks mate," Jones said. "I expect we'll be here for a couple of hours yet, trying to sort out what happened."

"Yeah, what a mess. I can often spot what caused it, but this one, I don't know..." he paused, turning to look at the mangled cars, "it's anybody's guess."

Jones laughed. "I know. My sergeant has been stomping round here for the last twenty minutes muttering about it not being possible. He even suggested it may not have been an accident. What the Yanks call 'road rage' he says. Still, looks like the family will live."

"Oh? How do you work that out?"

"The couple with the kiddie, the doctor said they'll probably be alright. Not like the other couple."

"Christ no, he got it all wrong," the fireman said. "We took the baby from the car the people died in, not the other one. The doctor's the one who got him out."

"Are you sure?"

"'Course I'm bloody sure. I had to help drag the doc out. Heavy bugger too."

"Oh Christ," Jones said. "The sarge is gonna go bloody ballistic."

"Sorry mate, but it looks like somebody dropped one there."

"Yeah, and guess who'll cop it? Still, cheers for letting me know."

"No probs," the fireman said and walked back to the fire engine. Blue lights and sirens off, the vehicle set off at a sedate pace. PC Jones watched it go and walked over towards his sergeant, who was standing looking at the wreckage of the two cars. This would not be good, Jones thought, not good at all.

In the distance, he spotted a tall figure climbing into a car. It was the doctor who had stopped, there was no mistaking that lanky sod. Maybe he could help.

"One moment, doctor," Jones called.

The doctor turned, looked at Jones for a second, and then slid into the car and drove away.

They never traced the car or the driver.

DAY SIXTEEN

Twoday 6.5.2834

Wednesday 15th February 2017

"Time," melanie said. "Hoods and masks on and put your oxygen pack beside you. It masses seven kilos now. Seventy kilos at ten-g."

Amrita and Jack pulled the rest of their suits on.

"Get strapped down," melanie said and closed the shuttle's door, leaving them with just the dim, red interior lights and a thin white beam from the porthole in the door.

melanie pointed to a spot in the middle of the bedding pile and said, "Go there," to Jack. "You're the biggest. We will be on each side of you."

Jack lay flat, and melanie draped webbing straps over him and Amrita before lying down and clipping together several straps over herself.

"Everything will force us back onto the floor," melanie said. "The straps are just in case there is any sideways movement."

"This is quite comfortable," Amrita said.

"Hmm," Jack said, not convinced. melanie and Amrita seemed to take the prospect very well. Almost as if they undertook trips for deranged lunatics as a matter of course.

A distant klaxon sounded. A sharp downward movement. Hard enough for Jack to want to question melanie's statement about, "everything will be forcing us back on the floor," as he felt himself lifting into the straps. The light through the porthole blinked into blackness.

Everything stopped; they were weightless for several seconds. Then the retros kicked in, and Jack was pressed back into the bedding, now like the sprung canvas of a trampoline and unlike the soft pile it had been.

The retros stopped, started again, and stopped.

"Lining us up on our destination," melanie said.

"Oh, good," Jack said. It felt like the shuttle was spinning like a top, but it might have been imagination. The next burst on the retros was not imaginary.

The soft bedding became an unrelenting steel plate under Jack's spine.

Just as that became bearable, a fully grown elephant was deposited on his chest. He blacked out.

When he came around, the elephant was gone, and the bedding was once again a cotton-wool mountain. There was a faint light in the porthole, then it went out.

"Are we down?" he said.

"Not quite," melanie said.

As she spoke, the gods of vengeance and mischief threw the shuttle into a cement mixer and gave it ten minutes.

"Jesus," Jack said. "What was that?"

"Top of the atmosphere," melanie said.

Steel plate replaced the cotton-wool mountain once more, and then a full-grown mastodon took over the elephant's job. Jack fled back into unconsciousness.

"Fuck me," he said as he awoke, back on the cotton wool.

"Maybe later," Amrita said.

"Behave," melanie said.

Another burst from the retros, and Jack was just watching the periphery of his vision going dark when it stopped. A few seconds later, a gentle jerk—minutes after that, a second, then a third. Everything went still, and there was gravity of a sort.

"Are we down now?" Jack said.

"No, that was the para-wing system," melanie said, undoing her straps. "We will be on the ground in about half an hour."

IST *Encounter*, en route to Gaia
00:30 GST

"This had better be good," Bianca said into her compad.

"*I would not call if it were not,*" Katelyn Fofana said. "*There have been several anomalies.*"

"Tell me."

"Enterprise *was supposed to collect the pilots delivering that shuttle. They received false orders, and* Encounter *has come out of retroverse to collect them.*"

"That I knew."

"*While collecting the pilots, a scheduled disposable drop-shuttle left* Encounter *for the surface. It would not have been dropped if it had not become necessary to pick up the pilots.*"

"Not exactly," Bianca said. "I had agreed to a fly-by drop for melanie."

"*Perhaps, but Caeil Ashbow is no longer on* Encounter."

Bianca smiled. "Clever," she said. "If we had not had to collect the two pilots, we would have been traveling faster when we dropped melanie.

"So, excellent. My daughters will soon join them. Things could not have gone better if I had planned for it."

"*Yes, I thought you might be pleased.*"

GCID Operational Base, Romstrum 3
04:30 GST

The shuttle, suspended from its ram airfoil, touched down with a puff of help from the almost depleted retros and bounced gently on its springs, as the canopy dropped behind it, and small winches began hauling the material in.

As the cargo door dropped, melanie stepped out, closely followed by Amrita and then Jack, who fell to his knees and threw up.

"If you knew what lives in the soil here, you wouldn't put your face that close," melanie said. Jack got to his feet.

Ingpor, the larger moon, was full and approaching apogee. It appeared bigger and brighter than Luna from Earth, and Jack looked around at his first alien planet.

There wasn't a lot to see; a perimeter fence, its location marked by pools of brightness from the ten-meter-high security lamps. In front of them stood a low, dark-painted warehouse, with a stream of bluish light coming from the partially open doors. A faint smell of ozone carried on the slight breeze, and the only noise was the soft whirr of a slow-running electric motor.

Kanpor, the smaller moon, was just above the horizon, a mix of red and green streaks, like the marbles Jack played with as a kid. It would add a little more illumination to the scene.

"Christ, it's hot," Jack said, hoping the motor powered a fan.

"Wait until it gets light," melanie said absently and went back into the shuttle. She returned seconds later.

"Does it get any better?" Jack asked.

"Depends on what you think of as better? If you mean 'hotter', then yes, a lot better."

"Fantastic," Jack said and looked over at the buildings. "They don't seem too keen on meeting us."

210

Three figures silhouetted themselves against the open warehouse door and then started walking across the hard-packed earth towards them.

"There you are," melanie said. "The welcome wagon cometh."

As they got closer, Jack could make out a petite woman in jungle combat fatigues, carrying a stubby black assault weapon. She walked between two similarly armed men.

"You haven't forgotten what I said on the way down, have you?" melanie asked.

"You mean the bit about...."

"That's the one," melanie said.

The trio stopped, but melanie walked on towards them. "Hello," she called, "I'm Sergeant Liddell; this is Lieutenant Sunter and Sergeant Carroll."

That was it, Jack decided. "Carroll" and Liddell." There were no coincidences. melanie knew about the books, but he would keep what he knew to himself until she came clean.

"Welcome to Romstrum," the woman said, "I'm Lieutenant Korenjic, and these are Sergeants Johannsen and Iwasaka."

Jack felt a prod in the back and said, "I'm pleased to meet you at last. That was a rough ride down, and I'm still a little shaky."

"Shall we get in out of the heat?" Korenjic said.

"Sure, shall we get the luggage?" Jack said.

"Leave it," Korenjic said. "I'll send someone out with a cart."

"Sir, can I get my small grip?" melanie said.

"Sure," Jack said. "Then follow us in." He turned and joined Korenjic for the walk back towards the warehouse.

"Right now, I could murder a cup of coffee," he said.

"That we can do," Korenjic replied, falling into step beside him while one sergeant trailed along just behind. The other one waited to help melanie.

As they walked, Jack heard the '*dub*' of a distant champagne cork taking flight and then something substantial hitting the floor. Then a croak and another thud.

Jack restrained the impulse to turn and look and said, "Have you been here long?"

Looking straight ahead, Korenjic said, "Only about twenty-four hours. Have you been here before?"

"No," Jack said, "five days ago, I didn't know this place even existed."

She turned to look at him and said, "Really? Only five days, but...."

"*Dub*." Her face exploded as the one-millimeter round that had entered just behind her left ear detonated inside her brain.

This time, Jack turned. The sergeant who had stayed to help melanie was missing a face, but the one who had walked with Amrita was alive and lying on the ground in obvious pain.

melanie strode over to the downed man and said, "Get on your knees, hands where I can see them."

The man levered himself onto his knees, raising his hands and putting them behind his neck.

"No," melanie said, "keep them out where I can see them."

The man complied.

"Who are you?" melanie asked.

"Me, I'm just a guy looking for a bit a' work. They just said it was like straight in an' out. Lift a vault or summink, I dunno, but I weren't looking for no heavy shit like this." He spoke English with an accent Jack thought might once have been east London but wasn't.

"You speak Gaian pretty good," melanie said.

"You gotta, the way things is, don'cha? Youse guys is all over."

"Okay," melanie said, "I have no real fight with you. Tell me what I need to know, and I can let you go. We might even do a bit of business."

"Sounds a peach," the man said. "What d'ya wanna know?"

"Who is behind this, and how many are there inside?"

"No idea who's jacking it. I was pulled in by this guy I knows, Alf Gallimon, but he ain't the brains, like; there's only a coupla guys would take on anyfink to do with Gines. Take your pick."

"You reckon this is a Gaian operation here, do you?"

"Dunno," the man said. "If it were real Gine, or Afearean, youse'd have twenny full shuttles down here an' a coupla ISTs in orbit an' the juice to go fight the fuckin Nel. Word on the street is some youse Gines 'ave gone rogue 'n' got your own firm. Nobody would've taken this on if youse were kosher Gine."

"Interesting," melanie said. "So, how many of your friends are there inside?"

"Four. Outa seven of us. Gallimon is the boss man, and 'e's gonna be real pissed: that was 'is secon' woman you just offed."

"I think that's going to be the least of his problems with me," melanie said. "Where are they holding them?"

"There's a dirt' great T3 shuttle in there, can't miss the fucker," the man gave a false laugh. "It's got free ramps open. Your lot is by the right 'an' side ramp. They're in cuffs an' stuff. An' look, you let me go, I'm off dis rock, I ain't telling no one nuffink about you guys."

"Of course not. How many ways into the building?"

"Two doors; one 'ere and one on to the road."

"Very good," melanie said. "You know if I find there are any over four in there, I will kill you, don't you?"

""Course I do. I ain't got no fight with youse neither, just a bit a business."

"Okay, good," melanie said and pulled the trigger. The man's body fell over backward.

They stood in silence for a moment, and Jack said, "What happened to 'I have no real fight with you', blah-de-blah. 'Might even be able to do business', blah-de-blah?"

"I lied. Same as he did when he said, 'you let me go, I'm off dis rock, I ain't telling no one nuffink about you guys'." melanie said in an excellent impersonation.

"I suppose that wasn't this, err, Lieutenant Koren?"

"Korenjic? No."

"Oh, okay," Jack said. "What do we do next? Go in and rescue them?" he asked.

"No. I need those idiots to come out here." She gestured towards the building.

"Do you know what worries me?" Jack said.

"Let me guess. Useless as they are, they have taken our people prisoner."

"Close enough."

melanie laughed. "Let's get into cover behind the bodies and wait until whoever is supposedly running this starts wondering what is going on and sends someone to find out."

"How long could that take?"

"Minutes, hours, days, who knows? As long as they do it before it gets light, I don't care."

"I wish I'd brought my Kindle now," Jack said.

"You have me," Amrita said.

"You can keep quiet," melanie said.

They lay in silence for a while, and melanie said, "Here comes the first one."

213

The figure by the open doorway was taking few chances. He was peering around the corner using a night scope, and eventually, he spotted the bodies.

He turned and shouted to someone further inside.

"Amateurs," melanie said quietly. "Keep still, and they won't be able to see you."

A second and then a third figure appeared at the door. There was a brief argument, and one of the three took over the night-scope and began looking around, further afield. Eventually, he spotted the shuttle and, realizing that it was a likely hiding spot, took an experimental shot at it.

The 'dub-dub-dub' from melanie's pistol was almost a single sound, and all three figures dropped to the ground.

"Leaving one," Jack said.

"Possibly. If there really were only four of them."

Four minutes passed before anything happened.

"I want to trade," a man yelled from behind the door. "You get your people back, and I walk clear."

"Not going to happen," melanie said so that only Amrita and Jack could hear her. "Okay," she called, "let's talk."

"Remind me never to do business with you," Jack said.

"Okay," the figure in the door yelled, "come on in."

"I don't think so," melanie called back, "you bring the lieutenant to the door—and I mean the real one this time—and when I'm happy there is something to trade, you can go. I have no fight with someone else picking up a bit of cash where they can."

"Wait there," the figure yelled and disappeared. Seconds later, he reappeared with a woman in green fatigues with both wrists and ankles in restraints.

"Now what?" he yelled.

"Unarmed man coming over with a retinal reader. If she's Korenjic, we have a deal."

"Okay, sounds good."

melanie scrabbled through her grip and dug out a small device. "You're up," she said to Jack. "Just put this bit over her right eye, and when it goes 'beep', let me know. Have a look around first though. If there's anyone else there that shouldn't be when it beeps, tell me it's a 'positive ID'. If it's just him, tell me it's, 'Okay'."

"Will do," Jack said, and taking the retinal reader, he set off towards the open door.

As Jack approached, he could see the man holding the supposed lieutenant looked more scared than Jack felt. Jack ignored him and placed the reader over the lieutenant's right eye.

Jack stood there, wondering what to do if the damned reader didn't go beep when he noticed the lieutenant was attractive in a girl-next-door way. At least, as cute as a woman gets in camouflage.

He dragged his attention away from her and looked around inside the warehouse. He could see the shuttle and two figures tied up at the base of one of the access ramps, but nobody else.

The retinal reader beeped.

"Okay," Jack called out.

"What's the situation with the others?" melanie called.

"Alive and well, just a bit dopey at the mo...," the man yelled.

"Not you, her," melanie interrupted.

"They're okay, I think," the lieutenant whispered.

"She thinks they're okay," Jack called.

"Good," melanie shouted. "If you want to go, you can; I'm not interested in you anymore."

The man thrust Lieutenant Korenjic into Jack's arms and ran for the door at the other side of the building. He made it halfway across the warehouse before melanie appeared at Jack's side and fired. The running man came down in a heap.

"I know. He lied as well," Jack said softly.

melanie gave Jack a very cool look. "Yeah, something like that," she said.

"I suppose we'd better get them out of their restraints and find out what happened," Jack suggested.

"Not yet" melanie said and applied a small device to the lieutenant's skin. "My scratch tester will confirm if it's Korenjic; I want to make sure it's her first."

"What about the retinal reader? Didn't that confirm who she is?"

"No. That's a communicator. I beeped it because we don't have a small retinal reader, and a DNA tester is a bit more complicated. I improvised."

"Thanks for telling me."

"I didn't have time. However, this is the real Lieutenant Lorina Korenjic."

"Of course I am, boss," Korenjic said.

"Hmm," melanie said. "I wouldn't have thought the Lorina Korenjic I know would have been taken prisoner so soon."

215

"Long story," Korenjic said.

"Yeah," melanie said. "This is Jack Fletcher."

"Hi Jack," Lorina said. "Tied up over there are Sergeants Miguel Iwasaka and Gary Johannsen."

"Okay, so shall I get them free?" Jack asked.

"Yes," melanie said. "We'll need to find some cutting gear; I doubt these bastards brought the keys."

"There's some by the ramp," Korenjic said, using her bound hands to point to some crates close by where the two sergeants were still tied up. Following her instructions, he found a device a little like a small angle grinder.

"If you cut my main wrist restraint first, sir, I'll be a lot quicker cutting the rest free," said the one whose name tag identified him as Sergeant Johannsen.

That made sense to Jack, so he cut the strap joining Johannsen's two bracelets and handed him the cutter. Within a couple of minutes, Johannsen had wielded the dangerous little implement within millimeters of the skin of the other two, and they were free. It took Iwasaka another minute of cutting to free Johannsen.

Amrita had joined them from collecting weapons dropped by the welcoming committee, and Jack said, "This is Amrita."

Lorina had a quizzical look. Jack suspected she hadn't been expecting anyone else and didn't know who this woman was.

"Amrita Ghatak," Amrita said.

Lorina smiled and said, "Oh, yes, hello," and shook Amrita's hand. Jack picked up on Lorina's reaction to Amrita's full name and decided to investigate later.

"I'll make coffee," Johannsen announced.

The sergeant left, and almost immediately, melanie joined them. "Their truck was just outside," she said. "I've loaded the bodies on board. Maybe tomorrow we'll take it out in the bush somewhere, and it can have a minor accident. Meanwhile, we need some cabins."

"Coffee first, though," Jack said.

"Okay, coffee first," melanie agreed with a resigned tone.

"Good," Johannsen said as he reappeared with a tray full of mugs and a large coffee pot, "because I need this."

"Me too," Jack said. "After that trip down, I really need something a little stronger."

"I sympathize, sir," Korenjic said. "We came down in a *Languid Bloom* class shuttle, and I thought that was bad. A disposable drop-shuttle, that's crazy."

"It was not fun," Jack said. "But better than all this calling me 'sir' crap? I'm a civilian, and I'm not used to it. I am 'Jack'. What you call each other is your problem."

"Not a problem," melanie said. "First names only from now on."

"Thank you," Jack said.

After an overly long silence melanie said, "So, the elephant in the room. What happened here?"

"Hmmm," Lorina said. "We got here almost thirteen hours ago, on time, at twenty-thirty yesterday. The T3 was here, and so were Gabriel Lee and Briony Sigurðardóttir. After the usual niceties, they left."

"Not best buddies of yours," Jack said, picking up on Lorina's tone.

"Briony picked a fight with Lorina some years ago, which is stupid in itself," melanie said. "Briony lost and has a scar to prove it."

"A scar she could have had removed but elected not to," Lorina said.

"Anyway, then what?" melanie said.

"They had sealed the vehicle," Lorina continued. "Even so, we went aboard and did a security sweep. First, a quick check to make sure there were no obvious problems, like a baby-nuke ticking down, and then we would have followed up with a close check and then an even closer check when the Finkel arrived."

"We won't have time; I'll do it," melanie said. "Then what?"

"Sergeant Johannsen... Gary, and I checked the upper deck while Miguel checked the holds."

"I walked into hold three, and next thing I'm trussed up, and my head is hurting like shit," Miguel Iwasaka said.

"What did they get you with?" melanie asked.

"An old-fashioned length of aluplas strut. The bastards were standing behind the door."

"What about you?" melanie asked Lorina.

"Gary and I were working our way around the cabins," Lorina said. "I saw him walk into one and heard a crash and I thought he'd fallen over something and went to check. He was lying on the floor, and as I went in, they got me too."

"If they were waiting for you, on a sealed shuttle," melanie said, "they either came here on the shuttle, or they were let on board after it arrived."

"That's the same conclusion I'd come to," Lorina said.

"It gets light in another hour," Miguel said. "Gary and I will get all the stuff from the drop shuttle."

"I will make a sweep and see what nasty surprises they left for us," melanie said.

Gary said, "I'll get the little truck, and we can move it all over in a couple of trips." He was walking away as he spoke.

"Bring the parafoil," melanie shouted after him, "and anything else that might be useful."

"Does that mean anything not attached to anything else?" Miguel said.

"It does," melanie said.

Gary reappeared on what looked like a platform with a stand-up driving position, Miguel jumped aboard, and the cart whirred out the door.

"While that is all happening," melanie said, "perhaps, Amrita, you could find yourself and Jack a cabin?"

"Sure," Amrita said.

"The cabins opposite side from the flight deck are free." Lorina said.

"Thank you," Amrita said. "Come on, Jack, let's get settled."

As soon as Amrita and Jack were out of earshot, Lorina turned to melanie and said, "Nice timing, by the way."

"Oh, ye of little faith," melanie said. "So, what happened? I tried calling you and thought it odd when you didn't reply."

"Mea culpa," Lorina said. "It was as I told you. But what was weird was that they kept us alive."

"They were expecting Sunter and had probably been given instructions not to kill him," melanie said.

"That's what I thought," Lorina said. "Now, what are you going to do with those two?"

"Amrita will leave on *Valiant Sky*," melanie said. "I am surprised she lasted as long as she did on *Encounter*. Bianca must have known who she was. She can go back to Earth at some point."

"Is the Earth ready for another one?" Lorina said. "But I was more interested in Caeil, Jack, I mean. What are you going to do with him?"

"I'm not sure," melanie said. "But he might be of some use to us."

"Okay, but does he know what's going on?"

"Not totally," melanie said.

"Shouldn't he?" Lorina asked. "If he is to be part of it."

"He should," melanie agreed. "The first stage, anyway."

"What does he know so far?"

"He has met a Nel and knows what they are. Amrita explained what they are doing on Earth. He knows Kaninchen is on the other side, that she is Venatori and that they are behind the Nel. He doesn't know that the Venatori are the real goal, just who they are and that they are bad news, but then most of the team don't know that, and I would like to keep it that way a little longer. Meanwhile, you, Gary and Miguel can bring him up to speed as far as the Nel are concerned. I think he regards me with a certain degree of suspicion."

"Can't think why," Lorina said without a smile.

"Does he know Amrita is leaving us?" Lorina said.

"He knows, and I suspect will be over it in a day," melanie said. "She is just like all his other relationships, bar one, short and emotionless."

"Okay, good."

"Is the team on schedule?"

"Yes, the last group will board shortly. Although I dread to think how that might pan out with Zara Chang and the Dee-Dum. They will probably have to disarm Chiyo three times a day."

"Okay," melanie said. "Is Sunter, with all his strays and misfits, alive and happy?"

"Probably. You'd need to ask him."

"Okay," melanie said. "Anything else?"

"Yes." Lorina said. "You knew where Caeil or Jack was all the time, didn't you?"

"I did," melanie said. "How did you come to that conclusion?"

"I know you," Lorina said. "The Colonel has been looking for him for years now. You found him this time, just as there is a hunter-squad looking for him, and in the time frame you predicted, I might add."

"So far, so good," melanie said. "Anything else?"

"You had Amrita Ghatak aboard *Encounter*. That was very convenient, and I bet she is just his type."

"Keep going," melanie said.

219

"You said, 'she is just like all his other relationships, bar one, short and emotionless." You didn't get to know about his love life that quickly. I doubt even Miss Ghatak could have extracted it as fast, either."

"Well done," melanie said.

"But didn't he notice the family resemblance?" Lorina said.

"Yes, there was a slight recognition, but not much."

"That is crazy," Lorina said.

"We have a bit of a problem with the luggage," Gary called out as the two men came back into the building, riding on the pile of gear on the trolley.

"We'll talk later," melanie said quietly to Lorina.

Gary held up one of melanie's packs and pointed to a neat bullet hole. "Must have come in the door and hit this bag."

"Typical," melanie said.

Gary handed melanie the pack, and she looked inside. "Nothing too serious," she said. "They just smashed my full-size DNA scanner. Fortunately, I shouldn't need it for now."

IST *Valiant Sky*, Mars orbit
08:00 GST

"We must go now," Rufus Koenig told Zara. "We don't have much time, and we need to get you down to the loading dock, then we need to get you..." He paused. "Let's just do it. It's quicker than explaining."

Zara nodded and ran after the retreating Rufus, who was already halfway to the elevator.

"Your luggage is already down on the dock and will be taken to your room," Rufus said as they descended. "There is rather a lot. You like to shop, apparently."

"Yeah, apparently," Zara replied.

"There is a shuttle coming in now," Rufus said. "It's empty, but it will show your friend Tamara Finkel that a shuttle has arrived from Earth.

"As soon as we get you and your luggage clear, we can bring in the second shuttle and its passengers."

There was something shifty in the way Rufus was behaving.

"What second shuttle?" Zara said. "Who is in it?"

Zara stared at Rufus steadily. He avoided looking back at her. "Greta and Georgia Kaninchen," he said after several seconds. "They have a silly nickname, I believe."

"The Dee-Dum."

"That's the one," Rufus said as the elevator stopped.

At the dock, two men were just finishing loading an enormous pile of cases, grips, bags, boxes, and trunks into a freight elevator.

"You go that way," Rufus said, pointing at the luggage.

Zara joined the men, the luggage and a small cart in the freight elevator and began the journey back to the floor she had just left. Only further round the corridor and in a larger space.

Zara selected two smaller bags and let the two men take the rest to storage. The two bags she carried to her cabin. Which was a lot smaller than her previous accommodation, but temporary. She unpacked a few items and went in search of the lounge, wondering what sort of reception she was going to get.

Nine pairs of eyes stared back at her as the door slid open and she walked in–nine pairs of largely hostile eyes.

"A surprise party, and it's not even my birthday," she said with a broad and overblown smile.

Setu Anastassiou laughed, Abdul looked confused, Zack and Cornelius looked to Elise, who glowered, Sophia smirked, Dan looked disappointed, Tamara examined her hair, and Chiyo, well, Chiyo scowled. A dark, hatred-filled scowl. That faded.

Setu and Sophia were the first on their feet. Natural good manners took over with Elise, and she joined them, releasing Zack and Cornelius from bondage; Dan joined them with one eye on the door, and Tamara followed. That was what she had thought might happen.

Chiyo walked over to stand before Zara. She stood still for several seconds, then smiled and wrapped her arms around the other woman's neck. "I knew it was you," she whispered.

IST Valiant Sky, **en route to Romstrum**
08:15 GST

"Just so you all know," Rufus Koenig told the bored-looking Gaian team. "Lieutenant Korenjic and Sergeants Miguel Iwasaka and Gary Johannsen arrived on Romstrum on schedule but were captured by locally employed forces unknown. Fortunately, Commander melanie rescued them some hours later."

The team sat, apparently dumbfounded, then Chiyo stood up.

"Solemn pact time," she said.

"Come on, Chiyo, we aren't at school now," Elise said.

"I don't care," Chiyo said. "We swear a solemn pact. We never, ever mention this to Lorina. Miguel and Gary are fair game, but never Lorina."

"I agree," Zara said.

"She has looked after us very well," Setu said.

"Dragging us all over the galaxy," Elise snapped.

"Come on, babe," Cornelius said, "she had no choice, and we've hardly suffered on the way back, have we?"

"No, but..." Elise said, then smiled. "Okay."

"What's going on?" Greta said from the door. "Chiyo come up with a new conspiracy?"

"No, just compiling a fantasy death list," Elise said. "Nel mainly."

Zara, standing on the edge of the group, said, "Both normal and pigmy varieties."

The sudden hush seemed to stop time.

The predominant natural hair color for Gaians, and Aetherians, was a very dark chestnut brown. During their formative years, most experimented with changing their hair color using either dyes or pharmaceutical methods. Some, like Tamara and Zara, continued the more extreme changes into adulthood. Most of the others used a minor enhancement to change the tone or provide decorative streaks, tips or highlights.

Greta and Georgia were natural blonds and, it had to be said, looked like short versions of the Nel.

Someone, and the smart money favored Chiyo, started calling them, "The Pigmy Nel."

Having one nickname was usually okay. Especially if it came across as in any way affectionate. 'Tweedledee and Tweedledum' even though nobody knew what it meant, never seemed affectionate, and shortening it to "The Dee-Dum" made it far worse somehow.

Both versions paled into insignificance when the new name spread, and the angrier the two sisters became, the faster it spread.

After a few bloody fights, nobody ever called them 'Pigmy Nel' to their faces. Until now.

Greta took two steps towards Zara. Zara Chang was a stupid little weakling who should never have been in GCID. She was going down. The others didn't like her, so there would be no interference.

Zara Chang took four steps towards Greta and stopped when they stood eye-to-eye.

"Your move Greta," Zara said quietly. "I want the cameras in this room to see you make the first move; then, I am going to make up for a lot of years while I further ruin that homely little face of yours."

Greta stared into Zara's eyes. What she expected was fear. A tiny tremor. Something, anything, to suggest she had the advantage. But she saw nothing; as if someone else was staring out at her from behind those big blue eyes.

Then it hit her. This wasn't meek little Zara Chang staring back at her. Mother had been right; she had to be.

Greta felt the color drain from her face. Saying nothing, she turned and then said to Georgia, "Come on. The air smells fresher in our cabin."

Zara stood firm until the door had closed behind the two sisters and then turned. The rest of the team stood staring, transfixed.

"Wow," Elise said. "Whatever you have been eating on Earth, I want some. Way to go, girl."

Chiyo grinned.

"Hey Chiyo, when you leave, make sure you don't leave the smile behind," Setu said.

GCID Operational Base, Romstrum 3
08:15 GST

Jack stood looking at the shuttle dominating the hangar floor. Not quite what he would have imagined at the mention of the word 'spaceship'.

A slab-sided orange cylinder thirty meters across and eight meters tall, with meter-high black lettering identifying it as *SV 3-8749* and the property of 'Isis Surveys'. A company, Amrita told him, that was a front for AIB black operations.

"Time to go in," Miguel said as he walked past towards the ramp. "The sun is up, and it can get up to eighty degrees outside."

Jack thought that wasn't that bad for an English Summer's Day when it occurred to him that Miguel meant Celsius.

He ran up the ramp, and the outer hold door closed.

Lorina sat on a crate in what the sign on the wall identified as HOLD 1. From the noise, Miguel and Gary were moving containers next door.

"So, Jack," Lorina said, "any thoughts on our mission?"

"None," Jack said. "I know the truth about the Nel, I know about Bianca and her dislike of my family, although I suspect what I know is only the tip of the iceberg, and I have heard mention of the Venna somethings."

"Venatori," Lorina said, sure that Jack knew the word well enough.

"That's them," Jack said. "But how you are going to stop these bastards killing everybody on Earth, I do not know."

"Admittedly, we are a small team, and there are lots of them," Lorina said. "They have one weak spot. A base, a headquarters, somewhere on Earth. If we could find that, we might stop them."

"Can you find it?"

"We don't know," Lorina said. "We will have to operate without GCID intelligence support."

"Bianca playing for the other team, I suppose."

"Exactly," Lorina said. "The Aetherian Intelligence Bureau are good, but GCID have more hands-on Earth experience."

"What happens if you find it?"

"We have fighting skills, but we are GCID troops. This means we are more field intelligence operatives; we reconnoiter, run surveillance, hack computer systems, sabotage installations and steal vital equipment."

"Oh good," Jack said. "I'll fit in much better with you guys than the other lot. I was a bank robber."

"Any good at it?"

"I didn't get caught and made a ton of money," Jack said. "Amongst us bank robbers, that's considered being good at it."

"I imagine it is," Lorina said.

Jack said, "'Lorina', is an unusual name. You don't have sisters named 'Alice' and 'Edith', do you?"

Lorina went a peculiar shade of puce, then said, "No, I don't."

224

"Not a serious question," Jack said, realizing he had hit a nerve. "Something I read once was about one of three sisters with those names."

"Really?" Lorina said. "It is an unusual name. Did you find a cabin?"

"Yes, thanks," Jack said. "And I can probably find it again."

"Let me show you around properly," Lorina said. "I can talk you through what we have here."

"Sounds good," Jack said.

Lorina nodded and set off.

"This is, or was, a standard military T3 shuttle," she began. "After decommissioning, Isis converted it into a survey vehicle. The survey companies maintain their vehicles to a high standard, and I think all it needs, externally, is to apply a radar-absorbent coating."

"Okay," Jack said. "If this is a shuttle, do we have one of the big ones, an IST thing, up in orbit for the inter-stellar stuff and the retroverse?"

"This one is retroverse capable, which is unusual."

"Okay," Jack said, "melanie told me about the retroverse and SQUID and some of that other stuff. I didn't understand it, even though she made my brain bleed, but I get the general idea."

"So, you know retro capable T3s are rare," Lorina said. "There are only two modified in this way; there was never an actual need for such a vehicle."

"Oh. Why not?" Jack asked.

"Terrans have those car things," Lorina said. "But for long journeys, they use airliners, rather than strapping wings onto a car. This is the equivalent of strapping wings and an engine onto a bus. It is totally useless for anything but this mission."

"Okay," Jack said.

"Sorry, this must all be difficult for you."

"What must?"

"All of it. Learning a whole new culture from scratch."

"Yes, I suppose so. The thing is, I'm not going to know a lot of stuff Gaians grow up with, so you'll have to be a little patient."

"No problem, sir... Jack. I need to remember that I need to explain things like military T3s and not just assume, you know."

"Yeah, I appreciate it," Jack said. "But I already like the idea that we can go from here to wherever we want without the need to use a transport vehicle like the *Encounter*."

"It will make life easier."

"I assume these aren't normally allowed into civilian hands?"

"Normal T3s, yes. Survey companies love them, so the military sells them their old ones.

"But not those like this one," she shrugged. "As I said, there are only two, and nobody knows where the other one is. melanie says she does, but..." She shrugged again.

"Okay," Jack said. "I suppose we ought to get on with our tour of inspection. I saw a circular corridor to a cabin and back outside, but that's all."

"Okay, then we shall start with the lower deck," Lorina said and set off in front of Jack around the corridor.

"Er, did you get kicked or something during the struggle?"

"No. Why?"

"I thought you were limping slightly," Jack said.

"Oh, that," Lorina said. "It's an old war wound."

"But it can't be that old a war wound," Jack said.

Flattery, Lorina thought, perhaps to cover up that you were checking out my butt.

"I broke my leg when I was twenty. That's about twelve in Terran years, and it wasn't set correctly. The doctors had to re-break it, then reset it."

"Twelve. That's young for war wound," Jack said while busy thinking of new topics so that he didn't keep digging.

"Yes. The Gaian army puts us in the front-line at nine."

"Yeah, I bet," Jack laughed.

The next door was open, and they walked into HOLD 2.

Miguel and Gary stood amongst the cases and sacks that melanie had brought down in the shuttle, trying to triage it all before putting it away.

"Another hold?" he said.

"It is," Lorina said. "There are six holds in total. There are normally seven, but one is now a hangar space for two fliers."

"What's a flier?" Jack asked.

"A small flying truck, I suppose you could call them, about eight meters long. They are for atmospheric use, but they can handle short extra-atmospheric journeys. We haven't checked them out yet."

"They'll come in useful," Jack said.

Several cases were open in the hold and the contents scattered around.

"Our friends from last night, I take it?" Jack asked.

226

"Yes. They were looking for a vault that is in one of the other holds. They didn't find it, by the way."

"Good. What was in the safe?"

"The keys for the main armaments," Lorina said.

"Which are?"

"Nobody wants heavy weapons falling into the wrong hands. So, each one has a key that is shipped separately.

"The weapons arrive shortly, with the others. Once fitted and wired in, we enter the keys, and everything operates as it should."

"Okay," Jack said. "So, why did the other guys want them?"

"I suspect they thought melanie was bringing the weapons. Or that they were already here. The weapons and the keys together would be worth a lot of money somewhere like the Jericho system."

"Or, I suppose, how about they were planning on stealing the whole shuttle?" Jack asked.

"Possible. These are easy to fly, and once into space, there is a crude, in-built, RAI to take it through the retroverse."

"Ah, I heard of them," Jacks said. "Pronounced like 'rye' and it means Restricted Artificial Intelligence."

"Very good," Lorina said. "Where did you come across that?"

"The pilot on the shuttle up to *Encounter* told me about them. She said they usually docked the shuttle, but she liked to dock manually on occasions to keep her hand in."

"That's the one," Lorina said.

"So, what would a shuttle like this be worth?" Jack asked.

"You could buy your own planet. Not an inhabited one, and it might not be exactly idyllic, but it would be your own."

"That much, huh?"

"Yes."

"Okay," Jack said. "And, what's this other stuff in here?"

"A lot of it is what melanie brought with her, materials for building new bulkheads, furniture, bedding...."

"Probably crushed after our journey," Jack interrupted.

"Yes, I hoped that would help," Lorina said.

"Then I have you to thank for saving my spine," Jack said.

"Sort of," Lorina said and looked back at the contents of the hold. "There are food packs, clothing, medical supplies, light weapons and ammunition, some electronic computers—for some reason—and spare parts. The rest arrives on *Valiant Sky*.

"We also have our personal weapons, of course, and a few other hand and assault guns."

"Okay," Jack said. "Onwards and upwards."

They walked back into the corridor. On the wall opposite was a logo, a five-armed, left-facing swastika, with characters at each of the arms' tip.

"What's that?" Jack asked.

"The transliterated version of the LiRo corporation logo. They make the main generator, the generator interface, the rabbit-punch, SQUID, and MAM propulsion systems. Although it's not all in there. Some of it is under the floor."

"melanie explained enough of that to make my brain itch," Jack said. "As far as I'm concerned, that's the engine room. Do we get a chief engineer called 'Scotty'?"

"No," Lorina said, shaking her head slowly, "and if we did, I would trade him in for Geordi La Forge because LeVar Burton is well fit."

"Yes, okay," Jack said with a grin. "Where next?"

"Do you want to see the vault they were looking for?"

"Why not?"

They walked around the corridor to a door marked "HOLD 6" and entered. A glossy black cube sat in one corner with a few tools scattered about.

"The vault, I suppose?" Jack said.

"Yes, and their attempts to break into it. You'd think they'd know better. It is impossible to get into a vault of that type with brute force. They just implode and destroy themselves and anything inside them."

"Why should they know better?"

"People like them all know about Gaian vaults."

Looking around, he saw a six-wheeled military vehicle, an armored personnel carrier by the look of it, sitting against the far wall. "Oh good, we got us some wheels," he said.

"We have," Lorina said with a giggle.

"Okay," Jack said, "That's my fix of cargo holds; what else is there?"

"We can look at the upper deck," Lorina said, leading the way forward to the stairs and a small freight elevator behind the front airlock.

The upper deck was a little less military in its décor, with a dark red floor covering and cream rather than gray walls. All part, Jack suspected, of its cover as a surveyor's vehicle.

Lorina explained that there were twenty cabins, each about three meters square, around the upper deck's outer circumference.

"We can squeeze three or four into a cabin," she said as she set off.

"How many are you expecting?" Jack asked in alarm.

"Twelve specialists are arriving the day after tomorrow," Lorina said. "They will then form the search party. When we find the base, we will bring in extra Aetherian soldiers and recruit Terran troops to help us take it."

"If you don't know where this base is," Jack said, "where are you going to start?"

"There are some probabilities that experts back on Aetheria have put forward," Lorina said. "So, where would you look?"

Jack laughed. "It has been a while since I needed to figure out where an alien race might hide their base on Earth. As I recall, I was six and decided that it was probably behind the oak tree because I could see Paul Smith's shoe sticking out."

"Even so," Lorina said. "I would be interested in finding out how you would approach this. Sometimes hearing a different perspective can be enlightening. Things that you would think of that I would not. Maybe narrow it down to a continent or two."

"Okay," Jack said. "I don't suppose you have any idea how many Nel there are in this base of theirs?"

"No," Lorina said. "But melanie has an intelligence asset inside the base who estimates it could be up to five thousand."

"Just a thought," Jack said. "I'm sort of new to this, but couldn't melanie ask her intelligence asset where they are?"

"You know what?" Lorina said. "I bet that never occurred to melanie. Problem solved."

"I take it you were being sarcastic," Jack said.

"You think?" Lorina said. "melanie's source believes that only a few transport flier pilots know where it is. Everybody else just gets delivered."

"Yeah, I should've thought that through," Jack said.

"No reason you should," Lorina said. "I'm sorry I was sarcastic."

"No need to apologize," Jack said. "I really should've thought it through, but if it is five thousand holed-up in there...."

He paused and stared at the wall for several seconds.

"Okay," Jack said eventually. "But this is straight off the top of my head, so no laughing."

"I swear I won't laugh," Lorina said.

"Probably best you prefix everything I say with 'probably'," Jack said, "but if the Nel were average height, I'd look in the middle of a big city with excellent transport connections to the rest of the world. So, Manhattan or, better yet, London."

"A city?"

"Yes, and a big one," Jack said. "The bigger the population, the easier to hide. I've been doing it for years."

"melanie found you," Lorina said.

"Yes, she did," Jack said. "Why can I not rid myself of the suspicion that melanie cheated?"

"I've no idea," Lorina said with a broad smile. "So why is London better? It's on an island off Europe. Why not New York?"

"Either would do, but London is centrally placed in the northern hemisphere. Europe, Asia, and Africa are to the east, America to the west. Look at the Earth from the other side of the globe, directly opposite London, and it's all sea, no land."

"Then, why not Paris? It's on the mainland."

"London is the biggest city in Europe. Moscow and Istanbul, which aren't really in Europe, are bigger but have their own problems. London is almost three times bigger than Berlin, which comes in at number two. Paris is tiny; it has a quarter of the population of London."

"Anyway, that doesn't apply as the Nel aren't average height," Jack said. "Which means they need somewhere far from the madding crowd, so I think they would hide the base in the US, for several reasons. They will need a mix of wide-open spaces and extensive road networks, and they will need reasonable freedom of movement."

"Why will they need these roads and freedom of movement?"

"Feeding five thousand people means moving a lot of produce."

"Using the technology used in space vehicles, they could recycle much of the food they need," Lorina said.

"You just put me off eating ever again," Jack said, looking green.

"We don't," Lorina said. "The Nel do, but you have a point about the roads. So, not bad, you have it down to one continent."

"I'm not done yet," Jack said. "I think they'd go for somewhere out in the middle, so Wyoming, Colorado, South Dakota, Nebraska or Kansas, but I'd need to look at a map first."

"Down to five states," Lorina said.

"If you stop putting 'probably' in front and put 'possibly', I'd say Colorado."

"Interesting," Lorina said. "Can you get closer?"

"Maybe if I had Google," Jack said and laughed. "No. Not really. Well, sort of. Finding large numbers of very tall people might not be that difficult. Newspapers and the internet can reveal all kinds of things.

"That's where I'll start, but, as I said, that's only off the top of my head."

"Well," Lorina said. "I'm certainly not laughing."

They had stopped walking and were standing outside a door opposite the cabins. Lorina slid it open with the touch of a button and said, "This is our infirmary with a semi-autonomous operating suite attached. It's new, and that certainly wasn't left behind by the surveyors."

The next few doors revealed a gym for which all the equipment was in one of the holds, then in rapid succession, two offices, a meeting room, and a mess-room. The last of these had five booths, each made up of six of the airline-style seats Jack had encountered before.

"Serves a double purpose," Lorina said. "We can use it for rough take-offs as well as a mess-room."

"Excellent," Jack said as they continued around the corridor. "It's not as bad in here as I thought it was going to be. I think this will come in useful."

"This," Lorina said, opening a door, "is the weapons control room, commonly known as 'the turret'."

Inside the small room were just two seats and enough screens and controls to keep even the most jaded Hollywood science-fiction movie buffs satisfied.

"Wow," Jack said and sat in one of the seats. He examined everything but, Lorina was pleased to note, touched nothing.

"Just the flight deck left," Lorina said. "I kept that until last." Her grin suggested it would be something special.

Lorina opened the door, and Jack's jaw dropped. "Wow," he said. "You know, I really must stop saying 'wow', it is really dumb coming from someone of my age."

The flight deck was even better than the one in the shuttle going up to *Encounter*.

He climbed into the center seat of the three seats cantilevered into the hemispherical black room, resisting the temptation to make the spaceship noises he'd gleaned from *Star Wars* and *Star Trek*.

"Having fun?" melanie said, walking in behind them.

"Too right," Jack said. "I like this. Can I have the other one?"

"You find it, and you can have it," melanie said. "Meanwhile, get some sleep, and we will all meet around eighteen hundred hours."

"If you are sure, boss?" Lorina said. "Everything that was outside is now inside and all the detection systems operating."

"I am sure everything is as it should be," melanie said. "Now, go get some sleep."

IST *Valiant Sky*, en route to Romstrum
12:15 GST

Greta Kaninchen watched the display screen, and as the spike appeared, she hit the button on her compad.

"Did it work?" Georgia asked.

"Probably," Greta said. "Those transmitters don't take that much power when the message is small."

"What did you say?"

"'A aboard'."

"Is that all?"

"What should I have put? 'Hi, mom, having a great time. By the way, you'll never guess, your other daughter, that psycho bitch Adriana is on board as well. What high jinx we will all have. Love and kisses, Greta. PS. Georgia says, Hi.'"

Georgia laughed.

"This is not funny, you cretin," Greta said.

"Really? I thought watching you back down to Zara Chang was quite amusing," Georgia said.

"Why didn't mother have you put down at birth?" Greta said.

"I sometimes wonder as well," Georgia said wistfully.

Shuttle *SV 3-8749*, Romstrum 3
16:50 GST

Lorina pinged melanie's office as she walked towards the door, and it slid silently open.

232

"I just love what you've done with the place," Lorina said as she walked in. The lighting ceiling, white walls and charcoal gray flooring were factory fresh. There was a metal and plastic desk, with nothing on it. Behind the desk stood one metal and plastic chair, with four identical chairs in front. Set in the wall were the doors to a built-in closet.

"Did you get your luggage?"

"I did."

"We haven't swept anywhere yet, as you might have guessed," Lorina said.

"No need in here," melanie said, sitting behind the desk and waving Lorina towards a guest chair. "There is an automatic sweeper installed, and it has dealt with the twenty-two bugs in place."

"Good," Lorina said, still standing. "I see that damned picture is in the usual place."

"It is, now sit down," melanie said.

"I was putting off the horrible reality of sitting in your office," Lorina said as she dropped into a chair, then wriggled to get comfortable.

melanie looked across at the one person in the universe she trusted implicitly, putting on her regular, almost statutory, protest at melanie's notoriously uncomfortable guest chairs.

What could she ever have seen in her?

Lorina was the scruffiest soldier in GCID; there were always bits of her uniform missing or undone or replaced by non-standard items. She never sat up straight, preferring to loll around, giving others the impression that her mind was tuned to a different station.

She was highly intelligent. Some likened her mind to a steel trap, but melanie disagreed. That was something that clamped down from nowhere. Lorina's intellect was a fluffy, woolly blanket that flowed with heavy oil viscosity in and around everyone in her team. She knew what was going on, she planned for every contingency, and she knew people far better than they would ever credit. She was usually one step ahead. Yet, despite all that, she was notoriously lousy at chess and poker.

Perhaps because of this weakness, within her command everybody respected and loved her. Although she had made more than her allotted number of powerful enemies, few of them would ever risk doing anything about it.

melanie knew, although she had trouble with the basic concept, that Lorina was her friend.

Lorina's capture on arrival on Romstrum had confused melanie a little. But, she reasoned, Lorina wasn't a field operative. She and Miguel, and occasionally Gary, had worked together to organize and plan melanie's missions for a long time, and they were good at it. They just weren't ready for a gang of thugs.

"What do you think?" melanie said when the wriggling had gone on long enough.

"I think I hate the chairs in your office," Lorina said. "No. I know I hate the chairs in your office. Where do you get them, some off-grid BDSM store?"

"What do you think of Jack?"

"Hmmm." Lorina said. "He is... odd."

"In what way?"

"I told him we were looking for the Nel base of operations on Earth.

"His response was that if the Nel were normal height, he'd look in New York or London. But as they aren't, he'd look in Colorado."

"Really," melanie said. "It took a team of Aetherian experts three days to come up with the same answer. He took seconds?"

"So, I asked him that, having figured out roughly where the base might be, how would he go about finding it, and he said something about a goggle or..."

"Google," melanie said.

"Google it was," Lorina continued. "But he also said, 'that's where I'll start.' Which was odd."

"You think he might be interested in helping us?"

"Possibly. Either that or he is considering going after the Nel on his own."

"I doubt that," melanie said.

"Normally, so would I, but he asked the sort of questions that someone who, deep down, thinks we are all total idiots and was planning on stealing a T3 shuttle might ask.

"I am probably totally wrong, but we will need to keep him under surveillance."

"Understood," melanie said. "A pity, as he might be of some use.

"Until now, my only interest had been saving Sarah and Benjamin's son, but he dealt with one of the Bellachi thugs who went after Amrita and him, and his mind might just be an asset."

"It might," Lorina said. "But give him a meaningful role. Put him in command of a project."

"You may have something," melanie said. "Except, Jack is not good with people. He is a bit of a loner, but not in the romantic fictional hero way, more the borderline sociopath way."

"I didn't pick up on that, and nor did Amrita, from what I can see."

"He likes and trusts women," melanie said. "From the reports I am now reading, he has never had a male friend. He cannot stand gatherings. Four or five people he can handle, but more than that, it's difficult for him."

"We'll think of something," Lorina said.

"We will," melanie said. "Anything else?"

"Yes," Lorina said. "This was odd. About twelve years ago, you asked me to read those books you like. I only managed the first one, *Alice in Wonderland*. They were for children, and I would rather read Dostoevsky's complete works, in Russian, than a children's book."

"You can't read Russian," melanie said.

Lorina shrugged, "And your point is?"

"I might dispute they were for children," melanie said. "The first one was, apparently, written for a child, but I suspect he also wrote them to be appreciated by adults."

"I'll take your word for it," Lorina said. "But I also read one of the notebooks you gave me, and it mentioned that Carroll had written them for a girl called Alice Liddell. I assume that's the child who you meant he wrote them for?"

melanie nodded.

"Okay, well, Alice had two sisters called Lorina and Edith. I honestly can't remember much else from any of it, but obviously I remember the coincidence of the names.

"So, I was a little surprised when Jack asked me if I had sisters called Edith and Alice. Remembering your obsession with those books, I thought I should mention it."

"Quite right," melanie said. "Jack has the books. I put them with the rest of his parents' possessions after Bianca had them murdered. When he escaped from the orphanage, he took them with him. I am rather pleased that he hadn't sold them. Although it is possible, he tried, and nobody would buy them."

"What is it with those books?" Lorina said. "I know you met with somebody in New York back in the dark ages, and he told you where and when to find the books, but why are you convinced that they are relevant to the search for Caeloeterra?"

"Because he told me they were."

FiT: THE EIGHTEENTH

McSorley's Bar, 15 East 7th Street NY. NY.
11:55 EST Sunday 17th March 1929
(15:55 GST Twoday 2.1.2695)

"Hello, Bill," melanie said as softly as she could in the noise of laughter, shouting and exuberant chatter. "You wanted to see me?"

Bill McSorley gave the glass a last wipe with his grubby apron and turned. It took a second glance before he realized who it was.

"Mary, mother of God, yez'll get me shot," he said as quietly as he could, "yez know women ain't welcome. An' yez talks like a feckin' tan so ye does."

"First," melanie said, "you called for me. Second, it is me and not some tourist, so you can turn down the brogue. And third, I do look like a man."

"A bit," Bill agreed, "but not like the fellas we'ze gets in here you don't," his accent segueing from Ireland to lower east side New York. "More like one of them phonies on Broadway."

melanie looked around; it never changed. Probably never would. Pages and scraps from newspapers and an eclectic mix of art covered the walls. A pair of Houdini's handcuffs forever linked onto the bar rail. Just along the bar, Ed Cummings sat on a rickety stool glowering at the wishbones, waiting for those who had not returned eleven years earlier.

As to be expected, on the day for those who were, or wanted to be, Irish, the place was full. A day to quench a thirst, and some were already close to drowning. One had already vomited, and they had emptied a sawdust bucket over the evidence.

"But sober," melanie said.

"They're all sober," Bill said. "We only got near-beer. Fucking prohibition. 'Course, da fucking guineas is doin' okay."

melanie laughed. "Sure, you have. And not a drop of poitín has passed their lips?"

"As if," Bill said, cracking a small smile.

"So, what have you got for me that you called me from the other side of the galaxy."

"So, is that where the fuckin" City of Angels is at?" Bill said.

237

"Might as well be," melanie said. "Sixty-four hours on the train to Chicago and another fifteen from there to here. I left home last Wednesday."

"Yeah?" Bill said. "I didn't know where you was at. But this guy was a bit insistent, if you knows what I mean, so I just put out the call."

"And what does he want?"

"Jeez, I dunno," Bill said. "He just said that he needed to talk to melanie and that I knew how to get in touch."

"Okay, I'm here, where is he?" melanie asked.

"He just showed," Bill said and melanie turned.

He was short, humanoid and wore a bright green suit of breeches over white stockings and buckled shoes. His tailcoat was outside a patterned vest and bow tie, also green, and all over a white shirt. He had red hair, a full beard, a top hat and a huge smile clamped around a clay pipe.

"You brought me here to meet a leprechaun?" melanie said.

"It's New York, it's St Patrick's day. What didya think he's gonna be dressed as?" Bill said, allowing the Irish to rear its head as he added, "A feckin black'n'tan bastard?"

"Good point," melanie said.

"melanie, hello," the leprechaun said with a cliché Irish accent.

"Hello," melanie said. "And you are?"

"My name is Fearganainm Buile-Hatadéantóir."

Bill snorted and walked away muttering.

"No, it's not," melanie said. "'Fearganainm' is Irish for something like, 'a nameless man'. The rest makes little sense."

"But it is the name by which Ranolde Baker and Elizabeth Grove, amongst others, knew me."

melanie shrugged. "Then it will suffice," she said.

"I am pleased to hear it," Fearganainm said, still smiling around the pipe.

"And what do you want?"

"Nothing," Fearganainm said.

melanie saw his mouth move. His lips made the right shapes for the words he was speaking. And they would continue doing so, but in a different conversation. There were stray ears, and eyes that could read lips, abroad.

"I understand you are having some difficulty with whom you call the Venatori?" melanie heard through her neurolink.

"A little," melanie said by the same medium.

"Maybe I can be of some assistance."

"Possibly. Do you want to be and what will it cost me?"

"I do and not a brass farthin'. Although I'm not sure I am not insulted by the implication."

melanie smiled. "Then tell me how you can help."

"First, I have now installed onto your database a set of coordinates and a date in the year nineteen sixty-nine, or twenty-seven fifty-four in the little-improved Gaian calendar. There you will meet a man with books that you should study.

"Second, in the Terran year nineteen seventy-eight, the Gaian year twenty-seven sixty-nine, a woman who will become known to you as Minolar Karachovski will invite you to a social gathering in this city. You must accept.

"I will be there, in both cases," melanie said.

"I sincerely hope so.

"Third, I have also installed a list of sixty-six Gaians, Aethereans, Terrans and one other, thirty-seven male and twenty-nine female, onto your database. The Gaians and Aethereans you will need to recruit early, to create your core team. The others will come along later. I will make sure of it."

"None of these people have been born yet," melanie said, after reviewing the list. "Except one, and she's long dead."

The leprechaun looked at melanie the way adults look at children who have said something outstandingly dumb.

"No," he said, patiently, "of course they haven't been born yet."

"And I need these people for what purpose?"

"To complete your true goal. To wipe the Venatori out of existence. All of us."

"Not that easy if I don't know where they are," melanie said.

"Caeloeterra," he said.

"Which is where?"

"You will find it all in good time. It's not that far, but then, it is a long way away."

"That's all I need," melanie snapped. "An Irish riddle."

"Not a riddle, when you read *Foundation and Empire*."

melanie paused. "No such book," she said.

"There will be," the leprechaun laughed, then disappeared without even a puff of smoke, which, it being St Paddy's Day in New York City, didn't seem that odd at all.

FiT: THE THIRTY-SIXTH

GCID HQ, Zone A4, Gaia
10:20 GST Oneday 5.1.2809
(Wednesday 5th December 2001)

"Sergeant Korenjic, do stand at ease," melanie said and looked up from the screen she was pretending to read. "Ah. You already are, I see, after a fashion."

melanie looked the woman up and then down.

"Sit down, Sergeant," melanie said, indicating a chair on the other side of the desk. Korenjic stomped forward and flopped into the chair as if even that were an effort.

"I see you are Earth born and thirty-seven years old here on Gaia. So, you'd be twenty-one on Earth.

"Twenty-one used to be the age of majority back there. They used to say that at twenty-one, you got 'the key to the door'. That you were an adult and all grown-up. Were you considering doing that, growing up, sometime soon, Sergeant?"

"What?" Korenjic snapped.

"It wasn't a hard question," melanie said. "According to your files, your level of competence in English is high enough to understand a simple question. Are you going to grow up sometime soon, or have you decided to be a childish brat forever?"

Lorina Korenjic said nothing, just glowered.

"Apparently, you also have anger management issues, especially if someone mentions your limp. Do you have a limp, Sergeant Korenjic?"

Lorina Korenjic said nothing.

"I asked you a question, Sergeant. Do you have a limp?"

"Yes," Korenjic said quietly.

"What? I couldn't hear you," melanie said.

"Yes," Korenjic said a little louder.

"'Yes', what?"

"Yes, ma'am."

"No. What is it you have?"

"Yes, I have a limp."

"Better," melanie said. "Stand and walk up and down."

Korenjic dragged herself to her feet and walked across the small room and then back the other way.

"Yes, you do; you have a limp. It is very slight, but there is a limp. Sit down."

Korenjic sat.

"Are you going to attack me for mentioning your limp?" melanie said.

"No."

"Is that because, if you do, I can smear you all over the walls?"

"It's a factor," Korenjic said.

"So, when one of your colleagues, who is not so capable of defending herself, has the temerity to mention this minor defect, you feel justified in attacking her and, without extensive and costly surgery, leaving her scarred for life?"

"Briony Sigurðardóttir is a stupid, vicious bitch and deserved everything she got."

"What she got was an immediate transfer to officer school," melanie said. "That must have put her in her place."

"If you are going to kick me out of GCID, just do it," Korenjic said.

"Would you like me to do that? Is that what causes all this juvenile behavior? You want to be kicked out of GCID because you haven't got the guts to quit?"

"No, that's not it at all," Korenjic yelled.

"Really? Because it would fit. You are a coward, Sergeant Korenjic. You attack a weaker colleague because she said something unkind, yet you won't attack me for making the same comment, and you want me to fire you because you are too weak to leave. Those are the actions of a coward."

"I am not a coward," Korenjic yelled, leaping to her feet. "It wasn't just one comment from one stupid girl, it was weeks of listening to her and her friends giggling away, making comments about me, my family, my sisters, and my limp. That day I had had enough. It just happened to be about my limp, and if the opportunity comes, I'll attack her and her three friends again and finish the job I started."

melanie sat, saying nothing. Korenjic was close to tears but had enough control that she wouldn't cry, not in front of melanie.

"But you still want me to find the easy way out of GCID for you?" melanie said, eventually.

"No, I don't. I want to stay in GCID because right now, that offers me the best chance of finding out what happened..." She stopped.

"'What happened'?"

Korenjic said nothing.

"'What happened'?" melanie repeated.

No response.

"'What happened', to whom?" melanie said.

"A personal matter," Korenjic said. "If you want me out, so be it. I'll go to Aetheria and join up there. Just get on with it."

"Let me see," melanie said and went back to the screen. "An impressive academic record. You enjoyed literature, in part. Although you seemed to believe Dickens was a hack who would write Terran soaps today."

"I still do," Korenjic muttered.

"And more recently, an exercise to write a 'school report' for William Shakespeare..."

"Oh," Korenjic said.

"...that reads, 'Will is a little oik with severe oral hygiene problems who has yet to realize that writing is not about using other people's plots and making up your own words, but the other way around.' Which is a little harsh and raises two questions. Where did you get the word 'oik'? and how do you know about his halitosis?"

"One of the instructors used the word, and I tracked it down. It's a British word meaning, er, unpleasant, or uncouth."

"Yes, I know what it means, and I have a shrewd idea who the instructor might have been. And the other reference?"

"He lived in Elizabethan England. I thought it was a given."

"How coincidental that around the time you wrote this, they suspected your friend Tamara Finkel of looking at some records where she had no business. Those records concerned the same period of Terran history."

Korenjic shrugged.

"As well as English, you seem to have done very well in academic subjects such as math, chemistry, and physics and physical activities, despite your gruesome disfigurement, but you are not a team player unless you are the captain. You are also a poor loser. Militarily, you rated high in virtually everything, apart from discipline. To paraphrase your commanding officer, you are undisciplined and resent authority in every form. There is a note suggesting this may be a family trait.

242

"Reading this, the only reason you made sergeant is that it is an automatic promotion; otherwise, you would still be a private or a civilian. And I understand why you were not considered for officer training. You set a lousy example," melanie said while making a show of tapping at the screen.

"Yeah, good. That it? Can I go now? There's a freighter leaving for Aetheria this evening, and I need to pack."

"No, Lieutenant Korenjic, you cannot go. I have a job for you."

"What is calling me 'lieutenant' supposed to achieve?"

"It is to indicate your new rank. Nothing more," melanie said.

Korenjic laughed. "Bullshit."

"Is that what you think?" melanie said.

"Of course it is. Why would you make me a lieutenant? You just got off telling me it surprised you I made sergeant and why I won't make lieutenant and then tell me I am a lieutenant. And I don't think you can just make me a lieutenant anyway."

"First of all," melanie said, "I could make you a general if that's what I needed. But I don't need a general. I need a lieutenant. And you are it."

"With all the faults you just mentioned, like cowardice?" Korenjic said.

"Yes," melanie replied. "Although I know as well as you that you are not a coward."

"Why? Why do you need me?"

"Apart from my personal interest in you and your siblings, I have someone in human resources who keeps a watchful eye on who is passing through our organization. I asked him to assess you. He recommended that I either take you on as my number two or send you to a prison planet."

"I didn't know we had prison planets."

"We don't," melanie said. "That was merely his recommendation. I would have had you executed. But I decided you would make an excellent number two."

"I still don't see why?" Korenjic said. "You are right. I stood no chance of getting into officer training."

"No, you didn't," melanie said and pointed at her office door. "But you see, out there, the people they send to officer training are those who will make good lieutenants. That is, lieutenants who obey orders and pass them on. They do not take risks, they

243

do not think, because they have more senior officers for that, and they do not command, because they have field sergeants for that.

"What they are there for is to act as an interface between a commander and the NCOs. So, the commander doesn't have to speak directly to a non-officer. It's something that somehow we have picked up from Terran armies, and they do it like that because it made sense in their thirteenth century."

"And in here?" Korenjic said.

"In here, I want somebody who takes risks, thinks, commands, cheats, lies, takes no shit, and gets things done. I want you."

"I don't cheat, and I don't lie," Korenjic said. "Often," she added.

"Don't worry, I'll teach you," melanie said.

"You really want me as one of your officers?"

"No, I want you as my officer, singular. You will be my closest aide and confidante. You will be party to what my actual mission is, and you will help me complete that mission."

"And I will be a lieutenant? For real?"

"Sort of," melanie said and watched Korenjic sag. "We will list you as a lieutenant and, when necessary, you will wear a lieutenant's uniform. You will carry out all the duties and responsibilities of a lieutenant-commander and have the power of a full commander. Your salary will be that of a lieutenant-commander."

Korenjic stiffened. "This is a trick, isn't it? Another wind up for the gimp? You aren't the commander at all, just some skinny bitch from the catering school."

melanie stood up.

"Means nothing," Korenjic said. "You might be as tall as her, but there is no way that she is going to make me an offer like that."

"I understand you need me to prove that I am melanie," melanie said, coming around the desk. She reached out and grabbed Korenjic by the upper part of her standard jacket and lifted her straight up, leaning back as she did so to counterbalance the woman's weight, and kept lifting until Korenjic was at arm's reach above her head.

"I'd like to see some skinny bitch from catering do that," melanie said.

"Put her down, melanie, there are easier ways, you know," Alzena Gandalf said from the door. She was short for a Gaian, and perhaps a little thicker set. Reddish hair surrounded her face, and its imperious features were softened by a generous smile.

melanie lowered Korenjic to the floor.

"Ah," melanie said. "Another woman who knows the meaning of the word 'oik'."

"Naturally," Alzena said, before turning to Lorina and saying, "Remember me?"

"Yes," the now perplexed and shaken young woman said.

"You don't think I'm from the catering school, do you?" Alzena said.

"You might be, you have the build," melanie said.

"Ignore her," Alzena said.

"No, you're not from the catering school," Korenjic said. "You're Lieutenant Commander Gandalf of the Aetherean Intelligence Bureau."

"You know this because?"

"You were a guest lecturer at the school, and I caught one of your talks."

"Three of my talks," Alzena said.

"Yes, ma'am, three of your talks."

"And you stayed awake. Why?"

Lorina shrugged. "You were interesting."

"Although you didn't agree with everything I said?"

"No ma'am, not everything."

"But you agree with me that she," Alzena waved a hand in melanie's direction, "is the commander."

"Yes, ma'am, she is the commander," Lorina said and turned to melanie. "Sorry, ma'am."

"Unless we have company, do not call me ma'am."

"No, ma'am."

"Otherwise, it's 'melanie' or 'boss'."

"Let me tell you a bit about how it works around here," Alzena said. "The bit about melanie's friend in HR is partly true, and that's how we get most of our people. You have been on our radar for a long time. Your whole family has. But we have not only been following your career for a long time, we have also been actively manipulating it."

"What? Why?"

"That you will figure out for yourself," melanie said. "And that way, you will understand and know that it is all the truth. My job is to lie and spread misinformation. If I tell you

245

everything, you will not believe me. You need to know the truth."

Lorina turned to Alzena, who smiled and nodded. "It's for real," Alzena said. "And my interview was a bit like this one, except for the lifting up off the ground bit. Thank God."

"Well, do you want it or not?"

"You don't get a choice," Alzena said. "Asking is a sort of nod to the normal world."

"Yes, boss," Lorina said. "Oh, yes, I want this. I have wanted this all my life."

"Good, you start now. Get your things and be back here in twenty minutes."

"Yes, boss," Lorina said and almost ran to the door. "You said the power of a commander, didn't you?"

"I did."

Lorina smiled and was gone.

"She'll do," Alzena said.

"Yes, she will do nicely," melanie said.

DAY SIXTEEN (Cont.)

Twoday 6.5.2834
Wednesday 15th February 2017

Jack walked into the hold to find Amrita, Gary, and Miguel sitting on two cases drinking coffee.

"Can I get you one?" Gary said.

"God, yes, please," Jack said. "The coven is in conference, so I thought I'd come and see what I could do down here."

"Not much," Miguel said. "We have made a start, but we will begin again tomorrow and pack away what we can and then get the rest tied down.

"We just need to create space for whatever comes in with the rest of the team and rig up a fast tie-down for that. Lorina says we are leaving as soon as the others arrive and that we might be in for a rough departure."

"Why does she expect a rough departure?" Jack asked.

"There is a Nel vehicle in the vicinity; it is more than possible they will attack as we leave, and we aren't armed at present."

"Okay," Jack said. "So, when are the others due?"

"Day after tomorrow, I think," Gary said as he handed Jack a mug of coffee.

"Is any of this yours?" Gary said, pointing at the pile of cases and boxes that melanie had brought with her.

"No," Jack said. "We left in a bit of a rush. I didn't have time to pack."

"Thought so," Miguel said. "All of this is the commander's stuff."

"Typical woman," Jack said. "Can't go away for the weekend without taking her entire wardrobe."

"Hey," Amrita said. "You have no idea how much I left behind on that freighter to help get you out of there."

Gary and Miguel both laughed.

"Now you are in trouble," Miguel said.

"Yeah, and I don't think anybody ever called the commander a 'typical woman' before," Gary added.

"Definitely not," Miguel said.

"So, what is it all?" Jack asked.

"Some will be her personal kit," Gary said. "The rest will be things she sourced on Earth. Which is a bit strange.

"You do know we are going back to Earth?" he added.

"Yes, I know," Jack said. "I'm going with you."

248

"Any idea what our plans are when we get there?" Miguel said.

"No," Jack said. "I'm only staying with you until we get back."

"Why is that?" Amrita said. She had that 'matron' tone again that Jack found so discomfiting.

"I haven't made a firm decision yet," Jack said, concentrating on a small area of the floor, "but I'm not sure it would work out if I stayed."

"It's your planet," Amrita said. "Don't you want to do something? Or are you just going to let the Nel do what they want?"

"I'm gonna do something," Jack said. "Right now, I don't know what, but I'll think of something."

"Yeah, but," Miguel said. "Lorina and I have been together five years, and she and melanie had been working on this for years when we met. Wouldn't it be easier to join with them rather than going alone?"

"Maybe," Jack said. "But, err, I dunno, I sort of prefer working alone."

"You think you could bring the Nel down single-handed?" Miguel said.

"Maybe," Jack said. "I'm an Earthling... Terran. I understand how things work there, and sometimes one person working alone can do more than a small army."

Shuttle *SV 3-8749*, Romstrum 3
17:00 GST

"He told you that the search for Caeloeterra was linked to three old books?" Lorina said. "At this point, a normal person would tell me what he said to persuade you of this, but it's never that easy with you. Is it?"

"No, it isn't," melanie said.

"Let me guess, there was a map of the galaxy tucked between the pages with a large "X" to mark the spot?"

"Not quite," melanie said. "I was told to go to the 32.7β sector on a specific date. I was told I would find a man with no memory who had those books."

"Yes, I know, and you found a drifting shuttle with a man, complete with no memory and the books. You then transformed that man with no memory into Benjamin Ashbow, Jack's father. Then what?"

"That I should study the books. Which I have done. There are a few odd coincidences in them, but nothing that suggests where Caeloeterra might be. However, their very existence is an anomaly, and it was that anomaly that pointed the way, eventually to Caeloeterra."

"How?" Lorina asked.

"That is a little contorted, I will admit," melanie said. "The books were, supposedly, written by Lewis Carroll and, supposedly, published by Macmillan in London. There is no record of anyone, anywhere, by that name who could have written those books. There is no record of the books themselves. Even Macmillan denies their existence."

"Long-shot here," Lorina said, "but could they have created them on another planet? It's the sort of thing that somebody on DV8 would dream up. Fake Terran antiquities."

"No," melanie said. "Analysis of the paper, ink, glue and leather shows the books all to be Terran late-nineteenth century. It is more likely fakes would be first editions, which would have a far higher value. The illustrations were supposedly by a contemporary artist called John Tenniel, and the art experts I have consulted, human and AI, are all of the opinion that Tenniel drew them."

"Meaning that they are genuine and were created on Earth," Lorina said, "but there is no record of them having been created on Earth."

"Exactly," melanie said. "There is no record of the books having been created on our Earth."

"Sounds like you really do have an anomaly there," Lorina said. "A bit like that poem? Jabber-something? Now, that was an anomaly all on its own."

"*Jabberwocky*," melanie said. "Yes, it was. That was in the second book, *Through the Looking Glass*. You said you only read the first book."

"It was in one of the notebooks," Lorina said. "I'm surprised you don't ..."

There was a long pause while Lorina stared fixedly at melanie.

"You just said, 'no record of the books having been created on our Earth', didn't you?" Lorina said. "You don't think they originated on this plane, do you?"

"No," melanie said.

"Do you have any hard evidence to suggest the books come from another plane?"

"I didn't," melanie said. "But I had my suspicions. Because an alternate plane fitted the available evidence. Because once you eliminate the impossible, whatever remains, no matter how improbable, must be the truth. Plus, the powers-that-be unofficially discouraged all research into alternate planes on Gaia."

"I'm a little confused," Lorina said. "Nobody else knows about these books. Just you, your best bud, Rufus Koenig, the team, perhaps, and me. That means Bianca doesn't know they exist, so why would Gaia block research into alternate planes?"

"Nothing to do with the books," melanie said. "They just don't want anybody else figuring out where they hid Caeloeterra."

FiT: THE TWENTY-FIRST

Shuttle SV 3-8749, Sector 32.7β.8A865β
11:55 GST Threeday 2.3.2754
(Tuesday 22nd July 1969)

Red Ball Explorer dipped out of the retroverse for three-point-five seconds, dropped the shuttle, and slipped back into the retroverse.

"External cams on, all sensors at extreme range and all clear, no, it's not," Sally Gomez, Captain of SV 3-8749, said.

"Is that some new definition of a report that hasn't made it into the manual yet?" Lieutenant Commander Caroline Hume asked quietly.

"No, ma'am," Sally said. "There are two vehicles out there."

"Wow," Caroline said. "Two? One would be a talking point for a few years, but two... Are they together?"

"No, ma'am. Opposite directions. One's an ILT, one of ours, which is odd. The other one, I didn't see it at first; it's just off-center from a noisy star, looks like another shuttle."

"Any transponder or IFF?"

"ILT info is coming in, ma'am, but nothing from the shuttle."

"Anything interesting?"

"The ILT is *Ballantyre*. From the data, it looks like it came out of retro at the same time as us, and is all powered up, ready to go back in. The other one seems to be drifting there, some power, but not engines."

"*Ballantyre* is a GCID vehicle," Caroline said. "Why is it dropping in and out of retro?"

"Looking for something I'd say," Sally said. "Who knows with the spooks?"

"Is the other one ours as well?" Caroline asked.

"No, ma'am. It's like a type two shuttle. Same mass, but different shape."

"Who else is around here?" Caroline said.

"No intel reports on any foreign incursions," Bradley Suzuki, ensconced in the turret, said over the comm. *"And we have both Gaian and Aetherean intel streams."*

"Illegally, I trust?" Caroline asked.

"Stupid question," Bradley muttered.

252

"Can *Ballantyre* see the shuttle?" Caroline asked.

"Possibly," Sally said. "This is a very dense sector, lots of crap from across the spectrum. But from where *Ballantyre* is sitting, the other vehicle could be masked by that noisy star."

"Only 'possibly', then?"

"'Fraid so. Spook boats have kit we not only can't get; we don't even know exists."

"So, we can't just fuck off around that star, saying we don't know about the shuttle?"

"Probably not," Sally said. "Why, is that an option?"

"Yeah, it's an option," Caroline said. "If GCID gets in on it, then we could spend the next year filling in forms."

"The power usage on the shuttle is about the level needed to keep basic habitation systems running. There could be crew," Sally said.

Caroline knew she had to think fast. If they had been out here alone, she would have made straight for the shuttle. But anything involving the Gaian government was bad news. The Gaian Central Intelligence Directorate was just like the government, but sneakier. She didn't want to get involved.

Sending *Ballantyre* a message and then leaving wouldn't do. They might just as well send the GCID a confession for every crime committed since they had banished the Venatori.

"Shit," she said out loud. "Call the shuttle on channels one-zero-one and six-zero-six; let's see what they have to say for themselves," Caroline said. "At the same time, call *Ballantyre* and tell them we just spotted this shuttle and are heading that way."

"Okey me dokey," Dyson Kelvin said from comms.

"Meanwhile, take us in closer, Sally. Not too close; I just want a look."

"Yes, ma'am," Sally said and turned the shuttle towards the distant vehicle.

"Do you want me to bring weapons to bear?" Bradley said.

"No," Caroline said. "Anyway, we don't have weapons. We only have one little meteor cannon, and once that starts to charge up, half the sector will know and if they are unfriendly, they'll flick straight back into the retro and shoot us up the ass."

"Okay, boss," Bradley said.

"I'm getting a response on one-zero-one," Dyson chipped in. *"Shall I feed it through?"*

"Yes, it seems like a good idea," Caroline said.

"Okay, boss."

Caroline waited and heard a voice say, *"Hello."*

"Hello," she responded. "This is Caroline Hume, Commander of the survey shuttle SV 3-8749. Who is that?"

"I have no idea," the voice said back. *"The tag on my suit says I am Julius Schutter, but I have no memories of who I am, or anything."*

"Is there anyone else on board?" Caroline said and flicked the microphone off while she spoke to Bradley. "Who's that spook you know in GCID?"

"Nobody, I'm all alone. And I have been here for six days as far as I can tell," Julius Schutter said.

"You mean, melanie?" Bradley said.

Flicking the microphone on, Caroline said, "Okay, Julius, we are about ten minutes away. Hang in there."

"Thank you," Julius said.

Caroline flicked off the microphone and said, "That's her, Bradley. Get her on the comm. I need to talk to her. I trust her a bit more than most of the GCID scum."

"You don't know her, so why do you trust her?" Bradley said.

"Because you do, you clugger," Caroline said and switched her attention to the main screen.

"I have melanie on the comm, boss," Bradley said.

"Thanks," Caroline said and switched to the comm channel that her call was on. "Commander, and how are we today?" she said.

"I am very well, Lieutenant-Commander Hume," melanie said.

"Good," Caroline said. "We are in Sector seven two..." She stopped as the realization hit her.

"Shit, you're on *Ballantyre*, aren't you?"

FiT: THE TWENTY-SECOND

ILT Ballantyre, **Sector 32.7β.8A865A**
11:55 GST Threeday 2.3.2754
(Tuesday 22nd July 1969)

"melanie, two minutes and we move to sub-sector 65β," amelia said over the comm.

"Thank you, amelia," melanie replied.

"Why do you do that?" Lieutenant Alzena Gandalf, sitting across the other side of the desk, asked. "Speak out loud, I mean."

"It's good manners," melanie said. "Using a neurolink to exclude another person is like those people who exclude another person by speaking to each other in a foreign language."

"That makes sense," Alzena said. "Although I'm not sure this, whatever it is, does."

"Would it please you to learn that it makes little sense to me, either?"

"No, that would make me very nervous."

"Then I suggest you do whatever it is you do to show that you are nervous."

"You still do not know why we are here?"

"No," melanie said. "Forty years ago, somebody gave me this date, and a set of coordinates, and suggested I be here."

"Forty years ago?"

"Yes."

"We are now in sub-sector 65β," amelia said over the comm. *"It's very crowded, and even our filters are having a hard time sorting out all the garbage.*

"What we have got is a T3 survey shuttle about five minutes away after the mother vehicle dropped out of the retroverse, from the readings. And I am now picking up its transponder data. It's a legitimate vehicle."

"Do you mean five minutes away direct?" melanie asked.

"No. For us both to emerge, that close would require a report to the Transport Safety Board."

"Is that bad?"

"Very, and I would have some difficulty explaining why we were here. Something we would all rather not contemplate."

255

"I understand," melanie said.

"And there might be something else beyond the shuttle, but there is too much noise to be sure."

"How far beyond the shuttle?" melanie asked.

"Another five minutes. Probably. Difficult to tell. It's sitting directly in front of a star producing high levels of radio transmission. The shuttle is off-center a little; they will be able to talk to it."

"Thanks, amelia," melanie said.

"Nothing else here; I'll take us to 661 in five minutes."

melanie paused then said, "amelia, stay in this sector a little longer. One of those vehicles might be what we are looking for."

"Of course," amelia said.

"What's up?" Alzena said.

"Not sure," melanie said. "But what are the chances of us popping up in a sector with another vehicle, any vehicle, let alone one of ours, five minutes away?"

"Astronomical?" Alzena said with a smile. It was an old joke. "And even more astronomical for there to be two."

"And what if I said that chance plays no part in this at all?" melanie said.

"I have Chief Surveyor Hume on the comm," amelia said. *"The call is from that shuttle out there."*

"Thank you, amelia," melanie said. *"Chief Surveyor Hume, this is melanie."*

"Commander, and how are we today?" Caroline said.

"I am well, Chief Surveyor Hume," melanie said.

"Good," Caroline said. *"We are in Sector seven two...."* She stopped as the realization hit her.

"Shit, you're on Ballantyre, *aren't you?"*

"Yes, I am," melanie said.

"Okay, there's a coincidence," Caroline said. *"Thing is, do you also know why we called you, or do I go through it to maintain the coincidence illusion?"*

"Go through it because I don't know what you have."

"Okay, then," Caroline said, unconvinced. *"Well, we have an unidentified vehicle sitting here. It's the size of a type two shuttle, but it's not either Gaian or Aetherian. There is, or so he claims, one person aboard, a Julius Schutter. He sounds human, but who can tell with damned AIs these days. Beggin' your pardon, an' all."*

"Might be of interest," melanie said. "You get all salvage and a special payment to preserve confidentiality..."

"*Hush money?*"

"If that's what you want to call it, then please do so," melanie said. "The money is for you and your crew. Mention of this to the crew of the *Red Ball Explorer* will undoubtedly result in them wanting the larger share. It will also annoy me. And, be advised, we make payments depending on the worth of what needs to be protected. It could be a lot of money, and when we have paid out, we expect it to be a once-only payment. There is no second installment, and should it come to my notice that the terms of the original agreement are not being met, I make sure that there is no future revival of interest in the subject. Ever."

"*I think you have made your point,*" Caroline said.

"Good. We will be with you in a few minutes; please tell Schutter to keep calm and that we will transfer his vehicle into our freight bay."

"*Not a problem,*" Caroline said. "*When do we get paid?*"

"Salvage as soon as I get there. The rest will take an hour beyond getting the vehicle into our bay."

***

An hour later, the shuttle was in *Ballantyre's* main freight bay. The medics had removed the sole, somewhat bewildered passenger and were now trying to tease out any memories of who he might be, but with little success.

The technicians had descended and were passing a constant stream of reports that the shuttle was totally clean. There was no trace of DNA beyond that of the passenger. Even the sewerage recycling had failed to reveal anything. Apart from the low-level computers that maintained the craft's orbit and environment, every AI and computer was clean. The two working systems' software was based on a pirated version of a system openly available on Jericho and other undesirable locations.

The signs in the corridors were all in English. There were a couple of syntax differences from the version used on Earth, Gaia and Aetheria, but slight.

As Neil Armstrong and Buzz Aldrin had only made their first tentative steps onto their moon two days earlier, melanie was confident that it had not originated on Earth. Problematically, it had not originated on Gaia or Aetheria either. It had design similarities with shuttles from both, and some components were

257

identical to the extent that those with the same part numbers were currently fitted to other shuttles.

melanie made her way around to the cabin with Julius Schutter's name on the door. It did not surprise her that the tiny room was immaculate. The bunk made, the closet doors closed and secured.

The bathroom through the cabin was equally spotless and looked as if it had never been used, suggesting the shuttle had arrived not long before Chief Surveyor Hume's *SV 3-8749* or *Ballantyre.*

On the desk sat a small pile of books. At the top, two hard cover notebooks in foolscap folio size, fractionally larger than either the European A4 or American legal pads, suggesting they were British in origin.

Each unlined page was covered in small but easily legible cursive handwriting with the occasional diagram or sketch. She wondered briefly if anyone on Gaia would recognize a pen if they saw it. These notebooks would take a while to read and digest, and now was neither the time nor the place.

Below them in the pile was a sheet of paper with a printed list of names and dates of birth. All of them in the future. melanie didn't need to read the list. She had memorized it when a man in a green top hat had met with her in McSorley's Bar in New York on Saint Patrick's Day 1929 and told her to be at this point in space, on this date.

Under the sheet of paper were three bound volumes. She opened the first and read the title before running it through *Ballantyre's* massive database. As she suspected, it found no match for a book called *Alice's Adventures in Wonderland,* nor a writer named Lewis Carroll.

DAY SIXTEEN (Cont.)

Twoday 6.5.2834

Wednesday 15th February 2017

"That one person might achieve a lot more working with a small team of specialists than on their own," Amrita said.

"I accept that," Jack said. "But it sort of depends on the one person, doesn't it?"

"I don't know," Amrita said. "Does it?"

"Yes, it does, when it's me," Jack said. He paused and looked around the room as if seeking inspiration but not finding it.

"I haven't had to talk about any of this since I was at school, and I find it difficult. But there are two factors here. The first is that I cannot handle large numbers of people."

He paused and said, "That doesn't quite explain it.

"I can sit in a theater or restaurant surrounded by strangers with no problem. I can mix with you three, but if Lorina and melanie came in, I would find it more difficult to speak. The thought of twelve people who all know each other being in the same room fills me with dread. It doesn't just make me apprehensive it terrifies me.

"Let me put that in perspective. I robbed banks on Earth. To do that, I got a job as a cleaner, working in the bank I was relieving of its ill-gotten gains. To steal the money, I used their computers when the staff had all gone home. Except, they don't all go home. There are security people, other cleaners, the occasional diligent employee working late. At any moment, they could have caught me, and I did that five or six nights a week for months at a time over three years. If they had caught me, I would have spent a long time in prison. Much of the time, I was frightened, but I dealt with it.

"Over the last few days, I traveled on spaceships, something I thought only existed in the movies. I went on a spacewalk, I met the Nel, I killed an assassin, and I have never killed anybody before, so I'm having a bit of a problem processing that. I rode a drop-shuttle, and I got to watch melanie shooting people in the head. Much of the time, I was frightened, but I dealt with it.

"But I cannot deal with meeting a dozen new people all at once."

"Sorry," Amrita said. "I didn't know it was that bad."

"There is no way you would," Jack said.

Amrita laughed. "Yeah, there was," she said.

"It probably doesn't help," Miguel said. "There's a couple of them scare me, too."

"Really?" Jack said.

Miguel shrugged. "Oh, yes. Chiyo terrifies me."

"Me too," Gary said.

"Bang really is mad," Miguel said.

"He is," Gary said, "and then there's the Dee-Dum."

His voice trailed off over the final word, and then came the silence.

Shuttle *SV 3-8749*, Romstrum 3
17:20 GST

Lorina opened her mouth to speak, changed her mind, and then opened her mouth again.

"Okay," Lorina said, trying unsuccessfully to keep any hint of skepticism from her voice. "But if the books come from another plane, it doesn't necessarily mean Caeloeterra is also on another plane? Gaia could block research into alternate planes for a dozen reasons."

"No, it does not," melanie said. "Although, I have always thought that Caeloeterra had to be on Earth, or at least an Earth. That is where the Venatori originated. It's like Gaians going to Earth. The gravity, the air... maybe not the quality, but the whole place, just makes them feel comfortable.

"Also, one other thing the leprechaun said was that Caeloeterra was, 'not that far, but then, it is a long way away'."

"Which means what?" Lorina said.

"That was my reaction, too, and he said that I should read *Foundation and Empire*."

"I have heard of that," Lorina said.

"I hadn't," melanie said. "Back then, it had yet to be written, but some years later, Isaac Asimov published the first of the *Foundation* series. One ongoing theme was the location of the Foundation. It was supposed to be at the furthest end of the universe from those seeking it, and the furthest point from any one place in the universe is also the nearest point."

"Really?" Lorina said. "How do you work that out?"

"Go in a straight line from here, as far as you can, and in the standard five-dimensional spheroid model of the universe, you will come back to here."

"Got it," Lorina said. "'It's not that far, but then, it is a long way away'."

"Exactly," melanie said. "Suggesting that Caeloeterra might be on Earth. But if it were on Earth and knowing the excesses to which the Venatori are prone, there was nowhere on the Earth we know where they could hide it."

"Makes sense, I suppose," Lorina said. "And conveniently adds to your theory."

"So, do you think Isaac Asimov was working for this leprechaun of yours?" Lorina said.

"He may have nudged Asimov in the right direction, or maybe it is just a coincidence. Having a pathological hatred of coincidences doesn't preclude their occurrence."

"No, that's true, and..." Lorina stopped and stared hard at melanie. "I just remembered. When I asked you if you had any hard evidence, you said, 'I didn't'. Which implies you do now. You are really sneaking them in today, aren't you?"

"Obviously not that well," melanie said. "As to the hard evidence, I have had that since Tamara and I were on *Valiant Sky* last year. We were in contact with another plane using a straightforward, phased-photon system, five-unit code, thirty-two characters, just enough to pass brief messages."

"I won't mention you cannot build the ends of a pha-pho system in different places because if I do, you will tell me how Tamara did it, and my head will hurt," Lorina asked. "Instead, I will ask who you talked to?"

"Me," melanie said. "I still am talking to me. The Aetherians built a faster system, and it's here, now," melanie waved her arms at the wall.

"How are you talking to you?" Lorina said.

"Not this me, but the me on that plane," melanie said. "Who else would I talk to?"

"Is that even possible," Lorina said. "Doesn't that create paradoxes or something?"

"No, that's time travel," melanie said.

"Oh, okay," Lorina said. "So, is Caeloeterra there? On this other plane?"

"Probably not," melanie said. "I am talking to one alternate plane, and we don't know how many there might be. But if you pick a number between twenty-seven and infinity, I will find you a theoretical physicist who will agree with you."

"Ah," Lorina said. "How do we find out on which of these Caeloeterra is located?"

"We might find out from the Nel if we can find that base. Or there is the leprechaun."

"Right," Lorina said. "So, we know it is, possibly, on another plane, but we don't know which one, or even how many there are, and if we knew that, we still wouldn't be able to get there."

"Getting there is not an insurmountable problem," melanie said. "The Aetherians and Saurians are putting a lot of UCs and resources into an answer. We know the Venatori have a way of getting there, and if we know there is a solution, it makes it easier to reproduce."

"Actually, we don't 'know' the Venatori can get there," Lorina said. "We would only know that if they really are there. But we don't have proof positive that they really are there."

"Your usual unassailable logic," melanie said. "But the Aetherians and Saurians accept the Venatori are there and have already found that the solution to getting from one plane to another is little more than a very sophisticated rabbit punch."

"That's okay then," Lorina said.

"But there was something else the leprechaun said that I find a little odd," melanie said.

"Just one!" Lorina shouted, and laughed.

"Okay, one of the odd things he said," melanie said with a smile, "was that my *raison d'être* was to wipe the Venatori out of existence. Then he added, 'All of us'."

"Even by his standards, that's an odd thing to say. Was he Venatori?"

"Possibly, but more likely connected in some way. I don't know."

"More riddles," Lorina said. "If he wants us to destroy them, why doesn't he tell us where they are. It isn't a game."

"Maybe it is for him," melanie said.

Shuttle *SV 3-8749*, Romstrum 3
17:30 GST

A silence that intense could only mean that someone had said something they shouldn't. Coupled with the sudden guilty looks between the three, Jack knew there was something here he had to grab onto.

263

"The what?" Jack asked as calmly as possible. He didn't want to spook anyone.

"It's nothing," Amrita said. "A nickname is all. We ought to be...."

"NAAAAH!" Jack made a klaxon sound. "Amrita. You are out." He turned to Gary and Miguel and said, "Talk!"

The two waffled for a few seconds until Amrita said, "Tell him, Gary."

"It's the name your father gave your sisters," Gary said.

"Whoa," Jack said. "What sisters?"

"That's the point," Gary said. "I wasn't supposed to mention them."

"Er, no, you weren't," Amrita said.

"You have two half-sisters," Miguel said. "Greta and Georgia...."

"Half-sisters?" Jack said. "Which of my parents was their parent?"

"Your mother was their mother, with Bianca Kaninchen," Amrita said.

"Oh, fuck," Jack said, his mouth dropping open. "Oh, double fuck, fuck, fuck."

"I know there is a certain reluctance among Terrans with accepting non-heterosexual relationships," Amrita said, "but it is generally accepted by Gaians as normal...."

"I don't care about that," Jack said. "I care about it being with Bianca Kaninchen. She's involved with the Nel and.... Shit...."

"She killed your parents, and now she wants you dead?" Amrita said with a wry smile.

"There is that," Jack said. "So, how do these half-sisters of mine fit in? Are they trying to kill me as well?"

"They might want to," Miguel said, "but they wouldn't have the guts to try. Not with melanie nearby."

"What was it you called them?" Jack said.

"The Dee-Dum," Miguel said. "Your father used to call them Tweedledee and Tweedledum...."

"Oh fuck," Jack said. "In fact, triple fuck."

"....and for some reason, and it got shortened to The Dee-Dum," Miguel finished lamely.

Jack slumped onto a box, and Gary delved into a crate and pulled out a flask.

"Aetherian vodka," he said. "For medicinal purposes."

"Gimme," Jack said, grabbing the flask and taking a large swallow. He looked slightly surprised and began coughing.

"Christ," he said, "that's bloody rough. What is it made from? Distilled gravel?"

"I'm not sure alcohol is good for...." Amrita said.

"Don't worry, love," Jack said when he stopped choking. "If that little revelation didn't kill me, a drop of vodka won't."

He took another swig and said, "Hmm. It's obviously an acquired taste."

"You've acquired enough," Amrita said, reaching out and grabbing the flask.

"Was it something I said?" Miguel asked.

"Not at all," Jack said. "There is just some weird shit going on."

"Anything we can help with?" Gary asked.

"No, mate, thanks," Jack said. "But I need to get the fuck out of here and back to Earth."

"That ship you are leaving on," Jack said. "Where's that going?"

"I have no idea where the final destination is, but it won't be Earth," Amrita said.

"Somewhere else then," Jack said. "Maybe I'll go somewhere else. As long as it is far away from melanie."

"What's melanie done?" Amrita said.

"I said there were two factors in my decision," Jack said. "The second one is melanie's lies. Mainly by omission, but them's still lies."

Shuttle *SV 3-8749*, Romstrum 3
17:40 GST

"There's a comforting thought," Lorina said. "If Caeloeterra is on an alternate plane, how does that affect the base plan?"

"It doesn't," melanie said. "Our primary objective hasn't changed at all. Nor has how we will achieve it. We were always a little shaky on how we were going to create the right situation for the dénouement."

"I think 'a little shaky', is an understatement of 'we might have a minor problem because the artificial black hole's containment field just failed', proportions," Lorina said. "The plan is, or was, to expose Zara for who she is—or should that be, isn't?—wait for

265

the avenging angels to sweep her up and whisk her back to Caeloeterra while we track them. What could possibly go wrong before, during, or after that?

"How are we going to track them across different planes? We were planning on another system in this galaxy.

"You said your cross-plane communications equipment draws a lot of power. That means even a simple beacon cannot run off the human body. How do we find her, and Caeloeterra, if we don't know which plane they are on?"

"We might find the answer in that Nel base."

"Fuck, melanie," Lorina said. "We might find the answer in those books of yours or the astrology section of *The New York Times*, but Zara's life depends on this. It needs a bit more. Finding anything in that Nel base is, at best, unlikely. Assuming that there really is a connection between the Nel and the Venatori."

"I meant to tell you...."

"Yes," Lorina said, eyes narrowing with suspicion.

"Two years ago, we picked up a distress transmission from a Nel shuttle. It had hit a meteor and was badly damaged."

"Yes, I remember," Lorina said. "It was out near the asteroid belt in the Terran system. The Nel denied it had happened. Said it was on a training exercise."

"The Kuiper Belt," melanie said. "Rufus Koenig didn't believe that it was a training exercise any more than we did."

"With all due respect," Lorina said, "Koenig wouldn't believe his own mother unless they strapped her into a multigraph."

"Perhaps," melanie said, smiling. The feud between Lorina and Rufus was well into its third year. "But being paranoid is no proof that they aren't out to get you. So, Rufus has been looking for the wreckage ever since.

"Three days ago, his people found a wrecked shuttle out in the belt. Nel crew, Bellachi workers, and Venatori passengers...."

"Venatori? They're sure?"

"Yes, they are sure," melanie said. "The Aetherians took DNA samples and discovered these weren't just Venatori. They were Hochadel."

"Why would the Hochadel have different DNA than the rest of the Venatori?"

"They are a different species," melanie said.

"That explains a lot." Lorina said. "Aren't the Hochadel the direct descendants of Egelwin?"

266

"Supposedly, yes," melanie confirmed.

"Now," Lorina said, "as I recall, the Hochadel have the rank, but when they were on Gaia, it was the Niederer Adel, the lower aristocracy, who made them powerful."

"Exactly," melanie said. "For a Hochadel to be in a shuttle somewhere as hazardous as that belt, it must have been for a good reason. Whatever that reason is, we have our link between the Nel, the Venatori and the Nemesis ship."

"That is encouraging," Lorina said. "But I'm still very much of the opinion that we will not find the location of the Venatori in that Nel base. I mean, really, would you trust the Nel with the location of anything?"

"Probably not," melanie said.

"So, I still believe that the only real benefit of finding that base is to draw Bianca out," Lorina said. "Then, if Caeloeterra is on another plane, we will need a means of finding which plane, then of traveling to that plane, and a tracking system.

"Even then, the whole thing only works if Bianca continues to think that Zara is who she believes her to be, and Zara is actually who we believe her to be."

"I understand your concerns," melanie said. "But, let me ask, do you think Zara is who we believe her to be?"

"I do," Lorina said. "That frightens me most. Because she will be in the most dreadful danger."

Shuttle SV 3-8749, **Romstrum 3**
17:40 GST

Amrita laughed. "No shit," she said. "I have known melanie a long time, and I would, and have, trusted her with my life frequently. We all do."

"I don't care," Jack said. "You all trust her because you know her. I don't know her at all, only as far as that she drugged me on a street corner in London and brought me here."

"Yes, but...." Amrita said.

"Never mind the bullshit," Jack said. "What does 'Tweedledee and Tweedledum' mean to you?"

"Nothing," Miguel and Gary said in such unison that, at any other time, Jack might have found the irony amusing."

267

"Maybe not," Jack said and turned to Amrita. "But you are staying quiet, I notice."

Amrita started to speak but decided it might be better to keep silent.

"It means something to me," Jack said. "And it means something to melanie, but she is in denial. I suppose melanie told you not to mention it to me. Which is what she does all the time."

"melanie has spent her entire life in espionage," Amrita said. "In her business, it is the norm to lie, to deny information to others.

"There is a story of a scorpion wanting to cross a river who asks a crocodile to take him. The crocodile refuses because she fears the scorpion will sting her, and they will both die. Eventually, the scorpion persuades the crocodile and halfway across, the scorpion stings the crocodile, and as they both drown, the crocodile asks the scorpion, 'Why?'

"'Because it is in my nature,' the scorpion responds. melanie is that scorpion."

"Fine," Jack said. "Then she'll drown alone because this crocodile has had enough bullshit."

Shuttle SV 3-8749, Romstrum 3
17:50 GST

Lorina and melanie reached the mess room first and sat opposite each other in one of the booths.

Lorina said, "From what Amrita is saying, through my now fried neurolink, Jack is really pissed. Are you going to mention anything about Caeloeterra to him?"

melanie opened her mouth to speak but stopped as Amrita, Miguel, Gary and a murderous-looking Jack walked in.

Amrita glanced at melanie and shrugged.

"How's it going down there?" Lorina said.

"Not a lot to do," Miguel said. "We have the list of what arrives next and how much space it will need. It will take a morning to prepare everything."

"Good," Lorina said. "The bulk arrives with the rest of the team in around thirty-eight hours, so as long as we have enough food, water, and places to sleep until then, all is well."

They all went to get coffee and joined melanie and Lorina. Except for Jack, who walked back towards the door.

"Jack, don't you want to join us?" melanie said.

"Unless you can tell me when the fuck I get back to Earth, not really," Jack said and carried on walking.

"That was top of the agenda," melanie said.

Jack stopped, turned and walked back to the table, "So, tell me," he said.

"It's a little more complicated than that," melanie said.

"Let me know when it isn't a little more complicated," Jack said and turned for the door.

"Jack, wait," Amrita said. "Listen to what melanie has to say, and if you don't like it, you can come with me when I go."

Jack shrugged and slid in next to Amrita and opposite melanie.

"As you are all aware," melanie said, "the plan is to go to Earth, find the Nel base and destroy it.

"Part one is to get to Earth," she continued. "First, we need to re-register this vehicle. That we can do tomorrow.

"Jack, perhaps you'd like to come along. See another planet?"

Jack shrugged, "Why not? What's involved?"

"We drive into the city and register the vehicle as Romstrum protected. It's like a Terran flag of convenience."

"How long will that take?"

"A few hours," melanie said. "The rest of the team arrive the following day, and we can leave immediately."

"Back to Earth?" Jack said.

"Yes, by a slightly circuitous route," melanie said.

"How circuitous?" Jack said.

"As circuitous as it needs to be," melanie said.

"Like the local variation on a straight answer, then?" Jack said.

There was a short and tangible pause melanie ended by saying, "Meanwhile, Colonel Kaninchen will be back on Gaia shortly. By then, she will know that the ambush achieved nothing. She will not be happy and will, we suspect, launch a two-pronged attack.

"Through channels, she will go to the government and announce that we are a rogue operation and must be stopped. She will also blame the Aetherians, claiming we are influencing Gaian soldiers in an illegal conflict.

269

"Simultaneously, she will alert the Nel that we are on the way to Earth and to be on the lookout.

"She'll do that?" Jack asked.

"Certainly," melanie said. "Bianca won't allow us to succeed if she can help it. She is going to be fighting for her own survival."

"Won't she ask for help from the local authorities?" Jack asked.

"Hardly," melanie said. "Romstrum is a planet not overly blessed with the rule of law; the indigenous species do not care what anybody else does as long as they are not disturbed. So, dealing with any of the criminal elements on this planet never works well."

"As I am more anxious than most to get back to Earth," Jack said, "can I suggest something that might speed things up?"

"Please do," melanie said.

"The Nel are going to be waiting for you when you get back to Earth. They probably know who you all are."

"There is little we can do about that," melanie said.

"Yeah, there is," Jack said. "They won't be looking for you if you are dead. So, fake your own deaths. You're military, and you will have access to things that go bang. Make it look like this thing had an accident and blew up."

"Not an accident," Lorina said. "Accidents are incredibly rare, but sabotage is possible."

"More than possible," melanie said. "Bianca's people hid several devices on this vehicle. One of them could provide a fake explosion, just before the retroverse, for instance."

"How do you mean, there are 'several hidden on this vehicle'?" Jack said.

"Bianca took out insurance," melanie said. "But they are all neutralized, for now."

'Okay, so how and when will you do it?" Jack asked.

"Just as we are entering the rabbit hole," melanie said. "In a real explosion, the rabbit-hole would pull in most of the debris, so we don't need much, and it might be worth keeping those bodies for some DNA samples to be left behind."

"Good, we have a plan," Lorina said.

"Should make a change," Jack said and walked out of the mess room.

Shuttle *SV 3-8749*, Romstrum 3
18:10 GST

"Well?" Lorina said once she and melanie were alone.

"I was unaware Jack suffered from some social anxiety disorder," melanie said.

"'Some social anxiety disorder,' you call it?" Lorina said. "Even you described him as a loner and borderline sociopath."

"Yes, I did," melanie said, "but I was unaware that it was going to cause him this degree of stress."

"No, I suppose not," Lorina said. "I think we can probably get around that, but only you can get us past the other, bigger problem."

"Which is what," melanie said.

"Fucking unbelievable, boss," Lorina said. "You. The other problem is you."

"I am not sure how," melanie said, looking perplexed.

"Because you lie to him all the time," Lorina said slowly, forcing the words home. "That has to stop. Tell him the truth and do it soon, or we will lose him."

"I have been honest...."

"No, no, no, no," Lorina yelled. "This is me you are talking to. I spend half my life extracting information from you, and it's never anything but a struggle. It isn't that you always lie, but you only tell me the bits you want me to hear. I have to complete the picture myself, and I'm getting good at it. But Jack doesn't have my resources. You either start telling him the fucking truth or lose him."

Shuttle *SV 3-8749*, Romstrum 3
18: 34 GST

"Is this stuff all assigned, or can I help myself?" Jack said.

"Looking at what's in here," Gary called back from the other side of the hold. "I'd say the QM mob dumped a load of stuff nobody is ever likely to ask for. So, you can help yourself."

"Good," Jack said.

"Why, what have you found?"

"Nothing," Jack said. "But I might."

Gary translated that to suggest Jack had found something but didn't want him or melanie to know.

"No problem, but if it's a weapon of any sort," Gary said, "let me know, and I will tell you if you need to tell melanie."

"Define weapon," Jack said.

"Okay, any guns, projectile and beam."

"No, no guns," Jack said. "I'm a bloody awful shot, so I try to stay away from them."

"You need one of Gary's pacifiers," Miguel said.

"What are they?"

"Think of a large caliber shotgun in a pistol," Gary said. "You cannot miss with one of them."

"Yes, that I could manage," Jack said.

"I'll dig out a couple for you," Gary said. He had walked over and saw Jack dropping a flat leather envelope into a bag at his feet. It wasn't a gun.

Shuttle *SV 3-8749*, Romstrum 3
18: 50 GST

"Where is Jack?" melanie said as Lorina walked into her office.

"In the hold, helping Miguel and Gary. Why?"

"No reason," melanie said. "We will be in that truck for a lot of time tomorrow; I'll talk to him then."

"You better had, boss," Lorina said.

"Right now, that bomb idea of his was hardly new, but I hadn't thought of it in this context."

"Yeah? It needs work," Lorina said. "And bombs."

"That's my cue to mention the little surprises I found onboard."

"Was it a decent haul?"

"Three thermobaric and two nuclear."

"That is it? No more hidden anywhere?"

"No. A couple of my people work in Section-J and fitted tells all over the vehicle. All I needed to do was check out where they had been disturbed."

"Those clowns from yesterday didn't add more?"

"Not a chance," melanie said. "They were just expendable foot soldiers and wouldn't have anything capable of damaging a military shuttle."

"Yet they took us out," Lorina said.

"Only because they were let onto a sealed shuttle by members of the GCID. That's the only way they could have."

"Thanks for that," Lorina said.

"No problem," melanie said. "The team is on schedule, I hope?"

"Yes, they'll be here on time."

There was a long pause, and Lorina said, "Do you think this will be it?"

"I hope so," melanie said.

FiT: THE FORTY-FOURTH

IST Valiant Sky, **Artemian orbit**
01:28 GST Fiveday 1.4.2833
Thursday 12th May 2016

melanie checked the equipment for the third time.

"It's fine, ma'am," Tamara Finkel said, not looking up from her detailed examination of a strand of blue hair, "but I doubt if it will last more than ten milliseconds."

"I know," melanie said, knowing she would find nothing wrong, but it filled the time. "That's long enough to find out if there is anybody there."

A panel glowed green on the wall, and Tamara leaned forward to adjust part of the display.

"Any time now, ma'am." Tamara said.

melanie sent 101.00, 000.01, 100.10, 100.10, 110.00. The Baudot-Murray five-unit code for >>Hello >>

She had thought that an appropriately sound-bite-sized phrase might be a good thing, but nothing suitable had come to mind, so 'Hello' in English had to suffice.

<<Hello. << came the response.

>>This is melanie. >> she sent.

<<So is this. <<

>>I am operating on a test rig. May we talk again in twenty-four hours? >>

<<I, too, am on a test rig. Twenty-four hours should be enough. <<

The exchange had lasted seven milliseconds.

"When you are ready," Tamara said.

"Already done. We did it," melanie said. "You did it, you wonderful blue-haired person you."

Tamara looked at melanie for several seconds and then burst into tears before collapsing over her console. melanie picked her up and set off for the sickbay.

.

DAY SEVENTEEN

Threeday 6.5.2834
Thursday 16ᵗʰ February 2017

Nel Military Base, Colorado
20:00 MST Wednesday
(04:00 GST)

Sitting in one of the hard metal seats directly behind the pilot, Vilishu wondered if the fear she was experiencing was from the sudden summons or the flight itself.

Lieutenants, especially female lieutenants, were not expected to know that the base even existed, so calls to attend Captain-Colonel Polikar, the base commander, never happened.

The craft came to a halt horizontally and began descending vertically. As it dropped through the moonless Colorado sky, Vilishu was reminded of the other reason for fear. Nel fliers.

This one was a very reliable Gaian civilian transport, which would have allayed Vilishu's fears were it not that the Nel had converted it into a military transport. Few words struck more fear into the hearts of the Nel than, 'the Nel had converted it....'

The drop ceased as abruptly as it had begun.

Vilishu peered over the pilot's shoulder. The instruments showed they were stationary.

An icon appeared on the screen, telling them to ease forward. As the flier passed through the holographic screen, the ineffective night vision system barely showed the image of rock and scrub that hid the cave mouth's existence from human eyes during daylight hours. They passed the open blast doors and, two hundred meters on, the pilot touched the flier down. For several seconds, they sat in darkness until the blast doors slid closed and the hangar lights came on. Vilishu breathed out for the first time in what seemed an age.

The ramp dropped, and Vilishu walked down to meet Captain-Colonel Polikar, her newly arrived superior officer and confessor. She kneeled and placed her forehead against Polikar's hand.

"Vilishu," Polikar said in the guttural tones of the Nel language. "You are under arrest for dereliction of duty. Your trial will be in one hour from now, and execution will follow immediately."

Vilishu froze. A Nel trial lacked any ambiguity, the verdict pre-determined. The proceedings provided a record of why they had carried out punishment. Guilt was assumed. Death the only sentence.

"Follow me," Polikar said and turned to walk away. Vilishu, programmed from birth, followed meekly. There was no need for her to be manacled or escorted. Her fate was settled; there was nothing she could or would do about it.

They boarded one of the small buggies. Polikar faced forward, behind the driver, Vilishu at the rear faced backward.

The buggy began the long ascent through the six sections of the main tunnel. The floor, walls, and ceiling were made from a locally produced ferrous alloy, with long insulating strips that provided extra grip for the buggies and divided the high voltage killing fields. At regular intervals, just in case, were gas outlets, some with igniters, some without.

They passed the slightly recessed seventh door and stopped in front of the troop hostel at the top.

Polikar stepped out of the buggy and signaled for Vilishu to follow. They walked through to the junior officers' mess-room, and Polikar pointed to a corner. There she stood, for an hour, ignored by her colleagues.

At the end of the hour, a Bellachi clerk summoned Vilishu into a small room dominated by an enormous desk. Behind it sat Polikar, her judge. To one side, Major Dekivalu, the prosecutor, sat at a smaller table. There was no defense counsel.

Dekivalu opened the proceedings by reading the charge. Desertion. She had abandoned her post and, without orders, boarded the ship of Colonel Bianca Kaninchen of the Gaian Central Intelligence Directorate.

In the Nel mentality, acting without orders was straying from the prescribed course and, thus, desertion.

Polikar looked at Vilishu's record for a minute and said, "Guilty. Sentence to be carried out immediately." He left the room.

"Follow me," Dekivalu told Vilishu.

He led her through several tunnels to a room some five meters to a side, where four Nel soldiers stood holding pistols.

"Stand there," Dekivalu told her, pointing to a mark on the floor. She did as she was told.

"In their compassion, the Nel High Command has decreed that even disgraced soldiers may be shot. For expedience, we shoot you with a poison dart," he explained.

He turned to the four soldiers. "Carry out your orders," he said. All four took aim and fired.

"Come on, Jack," melanie said, walking into the shuttle's mess-room, "let's get a move on."

"What's the bloody rush?" Jack complained as he tried to get one more cup of coffee inside him. "It's the middle of the bloody night."

"No, it is not. It's a two-hour drive each way to Daggrighnil City, and we have a shuttle arriving tomorrow, so let's go!"

Muttering loudly, Jack allowed himself to be led down to the personnel carrier in the hold.

The rear door was open, and Jack reached up to haul himself in.

"Wait," melanie said. "Put out your arm."

"What?" Jack said, not entirely understanding the demand.

"Your arm, that's the bit sticking out from your shoulder. Put it out in front of you."

Jack did as he was told, cautiously, and melanie tapped his arm with what looked like a pen.

"There," she said. "A broad-spectrum inoculation shot."

"Against what?"

"A broad spectrum of diseases," melanie said.

"I thought the exo-biologists all agreed that humans wouldn't be able to catch alien diseases."

"I wasn't aware they did?" melanie said. "But if so, that's Terran exo-biologists, I assume. Well, they should know, with their vast experience of interstellar travel."

"There is no need for sarcasm," Jack said.

"*Au contraire*," melanie said. "This is not your home planet. The native inhabitants are not human, but they have diseases, just as do you. Most are not harmful to humans, but a few, known as xenotic diseases, can be."

Jack knew he wouldn't win this one and said, "Okay, let's go."

melanie climbed in first, and Jack had put his foot on the step to follow when Gary came running over. "Is this what you wanted?" he said, handing Jack a black gun, more substantial than a pistol but smaller than the standard Gaian assault weapon.

"That is exactly what I wanted," Jack said with a smile.

278

"Good," Johannsen said, thrusting a small pack into his hand, "because here's the second one, two holsters, and enough ammunition to start a war."

"Bloody brilliant, Gary, thanks," Jack said and climbed in after melanie.

He slammed the door in the back of the truck and crouched to make his way to the cab. melanie sat in the central driver's seat, and Jack took the one to her left.

The shuttle's hold door slid open, and melanie dropped the truck's nose down the steep ramp. As the hangar doors in front of them wobbled open, the shuttle door behind them was closing.

melanie swung the truck left onto the road and accelerated quietly to a comfortable cruising speed.

"Improbable as it seems." Jack said, "it looks hot out there."

"To my horror, I know what you mean," melanie said. "It is hot. Sixty-one in the shade. But it will reach eighty degrees later today."

"Yeah, so Miguel told me," Jack said. "Is that survivable?"

"The human body can survive to almost one hundred thirty degrees Celsius if the humidity is below one percent."

"What's the humidity out there?"

"About fifteen percent."

"Lovely," Jack said. "I must come here on my holidays sometime."

"What is that?" melanie asked, nodding at the gun on Jack's lap.

"A violin," he said.

The whisper of the electric wheel motors was the only sound for several seconds.

"I understand it is a gun," melanie said. "What I meant, as you well know, is why do you have a gun?"

"Lorina has a gun, Miguel has a gun, Gary has a gun, and I bet you have a gun. I am not comfortable with the idea of you all having guns and me not."

"Yes, we all carry guns, and if you wanted one and had mentioned it to me, I would have provided you with a standard-issue one-millimeter pistol. It is an accurate weapon, carries nearly sixty rounds, and is much smaller than that."

"There is a problem with that," Jack said.

"Which is?"

"I'm a lousy shot. Couldn't hit the inside of a barn with a machine gun. This thing means I have some chance."

"That is true," melanie said. "Gary's rebuilds are extremely effective at short range. Did he tell you what it fires?"

"Not really."

"The ammunition he makes, illegally, I might add, is seven-millimeter cartridges with a load of fifty micrometer explosive balls. Be very wary where you fire those things. Let's just say you do not need to dispose of the bodies. Just hose the area down."

"Marvelous," Jack said, wondering if the standard one-millimeter pistol might not have been better.

Jack stared out of the window. There wasn't a lot to see. The broad highway was deserted as they drove along between two rows of hangars. Occasionally, a vehicle could be seen sitting on the landing pad outside, but mostly, it seemed anything vaguely interesting was tucked away out of sight. After a while, the buildings dropped away, leaving just scrub to each side of the road.

"So, what's Caeloeterra then?"

"I don't know," melanie said.

"Odd," Jack said. "Last night, when I overheard Lorina say the word 'Caeloeterra' to you, she was looking at me like a parent worried a child has picked up on a swear word and is going to say, 'Mummy, what does 'fuck' mean?' when the vicar visits next.

"Following our discussions of yesterday afternoon, Amrita chewed my ears off for several hours, telling me how you would be more honest with me and I should give you a chance.

"I thought I would go easy on you and start with something that we both know you are aware of. 'Caeloeterra'. Yet your immediate response is, 'I don't know'. So, the period of transparency and honesty lasted less than ten minutes. Is that a new record for you?"

"It's 'fewer than' ten minutes, not 'less than'," melanie said.

"Why do I suddenly doubt that?" Jack said. "Other than it was you that told me?"

He turned and looked out the side window.

"What I was in the process of saying," melanie said, "was that I don't *know* what Caeloeterra is, but I have a theory."

Jack snorted. "Of course you were," he said. "So, what's the theory?"

"To the few Gaians and Aetherians who have ever heard the word, 'Caeloeterra' is the Venatori equivalent of Heaven or

Asgard or any other fictional paradise. But I don't. I think it exists."

"The Venatori were that lot that took over Gaia, and then the Aetherians came and kicked them out?"

"They were."

"How did they get in in the first place?"

"That's a long story," melanie said.

"Okay, so give me the highlights," Jack said. "We got two hours of looking at fuck all."

"In that case, the Gaians and we Aetherians recruited people from Earth, using agents to find suitable candidates. Back in your twelfth century, a Gaian agent recruited a man called Egelwin and his extended family in Yorkshire, England."

"I know where fucking Yorkshire is," Jack said.

"I'm sure you do," melanie said. "A delightful county. Have you ever been to a place called Meltham?"

Jack turned slowly and looked at melanie. "You seem very well informed," he said. "You tell me."

"It's a little like Caeloeterra," melanie said. "We both know the name, and we would both prefer not to talk about it, but the truth always has to come out."

Jack stared ahead and then realized that they were traveling on the left-hand side of the road. Just like the British.

"As I was saying," melanie continued. "The Gaians recruited Egelwin and his tribe. Like us, Gaians get to choose their own last name on reaching maturity or gaining citizenship.

"Egelwin's family chose the name Venatori, which you will doubtless know is Latin for 'Hunters'. Over the next five hundred years, the Venatori prospered and grew until they controlled Gaia."

"And nobody noticed?" Jack said.

"No," melanie said. "The Venatori began with the civil service."

"Why, for God's sake?" Jack said.

"Because even in the most democratic system, the civil service provides a ready-made dictatorship waiting in the wings. Civil servants adhere to the notion that their consistency is a better form of government than the fleeting representation of the people's will in elections."

"That sounded suspiciously like a quote," Jack said.

"It was," melanie said. "From a paper, your father wrote."

"That's one way to stop me arguing, I suppose," Jack said. "Okay, now I see why the Venatori got to the civil service first. It's just that Terran civil servants seem to be the only people who get promoted for incompetence."

"No, that's universal," melanie said. "But did you know the British army once had a rifle they didn't like? They dubbed that 'The Civil Servant'."

"Why?" Jack said, well aware he was setting himself up.

"It didn't work and couldn't be fired," melanie said.

Jack laughed.

"Naturally, the Venatori didn't stop at the bureaucrats. They then moved onto the media and education, instilling the idea that a totalitarian system made sense, that it would be more comfortable that way. Those in charge, but without naming the Venatori, would make all the decisions for you. You need never worry, or even think, ever again."

"Big Brother," Jack said.

"Exactly," melanie said. "It took an Aetherian, Ranolde Baker, to realize that there was something rotten in the state of Gaia. Although it took him a considerable time to persuade the Aetherians that what was happening could have unfortunate long-term consequences for Aetheria."

"What were the Venatori trying to achieve?" Jack said. "Because if, as I suspect, they were after power rather than money, why Gaia?"

"Gaia wasn't their goal, just a means to an end.

"Gaia is an impenetrable fortress that could withstand an asteroid hit. Except no asteroid could get close, as Gaia can disappear into the retroverse at the first sign of danger. It is totally self-sufficient and produces its own food, water and oxygen. It has a power plant that will outlive most planets in this galaxy. It has the facilities to manufacture anything it needs, including any weapons. Finally, it is crewed by humans, the most feared species in the galaxy, with plenty more available on Earth.

"All that you could need to achieve the impossible. Galactic domination."

"Oh fuck," Jack said. "It was their *Death Star*."

"Exactly," melanie said.

Jack fell silent while he took that on board. Through the heavily tinted windscreen, a distant cloud of dust got closer. From the dust emerged a truck, balanced inside a single wheel, ten meters in diameter. They passed with a closing speed of over three hundred kilometers per hour.

"But that didn't happen, obviously," Jack said.

"No, it didn't," melanie said. "One night in August sixteen-twenty-eight on your calendar, a combined force of twenty-five thousand Gaian and Aetherian troops seized control of Gaia.

"The citizens had gone to bed in what they thought was a democracy but wasn't anymore, and woke up to find martial law had been imposed. Many powerful men and women were under arrest, and the whole democratic process had changed."

"Is that your way of saying the whole democratic process had changed into a dictatorship?"

"It is not," melanie said emphatically. "Democracy may not be perfect—I offer President Farthing of the United States of America as exhibit A—but it is the best system so far.

"Elections on Gaia were up and running in hours, and by the following day a newly elected democratic government was in place, and the true size of the Venatori grip on Gaia was revealed. They put those responsible on trial. That's when the lawyers got involved."

"Shit," Jack said.

"Shit is right," melanie said.

"In my experience," Jack said, "the Devil had two excellent jokes. Organized religion was the first, lawyers were the second."

melanie laughed. "I will remember that," she said.

"No doubt," Jack said. "And did they get off?"

"No. Public opinion was strongly against the culprits. Righteous indignation, coupled with relief at not being caught out oneself, makes for brave fellows. Even those on the fringes of the corruption were seen howling for blood."

"Literally?" Jack asked.

"Sometimes," melanie said. "But neither Gaia nor Aetheria allows the death penalty. While I am not in favor of state execution, except perhaps for assaults against children, I believe the galaxy would be a better place if they had exterminated the Venatori."

"What happened to them?"

"The government banished them. One hundred ninety-six days after the military coup, they gave the core Venatori and a few of the second level family members the keys to the *IST Constantinopolis*, and they disappeared."

"Did things return to normal?"

"Yes. As soon as the Venatori were gone, the Gaian army went back to their barracks, and that was that. The Aetherian troops had actually all gone within the first twenty-four hours."

"Just a second," Jack said. "Hadn't the Venatori infiltrated the army?"

"No," melanie said.

"Isn't that odd?" Jack said.

"Not really," melanie said, bringing the truck to a stop.

A twelve-meter-long cross between a snake, a centipede and a crocodile, with vibrant fur of red, green, yellow and blue, took its time crossing the road in front of them. Perhaps savoring the massive red and green scorpion leaking an oily yellow substance clamped into its jaws.

melanie waited patiently, ignoring the creature in the way Jack would have a crocodile of school children back in London.

The flowing row of black legs along the creature carried it and its prey off the far side of the road.

"Are those things dangerous?" Jack asked.

"No, not at all," melanie said.

"I'm Terran; I recognize sarcasm," Jack said.

"You would need to," melanie said.

"Okay," Jack said, trying to get back to the topic. "Where did the Venatori go?"

"Depends on who you ask," melanie said. "Trust me, our in-house conspiracy theorists will give yours a run for their money any day.

"You can choose. The *Constantinopolis* was mined and blew up in the retroverse; that one is state-sanctioned, unofficially. The Venatori didn't go at all and are still running Gaia to this day; that one's not state-sanctioned. They are out there in the galaxy somewhere, plotting their return. Finally, they went to another galaxy and transcended into a non-corporeal state. Take your pick."

"What's the majority verdict?" Jack asked.

"There isn't one," melanie said. "Fewer than one percent of the population share these theories. The majority, the average citizen, doesn't care. It was all over six hundred years ago—that's our years, by the way. Do the English ever wonder what happened to the supporters of Oliver Cromwell or if Victoria really had it off with the gamekeeper?"

"No, I suppose not," Jack said. "What does Bianca say? From the little I've seen of her, I take it that whatever she says is GCID policy, by default?"

"Yes, that is about right."

She stared ahead, silently, as if marshaling her thoughts.

"Bianca has frequently said that the Venatori are gone and best forgotten. This offers some idea of why one theory is covertly promoted by the state. Rather the proles have a long-dead government to blame than enjoying idle speculation about what really happened.

"She also says that any speculation about them is only a distraction from our real work, engaging the other assorted species who would like to harm Gaia in any way possible."

"Did you read that off a prompt card?" Jack asked.

"More or less. You asked me what Bianca says."

"True," Jack said. "What do you think? What do you think happened to them?"

FiT: THE SIXTH

Egelwin quieted his horse with a very gentle squeeze of the knees. Some of the group's younger members were getting restless, sitting looking at a seemingly empty stretch of moor. He would speak to them later. If the frilingi could stand still and keep their packhorses and the oxen for the wagons still, then so could a few edhilingui who thought they were above such things.

Soon, very soon, the Gaians would be here, and Egelwin and his family could leave from this place, this banishment.

The rest of the tribe, too, although the core reasons were ever so slightly different. For them, it meant they would no longer need to pay heed to that damned sheriff in York. Or the king. 'Henry the Lion' indeed. Bowing and scraping to his father-in-law in the south, and his wife Matilda leading him by the nose.

The opportunity to get off this planet had taken a little organization. The Gaians still thought this was all their idea, and that they were recruiting a bunch of savages. Mostly they were, Egelwin conceded, glancing back at the rest of his tribe. Mostly they were.

His horse shifted slightly. Uneasy. Sensing things were about to change.

How little it knew. In their patronizing way, the Gaians had explained that once induction was complete, the tribe could pick new names. Egelwin had looked through the names adopted by newly recruited Gaians and cringed. They liked those of past Gaians, sopping up to the vanity of these pathetic creatures who themselves had been savages scant generations before.

Egelwin had picked their new name from the Latin tongue they now used.

He heard the shout and a few horses protesting, whinnying and rearing, picking up on their riders' fear.

Looking up, he saw the two black discs descending slowly. He had asked that they did not drop at their usual rate; that it would cause panic, although even this measured approach seemed to manage that well.

The first of the ships landed, just out of longbow range, and the doors dropped to form ramps. Three men walked out, their hands raised, palms flat.

Egelwin urged his horse forward. He wasn't afraid, and his horse, although nervous, was under control. His immediate family followed.

Egelwin and his four sons rode up the ramp to where the Gaian officer waited, all false smiles.

"Willkamen, Keunig Egelwin," the Gaian said, getting the wording, title, and inflection wrong.

"Gratias Tibi," Egelwin replied in flawless Latin.

"Ah, you have made strides," the Gaian said, switching to Latin. "You will be picking a family name soon."

"I already have," Egelwin said, dropping from his horse to the deck.

"Excellent. May I enquire as to what it is?"

"Certainly," Egelwin said. "We will be the Venatori."

FiT: THE SEVENTH

Patrol Vehicle *Babylon*
09:55 GST Sixday 6.5.2178
(Friday 9th March 1629)

"No closer," Commander Soto said. "When they finally hit the rabbit-punch, I do not want to be sitting here with any farewell gifts coming my way at fifty percent lux."

"No ma'am," Captain Sutton, sitting in the pilot's seat, said. "Would they?"

"You can stake your pension that if we get close enough, they will do it," Soto said.

"That's a hell of a vehicle they took," the pilot said, looking at the display screen showing the *Constantinopolis* from its least attractive aspect.

"Yes, it is," Soto said. "And that scum gets it."

Not for the first-time, Soto wondered if, just maybe, she should suddenly detect a missile launch from the vehicle ahead and order return fire. *Babylon* was an old heap of junk, but she carried an impressive battery of missiles for this mission. Far more than they needed.

Maybe that was the unspoken plan. Why Ranolde Baker had given her this job. Why Babylon was the lone escort. Why an over-armed vehicle with a crew of six—a very loyal crew of six—and one passenger, were here.

It had been Colonel Baker who had started the entire chain of events that led to the expulsion of the Venatori family and their followers. He would not have missed the last moments.

If *Constantinopolis* disappeared in a small blue flash, there would be little overt dismay back on Gaia. And the crew would all swear that *Constantinopolis* had launched a pre-emptive attack. Baker would say nothing. Given his way, it would have been an execution rather than a banishment from the beginning.

"Funny, I thought I saw something launch just then," Sutton said.

Soto grinned mirthlessly. She wasn't the only one, but she knew she couldn't launch an attack on a vehicle carrying several thousand people because a few were evil.

"Nice try, pilot, but no, you didn't," she said.

288

"You sure, boss?" one of the two Chin-lo brothers said from the small weapons control room. *"I thought I saw something, too."*

"Here's the deal, guys," Soto said. "Anything, anything at all comes from the vehicle, and we will turn it into a mini nebula. But we play this by the book. Agreed?"

There was silence over the comm.

"Agreed?" A little more forcefully.

Mutterings from throughout the vehicle meant they agreed. And they would stay with the agreement. That was how it worked on a patrol vehicle like *Babylon*. They stuck together, they all got their say, but the Commander was boss.

"Do you think we will ever see them again?" Sutton asked.

Before Soto could answer, a slight shimmer, and the *Carthage* class freighter disappeared into the retroverse.

"If I may answer Captain Sutton's question, Commander?" Ranolde Baker said.

"Please do, Colonel," Soto said.

"People like the Venatori hate to lose," Baker said. *"They almost consider it an affront. So yes, I would say that it is quite probable we will see them again."*

FiT: THE THIRTY-FOURTH

Huddersfield Road, Meltham, W. Yorkshire
11:52 BST Friday 6th April 2001
11:52 GST Fourday 6.6.2807

Jack stopped the van in the narrow yard behind the butcher's shop and retrieved the grease and blood-stained warehouse coat from behind the seat. Like the van, the coat had once been white, but both had suffered years of abuse and needed replacement.

He took four boxes of meat from the back of the van. It was always four boxes on a Friday, and it would all be gone at closing time on Saturday. That was how Mister Hastings liked to do things. Get it in and back out again as quickly as possible.

Jack took the first two boxes into the little storeroom behind the shop counter and called, "Usual place, Mister Hasting?"

"Aye lad," Hastings called back from the front, not turning from telling one of his customers how to cook a piece of beef for the best results.

Jack dropped the boxes and went back out to the van for the other two. He dropped them next to the first pair and went through to the shop.

Mrs. Hastings, sitting in her little glass booth, signed the paperwork and gave Jack one of their home-made steak pies for his tea. Jack thanked her nicely; he omitted to mention the fox he fed, three times a week, four miles out of town.

Jack considered delivering to the areas of butchers' shops the public never saw the best of all possible arguments for vegetarianism. Not that he had ever been tempted.

"Okay, if I have my dinner in the yard?" Jack asked as he did every Monday, Wednesday and Friday.

"Don't see why not," Mister Hastings said, as he did every Monday, Wednesday and Friday.

Back in the van, Jack set up the little wooden table on the passenger seat. It came in useful for doing his paperwork and for somewhere to set his flask, sandwiches and other accouterments. Mrs. Hastings's pie he placed in the door pocket, making it easily accessible.

When all was complete, he walked round to the passenger door and retrieved a blue duffle bag from under the seat. He took off the once-white coat and donned a leather jacket, scarf and woollen hat. After checking the bag's contents, he walked out of the yard, down the alley and right onto the main road. The Lancaster and Lancashire Bank was the first door along, and, as usual on a Friday lunchtime, most of the citizens of Meltham were too busy with their dinners to be in the bank.

As Jack walked into the bank, he pulled the woollen hat down and the scarf up over the lower half of his face, then produced the shotgun from the duffel bag.

There wasn't much left of the original gun. Jack had reduced the barrels to a little over twelve inches and replaced the wooden stock and butt with a small metal pistol grip. Leaving just the cold, functional heart of a weapon.

The two cashiers behind their glass screens were taking advantage of the lunchtime lull to eat pots of yogurt. One other staff member sat with two customers at a low table, discussing their financial plight with feigned sympathy.

The customers were facing the door, the bright light from outside surrounded the staff member like a back-lit prophet. They hardly noticed as Jack walked past.

He had reached the counter before the cashiers gave up their conversation about their respective dates for the forthcoming Saturday night and switched on their plastic smiles. Jack tapped the note he had placed on the counter with the shotgun's business end as the smiles melted into abject terror.

The older girl took the note between trembling fingers, glanced at it, then the barrels of the gun and nodded. She started piling notes from the drawer onto the counter. As she did so, Jack looked at the younger girl, nodded, and waited until she, too, was piling up cash.

Then he turned towards the three at the table.

The bank employee was standing up. Gawping. Jack waved him back down with his left hand, then turned around to the cashiers. He opened the duffel bag and swept the money and his note under the glass partition and into the bag.

He turned to leave, but there was something about the bank employee in front of him. Something vaguely familiar.

The Walrus! The shape, that demeanor. It had to be the Walrus.

Jack turned, nodded his thanks to the two cashiers. They would have set off the alarms by now, and the police hot-footing it from Huddersfield. But this was too good to miss.

291

The couple, who thought the most significant problem they had to face was their overdraft, were transfixed when he strolled over to them.

"How do," Jack said. He was rubbish at accents, but they were too scared to be critical. "Now't to worry about."

He turned towards the Walrus.

"You," he said, "Get up."

The man shook his head, his body rippling as he did so.

"Get up, or I shoot you here," he said.

The man stood.

"Kneel," Jack said.

He dropped to his knees. He was muttering quietly to himself. Jack leaned closer and heard the word 'please' over and over.

"Still a fat bastard then, Walrus," he whispered.

Even though the kneeling man wore a very dark blue suit, there was no hiding the growing stain around his crotch.

Jack stood up, turned and walked towards the door, slipping the shotgun into the duffel bag, pulling the scarf down.

Outside, he turned left and left again into the alley, walking, not in any hurry, nothing to attract attention. As he went, he removed the leather jacket, the scarf and the hat and shoved them into the duffel bag.

He turned into the yard, still sauntering, opened the passenger door of the van, slid the duffel bag under the passenger seat, pushed a couple of greasy overalls in front of it and walked round to the driver's side. There, he donned his once white warehouse coat and climbed in. He poured a cup of tea from the flask, switched on to Radio One and immersed himself in the crossword that he had half-completed that morning while eating half of one of his sandwiches.

Which is how the police found him when they arrived five minutes later.

He told them what he could.

Yeah, someone had run up the alley, but he hadn't really noticed, just some kid with a leather jacket and an old grip or bag of some sort. Then there had been the sound of a bike. That he had noticed. He was a biker himself; he had a Honda six hundred, a real bike, but this was just a pop-pop, a two-stroke, not big, maybe a one-fifty, something like that.

Mister Hastings came out from the shop. He vouched for Jack and told the police he was harmless. Maybe not too bright, him coming from down south, London and the likes, but harmless.

The policeman made notes, and when, twenty minutes later, he pulled out of the yard and down the alley, one of them had held up the traffic to let him out and past the knot of police cars as he set off for Huddersfield.

DAY SEVENTEEN (Cont.)

Threeday 6.5.2834

Thursday 16th February 2017

Unknown

Vilishu awoke after another seemingly dreamless and momentary sleep. She was lying on the hard floor of a cave illuminated only by a dirty red glow coming through the entrance. A deep and rhythmic beat assaulted her ears. She was naked and stank of urine and feces; her dry tongue traced missing teeth.

The chain attached to the fetter on her left ankle snapped taut. She felt herself being dragged out of the cave for another day of rape, beatings, starvation and humiliation.

It was her third day in Heaven.

Romstrum 3
05:50 GST

"I think that some of the conspiracy theorists are right," melanie said.

"Which ones?"

"I believe the Venatori didn't go at all and are still running Gaia and that they are out there somewhere, plotting their return."

"Hmm," Jack said. "Isn't that two contradictory theories?"

"Yes, it is," melanie said. "The Venatori are running Gaia by proxy. Their supporters are doing their bidding. But the Venatori would like to come back and have their presence acknowledged."

"What's the attraction?" Jack said. "What do their supporters get out of it?"

"Power," melanie said.

"Yeah, I should have guessed," Jack said. "The trouble is, I just don't understand the attraction of power."

"You don't?"

"No," Jack said. "Money, I get. Even then, there is a limit to how much of it I want."

"Enough for three meals a day and a couple of beers with the lads on a Friday night?" melanie asked.

"Hardly," Jack laughed. "I like to live well, but I don't want a super-yacht or a helicopter or a Ferrari. I chartered a yacht once—I was bored silly after two days. Helicopters are bloody terrifying, and Ferraris are uncomfortable. I wouldn't mind a Bentley, though."

"You don't see the attraction of power?"

"Yes. No," Jack said. "What I mean is; I understand that power attracts some people; I just don't really understand why they want it."

melanie laughed. "Me neither."

They sat in what was almost companionable silence until Jack said, "Err, how do you know the Venatori have supporters on Gaia?"

"Names," melanie said.

"Is there any more on that?"

"There is," melanie said. "You remember I said that on being granted citizenship, the Egelwin tribe all elected to adopt the name Venatori?"

"Yes, I remember," Jack said. "It was only just now."

"People expected subsequent generations would revert to tradition. Instead, the family started its own tradition.

"The core family, the Hochadel, or upper nobility, the direct descendants of the original family, called itself 'Venatori'. Below them, the Niederer Adel, or lower nobility, were further split. The upper ranks of Niederer Adel used the name in other languages than Latin. 'Jaëger' and 'Hunter', for example, or the names of mythical hunters. While the lower ranking Niederer Adel took to adopting these names with the first letter changed. Such as 'Haëger' and 'Gunter'."

"That was my mother's name," Jack said.

"Yes, it was," melanie said.

"She was Venatori?"

"She came from a Venatori family," melanie said. "But your mother was not a believer."

"Which means?"

"Despite the preaching of certain elements in her family, Sarah did not believe that the Venatori were some glorious dynasty destined to rule."

"That's good to hear," Jack said. "But why do this? Why give yourself a name that is going to identify yourself as one of the bad guys?"

"Names are powerful things," melanie said. "Suppose your name was Himmler, and you were living in the late nineteen-thirties Berlin. Don't you think your name might get you into a few restaurants and clubs that you wouldn't have got into if you were called Schmidt?"

"And that was what having one of these names did?" Jack said.

"It was."

"Okay," Jack said. "But let's move on to late nineteen forties Berlin. If your name was Himmler, wouldn't you change it to Schmidt?"

"Yes, you would, wouldn't you," melanie said. "Unless you thought Hitler wasn't really dead and any day now, he was coming back with a weapon that would reassert his dominance."

"Gotcha," Jack said. "They thought the Venatori were coming back."

"They did, and while the faithful were waiting, their time was spent demonstrating just who had been keeping the Venatori's seat at the table warm."

"Fucking hell," Jack said. "All so they can get a reservation at a restaurant."

He fell silent. Somehow, he had hoped that the Gaians and the Aetherians might have grown up a bit from the squalling mob who inhabited the Earth. It seemed not.

"On the subject of names," Jack said. "Why don't you have a capital letter at the beginning of your name?"

"How do you know that?"

Jack pulled out a compad. "Several things have mentioned you by name, but always with a small, 'm'."

"An affectation, nothing more."

"Bull shit," Jack said. "What's your second name?"

"I choose not to have one," melanie said.

"I suppose that makes as much sense as everybody choosing their own name," Jack said.

"You did," melanie said.

Jack laughed. "Yeah, sort of," he said.

Jack sat silently for a few seconds and then said, "That's a point. Bianca's name is Kaninchen. Is that the word for 'Hunter' in Greek or something?"

"To the contrary," melanie said. "It's German for 'rabbit'. But Bianca doesn't need a name to get into anywhere. She is Bianca."

"Yeah, I suppose she is," Jack said. He was about to speak when he realized Bianca meant 'White'. Her name was 'White Rabbit'. Which was curiouser and curiouser. But not necessarily a coincidence. He said, "Final question. What is this really all about?"

"Finding Caeloeterra and destroying the Venatori," melanie said.

FiT: THE THIRTY-FIRST

Oxford Street, London
21:50 GMT Friday 21ˢᵗ February 1997
22:50 GST Fiveday 1.1.2801

John turned onto Poland Street and walked ten yards before stopping to check his money. He'd made seven pounds and forty-seven pence. Not bad for a few hours sitting down and looking pathetic and pretty.

There had been a few propositions, one from a woman; possibly. But that was the other side of looking good.

John was cold, and right now what he needed was to get home, get warm, and enjoy whatever some of the other guys had scored. Dylan said he would get something different, just in from Nicaragua or Colombia or some such place. It didn't matter. At least he didn't have to suffer all the stupid rules his tart of a mother and her new husband had laid down.

"Oh look, it's the pretty boy again," he heard a man's voice say. "Some faggot been reamin' your arse and given you some loose change, has he?"

John turned. There were two of them; they looked tough, well-muscled, drunk. He was sure he'd seen them earlier, and they'd made the usual unoriginal comments about how he should get a job.

"And we're the vice squad, and we fine you whatever you got for being a bum-boy," the other one said.

"It's all I got," John said.

"Shouldn't be a bum boy," the first one said, getting in close.

"Hey, you two, leave him alone and fuck off," a third voice said.

The two men turned from John and regarded the stranger. A tall kid, skinny; not a problem.

"You talkin' to us?" the first asked.

"Nobody else here, is there? You dumb fuck," the stranger said.

The two men launched themselves at the skinny kid who moved out of the way, tripping one, so he veered into his mate and bounced off before falling onto all fours.

300

The one who fell started climbing to his feet, but the skinny kid moved in and kicked him in the side of the knee. Grabbing his injured leg, the man fell over, screaming, while his mate moved in, adopting a judo stance.

The skinny kid laughed and said, "Ah so, you judo master," in a bad take on a Japanese accent.

"Enough to fix you, yer little shit," the man said. He was going to say more, but the skinny kid had jumped in and brought his knee up into the judo-man's testicles, very hard. The judo pose collapsed into a gasping ball of humanity.

Then the skinny kid kicked him in the head, and he fell silent, unlike his companion, who continued screaming. The kid moved over and kicked him until the screams were louder but muffled in the way of broken jaws.

"Time we got the fuck outta here," the kid said, grabbing John by the sleeve. "Place will be full of busies in two minutes."

The two walked away, John trying not to run.

As they passed through Golden Square on their way to Piccadilly Circus and the tube station, John said. "Thanks, man. Anything I can do for you..."

"Now you mention it," the skinny kid said, "I do sort of need somewhere to stay outta sight for a day or two. I pissed off Jorge Theophilus, and he wants a chat."

"Who?"

"Best, you don't know."

"I'm in a squat in Battersea. Would that do?"

"South of the river, fucking ace it would. Nobody would look for me there."

"Come on then," John said. "I'm John, John Fletcher."

He considered for a moment. Too many people knew William Dean and Danny Pollard. He needed to go back a bit.

"Caeil Ashbow," the kid said.

It was a little after four in the morning when Caeil woke up. He had passed on the party, as he had no intention of sticking anything in his veins. Come seven o'clock, he was going to be out of here.

But as he was awake...

He dressed quietly; he'd steal a bicycle, get out to the main roads and hitch a ride somewhere.

He looked over at John; he wanted to say 'thanks' for the crash.

John was staring at the ceiling, but Caeil knew he wasn't awake or even alive. Dead bodies were different somehow.

He had no pulse, and the body was cold. Probably an overdose; or maybe they'd cut whatever he'd used with something lethal. It happened. The boy had been dead a couple of hours. He'd call an ambulance once he was a few streets away.

He turned to go, then stopped. He felt bad, but needs must.

The backpack by the bed was heavy, and Jack checked it thoroughly. A few clothes, some in his size. At the bottom was a large wallet. Inside, Caeil found John's passport and driving license in the name of John Card Fletcher. Plus two check books with guarantee cards and nearly two hundred pounds in cash.

John was almost Caeil's height and build. Caeil's hair and coloring were darker, but that wasn't a problem. What Caeil had here wasn't just a backpack, but a new start.

It was almost seven o'clock before Caeil reached the top end of Cricklewood and Staples Corner. He needed to put distance between himself and London.

He trudged round to the bottom of the M1 motorway and prepared himself for a long wait.

A truck whisked away two girls who had arrived after him, but then a dark green Jaguar stopped. A woman driver, middle-aged, not the usual XJS driver.

"Where are you going?" she asked. She had a slight accent; Scandinavian maybe.

"North," he said.

"Anywhere in particular?"

"No," he said. "Just north."

"I'm going to Manchester."

"Perfect," Caeil said and climbed in.

They chatted as they headed north through a gray morning on the M1. He said he was looking for a job when he got there. He didn't know what.

"Take my card," the woman said. "I run an agency in Salford."

Caeil looked at the card and said, "Astrid Gunnarson. Okay, thank you. My name's John Fletcher, by the way, but everybody calls me Jack."

DAY SEVENTEEN (Cont.)

Threeday 6.5.2834

Thursday 16th February 2017

Shuttle *SV 3-8749*, Romstrum 3
06:00 GST

"You did what?" Lorina said, lowering the coffee cup from her mouth very slowly.

"Gave Jack a couple of my modified guns," Gary said.

"The commander will have you strapped to an anthill for that."

"What are you reading? *Beau Geste*?" Miguel laughed. "Nobody has ever strapped anyone to an anthill in this army."

"It's a new initiative," Lorina said. "But she will blow a dozen fuses when she hears."

"She was there, she knows," Gary said.

Romstrum 3
06:10 GST

"Okay," Jack said. "So, what about the Nel and their invasion?"

"I thought that was supposed to be your last question."

"I lied," Jack said.

"We still need to find their Terran base," melanie said. "When we do, we will wipe the Nel out. However, the main purpose of doing so is that it may lead us to the Venatori."

"How come?"

"Approximately two years ago, a Nel vehicle disappeared in the Kuiper Belt. In the last few days, the Aetherian shuttle *Baleful Moon* found that vehicle and identified two of its passengers as Venatori.

"This confirms a theory that there is a link between the Nel and the Venatori. That may mean that somewhere in the Nel base, we might find the location of Caeloeterra."

"Okay," Jack said. "I know you don't know what or where Caeloeterra is, but what do you think it is? I mean, is it a planet or another habitat, or don't you know that either?"

"Again, I have a theory," melanie said. "But not everyone agrees."

"Okay," Jack said.

"The name 'Caeloeterra' is bastardized Latin. It is a contraction of the phrase *'Caelo et in terra.'* Literally, 'Heaven on Earth'. Logically, it would be on Earth."

"Makes sense," Jack said. "How many of these Venatori are there?"

"I would guess maybe half a million."

"They would be hard-pressed to hide that sort of number," Jack said. "Even in Colorado."

"They would," melanie said. "Caeloeterra is not like the Nel base, some rabbit warren. Caeloeterra has to be a statement; it will be enormous and surrounded by vast open spaces where the Venatori can hunt and fight."

"So not Colorado then?" Jack said.

"Well, certainly not the one we know," melanie said.

"Fuck," Jack said. "Are you saying what I think you are saying?"

"To prevent this conversation degenerating into a Möbius loop," melanie said, "I meant an alternate plane."

"Fuck," Jack said again. "They exist then?"

"They do," melanie said.

Jack sat, his mind racing, staring out through the windscreen. The road was still as straight as ever, but had hit a very slight incline. Alongside it, the truck was passing another tiny enclave of hangars and landing pads. Beyond them was little but a flat desert without even a cactus or wandering monster to break the monotony. A range of mountains with what might have been snow on the peaks provided minimal relief in the far distance, but they were so far away even they were hazy.

"How do you know?"

"I've spoken to someone on another plane."

"Okay," Jack said. "That sounds conclusive."

"Also, I used to know someone who came from another plane," melanie said. "But he was murdered."

"Happens a lot around you," Jack said. "Did you kill him?"

"No, I did not," melanie said. "He was harmless. He had the soul of a poet."

"Yeah," Jack said. "I know a poet. He's not harmless, and he has no soul."

"Who is that?" melanie asked.

"Richard bloody Patterson."

"The Sitting-on-a-Bench man?"

"That's him," Jack said.

"I like that poem," melanie said:

"I'll tell thee everything I can

305

Concerning matters French
And of an aged, aged man
A-sitting on a bench.

"Who are you, aged man?" I cried,
"And tell me why you sit
Upon a bench in Gabian.
Pray, what's the sense in it?"

"Ugh," Jack said.

"What did he do to upset you?"

"I bought a house from him. While I was moving in, Rick had a look through a box of books I was bringing in.

"In the book was a poem called *A-Sitting on a Gate*. It was a parody of Wordsworth's *Resolution and Independence*. Patterson saw the poem, rushed home, wrote *A-Sitting on a Bench* and for reasons neither he nor I understand it became famous."

"What a terrible person," melanie said. "There is no greater crime in the galaxy than plagiarism. When this is all over, I shall send an armed squad to find Richard Patterson, kill him and all his family, then burn his house down. I will not tolerate such evil."

"Funny, I thought I was the sarcastic one," Jack said. He was going to keep his cool. She now had a perfect opportunity to talk about the books. She might lead up to it, or she might have forgotten *A-Sitting on a Gate*.

"Really?" melanie said. "Did you?"

Jack laughed and said, "So, what did your poet friend write?"

"Nonsense, mostly," melanie said:

"'Twas brillig, and the slithy toves
Did gyre and gimble in the wabe;
All mimsy were the borogoves,
And the mome raths outgrabe.

"That sort of thing."

Jack sat silently, wondering what to do next. Those lines were from *Alice Through the Looking-Glass*. As were the lines Patterson had copied. This was not melanie leading up to anything or forgetting. This was melanie playing games.

"Your friend was Lewis Carroll?" Jack said.

"Who?" melanie replied.

306

"Wrong answer, melanie," Jack said. "You know bloody well who Lewis Carroll is, and as you cannot be straight with me, I don't think we have anything further to discuss."

Romstrum 3
07:00 GST

A perfectly conical hill shimmered out of the heat haze, gaining substance as they got closer.

At the top of a gentle incline, the entrance to a tunnel overlooked the plain and the pair of blockhouses guarding the road. As they got nearer, melanie slowed down.

"We have an appointment," melanie said. "But these guys are often the last to know."

They were the first words spoken inside the vehicle for almost half an hour, and Jack ignored her.

They pulled into a slip road running around the back of the blockhouse and under a large canopied area. melanie climbed out of her seat and opened the back door, letting in a blast of hot air, before she slammed it shut after her.

A door opened in the blockhouse, and a spider, the size of a small pony, walked out.

"Oh, Jesus H fucking Christ," Jack said in a hoarse whisper, his mouth and throat suddenly parched.

He watched, almost frozen, as melanie and the spider chatted. melanie produced a compad that the spider examined and then offered what was possibly the eight-legged version of a salute.

melanie climbed in through the truck's back door to find two seven-millimeter gun barrels staring her in the face.

"What are you doing?" she asked, pushing the barrels away.

"When you disappeared, I thought they'd got you," Jack confessed.

"I assume you were on your way out to rescue me?"

"Like fuck I was. I was more concentrated on keeping my bodily functions under control."

"Eew. Too much information," melanie said. "I assume you suffer from arachnophobia?"

"No, I just like squealing like a girl sometimes," Jack said. "Too fucking right, I suffer from arachno-fucking-phobia."

"Strictly speaking, they aren't spiders. Box lungs would not work in a creature with that ratio of volume to surface area."

307

"I couldn't give a fuck what they aren't; they look like fucking spiders to me," Jack's voice had risen in pitch.

"Then I'll see what we can do about keeping you away from them."

"Fuck keeping me away from them; I can manage that on my own. Keep them the fuck away from me."

"As this is their homeworld, that might be a little difficult," melanie said. "But I have arranged for a pseudo-mammalian advisor at the ministry."

melanie pulled back onto the road, and they climbed a little before entering the tunnel and starting back down again on a well-surfaced road with excellent shadow-free lighting.

After a few kilometers, other roads joined the one they were on, and other traffic appeared, odd-looking trucks equipped for the desert. The road leveled out, and after another kilometer, they emerged overlooking what at first Jack took to be a valley.

He assumed they had passed through a mountain range, but the light looked wrong. Like the difference between winter and summer sunshine, this was not the same as the light had been.

Swiveling in his seat, Jack could peer up at the sky or where it should have been. He could see that the light didn't come from a single source, like a sun, but as if they had spread a billion diffused LEDs across the sky. It took Jack a while to realize that they weren't outside again, but in a vast cavern.

"It's twenty-two kilometers across and five from floor to roof," melanie said before Jack could ask.

"Good," Jack said.

The road turned and followed the valley's side down to a city of tall, irregular towers, with never a straight line or any geometric shapes that conformed to human understanding of the term. Towers arched across to rest on others or on the sidewalls of the cavern. They twisted like giant corkscrews, and one hung like a stalactite from the ceiling, with the point only meters above a lake.

They drove through wide boulevards, past parks and open areas with lakes and rivers that seemed to flow in continuous circles. To Jack's horror, wherever they went, the one consistent factor was the number of spider look-alikes. The majority weren't as large as the one at the gate, but that was not much comfort to Jack: he thought even examples as small as a Chihuahua were still too damned big.

"They are vegetarian," melanie said at one point.

"I couldn't give a flying fuck if they are all really nice people and help little old lady spiders across the street and do good works whenever possible. They are still spiders in my book, and they still give me the heebie-jeebies."

"Don't worry, I won't tell them that, back on your planet, you pulp their cousins with your shoe," melanie said with a chuckle.

"Wrong again," Jack said. "They scare the crap out of me, but I put them outside, alive, if they invade my space. Anyway, didn't you just get off telling me they weren't really spiders?"

"Whatever. We seem to be at the Transport Ministry building. The aliens' entrance is just around the corner."

As melanie spoke, she pulled up outside one of the less bizarre towers with an indecipherable sign that Jack assumed meant that this was indeed their destination.

melanie rooted around under one of the inward-facing seats in the truck's rear section and recovered a large leather satchel. She hoisted it up onto her shoulder, and the two climbed out of the vehicle.

"Don't forget your compad," melanie said. "It works as a translator too."

The entrance to the building accommodated as many species as possible with ramps and a variety of differently pitched staircases. One of these seemed ideal for humans.

In the Ministry building, a mammalian creature dressed in long and flowing robes that made it impossible to get any real idea of its shape greeted them. It had covered its head in a cowl, but what little of the face they could see suggested something a little like a green kangaroo.

The creature carried a translator that immediately paired with melanie's and Jack's compads. He, or she, Jack's translator, was having some problems determining the creature's gender, introduced him/herself as Ullpergoi, and apologized for any delay. The Ministry was experiencing some issues, and things were running a little late.

Introductions complete, Ullpergoi asked them to follow it— the translator had given up on the gender issue—to a small meeting room. As expected from a government department room, they were in a sterile box with shades of pale brown dominating. The only furniture was a black desk, a stool on one side and two chairs opposite.

"How may we help?" asked Ullpergoi once they were all seated.

"We wish to transfer ownership and re-register our vehicle under the protection of the Romstrum Government," melanie explained.

"I see no problem, providing you have the necessary documentation," Ullpergoi said.

melanie passed her compad to Ullpergoi, who held it to the desk. The compad beeped, the desk beeped, and Ullpergoi returned the compad to melanie.

"Your new registration number is now on your compad and with the hangar in which you berthed your ship. To activate the registration, there only remains the question of payment," Ullpergoi said.

"Certainly," melanie said and deftly pressed the compad a few times. "Here is the standard payment." Again, she passed the compad across the desk, and, after both had beeped, it was returned.

melanie reached into the satchel and retrieved a package wrapped in something akin to oilskin. She passed this across the desk and said, "Here is a small thank you for expediting this service, as I am sure you will."

"Very generous," Ullpergoi said, weighing the package in one hand/paw, "and I believe the activation has already happened."

melanie and Jack rose to their feet and turned towards the door.

"Tell me, Captain, would you like the name of your ship registered?" Ullpergoi said.

"No, thank you," melanie said, then, "Wait. Jack? Do you want to name it?"

Jack was about to say no but said, "Okay. Why not?"

"The naming document is on your compad," Ullpergoi said.

"Okay," Jack said and looked at the screen. He tapped in eleven letters and a space. Ullpergoi took the device and went through the double beep ritual on his desk.

"Your ship is now named, and I believe our business concluded," Ullpergoi said.

"Yes, I think so," Jack agreed.

On the way back down the steps to the truck, melanie said, "So what did you call it?"

"It's a surprise."

melanie stopped on the steps and said, "That's fifteen letters, punctuation marks, and spaces. You entered twelve, including one space."

Jack paused as well.

"So, I did," he said.

They climbed into the truck, and melanie said, "One more stop before we go back."

"The fire station?" Jack said. "To have your pants extinguished."

"Don't be childish," melanie said. "We are going to the alien quarter."

"More spiders?"

"The clue might be in the word 'alien'. The alien quarter is where the aliens, that means us, hang out, not the indigenous species."

"In that case, let's go," Jack said.

Nel Military Base, Colorado
00:15 MST
(08:15 GST)

Nel scripture was adamant. Faith was everything: losing faith removed God's protection and allowed for death, followed by an eternity in Heaven. The concept of Hell was redundant.

God had created the universe and everything in it. Inventors or philosophers or researchers were unnecessary: God had provided. Just not all at once. God made the Nel in His own image, but they were children who needed to develop towards being adults before understanding and appreciating God's bounty.

The Curiata, the most senior house of the Clergy, handed down God's gifts as the Nel became mature enough to handle them, and the need arose. One of the greatest gifts was that of controlled faith.

The priesthood had often struggled with the lay creatures who found difficulty accepting God's reality and omnipotence. Fortunately, God had provided for those who might lose faith—and who amongst them might not?—drugs and an electronic device hacked into the thalamus to fully enforce the acceptance of the scriptures.

For those who needed a little more persuasion came the coffin-like tanks. These introduced memories within the hippocampus and cerebellum and in the cerebral cortex,

311

premotor cortex, and basal ganglia. In effect, they could create whole new realities. They could create a taste of Heaven.

Tucked away in the deepest caves beneath the Rocky Mountains, Captain-Colonel Polikar stood looking at the twenty rows, each of twelve tanks. Across the room, two Scientists were lifting an unconscious human from a tank and then inserted a replacement. As they finished, two more Scientists entered with gurneys and made their way to a separate tank.

"We have arranged it to rotate a tank every four hundred fifty dekans," Scientist Flanoklar said. "For the sake of efficiency, we gear our deliveries to the planetary cycle. Therefore, we maximize the use of tanks so that every full delivery matches the number of tanks."

"Good," Polikar said. "So, what success have you had?"

"As with all scientific study, we continue varying the processes until God decides we should find the correct combination," Flanoklar said. Laying responsibility with God invariably worked. It diverted blame and provided an argument-proof firewall. Who was going to criticize God?

"I understand," Polikar said. "But have you any idea of where you will go when a solution is discovered?"

Flanoklar paused and considered this carefully. "I understand that a new Scientist outpost is being constructed on the edge of Arthronine space," he said. "Doubtless, God will see fit to send me there."

"And Chief Scientist Aragrantuth?"

"He is an old man and will return to Nel."

"I am sure it will disappoint him to be so far from the action," Polikar said.

"What action?"

"Have you not heard," Polikar said. "The Arthronine like to target Scientist outposts; they prefer the softer flesh of the Scientists over that of warriors. But you might survive."

Flanoklar turned pale and said, "Then it is God's will that if we find a working control system for the Terrans, I will die in some out-post."

"So, it would appear," Polikar said. "Just as long as poor Chief Scientist Aragrantuth will be back on Nel, away from the action. Eh?"

"Indeed," Flanoklar said.

"It is indeed unfortunate but unavoidable," Polikar added, "that testing until you find a suitable combination of drugs and implants will take so long. We can only hope that it does not take so long that God and the Emperor defeat the Arthronine without the need for these Terran cattle. If so, we will lose our opportunity to contribute and perhaps our opportunity to die in God's name."

"Is that possible?" Flanoklar asked.

"Oh yes," Polikar said. "But back to business. In which of these is Captain Vilishu?"

"None of these," Flanoklar said. "These are not full-function tanks. Just a stripped-down version for the Terran experiments.

Flanoklar led Polikar to a small side room with four considerably larger tanks.

"She has been inside for a relatively short while, at twenty-five times relative," Flanoklar said.

"Excellent," Polikar said. "Leave her in for the time being, and I will send an officer to get her. We will tell her, the General commuted her sentence, and we dragged her back from the brink of death. Now she's had a taste of Heaven, I think we'll find her following orders a little more diligently."

Daggrighnil City, Romstrum 3
08:15 GST

Just before the ramp to the surface started to climb, melanie swung the truck off the main road and into an area of much lower, squatter buildings.

"Pleasant neighborhood," Jack said as they drove past shops, bars, cafes and hotels. The back streets of Havana aside from the dearth of sixty-year-old Chevrolets.

"Nobody ever thinks they are going to be here for long, so nobody bothers to clean the place up. Then one day, they realize they've been here half a lifetime, and it's all too late," melanie said.

Turning up a narrow side road, they stopped in front of a two-story building. Many years before, they had repainted the façade with a *trompe-l'œil* Rousseau-style jungle, with fantastical creatures peering out from behind exotic foliage and flowers that might have been insects.

"Welcome to *The Plantation*," melanie said.

"Incredible," Jack said as they climbed out of the truck. "Who did that?"

313

"The owner," melanie said. "Or he was last time I was here. There are supposed to be flora and fauna from over one hundred different planets on there. Let's see if he is still alive."

In contrast to the beautifully decorated but run-down exterior, the interior of the bar was just run-down. A dozen humanoids were sitting at tables or standing in a group by the bar running along the entire back wall of the room. Behind the bar stood what looked like a lizard walking on its hind legs.

As they walked in, the lizard shouted something that sounded just a little unfriendly to Jack's ears. melanie yelled back in a similar vein, and the two exchanged greetings by patting each other on top of the head. It was quite a stretch for the lizard.

"This is Huret-jhi Rekagious Wiltyregch, but call him Billy," melanie advised.

Seconds before he got his head patted and learned how to smack a small dinosaur on the head, Jack said, "Really? You don't want me to call him by his real name?"

After the head patting, Billy joined melanie and Jack at a table and began reminiscing with melanie. Jack decided that his best policy was to sit and smile and nod and laugh when the other two did, but mostly the conversation involved people and incidents he had never heard of. Worse, the two knew the stories so well they rarely bothered getting more than halfway through one before going onto the next.

Jack had always been a people watcher. If it didn't involve talking to them.

He could waste hours sitting in a sidewalk café watching his fellow man, with all his multitude of idiosyncrasies, walking past. Fellow men were scarce on this occasion, but Billy's regulars were still worth a look. Long experience of this activity meant Jack never appeared to be watching anyone; he was just sitting there, minding his own business.

At the far end of the bar he saw two of the customers, looking more-or-less human, paying more attention to melanie than she would have liked. Hardly surprising, melanie stood out even in an alien environment like this.

What concerned him was that one of the two humans left and returned five minutes later with two others. All four were now more than a little interested in melanie, and they didn't look like they were autograph collectors.

Jack tried to gain melanie's attention without making it obvious.

314

"Yes, I know," she said, without looking at him.

"Who are they?" Jack asked.

"If it's the four, I suspect," Billy said, he had his back to them, "then I reckon they're Gaians. They say they's Tomalites, but they ain't."

"I don't suppose you brought your new toys in with you, did you?" melanie asked.

He hadn't. Going to a bar didn't automatically register with Jack as something that required packing a gun.

"Nope. Are you carrying?"

"Yes, I am, and it's probably just as well you aren't, with those cannon of yours," melanie said.

"Okay," Jack said, "let's see if they want to dance, shall we?"

He went to the bar, leaned against the counter and called the suddenly nervous humanoid bartender over. He ordered a beer that was delivered in seconds. The bartender returned to the other end of the room even faster.

The four men watched him intently – one of them moving up the bar and nearer to Jack for no apparent reason.

Jack took a swig from the bottle, took three paces towards the door, and stopped. The one who had moved up the bar had also taken three paces on an intercept course. Jack turned his head and grinned at the man, who stopped. Jack's right arm came out at forty-five degrees, his whole body turning as his arm came higher and released the bottle.

The bottle's base hit the man in the nose, crushing the cartilage and flinging him backward over a table.

Jack followed through on his advantage and covered the distance to the group's next man. This one wore a battered leather-like jacket that provided Jack with something to grab before smashing his forehead into the man's face.

Jack heard the crash of a table going down behind him and decided it had to be melanie making her move and, he hoped, putting a couple of bullets in the other two. He wasn't too sure if she had the build needed for a fight this close and personal.

The thought had barely registered when he swung his second and not totally conscious victim, still firmly in his grip, round by the lapels to use as a block against the third member of the foursome who had produced a large knife. Using an unconscious man massing around a hundred and fifteen kilograms, as a block, wasn't easy. Jack thought he needed a new plan when the fourth

315

member of the team crashed into the one wielding the knife at about chest height, bringing the two of them down.

Jack dropped his human shield and turned to see melanie standing there, looking pleased with herself. Billy had turned around for a better view, but he had remained seated throughout and was clearly having the best time.

melanie reached behind her and pulled out a small pistol. "Point this at them and if any of them move, keep pulling the trigger until they stop," she said, handing the gun to Jack before walking out of the bar.

"You two sure can put on a show. Have you worked together long?" Billy asked.

Jack turned and smiled at the lizard. "No, not long, not long at all."

"Really? In which case, Bianca Kaninchen had better watch out because you two are a natural."

"Thanks," Jack said.

melanie walked back in carrying a loose handful of thin plastic strips with which she began binding their four attackers. She stopped after three.

"Good shot," she said. "The one you threw the bottle at is dead. But we'll take him along as well."

"Where are we taking them?" Jack asked.

"Out to tea," melanie snapped. "Back to the shuttle, of course; where did you think?"

It took melanie and Jack a few minutes to carry and drag their prisoners out to the truck and tie them to the inward-facing seats in the rear. After bidding Billy farewell, accompanied by more head patting, they set off back up the road leading up the side of the valley.

About ten minutes in, Jack said, "Were you expecting someone might be there?"

"Not so much expecting," melanie said, "but not really surprised either. I thought that if there were any of them there, it might answer a lot of questions."

"Such as?"

"I don't know yet," melanie said. "I will talk to our new friends and see which way it all goes."

Jack said nothing.

"You can trust me, Jack," melanie said. "The problem we have is that Lorina and I have been working on this mission for a long time. There are several factors involved. I'm telling you as much as I can as fast as I can, and you'll just have to have a little patience if I can't tell you everything all at once. Because it simply isn't physically possible."

"Okay," Jack said while thinking that the last person he would trust was melanie. "Can you answer two questions for me?"

"If I can," melanie said.

"Why am I here?"

"I need you," melanie said. "Initially, because your parents were my friends and I had promised them that if anything happened to them, I would keep you alive. Now, I want you around for your mind. Besides, it would appear that you are a lot better in a fight than I would have guessed."

"I had a first-class teacher," Jack said. "Okay, second question. I got the Lewis Carroll books from your friend, my father. Which means you are as aware of them as I am. So, why do you deny knowing anything about them?"

"You won't believe this, Jack," melanie said. "But I don't know why. I suspect they have a critical role to play in what will happen, but I do not know what that role is, even if one exists."

"Why does that prevent you from talking to me about them?"

"I talked to your father about those books a lot," melanie said. "Bianca had him killed, and while I am not superstitious, I am careful, and I do not want the same thing happening to you."

Romstrum 3
09:30 GST

melanie drove the truck up to the barrier guarding the exit to Daggrighnil City and stopped.

"I won't be long," she said as she climbed past their prisoners to the back door and dropped out, letting in another blast of heat.

Jack had been watching melanie drive by using a single stick. Forward to accelerate, back to brake and right and left to steer. Jack slid into the middle seat, and as soon as he felt the blast of heat as melanie climbed back in, he pushed the stick gently forward.

The truck pulled away from the post, and, despite melanie yelling for him to stop, Jack took the vehicle up to speed.

melanie slid into the seat on Jack's right and closest to the stick.

"I'll take it from here," she said.

317

"No, you won't, melanie," Jack said. The heads-up display on the windscreen showed them driving at one hundred and fifty kilometers per hour.

"This is not like driving a Terran car," melanie said.

"I'm aware of that," Jack said. "It's simpler."

They drove for a few kilometers in silence, and then Jack said, "By the way, did you use your little scratch test thingy on that lot?" He indicated the back of the truck with his thumb.

"Yes, of course, I used the 'little scratch test thingy' on them," melanie said. "Why?"

"They're Terrans, aren't they?"

"How did you figure that out?" melanie said.

"All the Gaians I have seen are like me, tall, skinny and range in color from lightly toasted to well done. We have brown eyes and straight, dark hair.

"That lot are short, podgy and that gray-pink color we Terrans call 'white'. One has blue eyes, and one of them has curly hair.

"Adding injury to insult, one guy you shot soon after we arrived was a cockney."

"That's a Londoner, right?" melanie said.

"A bit more than that. It's a Londoner born within the sound of Bow Bells. That's the church of St Mary-le-Bow in Cheapside. But that burned down in the Great Fire of sixteen sixty-six. Now it means anyone from the East End of London."

"Interesting," melanie said.

Jack laughed, "Hardly," he said. "But there is a truck sitting about two hundred meters behind us. It was traveling faster than us and then matched our speed instead of overtaking. Now that's interesting."

Nel Military Base, Colorado
01:30 MST
(09:30 GST)

It took Vilishu a while to realize she was awake. There had been several dreams, some almost pleasant, and she had preferred to stay with them rather than face whatever realities being awake might present. Then it came back to her; the hard dark floor of the cave and the obscenities waiting for her outside.

Except she wasn't in the cave. She was in a bed, with soft sheets, with a pillow under her head, and she was warm. She ran her tongue over her teeth; they were intact. The aches and pains were gone. She could no longer be in Heaven.

She opened one eye and could see that her bed was in a pleasant, dimly lit room. A monitoring device stood beside the bed, letting off an occasional and strangely reassuring burp to indicate all was well.

"I see you're awake," a voice said softly, and she swiveled her head to see Major Dekivalu sitting at her bedside.

Vilishu tried to speak, her dry throat producing a series of harsh coughs instead. Dekivalu was at her side in an instant, a beaker with a drinking tube in his hand. Vilishu sucked on the sweet, almost oily texture of caztergon fruit, something reserved for special occasions.

"Where am I?" she whispered finally.

"In the base infirmary," Dekivalu replied. "General Hedasfarmu ordered a reprieve. Unfortunately, it came through seconds after they had carried out the sentence. We thought we had lost you. The doctor treating you said that you died for several minutes. Does this correspond with what you experienced?"

Vilishu considered her options. If she confessed she had indeed died and gone to Heaven, it would not go well. If she had been male, it might have been different. Then she might find herself elevated within the Military and enjoying the benefits that would bring with it. As a female, the more likely possibility was that her having visited Heaven might cause a sudden reversal in the reprieve, and she could find herself back there, permanently. If she had been gone 'several minutes' and had experienced several days, then she wanted to live a long life. A very, very long life.

"No, I don't think so," she said. "I just slept for a while."

"Quite so," Dekivalu said. "Perhaps it would help if you were to forget every aspect of this sorry episode."

"I have already forgotten it," Vilishu said and watched the man walk out of the small room.

**

In the corridor outside, Captain-Colonel Polikar stood waiting. "Well?" he demanded.

"She says she only slept and recalls nothing. She's lying, of course."

319

"Watch these test subjects with particular care, Dekivalu. This might be the way forward for the entire junior officer corps."

"Yes, sir."

Romstrum 3
09:45 GST

melanie looked at the rearview screen and said, "Yes, that is interesting."

"Would it be cynical of me to suggest they are following us?" Jack said.

"Not in the slightest," melanie said. "Whoever it is will know where the shuttle is located, so I suspect they are waiting until we get back to the hangar before making a move."

"Seems likely," Jack said. "It wouldn't occur to them to think that sitting behind us like that is going to get noticed?"

"They aren't paid enough to think," melanie said.

"No, I suppose not," Jack said. "Does that truck of theirs have any weak spots?"

"It's a slightly older version of this one, so very few," melanie said while reaching under her seat to pull out a gun of the sort either fired from a tripod or carried by Arnie Schwarzenegger.

"What the...?" Jack said.

"Heavy Assault Weapon," melanie said. "This is Chiyo's favorite. You'll meet her later. You'll like her."

"Okay," Jack said. "Will that thing stop the other thing?"

"I'm not sure," melanie said. "There's no turret or hatch on this, and I need to be outside, so we need to stop first."

"You'll cook out there," Jack said.

"I'll be okay for a short time. Can you create diversions?"

"I sure can," Jack said. They were coming up on the cluster of hangars they had passed on the way in.

"Hang on," Jack said.

He pulled the stick back, hard. The truck dropped from one hundred and fifty kilometers per hour to twenty in three seconds and seventy meters, causing the prisoners to yell.

The truck behind swerved and passed them, still braking hard.

As the other truck went past, Jack pushed the stick forward and hard right, turning through the closed gates of another hangar compound. The rough ground and battered gates causing the truck to bounce on its suspension with four of its six wheels off the ground.

Jack stopped the truck.

"Further round," melanie said.

"Wait," Jack said. "See if they follow or cut me off."

The second truck had reversed and turned in after Jack, crashing over the fallen gates and following them around the hangar.

"Stupid, but I like it," Jack said, accelerating round to the back of the building. As they approached the next corner, Jack saw the other truck appear in the rearview screen.

"Just around this corner," Jack said, and as soon as they were out of sight, he stopped. melanie was already climbing past the prisoners, the HAW in one hand and opened the rear door.

Jack waited for the blast of heat to end and pulled away, kicking up dust from the compound.

melanie landed running out of the truck, flicking the door shut as she went, the HAW in her other hand. The truck's rear end settled as it tore away, chucking up a vast cloud of dust.

She ducked behind a low wall, partially hidden by the dust, and propped the HAW on top.

Seconds later, as the pursuing truck came round the corner of the hangar, half airborne and barely under control, melanie pumped three rounds from the HAW into the cab. This should have smeared the driver all over the vehicle's inside, but the cab was armored, unlike most trucks of its type. Worse, the crew now knew she was outside and armed.

Once the truck passed, melanie walked back around the corner and crouched with her back towards where Jack would be coming. Seconds later, she heard the whine of the motors as Jack's truck came from the far end of the building. It came past, kicking up even more dust and hiding melanie from the pursuing vehicle.

The other truck was close behind and gaining, melanie decided. It came past her further out than before to run wide at the corner and avoid the spot where they believed melanie was still hiding.

As the truck went past, melanie pulled the trigger on the HAW three times and put one round into each of the Li-Ro two hundred kilowatt motors that formed the wheels on the right-hand side.

The motor cores fused, becoming brakes in the process. Inevitably, with all three wheels on one side braking, the vehicle tried to complete a U-turn in its own length.

At eighty kilometers per hour, physics dictated otherwise, and the truck rolled one and a half times before stopping, roof down.

melanie walked over to the truck, the HAW cradled in her arms and waited for the back door to open.

She shot the first one out as he tried to breathe in the seventy-two-degree heat, and his lungs failed. With no further movement, melanie walked to her own truck and climbed in.

"Warm enough out there for you?" Jack asked as he pulled forward and back onto the road.

Romstrum 3
11:30 GST

"It's the next one, Jack," melanie said, pointing at the hangar ahead.

"Okay," he said, reaching down to pull his two guns out from beneath the seat.

"You are learning fast," melanie said.

"Yeah," Jack said. "It seems people want us dead."

The gates swung open.

Nobody was visible.

"What happens now?" Jack asked.

"I've sent them a code from my neurolink, and they are just responding," melanie said. "It's too hot for anybody to come out."

A ramp slid out from the side of the shuttle, and Jack steered the truck round to drive up. As they neared the top, the shuttle's door slid open, long enough for him to get through before it closed again.

The hold was empty. melanie said, "Lorina is cooling the hold down before we get out, and they come in."

Two minutes later, the door opened, Lorina and Miguel walked in, and melanie and Jack jumped out of the truck.

Seconds later, Amrita and Gary appeared at the door.

"It's still not exactly chilly in here, is it?" Jack said.

"It's over seventy degrees out there now," Lorina said.

"Seventy?" Jack said, turning to melanie. "You told me it was sixty-five."

"They build us Aetherians very hardy," melanie said with a smile, "but meanwhile, we have three prisoners and a body in the back."

"You've only been gone a few hours; how did you manage that?" Amrita asked as she walked into the hold.

"Pure luck," Jack said. "Normally, when I go out, I come back with fish and chips or a curry. Prisoners and a dead body need that melanie presence."

"The prisoners will need some water and, after being driven by Jack, some first aid."

"You were driving?" Lorina said to Jack.

"I was," Jack said. "It's what we Terrans do. Drive."

"Yes, he was more than proficient," melanie said. "So, Amrita, why don't you take Jack up to the mess-room for a cup of tea or whatever his English soul craves?"

"And if it isn't tea, his English soul craves, not in the mess-room, please," Lorina said.

Without a word, Amrita grabbed Jack's hand and led him around to the stairs.

"So, has peace broken out between you?" Amrita demanded.

"After a fashion," Jack said. "I still may not stay, but we will get to Earth, and then I can decide."

"How about your problem with groups?"

"After today, I'll try and cope," Jack said. "But right now, as nobody outside of the UK, with the honorable exceptions of Australia, India and New Zealand, can make actual tea, a cup of coffee will keep me going."

***

As soon as Amrita and Jack had gone, melanie turned to Lorina and said, "Well, that was interesting. I have told him a lot more than I intended, but he seems happy."

"So, not everything, then?"

"No, not everything," meanie said as Miguel joined them. "But I have learned a lot about him. Such as he's okay in a fight."

"Really?" Lorina said.

"We went to see Billy, and those guys we have prisoner showed up looking for trouble," melanie said.

"Billy?" Miguel chipped in. "Is that old bandit still alive? Is *The Plantation* still standing?"

"Just about, in both cases," melanie said.

Gary emerged from the back of the truck with the three men on a steel wire linking their wrist restraints and helped lower them down onto the ground. Then he climbed back in.

"It was Jack who started the fight," melanie said. "Threw a bottle at the one still in the back of the truck and killed him at four meters."

Gary jumped down from the back out of the truck, dragging the body of the fourth man.

"That one," melanie said.

"Seriously," Gary said. "Is that even possible?"

"It can be," Miguel said with clinical detachment. "If you get the angle right, the bone or cartilage, whatever it is, can get pushed back into the brain."

"Then, on the way back, another truck tailed us," melanie said. "Jack was driving and drove around a compound with them in pursuit. I took them out with a round from the HAW in each wheel motor."

"How come he was driving?" Lorina said.

"I got out at the control point when we were leaving the city, and Jack took over. He could drive it straight off."

"It took me three days to learn to drive," Miguel said.

"Me too," Lorina said.

"You sure you went for lessons?" Miguel asked, then yelped as Lorina punched him.

Amrita and Jack came in carrying coffees for everybody.

"Are they part of the same crew that ambushed us?" Lorina asked, pointing at the three prisoners sitting on the floor of the hold.

"I think so," melanie said. "Terrans, according to the scratch test."

"What are Terrans doing on Romstrum?" Lorina said.

"That is what I will find out," melanie said. "Just as soon as I can get hold of a real DNA scanner."

Gary emerged from the truck carrying the HAW and yelled, "It's Jack, the beer bottle slayer!"

"The what?" Jack said.

"I hear you disposed of one of this lot with a beer bottle at six meters," Gary said.

"It was four meters," Jack said.

"I heard six," Gary persisted.

"It wasn't six; it was four meters," Jack yelled, holding up four fingers.

Amrita looked at Jack and said, "How many meters?"

"Four," Jack yelled, holding up four fingers yet again.

"I've just had an idea," Amrita said. "I reckon you can tell if they're Gaian or Terran without a DNA scanner." She whispered in melanie's ear.

melanie said, "That's an idea."

She walked up to the first of the prisoners. "How many can you count up to on your fingers?" she asked.

The prisoner ignored her, so she moved onto the second one, turned to Miguel, and pointed at the first prisoner. "If he hasn't answered by the time I get to the third one," melanie said, "shoot him."

"Yes, ma'am," Miguel said.

"How many can you count to on your fingers?" melanie asked the next prisoner.

He, too, remained silent, so Lorina moved on to the third while Miguel moved up behind the first one and placed the barrel of his gun against the man's head.

"How many can you cou.... "

"Ten. I can count up to ten," the first one yelled.

"Thank you," melanie said, "now if you'll shoot the second one, I'll see how this one does at...."

"Ten. We can all count to ten, for fuck's sake," the second one called.

"And you," Lorina leaned forward and half-whispered in the third man's ear, "how far can you count on your fingers?"

"Ten," he admitted grudgingly.

"Your right," Lorina said. "They are Terrans."

"What's going on?" Jack said. "Do you all have six fingers and haven't bothered telling me?"

"I'll show you," Amrita said. She held up her left hand, clenched into a fist.

"Gaian children learn a little game, so they can count to one thousand twenty-three on their fingers. Like this."

She raised her little finger. "One."

The little finger went down, and she raised her ring finger. "Two."

The little finger came up to join it. "Three."

"Got it," Jack yelled, "binary numbering using the fingers. So why do you learn that? I mean, I now know why golfers yell 'fore': it's a secret code for giving the finger."

"It is that," Amrita said. "I saw you standing there waving your fingers about and saying 'four', but I was reading fifteen. Then it occurred to me, Terran kids only learn to count to ten on their fingers. I thought that if they were Gaians, they'd know the game. If not, they wouldn't."

"Smart and beautiful," Jack said.

"Simple math where we come from," Amrita said.

"Math*sss*," Jack said, stressing the last consonant.

"We say 'math' in the singular form."

"I don't care," Jack said. "The word is 'mathematics', in the plural. We should shorten it in the plural. Just because the Americans say 'math' does not mean the whole damned galaxy has to."

"Just because the British get it wrong," Amrita retorted, 'doesn't mean the whole damned galaxy has to."

"Much as it grieves me," melanie said, "I agree with Jack on that one."

"The rest of us don't care much," Lorina said. "Can we stick to finding out who these guys are?"

"Yes indeed," melanie said. "Shall I begin?"

She walked across and stood behind them. "You're Terrans; what are you doing here?"

The three men ignored her, staring straight ahead. "Okay," melanie said, pacing up and down, "so, you reckon you are now prisoners of war, perhaps, and that we will do the honorable thing and look after you until the Nel come and set you free? Is that it?"

They said nothing, and melanie reached into her pocket and pulled out a small device. "Unfortunately, it isn't that sort of war. It's not a nice little game played by gentlemen who observe rules; that sort of crap disappeared a long time ago. This is the sort of war where there are no rules. So, let's find out which of you has been given the Nel treatment and which of you we might salvage."

She walked over to the first man and held the device up to his head. It beeped. She moved on to the second. As she did so, the third man, the one melanie had thrown into Jack's knife-wielding attacker back at The Plantation, tried to turn and run. The restraints brought him crashing down.

"Nice try," she said to the second man, still standing there, "Very nice indeed, but no coconut for you."

The second man's face grimaced in anger and frustration, and he snarled, "You better fuckin' kill me, bitch, 'cos I'll tear you apart if I get free."

melanie paused for a moment. "Funny thing. I had the same thought," she said as she swung the pistol up and pulled the trigger. A plume of blood, bone, and brains exited the back of the man's head to splash up against the wall behind.

As the body crashed onto the floor, melanie said. "Oh clever," and turned to the other two.

Gary was dragging the one who had fallen back to his feet, and the two survivors seemed bewildered, as if just woken from a deep sleep.

melanie turned to the first of the two standing men, "Name?"

"Er, Ball, Tony Ball, where the fuck am I?"

"No," melanie snapped. "I ask questions; you answer questions. Where are you from, and how did you get here?"

"Toronto, and I haven't a clue; I really don't know where I am."

"Where do you think you are?"

"I dunno, West Africa, maybe?"

"Who's he?" she pointed at the body on the floor.

Ball turned and looked at the body. "No idea. There isn't enough face left."

"You were standing next to him a few seconds ago."

"Look, lady, I don't remember anything much after I met up with Ernst Hartmann and a guy called Joe." Ball turned and looked at the other man standing next to him. "That's him, that's Joe."

melanie walked over and started digging around in the dead man's jacket. She found a wallet and opened it.

"This was Ernst Hartmann. What do you know about him?"

"Not much. Hartmann's a fixer; he gets merc. jobs. I've had a couple from him in the past. He said he had a short contract for me, couldn't say where, but it paid well."

"What's the last thing you remember clearly?"

"Hartmann took us to a place in the US, a small town where we were to meet the clients and then they were arranging onward travel. We met in a bar in this place, don't remember the name, and had a few drinks. That's it. Honest."

"Where was this?"

"Honest, I don't remember the name of the place."

"What state?"

"Iowa. It wasn't much more than a village."

melanie turned to the other man.

"Who are you?"

"Me, I'm Giuseppe Marafioti. Everybody calls me Joe, I'm from Milano. I went the same as him, same time we went to the bar together."

"Where?"

"I dunno, maybe Iowa, but I think it was Colorado, but the town, I dunno. Something like Greenville, maybe, I dunno."

"That's right," Ball suddenly interrupted, "it was Green City or something, but I reckon it was in Iowa."

melanie stared at the two men, then walked over to Gary Johannsen and asked him for a knife. He passed her a large and well-honed Bowie knife. She walked behind the two men and said, "Relax, I'm just going to cut your wrist straps."

She cut both men free and placed the knife on the ground. "You can do your own ankles," she said.

melanie turned towards the others. "They're harmless," she said. "We'll get them on an IST and take them home, eventually."

The two men finished cutting their ankles free, and Marafioti picked up the knife by the blade and walked over to pass it back to Gary. A meter from melanie's back, he spun the knife over, grasped the handle, and lunged. As he did so, melanie turned, brought up her pistol, and fired.

Inertia carried the Italian forward, and the blade sliced through melanie's jacket. Gary and Miguel leaped forward and grabbed Marafioti, who once again looked bemused and unaware of where he was. Gary snatched the knife and was about to use it on the man when melanie said, "Stop, Gary. It's not him."

Gary stopped and turned. "What?"

melanie nodded past where they stood. "It was him," she pointed at Ball's body slumped on the hangar floor, still half-kneeling. "He's the control, or one of them."

"Why didn't your detector tell you that to begin with?" Jack asked.

melanie laughed. "I don't have a detector. Just this translator."

"Christ, you mean you pulled the fake device stunt twice in twenty-four hours?" Jack asked.

melanie regarded him coolly. "Why not? You pulled the same 'cleaner in a bank' routine more than once."

"Yeah, I suppose," Jack said.

Lorina had been staring at the dead bodies lying on the floor. "Is that what we're facing?" she asked. "People who have been turned into automata?"

"At the moment, it's one form, yes. I'll go into a bit more detail when the others get here," melanie said.

"Hang on," Jack said. "Why did you give them a knife to cut those things? They were Gaian handcuffs; you can release them with your neuro-thingy."

"Yes, but I wanted to know which was the control," melanie said.

"That was bloody stupid," Jack said and glanced down at melanie's side. "That knife went in deep. Are you not hurt?"

"Yes, I think it did catch me," melanie said, pulling her jacket aside.

"You ought to check that out," Jack said. "It's not bleeding, which I think may not be so good."

"Hmm, I'll just go and sort something out."

"I'll come with you," Amrita said.

"If you would," melanie said. "It's nothing serious."

"Okay, boss," Lorina said as the two women left. Then she found herself somewhere comfortable to sit.

"What do you reckon with these bodies?" Gary asked, 'shall we chuck 'em in the airlock? We got the ones from when we arrived, they can all go together. Even if they are Terrans, it'll look like there's a bit of Gaian DNA floating around after the explosion?"

"Good idea," Jack said.

"We've thrown in a load of other junk already," Miguel added.

"That should all help," Jack said.

"What about me?" Joe Marafioti said. "I don't want to go out airlock. I did not mean to stab her."

"You won't," Jack said.

"But I think you need to be secured," Gary said. "Sorry, but we can't take a chance," and re-secured Marafioti's wrists.

"As long as no airlock, you do what you like," Marafioti said.

"Let's get these bodies into the airlock," Miguel said and got the cart. They loaded the corpses, and Miguel drove the cart away.

Lorina looked over at Jack and said, "Had a rough day?"

"Just a little," Jack said.

"I think an early supper and bed," Lorina said with a smirk.

"Good for you," Jack said, "I think I may have a couple more swigs of that vodka first."

"What vodka?" Lorina said, turning to look at Gary.

"Oops," Jack said. "I'll go find Amrita, I think."

Romstrum 3
12:30 GST

"I can manage this, okay," melanie said as she and Amrita walked up the stairs.

"I know you can," Amrita said. "I wanted to know how you got on with Jack?"

"You were right in your initial assessment. Jack might be of value to us," melanie said. "He's smart, and he can fight; it was he who instigated the ruckus in *The Plantation*."

"Interesting," Amrita said.

"How do you feel about leaving?"

"No problem. Why?"

"I wondered if you and Jack...."

"Ha," Amrita said with a huge grin. "You are funny sometimes. We've known Jack all his life. In many ways, he is still the little boy we had to protect. So, no, there is no romantic connection, either way.

"Julia was the love of his young life, and he was hers. But she was so right to go when she did. He is still not ready to settle down."

"That was my impression," melanie said. "But I needed to check."

Inside her room, melanie took off her jacket and examined it for cuts. The blade had missed that and caught the T-shirt underneath. melanie pulled that off and threw it into a corner.

"He meant business," Amrita said, looking at the twenty-centimeter-long cut in melanie's side.

melanie pried open the edges of the cut and looked inside. "He did, didn't he," she said. "It's just as well I don't bleed." She opened a cupboard and took out an aerosol.

"Yeah, this flooring is a pig to clean," Amrita said. "Any interesting conversations while you were out having fun?"

"He asked about Caeloeterra," melanie said.

"How did he find out about it?" Amrita said.

"He heard Lorina and me talking."

330

"*What did you tell him?*" Lorina said from her neurolink.

"The truth," melanie said, adding, "mostly."

"I saw no point in hiding it. He would have gnawed away at it until somebody, shall we call them Gary and Miguel, would have told him."

"*My money's on Miguel,*" Lorina said. "*Anything else come up?*"

"Yes," melanie said. "Jack still has the books. That's the actual books and all the notes."

"*Good. Maybe if I understood their significance, I'd be a little more enthusiastic.*"

"I agree," Amrita said.

"*Did you tell him you knew about them?*" Lorina asked.

"He knows I do," melanie said. "I told him I didn't know what their significance was, assuming they have one...."

"*Here we go, around and around,*" Lorina interrupted.

"... and he isn't happy about it," melanie continued. "But that is the truth."

"*I think Jack may be on his way up to see you,*" Lorina said over the comm.

"Thanks, Lorina," melanie said.

"Let me spray the glue into that," Amrita said and took the can from melanie and dropped to her knees.

The door slid open. Jack was standing there, gawping at melanie, naked to the waist, and with Amrita kneeling in front of her.

"Enjoying yourself?" melanie said, regarding Jack with an amused smile.

"Err!" he managed.

"Maybe it's time you let Jack into another little secret," Amrita said with a huge grin.

"*What's happening?*" Lorina said.

"Jack just walked in, and melanie is naked from the waist up," Amrita said.

"*Holy shit,*" Lorina said. "*I'm on my way up.*"

Jack was not unfamiliar with the female form. In fact, he had spent an inordinate amount of time since puberty becoming as familiar as possible.

This was different. To begin with, melanie's breasts, as well as being pert, had no nipples. More accurately, there were nipple shapes at the right place on each breast, but they were the same color as the surrounding flesh. And breasts were never that evenly matched in size and location.

Then there was that cut.

The inside of the wound that Amrita had been spraying was the same color as her skin. Even a little paler. It should have been red.

Jack decided that his best plan was to retreat, and he turned for the door.

"Wait a moment Jack," melanie said. "No need to leave. I don't have the same concept of modesty as you."

Jack turned and a breathless Lorina, who had arrived to watch the fun, pushed him back into the room.

"I think I had better explain," melanie said as she pulled on a clean T-shirt, "I'm an android."

"Really?" Jack said. "You mean like a robot?"

"No, not like a robot'," melanie said crisply. "Supposing you told me you were human, and I said, 'You mean like an orangutan'?"

"Okay," Jack said, conscious he had crossed some sort of line. "Sorry, I didn't know there was a difference."

melanie laughed. "No, I suppose there's no way you could. I should have told you before, but I am trying to keep the surprises to a maximum of two a day. I'm sorry about that bit of android snobbery. Robots are just machines with a computer running them. Androids are fully mobile, with sentient artificial intelligence. Usually."

Amrita giggled.

"Okay, well, now I know. And it's cool that the surprises are being spaced out reasonably well," Jack said.

"Yes, I do try," melanie said. "Look, sit down while I collect up a few things; we need to talk. Lorina has things to do in her office."

"Oh, boss?" Lorina wailed.

"Go," melanie said, and Lorina went.

"And I need to put some stuff together," Amrita said and followed Lorina out.

Jack sat and looked around him. melanie's quarters were spartan. A bare table, five chairs, cupboard doors, and one small photograph on the wall. He had thought the flat he had fitted out for Pierre Gomez in London was minimalist. But this...

But then, he supposed, that androids didn't need a lot. Not that he had a lot of experience with androids. In fact, apart from those in science-fiction movies and TV shows, and he wasn't sure that counted as experience, he had none.

He knew, or assumed, that androids were machine-like and didn't need, or want, anything beyond the purely functional. Yet, in this totally functional room, designed to accommodate melanie and a few humans for meetings, a picture was on the wall.

It didn't belong there. It did not fit.

He swung round in his seat and walked over for a closer look at the twenty-five-centimeter by fifteen-centimeter color photograph. Dominating the background were the two central wheels of a truck of some sort, with three children, pre-teens, sitting on a log in the middle-ground. They did not look happy.

In the lower border were the words 'VIRIDIAN ALE' in a no-nonsense sans-serif typeface. Below that 'G O was right. Remember Napoleon,' and the initials "AT" written in blue ink.

"What does all that mean?" Jack asked.

"That's for you to figure out," melanie said. "Any ideas?"

"Not a one," Jack said. "But that bit in blue is the first time I've seen anything written with an actual pen since meeting you."

"So why is it that when you find out that I'm an android, you become interested in a photograph on my wall?" melanie said. "I was expecting all sorts of questions, based on what you gleaned on the subject from TV and movies."

"The questions are there," Jack said. "But I don't know, they seem a little, err... personal, somehow."

"Interesting," melanie said.

"Not really," Jack said. "You're still you. I haven't asked you any personal stuff before; why would I do so now?"

"Good manners?" melanie suggested.

"Yes, I suppose," Jack said.

"You really are an astonishing man, Jack Fletcher," melanie said.

"Huh, that's rich, coming from you," Jack smiled, then looked embarrassed. "Astonishing woman," he added.

"Thank you," melanie said.

"And it explains a lot."

"Really? What?" melanie said.

"You are obviously super-intelligent."

"We aren't a lot more intelligent than humans. My IQ is around two ten, which means I'm good at IQ tests. Yours is just under one sixty, if you are interested, which means you aren't as good as I am at IQ tests." She shrugged.

"But we aren't as good as humans at anything that requires imagination. I can appreciate music, but I find it difficult to write. Although I can play with absolute precision, my playing lacks life."

"I've heard you lie," Jack said. "That requires imagination."

"Not in the same way," melanie said. "If I need to hide the truth, and I do, a lot, I substitute a set of equally plausible fictions for the facts. Usually, those fictions are truths borrowed from other situations and altered to fit the parameters I need. Humans can fabricate whole worlds of lies in such things as fiction in books, on TV or in the movies."

"I can think of a few news broadcasters and journalists who can do the same thing," Jack said. "But, as I know, the problem with lies is that you have to remember who you told what. Which is why I had to stick to the script so closely with my different personas."

"That I can understand, and there androids have a massive advantage," melanie said. "We can access all our memories more readily than humans, and we don't forget things the way you do. You may suddenly not be able to recall the name of someone you know well, or a birthday. We never forget things like that."

"But sometimes you seem to have forgotten things," Jack said.

"Those are built-in personality traits," melanie said. "Some of my facial expressions are as automatic as yours. Things like 'forgetting' are there to not appear to be too much smarter than humans. Early studies suggested that to prevent humans from being intimidated by us, we either look like filing cabinets or adopt human frailties."

"Okay," Jack said. "That was often the concern by science-fiction writers, that androids would be too smart for humans. Or that humans might think they... you, were too smart and become threatened."

"Yes, where the writer wasn't using the emancipation of androids as an analogy, perhaps."

"Yeah. Something like that," Jack said.

"That was a classic example of you doing the same thing," melanie said. "Pretending to not understand what I have said. Dumbing yourself down."

"It doesn't help to be too clever in my business," Jack said with a grin. "In fact, I know a few people who do that. I'll introduce you to one when we get back. You'll like her. A real flake called Amber Gullifoyle. She has a mind like a bloody razor when she thinks nobody is looking. She might be quite useful to us."

"Yes, let's do that," melanie said, turning to walk away.

Jack fell into step behind her and said, "Can I ask you a question?"

"Sure," melanie said.

"What do you dream about?"

She stopped so fast Jack almost walked into the back of her.

"Do not go there," she whispered and walked on. Jack said nothing.

DAY EIGHTEEN

Fourday 6.5.2834

Friday 17th February 2017

Romstrum 3
08:00 GST

Standing in Hold One, Lorina, Gary, and Miguel, all wearing space suits, watched on a monitor as the military gray shuttle fell to within a meter of the concrete apron, stopped, gave a tiny sigh, and then dropped onto its landing jacks.

The lock on the newcomer opened and disgorged automated flying flat trucks, each laden with metal and plastic crates.

As the first truck arrived, Lorina opened the hold door long enough for the truck to enter, then closed it again. She was going to be fighting a constant war. They needed the cargo doors open to get the supplies in, but they needed them shut to keep the heat out. Cold air jets set in the side of each door helped a little.

Working the cargo as it arrived, Gary and Miguel were winning the war but losing battles as they directed each load and made sure it was positioned correctly before the machines set off again.

After thirty minutes, during which the hold's temperature had risen to just over forty-five degrees, the last truck left, and Lorina closed the outer doors. She, Gary and Miguel moved into the corridor and left the hold to get back to an average temperature.

They moved on to Hold Two, where the temperature was down to ten degrees.

"The team's ready to come over," Lorina said, watching the monitor. "They are sending them over six at a time, in body sacks, on a cargo truck." She looked around. "Where's Amrita?"

"Here," Amrita said from the door, standing behind Jack and Joe Marafioti. "It's cold in here."

"It won't last," Lorina said. "You and Joe are to go back with the first pallet truck."

"Okay," Amrita said.

With a blast of heat as the door opened, a truck flew in with six silver bags standing up at the rear rail, and the door slammed shut behind it. As the truck landed, nozzles in the ceiling blew carbon dioxide over the cargo for five seconds.

Miguel and Gary leaped forward and opened the bags, each revealing a figure in uniform. Lorina waved them over before directing them through to the corridor.

"This is it," Amrita said to Jack. "Keep yourself safe. For me."

338

"I will," Jack said as he kissed her goodbye. He was sorry she was leaving, but knew it was inevitable. "You stay safe for me."

"Come on, you two," Lorina said. "Time to go."

Amrita stepped into one of the silver bags, and as soon as Miguel had finished sealing Joe Marafioti into his, he closed her bag. A second blast of heat struck them as the door opened to let the truck out.

"You okay, Jack?" Lorina said.

"Yeah, I'm okay," Jack said. "I liked her a lot."

"I know," Lorina said. "Now, if you have nothing better to do, can you wait and help get the next batch out?"

"Sure," Jack said, joining Miguel and Gary to wait as the room temperature began heading downward again.

"Wait until we move," Gary said. "It is hot out there, and so are those bags."

Jack nodded.

Moments later, Lorina called out a warning and opened the outer door. The cargo truck followed the blast of heat and landed a split second after the door slid closed. The freezing blast of carbon dioxide cooled the bags' exteriors, and Miguel and Gary grabbed one each.

They unclipped each bag at the top and pulled it down to pool around the occupant's feet and then pushed the flushed and disorientated soldier in Jack's direction.

Jack bundled each one into the corridor and directed them towards the stairs.

The last one tripped over the bag around her feet and stumbled into Jack. He caught hold to help her upright.

A pair of huge brown eyes gazed at Jack from inside a mess of blond hair.

"Hello," he said.

"Who the hell are you?" she said.

"Umm..." Jack said.

"Hi, Umm," she said and, pulling the wayward hair back into a cotton candy ponytail, she bounded towards Lorina.

"Who the fuck is that?" Jack said to Miguel.

"Zara Chang, the Ice Princess," Miguel said. "That didn't take long."

"What didn't?"

"Amrita only left about sixty seconds ago."

"No. Nothing like that," Jack said. "She looks like trouble."

"You got that right," Miguel said.

As he spoke, melanie appeared in the corridor and hugged Zara. All the confirmation Jack needed.

Romstrum 3
13:45 GST

melanie settled herself into the center seat of the flight deck and entered the codes for the main system operation. The hangar doors had been left open, and she taxied the vehicle out onto the landing pad.

Near the center of the pad, melanie stopped the vehicle, and without the need to touch any controls, lifted the shuttle vertically.

As the mess-room was filling with people he didn't know, Jack went back down to Hold One.

As usual, Miguel and Gary were there.

"Hey," Miguel said with a huge grin, "I thought you'd be up in the mess-room melting the Ice Princess."

"Very funny," Jack said. "Not my type. I'm not into blonds."

He turned and looked at the stack of crates and boxes Miguel and Gary were tying down.

"What's all this?" he said.

"I don't know," Miguel said. "But we will find out."

"We have an HCG set," Gary said, looking at a cube-shaped case.

"What's that?" Jack asked.

"Holographic camouflage generators," Miguel said. "More to the point, an Aetherian HCG. The Gaian ones are shit."

"There seems to be a load of chuglies," Gary said, moving on. "Twenty- four of them. That's not good."

"What's a chuglie?" Jack asked.

Gary was about to answer when Lorina came in and said, "Everybody in the mess-room or cabins, Bang and Tamara are about to sweep the lower deck and under-core.

Jack went to his cabin.

Ross-on-Wye, England
19:35 GMT
20:35 GST

"Albright," he said, answering the phone.

"Sir Quentin? This is Rufus Koenig," came a vaguely familiar voice.

"If this is about double-glazing, I have already told you people, no," Albright yelled and slammed down the receiver.

Picking up the handset again, he pressed a fifteen-digit number and, following a prompt, a further twelve digits.

After a pause, Albright said, "Koenig? What can I do for you?"

"I appreciate you are retired, Sir Quentin," Rufus said, "but do your people still have a man keeping a watch on the Caeil Ashbow files?"

"I imagine so," Sir Quentin said. "When I retired, young Morgan Cheshire was taking it on as part of his baggage. It's been dormant for years, of course. Why, may I ask?"

"Certainly. melanie has found Caeil Ashbow."

"As I believe I mentioned to Albrecht Torre at the time Ashbow absconded from Dotheboys Hall," Sir Quentin said, "I doubt melanie ever lost him. Although she may have mislaid him temporarily."

"I believe the school was actually 'St Jerome's', Sir Quentin."

"Yes. I am aware of that. I was attempting levity. 'Dotheboys' was a reference to the school in Nicholas Nickleby, the novel by Charles Dickens. There were parallels to be drawn."

"I see, sir," Rufus said. "Yes, regarding Caeil Ashbow, there has been other activity, and questions might be asked."

"Has there? Do you want me to speak to Sir Gwyn Lutwidge? He is Cheshire's superior."

"No sir," Koenig said. "We just wanted to let you know we were aware."

"Ah, thank you," Sir Quentin said and hung up, muttering, "Idiot," after the receiver was firmly down.

Romstrum 3
13:50 GST

Four kilometers down the road from the Gaian enclave, the camera on the roof of a large truck followed the disturbance in the air as the first shuttle left. A concise and innocuous message was transmitted from the truck.

A few minutes later, the orange shuttle took off, following a similar trajectory to the first. Inside the truck, an eight-legged creature with four arms and a heart-shaped head watched the departure on a monitor and sent a second short and innocuous message.

Shuttle *SV 3-8749*, leaving Romstrum 3
20:40 GST

Jack was in his cabin reading when melanie's face appeared on the screen in front of him.

"Can you go through to the mess-room?" she asked.

"Sure, what's up?" he said.

"Just about to go through the rabbit hole, and it could get rough this time."

"Okay," Jack said and walked around the corridor.

Lorina sat in the booth nearest the door and waved him to an empty seat next to her. As Jack sat down, restraints slid out and gripped him. After they had him pinned down, he realized that opposite him sat the Ice Princess, looking less than pleased at his presence.

"melanie says it could get turbulent, so we need to be strapped in," Lorina said.

"It doesn't normally, does it?" Jack asked.

"Not on an IST, but these little shuttles aren't really designed for...."

A massive fist of energy hit the underside of the floor, accelerating the vehicle hard, the inertial field generator whining in protest. Then it was all smooth.

"We're through," Lorina announced as the seat restraints slid open.

melanie appeared in the messroom and walked over to their table. "I think Bang overdid it a little," she said.

"What did he use, a nuclear warhead?" Jack asked as he stood up.

"No, two, that's why we got a bit shaken up. Still, it should be enough to persuade the curious that the bombs destroyed us going through the rabbit hole, which means we don't exist anymore. Exactly as ordered."

"Good," Jack said and headed for the door.

342

"Jack," melanie said, causing him to pause. "The briefing is in thirty minutes. Be there."

Arthronine vessel, Romstrum 3 deep orbit
20:43 GST

The Aetherian shuttle had followed a course towards the freighter *Valiant Sky* out beyond Ingpor, the larger moon of Romstrum. The crew of the Arthronine ship ignored it.

Eventually, the second shuttle came past them, following a different course from the preceding vehicle and traveling slower.

As it drew close, the airlock at the front of this shuttle opened, and the vehicle rotated one hundred and eighty degrees. Three large crates emerged, two opening to disgorge a haze of minor items, scraps of metal, packing cases, human bodies and odds and ends of machinery.

A violent magnetic pulse signaled the rabbit punch going into action, and, as the wave of magnetism swallowed the shuttle, a massive explosion reduced the objects it had deposited to a fine dust.

The captain of the Arthronine ship composed a message, translated it into Kanforkar and then into Arach, reporting the destruction of an unidentified, orange-painted vehicle, entering a rabbit-hole. Condolences to those concerned, but nothing could be done; the ship had been atomized.

That done, the Arthronine ship disappeared into a rabbit hole of its own making.

Shuttle *SV 3-8749*
20:45 GST

"Sit down," melanie said as she took her seat behind her desk.

Greta and Georgia Kaninchen sat.

"I want some distance between Romstrum and us," melanie said. "But in twelve hours, we will rendezvous with an Aetherian freighter that will deliver you to *Enterprise* or *Endeavour*."

Greta said, "What's happening, Commander?"

"I have terminated my temporary secondment to GCID and your mother," melanie said. "We are now an independent unit."

"Aided by the Aetherians?" Greta said.

"Naturally. I am Aetherian," melanie said.

"May I ask what happened?" Greta said.

"Certainly," melanie said. "I found Caeil, and we all know that the moment the Colonel has the opportunity, she will kill him as revenge against your mother, Sarah."

Neither sister spoke.

"Also," melanie continued, "I believe we can all agree that the Colonel is conspiring with elements of the Nel. Her reasons are unclear, but whatever they are, I will stop her. I cannot do so while operating within GCID, which, along with much of the federal government of Gaia, she controls."

"May I speak frankly?" Greta said.

melanie nodded.

"I have been concerned for some time," Greta said, "that *mutter* Bianca had become obsessed with hunting for Caeil Ashbow. Her hatred of Benji and *mutter* Sarah was consuming her. That she should extend that hatred to their child was, I thought, indicative of her poor mental state.

"Might I propose we join you? Our aim will be to take *mutter* Bianca to a secure mental facility."

melanie considered this for several seconds. "What is your attitude towards the Nel?" she said.

"I wanted to murder the only one I ever met," Greta said.

"In that case, we will work something out," melanie said.

Shuttle *SV 3-8749*
21:00 GST

"Guess what?" melanie said as Lorina walked into the office, and the door closed.

"Greta talked, Georgia said nothing, and they want to do a deal. They then said that dear old mommy isn't well in the head, and they want to look after her?"

"I really must find a replacement for you," melanie said.

"Oh, please," Lorina said. "I take it you will go along with their offer?"

"It is that or the airlock," melanie said.

"I vote for the airlock. I don't trust those two. Especially Greta. Nasty bitch."

"She speaks well of you," melanie said. "I think having them close to hand might have advantages. I will ask Tamara to make sure we monitor them at all times."

"Good," Lorina said. "We are all ready for the briefing."

"I will be there, with Jack," melanie said.

Shuttle *SV 3-8749*
21:15 GST

Lorina cast a critical eye around the conference room. She didn't like what she saw. This should be a briefing room, all gray bulkheads and non-slip flooring. Instead, she got frond-covered wallcovering, silk-smooth carpeting matching the fronds, a pale wood table and twenty-four sumptuous green padded armchairs.

She sighed and glowered at the bait set out in the center. Sandwiches—currently very fashionable on Gaia—tea, coffee, lire, jaxog, cake, biscuits, cookies, and enough varieties of fruit and nuts to make a health freak weep with joy.

She opened the door and said, "Okay, get in here, help yourselves, and try not to make too much of a mess. I shall assign some of you to cleaning duties, and the messier eaters stand the best chance."

The new arrivals filed in, sat down, and fell on the food as if newly released from a bread and water diet.

Lorina evicted those who had opted to take the three seats she had designated, with large signs, for melanie, herself, and Jack. She created order. As they ate and drank, the team took to fiddling with compads, chatting to their neighbors as if they hadn't seen them for months, as opposed to being with them on an IST for days.

As melanie and Jack were still missing, but on their way, Lorina considered some of the domestic issues. She banged on the table until the noise abated.

"Okay," she said, "Everyone got a cabin?"

There were shouts of assent.

"Any problems?"

"Yes."

"What?"

"We'd rather share."

"So, share."

"Okay, boss."

"Anything else?" Lorina asked.

"Yeah."

"What?"

"No greengages amongst the fruit."

"Tough, eat something else."

"Yes, boss."

The door slid open, and melanie and Jack walked in and took their seats, with Jack between Lorina and melanie.

"Okay, over to you," Lorina said to melanie and sat down.

"I think we'd better start with a few introductions. If, one at a time, you can all stand up and tell us your name and what you do?" melanie said and turned to Lorina.

"Excuse me, ma'am, but why?" Chiyo said. "We all know each other."

"I don't care if you all wipe each other's asses," Lorina said, her voice low but carrying well. "If the commander told you to introduce yourselves, you introduce yourselves. Understood?"

Chiyo stared at Lorina for all of five seconds before dropping her eyes. "Yes, ma'am," she mumbled.

"I want to hear you," Lorina said.

"Yes ma'am, sorry ma'am," Chiyo said, loudly.

"Okay," Lorina said as she stood. "Lieutenant Lorina Korenjic. I'm the planning, logistics, and communications specialist."

As she sat, Miguel stood and said, "Miguel Iwasaka, sergeant 3 and systems engineer."

"I'm Gary Johannsen; I'm also a sergeant 3 and the light armorer."

A woman with bright blue hair said, "I'm Tamara Finkel, sergeant 5, and I specialize in biotronics and systems and the weird stuff."

"Dan Olafsen, corporal 3," a shorter, wiry man with white hair and a goatee beard said. "I was a sergeant 3, but I got busted. I'm the demolition guy, and everyone calls me 'Bang'."

Three women stood up together. All three had the dark to mid-range Gaian olive skin, but while two had black hair, the third was blond. Jack knew who she was. The Ice Princess.

"We're the fire-triem," Chiyo said. "Specialists in sniper, surveillance, close-combat, unarmed combat, and urban warfare tactics. We're all sergeant 2, and I am Chiyo Lemasolai." She sat down.

"Sophia Gulab," the second one said, rather meekly, and sat.

"Zara Chang, but I'm actually a sergeant 6," said the blond and sat to engage in a good-natured squabble with Chiyo.

"I'm Setu Anastassiou, sergeant 7 and the doctor," said a rotund young man.

"Abdul Wei," a slightly older man with reddish hair and what Jack would have called a frank Zappa mustache said. "I'm the heavy armorer and a sergeant 4."

"Cornelius Vartanian," a bouncy younger man said as he sprang to his feet, "Sergeant 4 and a mechanical engineering specialist."

"Zaccaria Vartanian," a slightly older, bigger, longer-suffering version of Cornelius said as he rose, "but no relation. Also, a sergeant 4, no relation. I answer to 'Zack' or, because I'm a paramedic, to 'medic'."

"Actually, those two are brothers," the next woman said. "I'm Elise Jarmo, sergeant 4, and a mechanical engineering specialist. I'm also married to Cornelius, for now, but that might change." Laughs and female cheers.

"Greta Gunter-Kaninchen, captain 2 pilot," the first of the other two blonds said loudly.

"Georgia Gunter-Kaninchen, captain 2 pilot," Georgia said in a softer tone.

"melanie, the boss," melanie said.

"Jack Fletcher," Jack mumbled and sat down.

melanie stood and looked around the table, "I'd like to make a couple of corrections to what you have said. Lieutenant Korenjic is now Lieutenant Commander Korenjic, and you sergeants are now master sergeants. Which leaves Bang. They reduced you from sergeant to corporal for the wanton destruction of Colonel Grant's war memorial. Therefore, I'm very sorry, but you go up two ranks to master sergeant." They greeted this with a few cheers.

"Before we begin the briefing," melanie said, "I would like to introduce Jack properly."

Jack didn't want to be introduced. He didn't want them to notice him or put him in the spotlight. Attention by others was not recommended in his business. To make matters worse, the super-bitch Ice Princess was glowering at him.

"For those of you who don't know," melanie continued, "Jack is the elusive Caeil Ashbow. As you *will* know, Colonel Kaninchen has been looking for him since his parents died in a tragic car accident on Earth. As they share a birth mother, he is a half-brother to Greta and Georgia."

Jack knew that half of the newcomers were staring at him, and the other half were staring at his half-sisters, who stared back with sickly grins. He hadn't realized just how lucky he was not to have had a family so far in his life and then moved on to hoping an asteroid would destroy the shuttle, immediately.

"Jack grew up on Earth," melanie continued, "and has a lot to offer in terms of local knowledge. I'm going to leave it to Jack to tell you exactly what he did on Earth, but what I can say is that he has gained skills and experience in planning and executing what is best described as covert operations."

"Ma'am," Chiyo said. "Where does he fit into the chain of command? If at all."

"He is a civilian," melanie said. "But Jack's orders are to be regarded as orders from either Lieutenant Commander Korenjic or myself."

The looks being passed around made it clear that this news was not as popular as Bang's promotion.

"Next," melanie said, "The Nel. We are all aware of what the Nel are, but they are now excelling themselves.

"They are currently on Earth, although we do not know where, developing a psycontrol system, similar to the one they use on their own people, to control Terrans.

"The purpose is to turn the people of Earth into an army to fight the Arthronine."

Jack had heard what melanie was saying from Amrita. How the Nel would recruit four billion Terrans as foot-soldiers and reduce those who were not up to the task to factory workers or food.

He could keep one ear open for deviations from the original and spend the time having a better look at the new members of the crew.

"Is there a time-scale on this?" Zara Chang asked, and Jack started paying attention again.

"We don't know," melanie said. "Usually, Nel research takes time because researchers are often more worried about upsetting holy writ than making a scientific break-through. The process will also be complicated by the difference between Nel NOA and human NOA."

That was new, Jack decided and said, "What's a noah?"

348

"Neural Operating Architecture," melanie said. "That is like the DOS or Unix of the mind. Humans have around five hundred million different versions, although many have their similarities, like Windows 3.0, 3.1 and 3.2. The Nel have approximately one hundred and fifty NOAs, with each class or sub-class having its own."

"Separating the Alpha plus from the Epsilon, then?" Jack said.

"Say what?" Gary said.

"Jack was referencing *Brave New World*, written by Aldous Huxley," melanie said. "You should read it."

"Yes, boss," Gary said.

"Despite this," melanie continued, "while I am deeply suspicious of most Terran myths and superstitions, there seems to be an element of truth in the phrase, 'the luck of the Devil', and the Nel just might find some way around the NOA problem. If they do, from breakthrough to the first conversion, it could be a matter of weeks. They have the conversion equipment already there, and can ship more in as soon as they have the go-ahead."

"How long to recruit the entire population from there?" Setu asked.

"Again, difficult to say. The Earth's population is over seven billion and has a net growth of something like two hundred thousand people per day. To put that into perspective, that is equivalent to the entire population of Gaia every fifty days.

"If they could get the process down to sixty seconds and they needed to process the entire population in a year, they would need fifteen thousand processing stations. But that's only if the population were prepared to line up like cattle at the abattoir, which isn't likely."

"Exactly. So how are the Nel going to get seven billion people to walk through these processing stations?" Zack asked.

"The point is, they won't. It will have to be a relatively slow process to build up to a point where the Nel have enough home-grown soldiers to take over and push the rest of the population through at gunpoint. So maybe two years for the first part and another year until they are herding them through."

"How will they build up to something like that?" Elise asked.

"Gradually. The Nel could take over a small community and convert them, then send the converts out into the world to set up more stations, where they can start converting others and expand again. It's not too different from the method used by many religions."

"Then... what?" Zack asked.

"Then we speculate," melanie said. "But from breakthrough to world domination would be in the order of three years."

"I never thought I would say this," Miguel Iwasaka said, "but the best thing we could do is hit their homeworld with a planet buster and put them out of their misery. As well as ours."

melanie nodded, "Much as I would agree with you, such action might cause problems between the rest of the galaxy and us. It might just be the catalyst needed for a few species that bear grudges against Gaia to join forces.

"However, many feel that anything the other species can chuck at us might be better than allowing the Nel to continue living. They are not going to muster a Terran army just to wipe out the Arthronine. Once they have dealt with them, they will go after the rest of us.

"Ironically, because Gaia is a vehicle that can move, rather than a planet, whatever happens you have a better chance of survival than the fixed species, like us Aetherians. The problem is that the Nel have many supporters on Gaia who would assist in a takeover."

"Why?" Chiyo said. "Why would anyone help the Nel?"

"They wouldn't think of it as helping the Nel," melanie said. "They would think they were using the Nel to help them take over Gaia and that the Nel will leave once the new order is in place."

"If you want to control Gaia," Chiyo asked, "what's wrong with the existing system?"

"That is a question that has been asked many times," melanie said. "The standard answer is because the population rarely understand what is best for them."

There was a silence until Zara Chang asked. "What can we do?"

"Find the Nel base of operations on Earth and destroy it."

"Do you have any idea at all where on Earth it might be located?" Zara asked. "I mean a continent if not a country/"

"That's what we are here to find out," melanie said, looking around the table. "I suggest a short recess, maybe grab some coffee and reconvene in fifteen minutes."

350

Fifteen minutes after melanie had called the recess, Lorina called everyone back to the table.

melanie was last in and evicted Gary, telling him to sit in her space next to Jack.

"Next," melanie said, calling the meeting to order, "I want Jack to tell us a bit about himself."

Jack looked at her and was about to get up and leave when Lorina said, "You'll be fine."

Gary, sitting on the other side, said, "We're here, mate."

"Jack has had an interesting history," melanie said. "Orphaned after the car crash on Earth, he grew up in an orphanage in England, which, for those of you who don't know, is part of a small island to the left of the main Euro-Asian landmass that dominates the northern hemisphere.

"When we found him, Jack was... maybe you had better explain this bit," melanie said.

Jack glowered in melanie's direction. He felt flushed and wanted to deposit his last meal over the conference table. He hadn't wanted to be in the same room as these people, and he hadn't wanted to talk to them individually. How the hell was he supposed to speak to them all?

"I was, umm... robbing banks," he said.

He stopped, still glowering at melanie.

"Anything else?" melanie asked.

Jack shook his head.

Chiyo sniggered.

In the grand scheme of things, it was only a snigger. Jack turned his head and looked at Chiyo.

While melanie had been speaking earlier, the team had sat up straight and paid careful attention. Especially after the slight run-in between melanie and the one he had since identified as Chiyo. The one of whom melanie had said, 'You'll like her'.

Now, slumped in their seats like recalcitrant teens, the newcomers were displaying their displeasure at being kept behind after school. An insolence suggesting they were already knowledgeable in everything and he could teach them nothing.

Chiyo gave a stage yawn and muttered something indistinct. A couple of the others giggled.

In the past few seconds, Jack had decided that he would not stay with these people. melanie had just set him up. That and her constant lies meant that the whole situation was untenable. Now he had two choices.

He could skulk out of there with his tail between his legs. Or, better yet, he could really piss them off on his way out.

All his life, he had played out roles; Danny Pollard, London thug, John Fletcher, delivery boy, Pierre Gomez, none-too-bright office cleaner and David Massey, financial advisor.

Time to add a new one. Jack Fletcher, bank robber and leader of men.

Jack stood up, his shoulders went back, and he stopped fixating on an empty plate in the middle of the table. He slammed his compad down on the table and said,

"Fuck this."

"You, what's your name again?" he said, staring straight at Chiyo.

She ignored him. Jack picked up the plate in front of him and flung it down to land in front of her.

"You, I'm talking to you," he said.

Chiyo looked at Lorina, then melanie, and both were staring back at her intently. She looked at Jack,

"Master Sergeant Lemasolai," Chiyo said.

"So, Sergeant Lemasolai. You were saying something earlier, which I didn't quite catch. I don't recall you being asked to speak. I was, so please show me the courtesy of shutting the fuck up while I do so."

Chiyo was about to say something but thought better of it. Jack looked around the table at their disgruntled faces. Nobody else was going to say anything.

The temptation to leave it there was strong, but fuck it, he'd been kidnapped, lied to, exposed to spiders that would give him nightmares for years to come, told that his planet was about to be taken over and lied to some more. He wanted blood.

"I am up here to talk about what I do," he said. "I rob banks.

"With no false modesty, I can say that I was fucking good at robbing banks. Over the past five years, I have stolen over forty million pounds. That's over fifty-three million US dollars.

"Through investment, that puts my current personal wealth at over eighty-five million dollars. I have a flat in Pimlico in London. Pimlico is not fashionable, like Hampstead or St John's Wood. I have an apartment in Hoboken, over the river from

Manhattan. And there is a house in the south of France. The Languedoc, not Provence.

"I drive a twenty-five-year-old classic Range Rover and a three-year-old Audi R8. Not a Ferrari and certainly not a Lamborghini, although that is what an R8 is.

"I live well, eat well and drink well in moderation. I fly business-class because I think first-class is over-rated.

"There is a pattern there. I think that not only is first class over-rated, but it also draws attention. Anything that draws attention to me is dangerous. I think like that because I am a professional.

"I work alone. No partners. No helpers. No muscle. Just me."

Saying nothing, he walked a quarter of the way around the conference room and stopped behind Elise Jarmo.

"I have been robbing banks for years. During that time, I have never been questioned or arrested. I have never even been on the radar. No police force has my photograph, fingerprints, dental records or DNA on file. They don't know where I live, who I am, or even that I exist.

"Even melanie hasn't got all the answers, have you?"

"I know where you live," melanie said.

Jack said. "The flat in St. Andrew's Square isn't home."

"If that is true, then no, I don't know," melanie said.

"It's true," Jack said.

Jack walked on another quarter of the way around the table and stopped behind Setu.

"When melanie asked me to join this team," Jack said, "I told her I was not a team player. Teams scare me. There is no better place to hide incompetence than in a team. The other team members will cover up the weak links, even if it is detrimental to the team. They then call it 'team spirit'. What a fucking joke that is.

"melanie assured me that this would not be a problem here. She had a small team of dedicated specialists. 'Professionals', she said. I believed her.

"How dumb is that? I have been telling you I am a professional and how successful I have been. And then I believed something melanie told me.

"I was about to leave," Jack said and stopped walking. "I was about to board whatever brought you here and leave. But I didn't leave because melanie had told me she had a team of professionals arriving. Ha!

353

"Instead, we got you. A bunch of rank amateurs. Indolent children who fear the possibility that someone might see their incompetence.

"So, here is what happens now. I am stuck with you lot for the time being but, as soon as it is possible, melanie will take me back to Earth. You lot can fuck off to somewhere else in the galaxy, where you can't do any damage. I will find the Nel base, and I will destroy these fuckers.

"If you stay on Earth, please, for my sake, join the Nel. It will be much easier to destroy them if you are with them, rather than with me. Either way, stay away from me. You are now part of the problem."

Jack turned and strolled out of the room. The door closed behind him.

There was total silence.

"Any comments?" melanie said. "Chiyo, let's start with you."

Nel Military Base, Colorado
14:10 MST
(22:10 GST)

Captain-Colonel Polikar sat in his office watching recent news events from his home on Nel Prime. Vids were streamed occasionally, and he enjoyed watching them before passing them on for general consumption.

The news was good overall, although it was rarely anything but good. War production was up. There had been spontaneous gatherings to condemn Gaian interference. A few radicals who had been subverted by Gaian agents had been executed publicly. Polikar enjoyed watching Nel executions. They were protracted affairs, giving the condemned a little taste of what they should expect in Heaven.

He was not a genuine believer. He was a realist, and mixing with other species had shown there were more beliefs and more gods than there were different species. There was nothing to say the Nel philosophies were right, and, looking at the universe with the eyes of one who had traveled between the stars, he doubted if any of the countless alternatives were right either. Not that he would mention his doubts to anyone else; that was a sure way of finding out if the God of the Nel existed.

354

The door from his inner room opened, and two soldiers with dull, uninterested eyes walked through, carrying a covered stretcher that dripped red as they went. Another two followed with a second stretcher, then his secretary, Jalimek, who rushed to open the outer door.

The clean-up crew were still in the room and would be for some time. Last night had been fun. Next time, he'd get three or four of them. He smiled in anticipation.

Soon after the stretchers had departed, Jalimek announced that Fangothar from the Intelligence Department was requesting an audience.

Fangothar kneeled and placed his forehead against Polikar's hand. "Thank you for granting me this audience, Captain-Colonel."

"It will, I trust, be sufficiently important to justify taking me away from my other duties?"

"I believe so, sir."

"Get on with it, then."

"The Gaian shuttle on Romstrum 3 had a cargo delivered a few hours ago and soon afterward left the planet. There have been reports it exploded on entering the rabbit-hole, sir."

"I see. This explosion. What was the cause?"

"It is difficult to assess, sir. We have only the report of a Kormark freighter leaving the system and the evidence from one of our own vessels that there had been an explosion at the point in space specified. The small amount of debris remaining contained materials consistent with the Gaian vessel's construction, and there were traces of Gaian DNA present."

"It would sound, Fangothar, as if you have some doubts as to the authenticity of this explosion?"

"Minor doubts, sir, which is why I have requested this audience. Despite their un-Godliness, Gaian vessels do not explode on entering a rabbit-hole. Our records show that the last time this happened was millennia ago, and there was some question then whether it was an accident or an act of sabotage."

"Could not this have been an act of sabotage?"

Before Fangothar could answer, the inner door opened, and a team of five cleaners, three pushing trolleys, emerged and walked towards the outer door. Fangothar could see the third trolley was full of blood-soaked bedding.

"I cut myself shaving," Polikar said, with a grin that made Fangothar's chest tighten with fear. "Do continue."

"I believe sabotage to be far more likely than an accident, sir," Fangothar continued.

"Yes," Polikar said, "it is. You have done well, Major, but I suggest you keep this conversation very much to yourself. Any future similar observations you will bring to me, understood?"

"Yes sir, of course, sir."

Polikar waved the Major out, and a few seconds later, Jalimek entered the office.

"You heard?"

"Yes, sir," Jalimek replied.

"What of the Major?"

"Currently useful. Ambitious enough to want to get on but sufficiently aware of his own deficiencies not to over-stretch himself. He's also a friend of the General."

"So, it would appear my source on Gaia may have been telling the truth," Polikar said, "and this stupid stunt has been foiled. If that is the case, it is a pity in many ways.

"But for some reason, I doubt it is. That bitch Kaninchen is devious; she may try a double bluff. Although that tick-tock of hers is worse. They may still be out there and, if they are, they will come here. Tell the data facility there is to be no reduction in checking information from the surveillance net. None.

"Think of the political capital we might yet gain by capturing them."

"Yes, sir."

"Oh, the fun we might have, eh Jalimek?" Polikar glanced at the inner door and grinned.

"Oh yes, sir," Jalimek agreed and permitted himself a small smile.

"Now, get out," Polikar ordered and watched Jalimek tiptoe out of the door.

Fear is such a beautiful thing, he thought.

Shuttle *SV 3-8749*
22:20 GST

"What happened there?" melanie asked Lorina in the corridor near Jack's office.

Lorina was expecting her to be angry, but she seemed almost sanguine. "Damned if I know," she said. "Chiyo took a dislike to Jack, but I have no idea why."

"You think?" melanie smiled.

"I should have moved in as soon as Chiyo faked that yawn."

"Good thing you didn't," melanie said. "If we want Jack to work with us for real, then I want to know how he reacts under pressure."

"What next?" Lorina asked.

"You go talk to Jack. I'm going to see what's happening amongst the revolutionaries."

Shuttle *SV 3-8749*
22:22 GST

"Well, that went well," Elise said and looked at Chiyo. "What next? Gonna shoot the boss?"

"Yes, Chiyo, are you going to piss me off too," melanie said as she walked back into the conference room.

"Okay, boss, I'm sorry," Chiyo said.

"You will be if he walks," melanie said. "I suggest you all give some thought to getting him to stay."

melanie turned and walked out.

"Look, guys," Miguel said, "we've got to know him a bit and he's okay. He talks funny, but he's cool.

"He was helping sorting out cargo and just mucking in."

"melanie says he can handle himself in a fight." Gary added. "He killed a guy in the Plantation. Hit him in the face with a bottle. From four meters."

"He is sort of cute," Tamara said.

"Leave him to stew for a while, and I'll go talk to him," Greta said. "I am his sister."

"Oh, fuck," Chiyo said. "That won't end well."

Shuttle *SV 3-8749*
22:23 GST

"That was fun," Lorina said to Jack as she walked into his office.

"Was it?" Jack said, staring at his compad screen.

"No, not really," Lorina said. "So, what now?"

357

"As I said, drop me on Earth and stay out of my way."

"Is that what you really want?"

"Yes."

"Do you think you are going to find it easier dealing with a group of Terran mercenaries who will probably think you are insane because you want to kill aliens in Colorado?"

"Now you put it that way, probably not," Jack said and grinned.

"So, how are you going to resolve this?" Lorina said.

"I'm not," Jack said.

***

Lorina found melanie waiting in the corridor.

"You heard?" Lorina said.

"I did."

"What now?"

"I will talk to him," melanie said.

"Jack," melanie said as she walked into his cabin. "Can we talk?"

"Sure," Jack said. "You can talk about how soon we get to Earth."

"As soon as we can," melanie said. "I suspect Bianca will have arranged it so getting back there might be a little difficult for us."

"Then get me onto another ship, or vehicle, or whatever."

"It isn't just us they will look for," melanie said. "If I put you onto another vehicle, even an Aetherian one, the Nel will find you and pass you straight to Bianca."

"How will they find me?" Jack said.

"The police on Earth may not have your DNA, but Bianca does."

"So, find me somewhere to hide out for a while," Jack said.

"You have that here," melanie said.

"No good," Jack said. "Here is infected with that bunch of amateur clowns you call soldiers. Whatever is wrong with them might be contagious."

"There is nowhere else that you would survive for more than twenty-four hours, so you need to accept this as the least bad option."

"Isn't there somewhere you could leave *them*?" he asked brightly.

"No," melanie said. "Here, with us, is your best option."

358

"Even better than being left on Earth?"

"Yes. You would have been dead by now," melanie said. "Jacob Scallon was lazy and incompetent, and would never have found you. But the squad Bianca had put on your trail was getting close. That is why I stepped in."

"Mmm, okay," Jack said. "So, is there anywhere, like an uninhabited planet we can stay on until we can go back? Somewhere I can stay away from them and you?"

"There is," melanie said. "We are heading there now. This vehicle still needs some work, and we can finish that off while we wait and see if the blockade lifts."

"That will do," Jack said.

"I was hoping for your help on this," melanie said.

"Why?" Jack asked. "You have your *team* out there."

"They have their uses," melanie said. "But I need your mind."

"Why?" Jack said.

"Because some people think a little differently," melanie said. "That team you dislike are all sergeants. GCID soldiers start as army privates and become sergeants or go back to the army at the end of basic training. Some go on to officer training.

"Lorina is my first and only officer. She didn't go to officer training. They would never have let her in because she thinks for herself. Lorina frightens people, not because she is a fighter, but because she is a thinker.

"You are like them. Only better."

Jack snorted.

"That is why I want you in on this. You have the skills I need, and that lot have the skills I need. The only actual difference is that the idea of working with others doesn't scare them. It scares the shit out of you."

"I'm not scared of them," Jack said.

"I didn't say you were," melanie said. "I said you scared of working with them."

"So, what was Chiyo's problem?"

"She wasn't scared of you," melanie said. "She doesn't like you, for some reason."

"Why the fuck not?"

"Who knows? But Chiyo's liking you or otherwise does not alter the fact that I still want you on this team. You showed them and me you don't take prisoners. I like that. They respect that."

"So, what now?" Jack said.

"They respect what you did; now they need to respect you."

359

"Why do I need their respect?" Jack said.

"That's a stupid question, as you well know."

Jack thought it over and shrugged. "No, it's not," he said. "I don't want or need their respect. As soon as we get to Earth, I'm gone. In the meantime, I suggest we just ignore each other."

"I could go in there now and order them to crawl around here and beg your forgiveness," melanie said, "but I don't think you like other people fighting your battles for you."

"No, I don't," Jack said. "But it doesn't matter. You still don't get it, do you melanie? I have no interest in them. In the same way, they don't like or respect me. Why should they? They don't know me; they just know the rest of their little clique."

"Lorina, Miguel and Gary know, like and respect you, and they are probably in there right now, telling the others what a bunch of pricks they are."

"They didn't have much to say when Chiyo was kicking off."

"No," melanie said. "Nor did I. You didn't need any help. When you said, 'You, I'm talking to you', it wasn't only Chiyo who took notice. We all did."

"Hmmm," Jack said.

"So, what will you do if they come round here of their own volition and apologize?"

"I don't know," Jack said. "That lot in there are just like so many of the people I've dealt with over the years. They have all the answers and think that is enough."

"Isn't it?"

"No, it isn't. Life isn't about the answers; it's all about the questions."

"Very profound," melanie said. "What does it mean?"

"There is always an answer to a question. If you can't figure it out, you can always just Google it. Coming up with the questions is the tricky part."

"You think?" melanie said.

"I know," Jack said. "Pythagoras didn't just come to the idea that the Earth was a sphere...."

"It wasn't Pythagoras; it was Anaxagoras."

"The history books all say it was Pythagoras," Jack said.

"Maybe, but the people who wrote the history books weren't there, the Saurians were, and it was Anaxagoras."

"Okay," Jack said, "So Anaxagoras, at some point, thought, 'I wonder if the Earth is really flat?' A question. That was the leap, the clever bit. Once the question is asked, then comes the long slow bit of providing the correct answer.

"Maybe, yes, the Earth is flat and riding on the backs of four fucking great elephants riding on the back of a giant turtle, but at least the question had been let out of the box, and the answer eventually proved."

"I understand what you are saying," melanie said. "That you know the questions."

"No," Jack said. "I don't know the questions, but I can often work out what the questions are or will be or should be."

"Oh, good," melanie said. "So, you will know my next question is, 'How does that help?'"

"Yes, I knew that," Jack said. "It was rather obvious."

"Do you have an answer, or are you going to Google it?"

"No, I'm not," Jack said. "It's still about the questions."

"It is?"

"Yes, it is," Jack said. "Right now, they are in that conference room working themselves up with a dose of righteous indignation. But eventually, a few of the voices of reason will kick in and start asking why *you* want me here."

"What will they conclude?"

"I doubt they will. The question, 'why does melanie want this guy here?' will have done its work by existing. It will have established the point that I am here because that's what you want. That will be enough; they will stop caring why."

"And then?"

"The question will then be, how do they make this right? You wanting me here and them attempting to drive me away will make them believe that this is all their fault. So, they will need to put it right."

"Are you sure?"

"No, but I reckon by eleven o'clock, someone, probably a sister or two, will be here."

"We shall see," melanie said.

Shuttle *SV 3-8749*
22:55 GST

When Jack answered the ping from the door, it slid open to reveal Greta and Georgia standing outside.

"Smart-arse," melanie muttered.

361

"Come in," Jack said. "What can I do for you?"

"The others have asked us to speak to you," Greta said.

Jack pointed at a couple of chairs and said, "Please, sit down."

The two women sat, and Jack said, "Now, who has asked you to do what?"

Greta seemed slightly thrown and said, "Er, the others, the rest of the team, they, um, wanted us to talk to you."

"Okay," Jack said, "you are talking to me."

The sisters sat and stared at Jack for a while until Jack said, "Did they want you to talk to me about anything specific, or just pass the time?"

"Yes," Greta said, realizing she wasn't doing as well as she would have liked. "If you are prepared to forget what happened, so are they."

"Really?" Jack said with an enormous smile. "Well, what can I say? Okay, that seems very reasonable." The smile disappeared. "Please tell 'the others' goodbye. Oh, and to stay the fuck off my planet."

"Okay, okay," Greta said. "What do you want? They will do anything."

"I have already told you what I want," Jack said, speaking slowly and loudly, "I want to get off this damned vehicle."

"May I say something?" melanie said.

"Would it make any difference if I said, 'no'?" Jack said.

"No."

"Then go ahead," Jack shrugged.

"We can get you to Earth, but it will take a while," melanie said. "So, what is it you need when you get there?"

"A professional team who are prepared to listen, to understand what our objectives are, and to tell me what I need to know to accomplish those objectives."

"Which is precisely what you have out there," melanie said.

"Yeah?" Jack said. "I must have missed them.

"Greta," melanie said abruptly, "you and Georgia go back to the mess-room. I'll be there shortly."

melanie and Jack stood silently until the twins had left and the door had closed firmly.

"It will take time before we can get to Earth," melanie said. "But maybe with your help, we can get there sooner."

Jack shrugged.

362

"Come on, Jack," melanie said. "You've given them a fright; now why don't you go out there and show them you are a leader and not a bully."

"I don't like Greta at all," Jack said, ignoring melanie. "You don't suppose my sisters, bless them, will pass information back to mummy, do you?"

"Possibly," melanie said. "Probably. Definitely. That's why they are here."

"What is it about all of this that you aren't telling me?"

"I've told you everything I can," melanie said.

"Politician's answer."

"It is," melanie said. "But as and when you need to know, or earn the right to know, or you figure it out for yourself, I will tell you the truth. Here's the point, Jack, I was created to do one job. Just one. I'm still doing it, and I will finish it.

"I will not let you, this team or anyone else get in the way. So, I will lie for you, and to you, for as long as it takes to complete my task. Understood?"

"Yes," Jack said. "Understood. Thank you, melanie. Now that was the most honest thing you have ever said."

"It was," melanie agreed.

"In that case, could you inform the team that I want them in the conference room at eleven-thirty?"

"It would be my pleasure," melanie said.

Shuttle *SV 3-8749*
23:30 GST

Jack entered the conference room and found the entire company sitting at the table waiting. He walked over and stood behind his seat, between Lorina and melanie.

He looked around the table. They all sat, staring back at him. Not exactly hostile, but still a little surly at having had their bluff called. Although he could only speculate what Lorina, melanie, and his sisters had said to them to get that far.

Lorina was also watching the team. Gary and Miguel were on side, she knew. The others were not looking happy. Some, like Chiyo Lemasolai, looked positively murderous. Then she spotted one face looking not the slightest bit murderous. In fact, quite the reverse. Well, well, she thought, what have we got here?

Jack said, "Hello. As melanie said earlier, my name is Caeil Ashbow, but I answer to Jack Fletcher. I'm a civilian, despite which melanie has asked me to help with this operation.

"If any of you do not want to work with me, say so now. If that is your decision, we will find you somewhere secure, if not terribly comfortable, to wait out this operation. Are you all absolutely clear on this?"

Jack looked at each one, in turn, only moving on when he had made eye contact. None of them indicated dissent.

"Good," Jack said. "First thing you need to know. As melanie told you, I am here as a civilian advisor. I will issue orders only when essential. In situations where I am reliant on your expertise, I will expect to follow your orders.

"The other thing you need to remember is that I am a civilian. I'm not in the GCID or any army, so I'm going to call you all by your first names. I expect you to call me 'Jack' to my face. You can call me what the fuck you like behind my back. This I want extending out to the officers as well."

Jack turned and looked at both melanie and Lorina, who both nodded their agreement. He ignored his sisters.

"The next thing you need to know is that although I am an advisor, I don't have any of the answers. Not one."

He paused and waited. "So, doesn't anybody want to ask what the fuck it is I do?"

Nothing.

"Chiyo? I expected more of you," he said.

"Okay," Chiyo said. "What the fuck do you do?"

"I'm glad you asked, Chiyo," Jack said. "Because, from now on, I ask the questions. The awkward questions, the questions you haven't thought of, the ones you have ignored because they are too much trouble."

Jack looked around. There was a shift.

"I'm going to start," Jack said, "by asking you, what do we do next?"

They stared back at him.

"Nothing? You have no clue?"

"Okay. From what melanie told us earlier, we all have some idea what the Nel are doing on Earth. I'm sure we can all work out that we need to stop them, not just for the Earth's sake, but for Gaia's too. But we need to accomplish this without Earth's people realizing they are hosting a turf war between what they

364

would see as two alien races. How we do that is a question for another time.

"Let's get there first.

"As we were entering the rabbit hole, there was a detonation directly behind us. melanie and Bang Olafsen created this and involved, I am told, two nuclear warheads, some old junk we had lying around, and a couple of dead bodies melanie had acquired. This, we hope, would be enough that anyone investigating will think this vehicle blew up just as we went into the rabbit hole. So, now we are officially dead.

"Therefore, my first question is, were the Nel fooled?"

"No," Lorina said.

"You sound very positive," Jack said.

"I am," Lorina said. "There is a surveillance net surrounding Earth. They have brought it up to a higher level of awareness in the last few hours. Suggesting they do not think they destroyed us leaving Romstrum."

"This surveillance net," Jack said. "What is it?"

"The Nel have twenty-six surveillance satellites hidden away within all the Terran junk orbiting Earth," melanie said. "They carry a mixture of active and passive systems. The satellites transmit all their data to a central site where, typically, five hundred Nel and assorted allies plus six AIs analyze what comes in.

"Because of the amount of debris, both Terran and natural, orbiting Earth, plus the Gaian, Aetherian and Nel vehicles, most estimates suggest that if they look at twenty percent of data, they've had a busy day. But it could go up to eighty or ninety percent now. If they suspect we are still around, they will bring in whatever staff they need to cover all the data coming in from those satellites. Which means they would spot us easily and quickly."

"How long will they keep that until they decide maybe we *were* killed leaving Romstrum?" Jack asked.

"It won't quite work like that," Chiyo said. "I spent some time working on a Gaian planetary defense net.

"Right now, the Nel will watch every section of the sky across the spectrum and around the clock. Ideally, the system will work with close to a one hundred percent detection rate. Even when new and the system is protecting the home planet, the best you can hope for is ninety-eight percent. Give it a few weeks and that will drop.

"Even though a RAI carries out most of the grunt work, the checking of the 'possible' sightings by a fully sentient individual is tedious and it takes very little time for the detection rate to drop below eighty percent."

"How long is 'very little time' do you think?" Jack asked.

"Three or four weeks," Chiyo said. "But that was for people who were operating a net for their own protection. The Nel aren't. They are running a net where there is no downside to the operators if anything gets through the net."

"Okay, so how long before the Nel system gets down to a level where we might get through?"

"Four or five weeks," Chiyo said.

"I believe Chiyo has a valid point," melanie said. "Politics will also kick in, and those who have lost resources to boost the surveillance team now, will start demanding them back, just to make sure the loan doesn't become a permanent fixture."

"Okay," Jack said. "When you all arrived, I saw a lot of cargo come aboard, and I think it was Miguel who told me that some of it had to be installed."

Nods from the assembled group.

"Next question. How long is it going to take to get all that stuff installed?"

Jack looked at them, and they stared back.

"That wasn't a rhetorical question," he said.

Elise Jarmo went into a huddle with Cornelius Vartanian, her husband and fellow mechanical engineer, and Abdul Wei, the heavy armorer. They tossed numbers and jobs and times around like manic jugglers until Jack said, "Just whether it's days, weeks or months would do."

"It could be as long as four weeks," Cornelius said, "but we'll get some priority lists together and see what we can come up with."

"Gaian weeks or Terran weeks?" Jack said.

"Gaian," Elise said. "But we'll have a more detailed look later when we have our lists."

"That's fine," Jack said. "Which brings us to my next question or two. Are we going somewhere we can get this kit fitted without looking over our collective shoulders all the time, and when will we get there?"

"Yes, we are, and in about a week, we have a minor detour on the way," melanie said.

366

"Okay, so we have four, maybe five weeks until we head for Earth," Jack said. "Therefore, our next question is, will the efficiency of the net have dropped sufficiently in the next five weeks for us to get through?"

"Not necessarily," Chiyo said. "They could still be looking at thirty to forty percent of the data."

"Is that too high?"

"Yes, it is," melanie said.

"Okay," Jack said. "Back to basics. What does this system do... err, how does it work?"

"The satellites use two forms of detection," melanie said, "The active systems are the ones that send out a signal of some sort and see what comes back, like radar. They aren't a real problem because the shuttle's exterior has a broad-spectrum coating that will absorb the signal.

"The passive systems detect any form of radiation being given off by the shuttle. That's anything from infra-red to ultra-violet and includes radio, heat, light, and whatever the engines are leaking. However, like all Gaian military vehicles, this vehicle has a lining in the outer casing to prevent most radiation from getting in. Or getting out and being detected."

"You said 'most'." Jack said.

"There are a few exceptions," Greta continued. "Heat from the outer hull itself or from the primary drive. The two ways of slowing a vehicle are by gently easing it into the atmosphere or using the engines. Both generate a lot of heat. Also, this vehicle has a mass causing slight curvatures in light. Even starlight."

"Can we overcome these problems?"

"No. We can reduce our chances of being detected; what we can't do is guarantee we are not in the percentage that is scrutinized."

"Okay. Anything else?"

"Yes, they can still see us," Lorina said.

"Ah, yes," Jack said, "We can get away without being detected by the most sophisticated equipment available but still be spotted by a bloke with a pair of binoculars?"

"The Nel use a bit more than that," Chiyo said. "Each one of those satellites has a bank of cameras constantly photographing the sky and looking for anything moving, blocking out the stars."

"Can we get around that one?"

"Possibly," melanie said. "But the chances of avoiding all the different systems are low."

367

"Miguel," Jack said. "Didn't you say we had some sort of holographic camouflage kit in the hold? Wouldn't that help?"

"No, they are only effective in an atmosphere," Miguel said.

"Okay," Jack said, "Are Gaian and Aetherian freighters getting in and out?"

"Yes, they are," melanie said. "Meaning the freighters are going into Mars orbit, and then shuttles are going to and from the Earth."

"This is a shuttle. Couldn't this be one of those shuttles? What was that thing with *Encounter*, err... 'ganging?"

"No," melanie said. "The Nel run visual inspections on shuttles. This would never pass."

"Okay, so could we not go down on one of the commercial shuttles."

"Technically, yes," melanie said.

"Not from a Gaian freighter," Lorina said. "We might just as well send Bianca a message detailing our arrival time and place."

"Yes. I suppose so," Jack said.

"Even an Aetherian freighter has its risks," melanie said. "Unless we use *Valiant Sky*, which has a meticulously screened crew, there is always the risk of a Gaian informant being aboard. The Nel would subject *Valiant Sky*, and any shuttles launched from it, to excessive scrutiny. There is also the factor that taking this shuttle will mean that if this operation goes wrong, we have a formidable vehicle and can fight our way out."

"Okay," Jack said. "That makes sense."

"Can we ask questions?" Elise said.

"Looks like it," Jack said, and grinned at her.

"Is there a way in?"

"Absolutely," Jack said.

"How?"

"I don't have the faintest idea," Jack said. "You tell me?" Elise looked blank.

"Okay," Jack said. "What's stopping us from getting in?"

"The surveillance net," Elise said.

"Can we not disable the surveillance net?"

"I doubt it." Elise said.

"Does it have a weak link?" Jack said. "Chiyo, you mentioned that they use a data collection center with five hundred Nel. That sounds like five hundred weak links. Couldn't that be destroyed or disrupted?"

"It's in Brazil," melanie said. "Which is on Earth."

"So, we go and blow that up, and then we can get this shuttle in," Jack said.

"But we'd need to get the shuttle in before we blew it up," Chiyo said.

"Would we, though?" Jack said.

FiT: THE THIRTEENTH

Charles Lutwidge Dodgson picked up his pen and wrote, "One thing was certain, that the white kitten had had nothing to do with it—it was the black kitten's fault entirely."

"Good afternoon, Mister Dodgson," Alice Liddell said. "May I speak with you?"

Dodgson looked up, then sprang to his feet and bowed. Alice responded with a curtsey.

"Miss Alice," Dodgson said. "How is this possible? How are you here?"

Alice was in Oxford, at home with her parents. Yet there she stood, her hair falling across the patterned shawl wrapped around her shoulders.

"I am not exactly here," Alice said.

"How can you be here, inexactly?"

"There are many things that are possible, even those that are inexact," Alice said. "Things that will be beyond your understanding. But all will become clear one day."

"Is this a dream?" Dodgson asked.

"No, Mister Dodgson, it is not," Alice said. "It is beyond dreaming. Now, we have something to discuss."

"Certainly, Miss Alice," Dodgson said. "But pray be seated first, and perhaps some refreshment?"

"Thank you, I will sit," Alice said. "I have no need for refreshment, but thank you for your offer."

"What is it you wish to discuss?" Dodgson asked as he seated himself after Alice had lowered herself into the chair on the other side of the desk.

"You are familiar with the concept of other places? For example, where the faerie folk exist?" Alice said.

"I am familiar with the Eddic poem Grímnismál and know of Álfheim," Dodgson said.

"That is close enough," Alice said. "In your new work, Alice will visit another place by traveling through a looking glass, will she not?"

370

"She will indeed," Dodgson said.

"Good," Alice said. "Now imagine yourself standing between two looking glasses and seeing your image repeated towards infinity."

"I visited the Great Exhibition as a young man and saw the Hall of Mirrors," Dodgson said. "I am familiar with the result and I also have a passing acquaintance with the mathematics involved."

"Of course," Alice said. "What you must now understand is that this is how the universe is set out.

"At this moment, there are many versions of you writing at your desk, but only one where I am speaking to you."

Dodgson stared at Alice, not seeing her, his mind catching up with what she had told him.

"I understand," Dodgson said, not sure if he really did.

"One hundred years from today, and beyond the most distant land, a woman called melanie, with whom you have a peculiar connection, and yet she has never heard of Lewis Carroll, will meet a man with no memory and a copy of your books."

"How can you know this?" Dodgson demanded.

"We know what is, what has been and what will be," Alice said. "To explain this would require many days and perhaps months to explain to one even of your elevated intellect. We ask that you accept our word on this."

Dodgson nodded.

"The woman will use your writings as a cipher, and, to that end, we would like to make sure that you employ certain keywords and phrases in your new work."

"What words?" Dodgson asked warily. "You wish to put your words into my work."

"Not at all, dear Mister Dodgson," Alice said. "We do not possess the wit for such action. These are your words. Your ideas, we merely beg leave to suggest certain phrases and plot lines that will become useful in the future."

"Can you offer some examples?"

"Certainly," Alice said. "Some fifteen years ago, you penned a piece that went,

Twas bryllyg, and ye slythy toves
Did gyre and gymble in ye wabe:
All mimsy were ye borogoves;
And ye mome raths outgrabe."

"I recall," Dodgson said.

371

"We would consider it beneficial if that piece were completed."

Dodgson considered for several seconds and said, "Yes, I can see it finding a place. It would need to be expanded and the mock-medieval taken out, but it would fit very nicely in *Through the Looking-Glass, and What Alice Found There*. Very nicely, indeed."

"Excellent," Alice said. "And what would you call this piece?"

"I have no idea at present," Dodgson said. "Would you care to offer a solution?"

"Yes," Alice said. "I would be honored to suggest you call it *Jabberwocky*."

"*Jabberwocky*," Dodgson said. "Yes, that is an excellent word. You know, 'jabber' means loud discussion, and the Anglo-Saxon word 'wocer' means 'offspring'. Perhaps the *Jabberwocky* will cause much noisy discussion by my young friends."

"I think it might, Mister Dodgson," Alice said.

"I do believe I know how it might continue," Dodgson said as he picked up his pen and stared at the blank paper in front of him. Frumious words and manxome phrases whiffled through his mind as Alice dissolved into the ether.

The end

Acknowledgements

My thanks to Jennie who, on a warm summer's afternoon in the south of France, gave me an idea that changed the whole story.

To Dori, and her long-suffering family in Colorado, language coach and location finder.

To the nameless, faceless people in OWA (Organizations with Acronyms) who... well, you know.

Many thanks to the dedicated beta readers without whom this all falls down.

To Daryl Blasi for producing wonderful covers.

Last, but far from least, my wife Patricia, for her countless hours working through the MS looking for typos and anomalies in a plot where anomalies are the norm, nothing is what it seems, and everybody lies.

About the Author

Patrick J Stoner was a telephone engineer, drove buses in Europe and Asia, fixed fruit machines in Australia and organized trade shows in the UK before developing new products for an international telecommunications company.

He has lived in Australia, the USA, France and the UK. Now he lives on the south coast of England doing what he wants to do, which is write.

To the reader

If you have enjoyed this book, please consider leaving a review, however short, on Amazon, Goodreads or wherever else you post.

If you would like to know more about Jack's adventures and discover how he and his renegade band of highly specialized misfits dealt with the Nel, Bianca and the Venatori, look out for the second book in the series: *The Vorpal Sword Revelation.* A small taster follows.

JABBERWOCK CONTINUUM TWO:

THE
VORPAL SWORD
REVELATION

Shuttle SV 3-8749
01:50 GST

"How did the briefing go?" Rufus Koenig said over the comm.

"Not well," melanie replied. "We've only just finished for the day."

"Over two hours for a briefing?" Rufus said. "What the hell did you talk about?"

"Jack got a little annoyed at Chiyo and stormed out. But it was all reasonably civilized later."

"I have only had the pleasure of meeting Sergeant Lemasolai once, and I, too, found her a little tiresome.

"So, how long are you staying in hiding?"

"We won't be going anywhere for thirty days or so, by which time Jack will, I trust, have forced the others to figure out a way to get us past the surveillance net."

"I thought he was there as a consultant?"

"Me too, but he kept asking them questions, and they started coming up with ideas."

"Ideas are cheap. What about solutions?"

"I suspect Jack has figured out something or is halfway there and wants the others to find the solution."

"Well done, and keep me informed," Rufus said.

Rufus cut the connection, and melanie opened the door as Lorina arrived.

"I pinged you," Lorina said.

"Yes, I know," melanie said. "I was talking to Rufus."

"Oh, Rufus," Lorina said. "Did you say, 'Thank you, Master Koenig,' like a good girl?"

"You really don't like him, do you?" melanie said.

"Not much," Lorina said, shaking her head emphatically.

"Why not?"

"No reason. He's a damned useful ally, and I trust him, but I just don't like him."

"It's not compulsory," melanie said. "Anything else?"

"Yes. Tamara has hacked into a Bellachi vehicle in Mars orbit and extracted a lot of intel.

"Looks like the Nel weren't persuaded by your disappearing act, and right now, their analysis center for Terran satellite data is bursting at the seams with extra staff, AIs, and equipment. That means whoever is in charge down there is building up a lot of power. The others won't like it, so give it a few weeks, and they'll begin dragging their people back where they belong, just in case they lose them permanently."

"That's okay," melanie said. "Was that all?"

"Almost. What did you think of Jack's question session?"

"I think he might know more of the answers than he lets on."

"That's what I thought," Lorina said. "And I nearly forgot. Just in case I ever need a bit of extra cash, Bianca has settled a one million UC bounty on you, dead or alive."

"Excellent," melanie said.

"It would be if she hadn't settled another million on me."

"At least she appreciates your value now," melanie said.

"You know, you have a point there."

"You wanted to see me, boss?" Zara said as she walked into melanie's office.

"I did," melanie said, waving her into a seat next to Lorina. "How was Jericho?"

"No different from usual," Zara said. "Although what you really mean is, did I contact Matthew Black—is his name really Matt Black?—and did I get the information you wanted?"

"That's odd," Lorina said, looking straight at melanie. "When I told you Zara was on Jericho, you expressed surprise. But you actually knew all the time."

"I know, it's dreadful," melanie said to Lorina, then turned to Zara and said, "No, it's a cover name; his real name is Gloss White. Yes, I want to know."

"Hmm," Zara said. "Well, Ariella Gorbachev arrived on Jericho almost two years ago, according to Black, and checked in with him. She then began hanging around the Loose Cannon in Hull 5 and other places where crew gets recruited off the books.

"She did so for nearly three months and then disappeared the same day the freighter *Cyrene* left Jericho, supposedly for the Terran system."

"The Venatori are at least predictable," melanie said. "Cyrene was the huntress daughter of King Hypseus."

"I'm going to regret asking this," Lorina said, "but who was King Hypseus?"

"Oddly enough, a grandson of Gaia, his father was Peneus, the river god, and his mother was the naiad Creusa."

"That could have been worse," Lorina said. "So, you think Ariella ended up where?"

"Caeloeterra," melanie said.

☐

--oOo--

melanie and Jack, despite still being at odds, travel with the rest of the team to Tranasyne where melanie needs a cutting from an intelligent - and belligerent - plant. Putting part of the team in danger.

They continue on to Garadana where they plot ways of getting to Earth through the Nel surveillance net, and between them come up with an idea that just might work. As long as they can figure out how to make a fifty-ton snowball!

www.ingramcontent.com/pod-product-compliance
Lightning Source LLC
Chambersburg PA
CBHW060150260626
47160CB00001B/198